To My dear !
Hope you en
Blessings,
Judy

A Quiet Roar

by
Randall Arthur

A Quiet Roar

By Randall Arthur

www.RandallArthur.com

Published by
Life Image Publishers
P.O. Box 1160
Stockbridge, GA 30281

ISBN 978-0-9850257-7-9
Printed in the United States of America
Cover photo by Stephanie Williams
Cover art by OliviaProDesign

Dedicated to my mom,
Flora Dean,
a grand lady who celebrated
her 100th birthday
on November 1, 2018.

And to
the Fairhope Center
for the Writing Arts.
Thank you for your
getaway gift. I'll always
be indebted.

Other Books by Randall Arthur
www.RandallArthur.com

Novels
Wisdom Hunter
Jordan's Crossing
Brotherhood of Betrayal
Forgotten Road

Nonfiction
46 Stones - Letting Go Of Hurtful
Notions, Tendencies, And Beliefs
In the Evangelical Church

Children's Book
ABCs On The Move

PROLOUGE

Bamako
Capital City of Mali, Africa
Thursday, May 8, 2014

"Thirteen! I can't believe it! I've got a teenager, a real live teenager!" Angela Carter enthused, her eyes wide and cheerful.

Jake smiled at his mother's proclamation. He had turned thirteen five days ago. And his mom was still making a big deal out of the milestone. Crawling into the front seat of their Toyota Land Cruiser after a day of classes at the American International School, he looked at his mom behind the wheel. "You don't have to keep saying that, you know." He tried to suppress another grin.

"Yeah…well…my baby is growing up," she said, reaching over and playfully squeezing his leg. "And I can be amazed for as long as I want to be."

Jake rolled his eyes. He tousled his bushy dark hair and threw his backpack into the backseat. As his mom pulled out of the school compound onto the busy four-lane road, he lovingly fist-bumped her on the shoulder. He then let out an exaggerated sigh and leaned back onto the seat.

"How was your day?" his mom asked.

Jake stretched his arms upward until his hands touched the roof of the car. "You know; always a little drama. I mean, after all, we are teenagers." He shook his hands in the air and snickered.

"So, what was the drama today?"

"Well…," Jake answered as he curled his legs up into the seat and twisted to face his mom. "Gretchen and Michael are still feuding with each other. It's really funny. Michael keeps telling her that her left elbow is bigger than her right one. And she doesn't know if he's being serious or not. And it's driving her crazy. She even asked Mrs. Hargrove today to stand behind her and tell her if it's true."

Jake watched his mom lightheartedly shake her head while mildly groaning. He didn't know if her reaction was a sign of amazement at teenage behavior or a sign of empathy for Gretchen. Knowing his mom, he was pretty sure it was the latter.

"By the way," his mom interjected, slightly changing the subject, "How's Mrs. Hargrove's husband? Have you heard if he's doing any better?"

Jake looked out the window and then back at his mom. "I think he's had a relapse. But Mrs. Hargrove doesn't talk about it. I think the hush-hush has something to do with Mr. Hargrove's work at the embassy. Anyway, I've heard they might call it quits at the end of the school year and move back to the States."

"So, in about four or five weeks then?"

"Yeah, I guess."

Jake expected his mom to highlight the fact that such was the nature of the expat community. That the expats were always coming and going. That hellos and goodbyes were as common as Mali gold miners.

Instead, he heard her say, "Why don't we pray for them."

"Now?" Jake looked ahead out the window. They were heading to the extreme southwest corner of the city for his weekly cello lesson. "Sure," he said.

He closed his eyes, peeking only a couple of times to make sure his mom was watching the road. He listened to her pray aloud that God would grant the Hargroves divine wisdom as they tried to figure out the best course for their life, and that He would surround them with friends and associates who would support them every step of the way.

When she finished praying, they rode in silence for awhile as they each got lost in their own thoughts.

Staring out the window at the great Niger River, Jake tried to gear his mind up for the cello lesson. It would be his next to last lesson for the school year. He would then enjoy a much-appreciated break. He started taking cello lessons almost two years ago, right before his dad died with malaria. Following the loss of his dad, he clung to the instrument as an outlet for his anger and grief. At that time, the weekly lessons couldn't come soon enough. The instrument still provided a therapeutic release, but the lessons themselves were no longer part of that therapy. He had now reached a level of dexterity that allowed him—to varying degrees—to play pretty much any music he wanted to play to pacify his moods of melancholy, joy, or sadness.

As his mom turned south onto the ten-mile-long dirt road leading to the music teacher's house, Jake once again thought of his dad - Scott Nicholas Carter. Jake still missed him, more than anyone would ever know. He missed the nightly father-son prayer time. He missed the hiking expeditions. He missed the movie nights. He missed the optimistic spirit his dad exhibited in everything he did. He missed the logical way his dad thought about things, and explained things. He missed the heartfelt father-son conversations.

To Jake, the man had been bigger than life. He had been his hero.

Jake stared quietly ahead as the Toyota approached a washboard curve. The thoughts of his dad yielded a fresh cloud of sorrow.

He started to ask his mom if the clouds of grief would ever go away, but was distracted when he saw a young teenage boy on bended knees, leaning over a goat, in the middle of the road. The boy was just on the other side of a short concrete bridge. Was the goat dead? The boy was dressed in a dirty brown tunic and dirty trousers. The boy looked up when he heard the Toyota coming and tried to lift the goat off the road. Did Jake see tears reflecting off the boy's black face? Had his goat been run over? There didn't seem to be anyone else around to lend a hand.

Jake's mom immediately slowed the Land Cruiser to a crawl, the dust from the road whirling to the front of the vehicle.

Jake looked at his mother. "Should I try to help?" Because of the controversial and high-profile work his mom did, she often received threats on her life. Jake knew she always tried to exercise caution when in public.

His mom, looking tentative about the situation, slowly pulled over onto the shoulder of the road—close to a field of tall, thick shrubs—and nodded that it was okay.

As Jake reached for the door handle, he saw his mother out of his peripheral vision reach under the seat to retrieve her 9mm Glock. Just in case.

Jake jumped out of the car, in the sweltering heat, and moved toward the boy. "Do you need help?" he asked in French, the national language of Mali.

The Muslim teenager looked in Jake's direction and nodded.

When Jake walked up to the boy, he bent over and lifted the back end of the goat while the boy lifted the front end. Jake was nearly overcome at that moment by an unexpected stench. He did not know if the odor came from the boy or the animal. He tried not to wince.

The black teen nodded for Jake to reverse direction and head toward the bridge embankment.

Not exactly sure what the boy was doing, Jake complied, trying all the while not to inhale deeply.

With the goat in their arms, they sidestepped their way toward the bank leading down to a dry creek bed.

Jake struggled to not slip on the dirt as they carried the goat down the bank. He was caught totally off guard, and momentarily froze, when seven or eight men in tunics and head scarves rushed from beneath the bridge and grabbed him. He was instantly overpowered. The goat was shoved from his arms. Fear blitzed his body. Flushed with adrenalin, he started thrashing, and screaming for his mom. His hands were quickly twisted and tied behind his back. Before he knew what was happening, his head was stretched backward and the blade of a razor-sharp machete was pressed against his neck.

On his tiptoes, Jake closed his eyes and sucked air frantically through his nose. His pants were already being ripped off by the time he heard his mother rushing down the bank, screaming his name. Jake managed to look in her direction. Her eyes carried the flames of panic.

"Let him go!" she screamed, sweeping the Glock from man to man. "Let him go NOW!"

The man holding the machete to Jake's throat swung Jake to face the gun. "Drop the gun or I'll cut his throat!" the man shouted in the indigenous Bambara language.

Jake emitted a ghostly, high-pitched cry.

Another man stepped out of the shadow, aiming a rifle at Angela's head. "Put the gun down," he repeated the feverish demand.

Jake suddenly realized he was naked from the waist down. His eyes rolled back in his head as he breathed his next breath in absolute terror.

PART I

1

Monday, March 23, 2015
Lyons, Georgia

Standing in the kitchen of his three-bedroom wood-siding home in rural Georgia, 61-year-old Ray Huxley was still reeling from the announcement he and the others had received from the church pulpit twenty-four hours earlier.

"He can't do that, can he?" Ray bellowed for the umpteenth time, squeezing the top of his head with its few remaining wisps of white hair. "I mean, it's....it's not right! And there's nothing nobody can say that will make it right! Absolutely nothing!" Ray—stout and hard as iron—smacked his fist into his calloused palm. "I don't see that I have any other choice now. I don't want to do it. But I'm not going to just stand around and condone such a god-awful decision! I'll call the rest of the men this evening and tell them I'm stepping down and leaving the church if Floyd doesn't reverse his decision!"

Evelyn, Ray's wife, pursed her lips and slumped her thick shoulders beneath her loose-fitting cotton dress. "I think I'm going to give her a chance."

"You're what?" Ray retorted in disbelief, nearly twisting his neck too hard.

"I said, I think I'm going to give her a chance," Evelyn repeated, projecting her voice just above a whisper.

Ray's brow rippled like water blown by the wind. "For God's sake, Evelyn," he erupted, "how can you..."

"I think I see old man Baxter's point," she interrupted softly.

"Old man Baxter's point!" Ray nearly shouted. "He stands up in church and says, 'I've owned the church building and the property it's on for forty years and I'm bringing in a woman pastor; you can like it or you can leave.'"

"No," Evelyn whispered.

"No?"

"No, not that point. I mean the other point; the one about Pastor Phillips and Pastor Crawford."

"Okay, so both of the previous pastors had a hard time keeping their zippers zipped. But that doesn't mean it's okay to put a woman in the pulpit!"

"We've lost so many people already, Ray. Why not try to start over with a lady pastor? I can't see that it's going to make things worse than they already are."

"Evelyn, it's Central Baptist for heaven's sake! It's the town's most prominent church!"

"And your point?"

"My point! Number one; it's not right! Number two; it'll make us the laughing stock of the whole county, maybe the whole dadgum state. Number three; so many people could leave that there might not even be a congregation left! Shall I go on?"

"Well, at least she's not going to cost us any money," Evelyn offered with a partial smile.

Ray looked at his plump wife, shook his head, and bolted out of the house to stew in the evening sun.

* * *

"It's for you, Ray," Evelyn called from the kitchen later that evening. She raised her voice again to make sure Ray heard her from his green recliner in front of the television.

Ray raised his head and twisted to look at her.

Evelyn gestured at the cordless phone she was holding in her dishwater-covered hands.

Ray fumbled with the TV remote, pressed the mute button, and heaved himself out of the recliner and into the kitchen. He took the phone and pushed the speaker button so he could hear better. "Hello," he huffed.

"Ray, this is Eric Sawyer over at the Vidalia Times. I understand your congregation had a real interesting meeting yesterday morning. If what I've heard is true, I think the story is probably worthy of a front page article. I'm wondering, since you're the chairman of the deacons, if I could meet with you sometime tomorrow and get some details."

Ray rubbed his thick eyebrows and inhaled deeply. The gossip had already begun. Should he just ignore the call and allow the gossip to take its course? After all, he was planning to officially withdraw his church membership anyway. Or, before he stepped down from his ten-year stint of heading the deacon board, should he first offer up his side of the story and put all the blame on Floyd Baxter, exactly where it belonged? He squeezed his forehead for four or five seconds. "Where do you want to meet, and what time, Eric?"

"What about twelve noon at Roxy's diner?"

"Just you and me. I'll meet you there at noon."

Ray returned the phone to its base.

"And you don't think this will just stir the fire even more?" Evelyn queried after overhearing the call.

Ray tried to avoid eye contact with her. "Oh, I'm sure it'll stir the fire," Ray seethed, heading back to the living room. "But maybe that's exactly what Floyd Baxter needs right now to make him think twice and change his mind."

2

Tuesday, March 24

At his age, Ray felt healthy and strong. His job as a self-employed tractor mechanic—working out of a big steel-and-concrete garage in his backyard—kept him active. Unlike most people he knew, he was only using one prescription drug. It was a blood pressure pill.

Before he left the house for his appointment with Eric, he came close to swallowing an extra one of those pills.

He finally crawled into the cab of his old Chevy pickup and headed across the small town.

*   *   *

Ray arrived at the dull cinder-block diner, south of town, ten minutes early. He needed the extra minutes alone to just sit in the truck and try to calm his nerves.

When he finally entered the mom-and-pop restaurant and sat down at a red vinyl booth, he was feeling certain that what he was about to do was right, especially in the eyes of God. And that's what was important, regardless of the repercussions. He was mentally rehearsing the details of the disastrous Sunday morning church service when Eric walked up.

"Ray Huxley," the young journalist said flatly.

Ray looked up. "Eric," he reciprocated, extending his hand for a firm shake. They knew each other by name and face, but that was all. Eric was an intelligent-looking young man who had an irresistible smile and a head full of bushy blonde hair.

Eric slid into the booth, on the opposite side from Ray. "Thanks for meeting with me."

Ray nodded.

Almost immediately a middle-aged red-headed waitress, wearing a red-and-white checkered apron, appeared at the table.

Ray ordered a burger and a glass of iced tea.

Eric ordered just a Coke. "I was planning to eat lunch with you, but just as I was walking out the door, my boss gave me a new assignment down in the lower part of the county. So I've got about thirty minutes. And then I'll have to run."

Ray nodded again, trying to manage his nerves.

Not wasting time on pleasantries, Eric jumped right into the topic at hand. "Anyway, I just need to know up front if I can use your name in the article, or if I need to quote you as an anonymous source. Either way, it's your call."

Ray thought about it. If he was going to spill information to a newspaper reporter then he needed to be man enough to stand publicly behind his words. Besides, he wanted Floyd Baxter to know he was not going down without a fight. "If it's all right, just quote me as the 'chairman of the deacon board,' without spelling out my name. That should be sufficient. All those who know anything about the church will know it's me. And everybody else will figure it out pretty quickly."

Eric clicked open a cheap pen and wrote 'chairman of the deacons.' "Okay, well if you don't mind, just start from the beginning and tell me what you remember."

Ray took a deep breath. "Well, as you probably know, our church has been without a pastor now for about four months. The men of the church have been standing in until we find someone permanent." Ray cleared his throat. "Last Sunday, Floyd Baxter was the one filling the pulpit."

Eric interrupted. "Floyd Baxter, the owner of the Prime Vidalia Onions enterprise?"

"Yeah, the one and the same."

There was a hint of surprise in Eric's voice. "Does he often fill the pulpit?"

"He's not one of the men that normally fills in, no. But, he has stepped up recently on two or three occasions."

"He actually preaches?" The surprise in Eric's voice was more pronounced this time.

Ray wrinkled his lips. "Well, he doesn't actually preach. He more or less just refers to the Sunday School quarterly, and teaches like he would if he was in a Sunday School class."

Eric was jotting down notes when the waitress returned with their drinks served in green mason jars.

"Okay, go on," Eric coaxed when the lady turned and walked away.

"Well, like I said, he filled in last Sunday morning. Except he didn't teach this time. Instead, he told us he had an important announcement to make. He then proceeded to remind us that he and his older brother, Cecil—a millionaire in the onion business as well, before he died—were the ones who forty years ago built the church building as a gift to the congregation. And that they had built it on their property." Ray sidetracked. "The plan all along has been for the building and the property to be bequeathed to the congregation when the brothers have passed away."

"And?"

"And, at the moment, the deed for everything that's considered Central Baptist Church property—the building and the four acres it's on—is still in Floyd's name. He reminded all the old members of that fact, and shared it for the first time with the newer members. He then went on to tell us he had made a major decision regarding the church, and there was nothing any of us could do about it. We could either accept the decision, or we could leave the church." Ray paused and took a sip of his tea.

Eric, spellbound, held eye contact.

"He said he's bringing in a lady pastor." Ray felt more than a tinge of shame and humiliation as he spoke the words out loud. "He said he's personally going to provide her with a house, a car, and a salary."

"A lady pastor at Lyons Central Baptist," Eric echoed, more to himself than to Ray.

"I know." Ray took another quick sip of tea as if to cleanse his mouth. "It's more than a scandal. It's down right wrong. It's dangerous, and it's blasphemous. It's going to completely destroy the church, and I wouldn't be surprised if it brings God's judgment down on the whole town."

"Did Mr. Baxter say who the lady is?"

Ray shook his head. "He wouldn't give us a name. He only told us she's a missionary from Africa."

Eric's eyes lit up. He almost faltered with his next question. "Is she white or is she..."

Ray physically jerked. "My God, son! Even Floyd Baxter wouldn't be crazy enough to put a black woman in charge of the most influential church in town." Sensing immediately that Eric was going to ask if he was sure, Ray added, "Floyd briefly mentioned that the woman was originally from north Georgia which, if I remember correctly, is pretty much an all-white part of the state."

Eric took a gulp of Coke. "Did he say anything else about her?"

"He said she was widowed about three years ago. He also said she would be flying into Atlanta on Tuesday, March the thirty-first, a week from now. And that her first Sunday in the pulpit would be Easter Sunday, April the fifth."

Eric suddenly grinned as if he had providentially come across a journalist's goldmine.

Ray saw it in Eric's expression. It was easy to believe that Eric was envisioning an ongoing series of articles that would sell a ton of newspapers, particularly in light of all the scandalous articles that had been written in the last twenty-four months about the two previous pastors. Ray again felt nauseated.

"Anything else?" Eric was now looking for every bit of information he could find.

"Yeah, he said her initial stay would be for two years. After that, the congregation could vote whether to keep her or let her go."

"Two years?"

Ray took a bite of his burger that was delivered to the table on a yellow Melmac plate. "Two years. But it's my bet she won't last two months."

Eric was energetically scribbling his notes. "And did he say what his connection was, or is, to this lady missionary?"

"No, he wouldn't answer that question."

"So, the church doesn't know the lady's name or age? And doesn't even know her connection to Mr. Baxter?"

Ray sighed. "Floyd has left us with a lot of unanswered questions. And quite honestly, I don't understand why he would do something like this."

"Ah, the why!" Eric highlighted. "I'd think that would be the biggest question on everyone's mind right now. Surely he's given some indication as to what his motive is behind all this."

"Like the rest of us, he's still frustrated over the last two pastors we've had. But to give up on all the good male candidates we could pull in from around the state is just completely insane. It doesn't make any sense."

Eric finished off his Coke. "How old is Mr. Baxter these days? I'm just curious."

Ray got the impression Eric might be wondering if old man Baxter was still mentally competent, but was just too hesitant to ask. Ray could certainly sympathize. He had wondered the same thing. "He's at least eighty, if not eighty-one or eighty-two. And as far as everyone can tell, his mind is still sharp as a tack."

Eric bunched his lips, then looked at the time on his smartphone. "I only have a few minutes left. So my last question, at least for the day, is: What was the overall reaction of the congregation?"

Ray scowled. "Shock. Confusion. Disbelief. Anger."

"And you personally?"

"I'm so disgusted that I've already told the deacon board I'm leaving the church if Baxter doesn't change his mind by this weekend. I'll simply dust off my hands and walk away."

"Do you think a lot of people will follow suit?"

"I'll honestly be surprised if more than ten or eleven people stay. And that's the God's honest truth."

* * *

Ray spent the evening heatedly talking about the church issue with several friends over the phone and in his garage.

Evelyn talked about the matter with her friends equally so.

So did everybody else in the church, it seemed.

The cauldron of gossip, speculation, and personal opinions was already boiling over. Everywhere. And on everybody.

The town of Lyons was abuzz.

3

Two days later, on Thursday morning, the town of Vidalia, along with Lyons and the other parts of Toombs County, awakened to Eric's front-page article in the well-established *Vidalia Times*.

Floyd Baxter, a long time subscriber to the paper, received a copy at the front door of his 4,000 square foot lakeside, brick home. Enjoying his morning cup of black coffee while sitting in his den in a leather recliner, he read the article and smiled.

African Missionary
Splits Lyons Central Baptist

Unless Floyd Baxter, owner of
Prime Vidalia Onions Corporation,
changes his mind, the Central Baptist
Church of Lyons will be pastored
by a female pastor, beginning Easter
Sunday, April 5. Deed holder to all
Central Baptist Church property,
Mr. Baxter announced the unilateral
decision to the congregation last
Sunday morning that he is personally
hiring the lady, paying her salary, and

covering her housing costs. Mr. Baxter refused to give the Central Baptist congregation the lady's name, age, race, or credentials. He divulged only the fact that the woman has been a missionary in Africa, and is now widowed.

The Central Baptist deacon chairman is leading the opposition to Baxter's decision, announcing he will withdraw from the church membership unless Baxter reverses his decision.

Mr. Baxter has refused to take the *Times*' calls to affirm or deny the allegations.

A call to the Evangelical Baptist Alliance state office revealed that state officers have received no information about the Lyons Central Baptist incident, but promised to launch an immediate inquiry.

The article was accompanied by a black and white photo of Central Baptist's conventional brick building, its steeple rising to the sky. The marquee of the church, with the church name in huge black letters, was highlighted in the picture.

Floyd Baxter adjusted his tall slim body in the recliner and read the article two more times to make sure he did not miss anything. He smiled openly. Unable to shake his grin, he stretched out in the leather recliner, closed his eyes, and savored the moments.

4

Sunday, March 29

Ray's wife, Evelyn, sat at her bedroom makeup mirror brushing her graying hair, readying herself for church. It was still one week before the arrival of the mysterious lady pastor. And Evelyn continued to muse over the fact that, at 59 years old, she still was not sure what she actually believed about female pastors. She had just always accepted the teaching of the male pastors and the deeply-rooted tradition of the Evangelical Baptist Alliance declaring that ladies were simply out of place as leaders in the pulpit. She realized that until now, though, she had never had a reason or a motivation to even question the accuracy of such a teaching. But as she doused hairspray across her hair, she felt a flood of new questions rising in her soul and an inexplicable excitement beckoning her spirit. All the wild speculations and opinions surging openly through the community only heightened her feelings.

Evelyn tried to squelch her grin. Despite the fact that Lyons Central Baptist had for years supported foreign missionaries through the annual winter and spring Helping-Hands mission offerings, she herself had never personally seen a missionary. Neither had most of the other people in the

church. Nevertheless, Ray and her nineteen-year-old son, Billy
—along with plenty of others in the community—were
speculating that the missionary lady would probably be a
grandmother-type character wearing a Quaker-like dress and
sporting long stringy gray hair piled in a bun.

Evelyn grinned again.

So what? Maybe the lady would indeed fit such a
description. Evelyn could even imagine that she might.

Yet, perhaps this was the kind of leader the congregation
needed right now to help give the people who remained a sense
of calm and reassurance.

Evelyn applied a generous portion of red lipstick to her
breaking smile, then grabbed her Bible.

As she passed through the kitchen where Ray was busy at
the sink drying breakfast dishes she said, "Are you sure you
don't want to go with me? There's been a lot of pressure on old
man Baxter to change his mind. It's certainly going to be
interesting to see what happens."

Ray paused, then underscored his point for the dozenth
time. "Evelyn, I've already made my declaration to God, the
newspaper, the deacon board, and everybody else. I'm not going
to set foot in that church again until Floyd Baxter takes it off
its wayward path. And I'm not going back on my word."

"All right then. Well, I'll let you know what happens." She
was truly sorry Ray was hurting so badly. Yet, at the same time,
she couldn't deny her own sense of innocent rebellion. She felt
almost like a teenager again.

*　　*　　*

As Evelyn approached the church parking lot, located on the backside of the building, she was shocked. Perhaps she shouldn't have been. Instead of the sparse number of cars everybody expected, the asphalt parking lot was nearly overflowing. Cars were even parked on the street.

Eventually finding a parking space in the overflow lot, Evelyn tried to remember the last time such a sizable crowd had shown up for a Sunday morning worship service. She found herself grinning again with nervous excitement. Not wasting a minute she walked briskly to the main auditorium.

The crowd in the burgundy-carpeted sanctuary was huge. Pockets of whispered conversations were occurring throughout the building. Evelyn, with a bit of difficulty, finally found an empty seat on the front pew, one of the seats most church goers avoided at all cost.

With a few minutes to spare before the 11:00 starting time, Evelyn shifted in her cushioned seat to observe the crowd. Chatter persisted all over the room. She saw church members that, as far as she knew, had not been in church for months, maybe years. She also saw a few new faces she did not recognize.

Evelyn felt a sudden tap on her shoulder, followed by a whisper in her right ear. "Did you hear that Troy and Walter are planning to stand up in the service and call Floyd out publicly?"

Evelyn turned and saw that it was her friend, another deacon's wife. Evelyn started to respond, but the lady, a short delicate blonde, was already circulating the news to someone else.

Evelyn then spotted Troy and Walter, two of the church's five deacons, at the back of the sanctuary talking nervously together. She looked for Floyd. She knew, according to the church calendar, that he was scheduled to lead the service again. But she didn't see him anywhere.

As the wall-mounted clock in the auditorium hit the 11:00 AM mark, the tension in the crowd—numbering at least two hundred people or more—was fully palpable. Evelyn found herself nibbling at a fingernail, something she would normally never do.

Evelyn still didn't see Floyd anywhere. She looked over at her friend who had earlier whispered the news about Troy and Walter, and shrugged her shoulders in question. The friend lifted her eyebrows and shrugged back.

The church's tall lanky song leader, taking a signal from someone—probably one of the deacons—stepped to the microphone and nervously welcomed everyone to the meeting. Normally talkative, the man skipped any pleasantries or trite remarks and announced the first hymn - 'I Shall Not Be Moved.'

Understanding the significance of the words, the majority of the people, it seemed, launched into the song at full volume. Evelyn was nearly taken aback. She hadn't heard the congregation sing with such stiff resolution since the bygone days of week-long revival meetings. In unison, the men were suddenly booming the lyrics, "Just like a tree that's planted by the water, I shall not be moved."

The music leader, visibly enlivened, led in two more hymns - 'Keep On The Firing Line' and 'Stand Up For Jesus.' The messages of both songs were obviously intentional. And the vocal intensity of the crowd only seemed to increase with each verse. The multitude of voices reached a crescendo at the end of the third song, "This day the noise of battle; the next the victor's song. To those who vanquish evil, a crown of life shall be. They with the King of glory shall reign eternally."

Evelyn looked around. Well, there was certainly no doubt about the general sentiment; the voice of the people had loudly spoken. One man was so worked up he was wiping his brow with a handkerchief. Evelyn inhaled deeply. From all appearances, the meeting definitely was not going to be for the faint of heart.

The song leader suddenly appeared a little anxious, as if he wasn't sure what to do next. Floyd Baxter still wasn't anywhere to be found. The song leader looked out at one of the deacons for guidance.

The deacon, Jim Manley, mounted the steps to the pulpit, while trying to look calm. At forty-five and hugely overweight, the deacon adjusted the microphone, cleared his throat, and said, "I too want to welcome you to our Sunday morning service." He then suddenly looked uncertain himself. "I guess I just need to go ahead," he proceeded, "and say up front that Floyd Baxter, the man who was supposed to lead the service this morning, isn't here yet. And we're not sure why." Jim turned his head from the microphone and again cleared his throat, apparently debating his next words. "Most of you, I am sure, know what's happening in our church. And that's probably why you're here. And you want to know what the deacon board is planning to do about it. Well, before Floyd possibly shows up, I'll go ahead and tell you. But first, I want to remind everyone that Floyd does indeed, as he announced last Sunday, hold the deed to all the church property. He is the sole owner of the buildings and the land. And he's the one forcing our congregation into this awkward and unprecedented situation, claiming he's going to install a lady pastor here at our church as early as next Sunday."

Evelyn felt her palms sweating. She rubbed them on her dress.

"Our congregation, of course, totally opposes such an absurd and half-baked move," Jim declared, smacking the podium with his fist. "Leading the opposition, our deacon-board chairman, Ray Huxley, has already stated his intentions. He's planning to officially and permanently step down and leave the church if Floyd Baxter doesn't reverse his decision by the end of the day. As far as the other four deacons are concerned, Jack Evans and I will move into an inactive status beginning next Sunday and will remain inactive for as long as Floyd pushes his agenda. We will boycott all church services as long as the church is being led by a woman. Our other two deacons, Troy Bingum and Walter Johnson, on the other hand have decided to remain on active status. They will attend all the church services. But...with an agenda. Their goal, to put it mildly, will be to disrupt, disturb, and derail the services in any way, and every way they possibly can. Hopefully, Floyd and his lady minister will be persuaded pretty quickly to abandon their wild idea and turn the church back over to those of us who will keep the church rooted in its Biblical heritage."

Evelyn flinched as a volley of applause and vigorous "Amens" ignited all over the building.

Jim tried to continue, but had to wait for the commotion to settle down. "Several of you," he finally picked up again, "have asked what you can personally do to help support the opposition. Well, Troy and Walter are inviting you to stay and join them as they put up a fight. Jack and I are asking others of you to boycott the church with us. Obviously, because of Floyd's deep pockets, we're not going to be able to cripple the church financially. But a boycott, especially by the musicians, ushers, Sunday school teachers, nursery workers, youth workers, kitchen workers, and all the other volunteer staff, can wreak havoc and help squash Floyd's plan. Our ultimate goal is to simply take the church back into our own hands and find a God-ordained pastor...a strong man who will rightly bring honor to God and His Word."

Another round of applause, this time accompanied by foot stomping, rippled shamelessly from everywhere in the room.

Evelyn looked around again. She decided there on the spot that she, for one, wasn't about to miss next Sunday's service. Shoot...a team of wild horses wouldn't be able to keep her away.

Jim then resolutely flipped open the pages of his King James Bible. "I'd like to read First Timothy, chapter two, verses eleven and twelve," he told the people. He waited a few seconds, giving those who had brought their Bibles a chance to turn to the passage. He then read slowly and emphatically, "Let the woman learn in silence with all subjection. But I suffer not a woman to teach nor to usurp authority over the man, but to be in silence." Without adding further comment, he said, "I know it's highly unusual at this point in our service, but I believe the spiritual thing for us to do right now is to gather around the altar in prayer and let God know we intend to stand in agreement with His Word, and then petition Him for divine help."

5

The Tuesday, March 31st, edition of the *Vidalia Times* featured another front-page "Central Baptist" article by Eric Sawyer.

As before, Floyd Baxter read the article multiple times in the privacy of his home.

Lyons Central Baptist
Deacons Fight Back

The Sunday morning service at Lyons Central Baptist was a resolute effort against Floyd Baxter's decision to unilaterally install a lady pastor on Easter Sunday. Mr. Baxter, who was scheduled to lead the service, failed to make an appearance. Deacon Jim Manley took control of the service in Baxter's absence. Manley promptly called for a boycott of all future church services, especially by Sunday school, nursery, and youth workers until Baxter rescinds his "absurd

and half-baked" decision. Some,
though, are being asked to stay
and fight and help expedite the
rescission.

The large audience was then
called to a time of prayer around
the church altar, asking the Almighty
to miraculously intervene and stop
Baxter's move of "insanity."

As of this moment, Ray Huxley,
the former chairman of the deacon
board for ten years, has resigned
and withdrawn his membership
from the church.

Unless things change, the
Central Baptist Church of Lyons,
and those who choose to stay,
will have a lady pastor starting
next Sunday.

When Floyd Baxter finally laid the newspaper down on his kitchen table, it seemed to him that he now had everyone's undivided attention. And hopefully, that would be a good thing.

He picked up his mobile phone and called one of his drivers. "You'll need to leave this morning by eleven-thirty. It'll take you at least three hours, maybe more—depending on Atlanta traffic—to get to the airport. And I don't want you to be late. She's been en route for nearly twenty hours. So, I want you to be there waiting on her when she comes through customs. I don't want her to have to wait for you, not for a minute. Understood? Oh, and by the way, don't talk her ears off. Let her sleep. She'll be so exhausted, she won't be able to hold her eyes open, I'm sure."

The driver had already received all the lady's flight information. He had only one question. "Shall I hold up a sign with her name on it?"

"Yes," Floyd answered, "Just hold it up so she can see it when she enters the arrival hall."

6

Thursday, April 2

Thanks to Eric Sawyer's ongoing articles in the newspaper, the events surrounding Lyons Central Baptist dominated conversations throughout the county.

As Easter Sunday rapidly approached, the deacons at Central Baptist were nothing less than obsessed by the matter.

Deacon Troy Bingum, a contractor by trade, took off work early on Thursday. He was sitting in his Ford pickup truck waiting for Walter. He had persuaded Walter to meet him downtown at the Dollar General Market. Troy had decided they should immediately start searching for the newly-arrived missionary and personally confront her without delay.

As Troy waited, he rolled down his truck window. The 73 degree weather with clear blue skies was absolutely gorgeous. Spring was his favorite season. The clean, fresh air and the sunshine only invigorated his spirit and added a fresh determination to his cause. He switched on the radio and was listening to Gospel music when Walter knocked hard on the side of the truck, from behind, and made him jerk.

"All right, what you got in mind?" Walter goaded.

"Sheee...come around and get in," Troy instructed, trying not to call Walter a "jerk" for scaring him.

Walter went around, crawled in, and closed the door.

"Okay, here's the plan," Troy told him. "First, let's question the hotels in the area. We'll go to the Lincoln Motel here in Lyons first. If she's not there, we'll drive over to Vidalia and inquire at the hotels there. If we strike out, then I'll come up with another idea."

"Let's do it," Walter hailed, as if in a football huddle.

Wasting no time, Troy threw the truck in gear and proceeded to the Lincoln Motel, a small red-brick motel left over from the fifties. With Walter at his side, Troy approached the motel owner, an elderly man from India who smelled of curry, sitting behind the front desk. Troy hoped the man, probably a Hindu or something, knew little or nothing about the Central Baptist debacle. "Can you tell me if a single lady has checked in during the last day or so, maybe with a lot of luggage? She'll most likely be a guest for several days. She's in the process of moving to town. We're here to greet her, and talk to her about her upcoming job."

The dark-haired man, with pockmarks across his face, stared at both Troy and Walter, and looked wary of the request. He started to say something, retracted, then finally said, "There's no one here of that description. All my customers right now are construction workers. All men."

"All right; thanks," Troy offered. He turned with Walter and walked back to the truck.

"So...that was easy," Walter critiqued.

"Yeah...let's head over to Vidalia then, and see what we can find there."

Over the next hour, Troy led them on a search to the front desks of the AmericInn, Econo Inn, Royal Inn, Comfort Inn, Quality Inn, and Hampton Inn.

But they struck out all around.

Most of the desk clerks refused to help, especially when neither Troy nor Walter could produce the lady's name, a physical description, or even say if the lady was with or without children.

Only one clerk offered any assistance. That particular clerk, a young college kid studying at Vidalia Tech, went so far as to allow the men to question the two lone female guests at his hotel. Neither of the guests, though, was a foreign missionary who had just flown in from Africa.

Back in the truck, Troy sighed, trying to remain energetic. "All right, we have about an hour left before offices start shutting down for the day. So, let's go to the Lyons courthouse, look at the Property Tax records, and find out if Baxter has bought any single family homes during the last few months."

"I like it," Walter cajoled.

They took a quick restroom break and then headed back to Lyons.

Once they reached the courthouse, it took less than twenty minutes to find the documents they were looking for. According to the files, Floyd Baxter had indeed purchased a single family home twelve weeks earlier. It was in downtown Lyons, on West Oglethorpe Avenue.

Troy dictated the address. Walter wrote it down.

Within ten minutes they were parked in front of the house. It was a beautiful medium-sized brick home. It looked as if it had been freshly renovated on the outside - roofed, painted, power washed, and landscaped. The newly stenciled name on the mailbox was 'Rose.'

There was no car in the driveway or carport.

Still, Walter said, "Let's do it; let's see if someone's at home."

The men walked to the front door and rang the doorbell.

No one answered.

They rang again. The curtains were open, so they eventually peaked through the living-room window. The inside had been newly renovated as well - new paint, new carpet, new furniture. But the residence appeared empty.

"What do you think," Walter asked.

Troy squinted and scratched his brow. "I think I want to make a phone call," he offered. "I want to try to reach Samuel Beck. Do you know him? He works for old man Baxter. And he's anything but a 'yes' man. If any of Baxter's employees will give us a heads up and let us know where the lady is staying, Samuel is our best bet."

"Call him," Walter urged.

Troy fiddled with his smartphone for about three minutes and finally got Samuel on the other end.

"Sam, this is Troy Bingum. Yeah…it's been awhile. Hey… I'm wondering if you can tell me where Floyd Baxter is housing this new lady he's flown in from Africa?" There was a pause. "You don't know anything about her? Are you sure? All right…thanks, then."

"I don't know about you," Walter jumped in, "But I think it's about time we made a personal visit to old man Baxter's place."

Troy looked at the time on his phone. He nodded. "He should be at home right about now."

When they arrived at the entry way to Baxter's estate, the huge automated metal gates at the head of the driveway were closed and locked.

"I've never seen those gates closed before," Walter noted.

Troy shook his head. "Me neither."

Walter was ticked. "So, I'm guessing then that Baxter is housing the lady inside his own house, at least for the time being."

"Yeah...I think you might be right."

"So, what do we do now?"

"You know what just came to me?" Troy huffed. "Baxter's been a widower for, what, about five years now? And I'm just remembering that he travels overseas a couple of times a year on so-called business trips. I'm suddenly wondering if this lady is someone he's met on the side. A mistress perhaps? A love interest?"

Walter listened.

"Maybe...," Troy persisted, "just maybe there is a not-so-pretty seed here that needs to be planted in the minds of those who still give old Floyd the benefit of the doubt."

"Maybe so," Walter said slowly, with a sinister smirk.

7

On Saturday night, Ray Huxley begged Evelyn in their living room to change her mind about attending the Easter Sunday service.

"I really wish you wouldn't go," he told her, grunting with emotion.

Evelyn gently sighed, pursed her lips, and conveyed her intentions with her eyes.

"Then at least plan to fight alongside Troy, Walter, and the others," Ray pleaded. "This just isn't right, Evelyn. You know it! God knows it! At least be on the right side!"

Evelyn was tired of arguing. So, she stood to leave the room. But first she tenderly grabbed Ray's clean-shaven chin and said, "How many years have we been together, Ray?"

"Thirty-seven," he said, trying to lower his voice.

"And have I ever fought you on anything in all those years?" she whispered, almost crying.

"No, so why start now...?"

"Shhh..." She stopped him, placing a finger across his lips. "Just listen to me." She paused to let him focus. "For thirty-seven years I've been your biggest cheerleader. There's not a man in the world I respect more. I love you as much as anyone can possibly love another human being. Always have. And always will. But regarding this particular issue—I don't know—

everything in me is saying I should give this woman a chance. So, that's what I'm going to do. I know it's an extremely black and white issue for most people. But for me, at least for the time being, it's a confusing issue, even after reading all the Bible verses. So, I'm not going to just cast the woman aside right now." She paused again. "So, I guess I'll just have to figure it out as I go. And I'll ask that you try to be patient with me. All right?"

A breath of frustration wheezed from Ray's unhappy face. He slowly nodded his consent. "All right, but you know this isn't easy for me."

Evelyn took his calloused hand. "I know, she said. You're a good man, Ray."

They embraced with tenderness as they stood alone in the dimly lit room.

*   *   *

That night, Evelyn could hardly sleep.
Neither could Kathleen Rose.

8

Easter Sunday Morning
April 5

As expectant as she had ever been, Evelyn arrived at the church an hour early.

Many of the church's men were already standing outside, on the sidewalks and on the lawn, in pockets of protest. A couple of the men were holding up cardboard signs, with painted letters that read 'God Will Judge Us For This!'

A policeman had been called in by somebody, probably to monitor the situation and make sure things didn't get out of hand. The officer, a middle-aged serious-looking man, was standing at a distance silently observing.

Evelyn anxiously went into the sanctuary. "Is she here, yet?" she asked one of her lady friends standing at a back pew.

"Nobody's seen her yet. Nobody's seen Baxter either."

Evelyn wrung her hands. "I'm so nervous, I can hardly stand it. What do you think she'll be like?"

"I don't know, but I hope she's a strong lady. Or I don't think she's going to have a chance."

Evelyn thoughtfully concurred. She exchanged a few more words of excitement and trepidation, then found another lady to share her feelings with. And then another. And another. She forged her way, conversation by conversation, toward the front of the auditorium. She explicitly wanted to stake out a front-row seat. She didn't want to miss a thing.

When she laid her purse and Bible down on the front pew, she felt the excitement building in the room. Along with a lot of anxious uncertainty.

With thirty minutes to go, the sanctuary was filling up quickly, primarily with women and young people—especially college students, a whole crowd of them. Evelyn spotted only three adult men inside the building.

Evelyn was almost sure that most of the people gathered at the moment were people who would take a passive, if not supportive, position regarding the new pastor. She started to relax a little bit. Then she saw Troy and Walter enter the room.

Without acknowledging anyone with even a handshake or nod, the two men, dressed in Sunday suits, marched to the first pew on the left side facing the pastor's chair on the platform. The men marked their seats with their Bibles and some placards turned upside down. And just as quickly as they came in, they exited. They left, however, through the rear door toward the parking lot.

Instinctively, Evelyn closed her eyes. "Dear God," she whispered inside her head, "Let them give her a chance. At least for the first service. Please don't let things get worse than they already are. Our church truly needs your help right now. Please!"

Evelyn then just sat quietly and observed as most of the auditorium seats swiftly disappeared behind tense and curious faces.

At ten minutes till eleven, Evelyn noticed that the song leader and the pianist were not in their places. Normally at this time they would be on the platform, or at the baby grand piano, going over the music agenda for the morning. She squinted and looked around again. The building was now full—again primarily with women and college-aged young people.

And then, as if following some invisible cue, everyone went quiet, unusually quiet. And, yet, there wasn't a single soul on the platform leading or directing. It was bizarre. Actually, the platform with its massive oak podium and ornately carved chairs looked chillingly abandoned, as if it had not been used in months.

Evelyn felt her shoulders tense up. She tried to relax.

She looked at her watch. It was about five before eleven. And then, without warning, a powerful commotion of shouting and yelling erupted outside. Evelyn jerked so forcefully that it unnerved her. It was a storm of men's voices, a whole crowd of them.

But it was the intensity and meanness of the voices that frightened her.

Evelyn heard gasps all over the auditorium. Everyone could hear the outside ruckus.

Evelyn squeezed her hands together and tried to breathe. And then she made a bold decision. She was a millisecond away from jumping up from her pew and rushing outside to be a peacemaker when the most eerie thing happened. The cacophony of shouting male voices instantly stopped.

Evelyn twisted her head and strained to hear what was unfolding. She was sure everyone else in the room was trying to decipher what was taking place as well.

Was the on-duty policeman quelling the uproar? Or were there multiple officers involved at this point who were forcing everyone to remain civil?

And then...

And then, the heavy wooden door leading to the platform opened.

9

The mahogany door opened, followed by a full second or two of non movement.

Then Floyd Baxter, dressed in an expensive new suit, suddenly stepped through and held the door open. In the next few seconds, the air in the room couldn't have been charged with a greater surprise.

A tall, lithe and fit lady, dressed in an elegant knee-length black dress, stepped through.

Lyons and Vidalia together boasted a population of a little over 15,000 souls. And half those were females. Yet, Evelyn, in all her 48 years of living in the region, had never seen a woman so beautiful. The lady's beauty—from head to toe—actually took her breath away. Evelyn had always believed that female images like this were captured only in air-brushed photos.

With an unmistakable tone of humility, the lady—at Floyd's gentle gesture—walked over to the pastor's chair and sat down.

Evelyn couldn't take her eyes off the lady. The lady's hair fell nearly to the middle of her back. It was the darkest, thickest, most lustrous hair Evelyn had ever witnessed. It was the kind of full-bodied and weighted hair that fell in natural sheaths without being brushed. Snatches of light reflected off the strands and shone across the room.

The woman's skin color looked like a natural sun-kissed tan. Her skin was so smooth it glistened as if massaged with coconut oil. Her eyes were striking, even across the room, and possessed the piercing blue of giant sapphires. The lady was unquestionably ravishing. She would have been seriously jaw-dropping if dressed only in a pile of rags.

Evelyn suddenly noticed that the entire audience was completely silent, no doubt lost in their own world of surprise, appreciation, or perhaps even jealousy.

Evelyn now guessed why the men on the outside of the building had gone quiet. They had most likely been intimidated, bewildered, and silenced by the lady's overpowering magnetism. Evelyn caught herself nearly laughing out loud at the irony of it all. She smiled. She couldn't help it.

While everyone was staring at the lady, Floyd Baxter—seeing no one else up front to lead—assumed a position behind the wooden podium.

"Good morning," he said, looking totally relaxed, but not showing a lot of emotion. "I see several new faces here this morning. I want to welcome you in particular. Actually I want to welcome everyone, new and old alike, to what I truly hope will be a new beginning for me, for you, and for our entire church family."

Without pointing out the obvious—that the song leader and pianist had decided to boycott the service—Baxter simply opened the pages of a hymnal and announced the first song of Easter Sunday morning.

"Everyone stand if you will. Join with me and let's sing a-cappella - Christ Arose!"

The new lady pastor reached down, picked up one of the old green hymnals from beside her chair, and stood along with everyone else.

Not the greatest singer in the house, Floyd nevertheless plunged into the old hymn with the gusto of a rekindled heart.

The audience followed. So did the tall, dark-haired beauty. As the lady sang, she softly scanned the audience. She occasionally made eye contact with particular individuals and smiled. Her brilliant white smile, from Evelyn's point of view, was confident but meek.

Evelyn noticed that the woman, in contradiction to her beauty, carried a stark aura of brokenness. Yet somehow it only added depth to the woman's mystique.

So, this was going to be their new pastor? The lady looked to be about 40. And, of all ladies, this one had been a missionary? In Africa? Evelyn couldn't imagine. Evelyn nearly chuckled again as she remembered everyone's speculation that the lady would probably be a homely looking grandmother-type.

Evelyn could hardly wait to hear the lady speak, and get a glimpse of her personality.

Floyd promptly led in two more songs - 'Because He Lives' and 'All Hail The Power Of Jesus' Name.'

Evelyn looked over and suddenly noticed that Troy and Walter's Bibles and placards had remained untouched, and that the two men were nowhere to be seen. Had the new pastor's physical radiance actually scared them away? Or were they outside right now with the other men making new plans?

Evelyn prayed again inside her head. 'Lord, I'm not sure what's happening here. But I think I'm liking it. Please do something here that will be seen as a miracle. Please! I ask it in Jesus' name. Amen.'

With no offering to be collected or announcements to be made, Floyd—at the completion of the third song—looked out over the audience and apparently made an assessment of some kind.

"Well, perhaps it's that time," he finally declared.

10

As she was being introduced—only briefly, at her request —Kathleen Rose closed her eyes and took a deep breath. Her thoughts were running in a hundred directions. Mr. Baxter had contacted her in Africa ten months ago following the life changing tragedy that had left her feeling utterly alone in the world, and told her he was praying for her, then revealed—to her complete surprise and amazement—that he was the one who had been her 'secret' financial supporter throughout the last thirty-seven years—through foster home, college, and adulthood. Yet, he had refused to tell her 'why.' He had left her totally bemused.

Then two months ago he had contacted her again at her home in Africa and told her he wanted to help her now in a different way. He wanted her to consider leaving the continent for a couple of years, to simply get away from all the heartache and danger, and come and live in south central Georgia. He assured her he would provide financially for all her needs during the time of sanctuary. The invitation had come at a time when she was emotionally unhinged. She had desperately needed for someone, like Baxter, to step in and help guide her. So, without a lot of strength left, she had accepted his offer.

Mr. Baxter had then asked if she would, at the same time, attempt to serve a noble purpose, albeit not an easy one, during her stay. She had never been a lady to live without a cause, even in pain, so she had accepted the offer—even after hearing the awkward details.

Now she was wondering if her agreement to 'serve the noble purpose' had been a right one, especially after encountering the thunderous loathing of the men outside.

She took another deep breath. She knew it was too late now to step away or to back out. A home and a car had been purchased for her. And she had already turned her African ministry over to another missionary couple for the next two years.

So here she was in the deep south, in a town she had never heard of until a few months ago. It was almost surreal.

Trying to keep her feelings from upending her composure, she lifted her head and again looked out over the crowd at the curious faces. She knew the first words that came out of her mouth should be 'I know this is not easy for you. I know that many in your community do not even believe this is right.' She knew she should perhaps even take this first Sunday—in the still-crazy notion that there would be future ones—and tell the people a little bit about herself. To tell them why she was here.

But she was still too emotionally raw. She just couldn't do it.

And then she was jarred to alertness by the announcement of her name "Kathleen Rose," followed by a welcoming applause from the people.

Evelyn Huxley was the last one to stop clapping. She then watched the lady step to the masculine-sized podium, open a

Bible and lay out some notes. Evelyn was transfixed as the lady stood in stoic silence as if contemplating her opening words.

Evelyn stupidly noticed at that precise moment that the woman was not wearing any jewelry, and maybe not even any makeup. Definitely not any lipstick. Yet again, Evelyn was at a loss for words regarding the lady's exquisite beauty. With or without makeup, the woman was absolutely resplendent from head to foot.

Evelyn swiftly blocked out everything else in the world when the lady opened her mouth to speak.

11

"Good morning," the lady said clearly and confidently into the podium-mounted microphone.

Several in the audience returned a hearty "good morning."

An air of hopefulness suddenly filled the room.

Kathleen Rose smiled softly.

Evelyn Huxley actually felt a beam of delight spread across her own face.

"How many here recognize the name Theophilus?" Kathleen asked, now staring fully at the crowd.

Evelyn's brow wrinkled. What?

No one in the audience responded with their voice or their hand.

"Let me backtrack then," Kathleen said gently. "As you probably know, there are twenty-seven books in the New Testament. It's pretty clear that twenty-five of those books were written by apostles, the original eyewitnesses of Jesus' life and ministry.

"The two books that were not written by one of the apostles are the books of Luke and Acts. Both of these books were written by a man named Luke. But who was Luke if he wasn't an apostle? Well, according to Colossians, Timothy, and Philemon he was a co-worker with Paul and a significant leader in the church approximately twenty years after the ascension of Christ.

"So, why are his books included in the New Testament?

"As we do a little research, we learn from Luke in his own words—in Luke chapter one, verse two—that as a Gospel preacher he was NOT an eyewitness of Jesus' life and ministry as were all the other apostles. Rather, his faith relied on the reports of the apostles, just as mine does and yours does."

Evelyn heard Bible pages ruffle all around her.

Kathleen turned a page in her notes.

"On a side note, we learn according to Paul's report in Colossians that Luke was a doctor. Thus, it is safe to assume Luke was a thoughtful, meticulous, and analytical individual with an intelligent mind.

"So why is all this important to know on Easter Sunday?

"Because Luke had a friend named Theophilus who was a Roman official. We know Theophilus was a Roman official because of the Roman title of 'most excellent' that Luke gives him in Luke chapter one, verse three. And as a convert to Christianity, Theophilus—in an influential position for the cause of Christ—was for some unknown reason overcome with major doubts about the stories of Jesus, including the story of the resurrection. Could Theophilus really rely on these stories, stories that others had passed down to him? Or was it possible he was simply believing a trail of bogus nonsense?

"Luke is so moved by this man's lapse of faith that he tells the man—in Luke chapter one, verse three—that he, as a doctor who needs to know details, has already carefully investigated these passed down stories, including the resurrection story, to make sure they are authentic."

Evelyn wasn't sure why, but she started to weep tears of joy.

"The word 'investigated' that Luke uses here," Kathleen continued, "means 'to follow alongside.' Or, in other words, Luke had undertaken the great task of researching these stories.

"How had he done this?

"He had done it in three ways. First, verse two makes it clear that he had examined the writings of Paul, Matthew, John, and Mark—who wrote for Peter. He had tested these writings thoroughly for non truths. Second, chapter three reveals that he had researched the claimed genealogical records of Christ to confirm the Messianic bloodline. And third, the text strongly implies that he had actually found and interviewed surviving individuals who had been part of these stories—possibly Jesus' half-brothers; the widow's son who had been raised from the dead; some of the people among the five thousand who had been fed by the few pieces of fish and bread; some of the seventy-two disciples who had been sent out to heal the sick; the man healed of leprosy who had returned to thank Jesus; significant individuals who had witnessed the crucifixion; and, yes, even those who had with their own eyes seen Jesus in his resurrected body.

"Luke had researched all these stories rigorously, including the resurrection story. And he had found them to be authentic, true, and without embellishment.

"And he now tells Theophilus, 'I am writing to you and lifting up all these stories once again so that you may know the certainty of the things about which you have been instructed.'"

Kathleen closed her notes.

"Or we can look at it this way: Luke was a first century historian and investigative journalist who shouted to Theophilus —and to us—that all the stories passed down from the original twelve apostles are indeed true.

"So why does God include this book in the Bible? It's to let us know that all the other books, with the stories they present, were written by men of integrity who did not lie.

"So on this Easter Sunday, as we celebrate the resurrection of Christ, we can rest assured that the story has been checked out and authenticated by an objective third-party investigator who had access to eyewitnesses, a man who was meticulous in his research.

"I pray this morning that this truth will bolster your faith and reassure you as a follower of Christ."

After sharing a few more poignant details, Kathleen wrapped up her first sermon. She then prayed aloud that every one in the building, including herself, would trust God's Word every day as a solid unshakeable foundation for life.

As Kathleen turned to walk back to her seat, a holy hush settled over the whole room.

Evelyn detected that everyone was stunned, actually aghast, in a great way. Evelyn realized that in all her years of attending Central Baptist, this was one of the best sermons she had ever heard. Most of the church's male pastors through the years had basically yelled at the flock, telling them what they should and shouldn't do, but had seldom offered thought-provoking facts and insights.

Floyd Baxter returned to the podium. With a look of irrepressible satisfaction in his eyes, he thanked Kathleen and then welcomed everyone to return on Wednesday evening to an open-house meeting where they could interact with Kathleen one-on-one.

"Before we dismiss with a final prayer," Baxter concluded, "Please know that everyone is invited to come to the front this morning and welcome Kathleen to our great state of Georgia and to our Central Baptist community."

Without opening the floor for public questions, which Evelyn—and probably everyone else—was hoping for, Baxter brought the meeting to a close with a benedictory prayer.

Not waiting around, Evelyn went immediately to the platform. She was the first in line to welcome Kathleen face-to-face.

As soon as Baxter finished sharing some private words with the lady, Evelyn stepped forward.

Responding to Evelyn's move, Kathleen with a genuine smile extended her hand.

Evelyn ignored the lady's hand and instead embraced her with a massive hug. "I don't know how or why you ended up here in Lyons, Georgia, but please, please know that I believe you will be a breath of fresh air to our community. And I mean that with all my heart."

"You're very kind," Kathleen said, her eyes conveying as much sincerity as her words.

Up close, Evelyn wanted to tell Kathleen, 'you are beautiful; your words are beautiful,' but instead she said, "I'll definitely look forward to getting to know you. I really, really mean it."

Evelyn sensed at that point that there was already a line of people behind her waiting their turn. So she quelled her desire to say more. She smiled and started to turn away. In that instance she happened to see something on the right side of Kathleen's neck that made her do a visual retake. It was a scar, a nasty-looking scar about three to four inches long hiding in the shadows of her hair.

Evelyn caught herself staring at the disfigurement. She then noticed that Kathleen was aware of her gaze.

Kathleen said nothing.

Evelyn collected herself and moved on. Her mind was suddenly ablaze with a dozen new questions.

12

"I'm so upset, yet I am so proud at the same time," Evelyn huffed.

Ray watched as his wife moved about the cluttered kitchen —as she put beans in a pot and removed the ham from the oven—preparing a big Easter lunch for the family.

"Troy, Walter, and a bunch of the other men," Evelyn continued her rant, "made absolute fools of themselves. They nearly assaulted the lady, it sounded like, when she first arrived. And after the service they marched around the church side- walks holding up their tacky protest signs for the whole town to see. I'm embarrassed to know they're the key men in my church. And it's going to be hard for me to forgive them. Yet, Kathleen never defended herself. She just ignored them. And acted like a decent and gracious human being."

Standing at the kitchen sink, washing potatoes, Ray wanted to shout back, but he dampened his voice. "I think you're being a little irrational, maybe, right now," he ventured.

He saw Evelyn put her hands on her hips for an instant and stare at him with utter conviction. "And I'm a little embarrassed by you too, Ray!" she retorted.

"Evelyn! For God's sake! I'm only trying to do what is right!"

"I'm not so sure," she declared as she threw a pan of biscuits into the oven, accidentally letting the oven door slam. "I think maybe it's just your manly pride that's getting in the way."

"But a woman is not supposed to lead a group of men!" Ray declared for the hundredth time. "That's what the Bible teaches!"

Evelyn nearly barked. "The lady...Kathleen rather...didn't assume anything! Didn't demand anything! Didn't decide anything! Didn't plan anything! She just opened the Word! And it was the best sermon I've heard in years!"

Ray could feel his eyes roll painfully inside his head. It was already happening. The lady's presence in the pulpit was already dividing families as well as the congregation. He knew at this point that it was futile to argue. Evelyn was just too emotional. She couldn't reason right now; it was that simple.

*   *   *

On Tuesday morning, people all over Toombs county—in homes, convenience stores, hospital waiting rooms, office complexes, and diners—eagerly read Eric's latest article.

An Unforgettable First
For Lyons Central Baptist

The new pastor at Lyons Central
Baptist is 41-year-old Kathleen Rose,
holding a Masters degree in Theology.

The discord at the church regarding
lady pastors, however, rages on and
was only highlighted on Easter
Sunday, Rose's first Sunday, when
the men of the church in significant
numbers marched outside around
the sanctuary, holding bright red
protest signs. There was a minor
altercation when Rose first arrived
on church property and some of
the men attempted to bar her from
entering the building. Police were
on hand and quickly brought matters
under control. No one was hurt.

Those attending the service—a
near capacity crowd of women, and
college students—left the church
service singing the new pastor's
praises, saying she is beautiful,
smart, and gracious. They all say
they will be back.

The men of the church, however, plan to keep protesting.

Floyd Baxter, the deed holder
to the church property, and the
source of funding for Pastor Rose,
invites everyone to an open house
at the church's fellowship hall on

Wednesday evening to meet and
interact with the new pastor.

Floyd Baxter still refuses to give
out detailed information about the
lady.

Eric sat at his desk inside the cramped newspaper office on
First Street. The morning sun filtered through the blinds of a
corner window and highlighted dust on a pile of unused books
atop his workstation.

Eric took a sip of black coffee. According to his old habit,
he scrutinized his published article for mistakes. He spotted a
typo for which he promptly berated himself. He always
wanted to produce a flawless article, even after three years in the
business.

He took another sip of coffee. He still loved what he did.
He especially loved the work when he could be part of a
controversial story that provoked ongoing conversations and
debates, and made people think. He knew the 'Central
Baptist' story fell into this category, simply because of the sheer
number of response letters and emails the office had already
received. Half the letters were pro; half were con. But they
were all laced with emotion.

At some level the 'Central Baptist' story had even moved
him. He had been raised a Presbyterian, but had stopped
attending church nearly thirteen years ago when he was fifteen.
It wasn't that he had ever dismissed the value of religious
teachings such as kindness, generosity, and patience. He had

simply found church gatherings to be too boring, too stuffy, and too pretentious.

Yet, here was a story that was bringing excitement and tension to one of the largest churches in the county, a county where religion was a vital part of everyday culture.

Heck...even he had found the Central Baptist's Easter service to be absorbing and thought provoking, not to mention historic. He had honestly wanted to add more to his latest article, but had been afraid he would deviate from reporting just the bare facts.

Reflecting on the details of the Easter event, Eric leaned back in his swivel chair and kicked his feet onto his metal desk.

He grinned.

And then on impulse, he put his feet back down and leaned over to his desktop computer. He typed 'Kathleen Rose' into the Google search engine. He scanned the first two pages of website addresses that popped up. He didn't see a single article that looked related to the Kathleen Rose who now resided in Lyons.

He clicked on 'images.' An array of photos appeared. He scrolled downward. Not one of the female pictures—ancient or current—looked anything like the newcomer to Toombs County.

Eric moved the cursor back up to the search box and added the word 'Africa' behind Kathleen Rose's name. Again, not a single reference, article, or photo that materialized looked as if it was connected to the new minister.

"That's a little strange," Eric whispered audibly.

But then again, the lady had been a missionary in Africa. As far as he knew, she had probably lived in the African bush, pretty much off the grid. So, in her case, maybe a nonexistent footprint on the internet wasn't that uncommon.

On the other hand, the lady came across as too beautiful, too sophisticated, and too intelligent to have lived in the bush regions of Africa. So, could she have lived and worked in a big city? In that case, wouldn't she have an internet presence of some kind, even if it was minimal? Maybe she did. Maybe it was just buried in the hundreds of pages of internet listings. Maybe when he had more time, he would search those pages.

Or maybe he would just attend the open house tomorrow night and question the lady himself.

He looked at the time on his smartphone. He quickly jumped to his feet. He was scheduled for an interview in fifteen minutes with the track-and-field coach at Vidalia High School. He had to scoot.

13

Kathleen jerked violently awake, and gasped fiercely as she fought for her next breath.

It took her several seconds to realize she had been deep in a nightmare. With her heart racing, she sat up in bed and shook her head. But she couldn't rid her brain of the visual images - her son screaming for help, the machete covered in blood, the blistering red eyes of hate, the unspeakable barbarism.

Kathleen took a weighty breath and placed her feet on the carpet. She looked at the alarm clock. The time was 5:30 AM.

She looked around and remembered she was in Mr. Baxter's guest house. She massaged her temples and burst into tears.

How could she do this? How could she keep living and maintain her sanity? She knew she would never be able to forgive herself. Not in a lifetime. Not in two. The guilt and self-loathing were simply too much.

She took another deep breath and slowly looked around again. She wiped the tears from her eyes, then navigated her way through the predawn twilight to the small kitchen where she switched on a light. Still feeling the unrelenting weight of her mental anguish, she added water to an electric tea kettle.

As she waited for the water to boil, to make a cup of hot tea, she stared out the window at the early morning silhouette of the pond out back. How would she ever be able to find tranquility? Here? Or any place? She sniffled. She would just have to survive, as she had done in Mali, one hellish breath at a time.

And then she remembered that today would at least be a day of distractions. In a few hours, she would be moving into her new place on West Oglethorpe Avenue. And then there would be the open-house fellowship in the evening.

As she heard the water come to a boil, she thought specifically about the evening gathering. She wasn't worried about any potential tension or conflict that might arise during the event; she was certainly strong enough to handle that. But she was concerned that the people might expect her to tell more about herself, and her past, than she was ready to divulge.

As she poured hot water into a blue china tea cup, she fought not to, but choked up. Before she could drop a tea bag into the water she started sobbing.

*　　*　　*

Kathleen and Floyd, when they finished their chore, stood on the tiny front porch of Kathleen's new downtown residence. Kathleen looked at her watch. It was only 2:30 PM. It had only taken about five hours to purchase the final piece of furniture, buy some kitchenware, unpack suitcases, and set everything up at the house.

"Thanks for all your help; I really mean it," Kathleen said softly to Floyd. "You're still a mystery to me, though. I just don't understand why you can't, or won't, tell me how you found out about me as a foster child and why you've insisted on supporting me all these years. I wish..."

Floyd was already firmly shaking his head. "Not necessary to go there," he stated.

Kathleen produced a flustered grin. "Just like always. All right, be that way then." Kathleen went silent for a second or two, then changed the subject. "Thanks again," she said, gesturing at the house. "I know that getting out of Mali was a right decision. At least for awhile. But it's still not going to be easy; so just keep praying for me."

Baxter squinted in the afternoon sunlight. "At least you won't have to be looking over your shoulder every day, all day. And I'm almost certain they won't be able to track you to south central Georgia. Especially since they will be trying to use your real name. Anyway, try to get a little rest and we'll see you this evening."

Kathleen nodded and offered up a soft smile, ready to settle into her new place and be alone for a few hours. "All right; will do. See you in a little bit."

At 5:00 PM, an hour before the evening meeting, Kathleen sat down on the plush leather couch in her new study, a former bedroom that had been converted into a library-office space for her.

Already dressed for the evening, Kathleen looked around the room. The rich yellow curtains, the thick floral rug, the classic oak secretary, and matching oak bookshelves all created a space conducive to rest and meditation. She already knew it would become her favorite room in the house, a private sanctuary for her soul.

She suddenly stared at length at one of the miniature drawers in the oak secretary. She knew she shouldn't, especially right before the meeting, but she did. She opened the small drawer and slowly retrieved the well-worn photograph. The 4" X 6" had been taken three and half years ago. It was a picture of her then 46-year-old husband, Nicholas, and her 10-year-old son, Jake. The photo—the last one of the two boys together—had become her most treasured possession on earth.

She stared into the two pairs of eyes. Her chest swelled. And then her mind started helplessly thrusting the sword of self-hate. And, as always, every slash pierced her soul with unrelenting guilt.

Falling on her knees beside the couch, she whispered to herself through tears, "Why? Why didn't I stop it? Why? Why?"

As predictable as the coming of night, the images blitzed her head - waking up, surrounded by doctors and nurses, in the Mali hospital; trying hysterically to deny what had happened; literally fighting to try to get back to the bridge; and then wishing with every fiber in her body that she had not survived.

For several minutes following the barrage of African flashbacks, she mumbled incoherently, to the point of exhaustion. Then collapsed prostrate on the study floor in her dress.

14

Deacon Troy Bingum tried to wrestle his thoughts into submission. Right before he left the house to come to the Wednesday meeting, he got calls from both Jim Manley and Jack Evans reminding him of his purpose for attending the service.

As he sat courageously on the front pew this time—in a packed out crowd of women and college students—he knew his assignment was to intimidate and disrupt. Yet, the lady pastor had a presence about her that secretly intimidated him. And the fact that she was so downright attractive didn't help matters. She possessed the type of breathtaking beauty that made men weak. None of the other men in the church had even mentioned the lady's physical allure, but they were all affected. Troy could tell. He could tell by their involuntary gulps, their obvious efforts to not stare, and their reversion to an almost high-school-like shyness when in her presence. Yet, they expected him and Walter to somehow completely circumvent the lady's dynamic beauty and treat her with disrespect.

He would never tell a soul, but he was glad to be one of the two deacons assigned to sit in the meetings. He could enjoy the lady's physical enchantment while trying to muster up the boldness to confront her.

A Quiet Roar

A protest placard that read 'This Is Evil' was lying on the pew right beside him, unused from Sunday morning. He wanted to pick it up and hold it high. But at that precise moment Kathleen Rose walked into the auditorium. Troy momentarily forgot about the placard.

The lady, looking like a flawless piece of physical art, entered the room from beside the platform. She walked directly to the front pew where Troy was sitting and sat down about three feet from him. Troy swallowed hard. The outline of the lady's sultry physique simply could not be hidden, not even by the modest red dress she was wearing.

Troy puffed a sigh of resolution.

He had to be strong. He had to be.

For the moment, though, he decided to just sit quietly and observe.

Evelyn was sitting on the front pew on the opposite side of the room. She noticed that Troy looked completely caught off guard by the fact that Kathleen, certainly knowing who he was through old man Baxter's reports, plopped down right beside him as if she didn't have a fearful bone in her body.

Evelyn wondered if Kathleen would say anything to him, but then noticed that Kathleen looked as if she was lost in her own world. She actually looked as if she had been crying. Evelyn had no idea how to interpret Kathleen's demeanor. She started to pray for her when Floyd Baxter suddenly appeared up front at a mobile podium, positioned at floor level.

"All right; it's time to start," Floyd announced. "So, let's just jump right in. I'll go ahead and say this will be the last time I'll introduce Pastor Rose. And it might very well be the last time I'll stand up front." Baxter then gestured with a sweeping hand toward Kathleen. "Kathleen's the new pastor now. So, from now on she will be the one to introduce the meetings. And she can introduce them any way she sees fit. I want to thank everyone for being here. And again, as an old man who has been around the block a time or two, I think our church is on the verge of a life-changing season that none of us will ever forget. With that said, I'll now ask Pastor Rose to come to the podium." Floyd led in an exuberant round of applause.

Evelyn clapped along with everyone else. She then looked over at Kathleen and saw Kathleen brush her hair out of her face and stand up. She watched as Kathleen, with a serious but distraught countenance of some sort, walked to the podium.

Kathleen manufactured a soothing smile and picked up the handheld mike. "I'm aware that my presence here at Lyons Central Baptist is quite controversial, especially carrying the title of pastor. So, with everyone's permission, I would like for each of you to just call me Kathleen."

There was a second or two of silence.

Before Kathleen could continue, a young male voice—probably that of one of the college students—cried out from somewhere in the center of the auditorium as if leading a cheer, "Pastor Rose! Pastor Rose! Pastor Rose!"

Evelyn turned around. She saw the young man stand up, motioning for those around him to stand and join in the mantra.

Before it could be squelched or discouraged, a swell of a hundred or more people was standing and chanting robustly, "Pastor Rose! Pastor Rose! Pastor Rose!"

Kathleen, seemingly stupefied, eventually motioned for everyone to please be seated. "Please, please. I do appreciate the vote of confidence. But let's do be sensitive to those in the congregation who are not so supportive. I believe you will agree that our goal should be unity, not division. And with that as our goal, I would like for us to begin our venture together as gently and as inoffensively as possible. After all, we want this church to be known to everyone in the community as a place of solid strength and contagious inspiration. So, join me if you will and let's work toward that end."

A few people who had not stood and chanted earlier started clapping.

"Let's do it!" someone shouted.

Kathleen nodded tenderly.

Troy had vowed to keep quiet, at least for a while. But almost on impulse, he stood and said, "What you're doing isn't right, though." He had wanted to sound tough. But, even to himself, his words sounded more like a father speaking mercifully to a young daughter.

Still, everyone in the room went quiet.

77

Kathleen turned immediately and gave her full and undivided attention to him. "What is your name?" she asked.

Troy wanted to say 'that's not important right now.' Instead, he said, "Troy Bingum. I'm one of the deacons."

"Troy," Kathleen stated without hesitation. "I have a couple of questions for you. I can ask them now, publicly. Or I can ask them privately when we break free for the one-on-one interaction. What is best for you?"

Troy suddenly sensed that Kathleen was giving him the option of avoiding any public embarrassment. Could he really not match wits with her? Did he even want to try in front of all these people? "Perhaps we can talk in detail after the meeting," he conceded, trying to sound wise.

"We can take all the time you need. Just track me down afterward," Kathleen reassured him.

Troy nodded his consent, again trying to look authoritative and settled.

"All right, well, this particular gathering has been designated," Kathleen said to the crowd, "for you to ask questions. So, perhaps I can take a few general questions from the floor. And then we'll break up. And you can approach me with any one-on-one questions you might have." Kathleen eyed the people with sincerity. "I'll look forward to the interaction and to learning about you as well."

The more Evelyn saw and heard, the more she was impressed by Kathleen Rose. The lady was kind, attentive, smart, and strong. She just seemed to be special all around.

"Well, let's open the floor for a few questions," Kathleen suddenly announced.

There was only a second of silence.

"Yes," Kathleen said, pointing to a hand instantly raised somewhere in the back.

"My name is Ric," another young man, again probably a college student, spoke up. "We have heard that you are a widow. Is that true? If so, can you tell us a little about your husband? How long were you married? What did he do? How did he die?"

Kathleen remain poised.

"Yes, I am a widow. My husband and I were married for twelve years. We moved to Africa as missionaries in 2000, shortly after our wedding. He founded a school of higher learning for those wanting to pursue degrees in Theology. In 2012, though, he contracted cerebral malaria. He was dead within two months. That was almost three years ago."

"What was your husband's name?" a teenage girl asked.

"His name was Nick. He was a very, very special man." Kathleen ignored a tear that surfaced at the corner of her eye.

"Where in Africa did you serve?" an older female queried.

"For security reasons I won't reveal the name of the country. That's because ninety percent of the people who live there are Muslim. So the Christians, especially the missionaries and pastors, in the country have to be extremely discreet. "You know," she added, "as wise as serpents and as harmless as doves."

"Did you teach at this school of theology that you referred to?" This time the question came from one of the handful of men in the audience.

"On occasions. Yes, I did."

"So, you have a teaching degree?" another young lady questioned.

Kathleen hesitated. "I have a Masters in Theology. Yes."

Absorbing every word from the front pew, Evelyn realized that her respect for the lady was increasing with every answer she heard.

"How do you know Floyd Baxter?" a man's voice suddenly intoned. The words were tense.

Evelyn twisted to look at the questioner. It was deacon Walter Johnson, sitting in the middle of the crowd.

Kathleen had strongly expected that someone would ask this question, privately if not publicly. She had already consulted with Floyd Baxter about providing a proper answer. "He's been one of my financial supporters for several years."

"Did he meet you and start supporting you AFTER your husband died, maybe while on a business trip of some kind?" Walter pushed.

What was the man implying? Kathleen had definitely not suspected this line of questioning. She wanted to say, 'You're trying to plant an idea that is way out of line, sir!' But she backed off. "The first time I saw Mr. Baxter in person," she offered firmly but graciously, "was a week ago here in Lyons, Georgia. He called me in Africa, I believe, five times over the last couple of years to offer words of encouragement. That is the full extent of our one-on-one communication...up until I arrived last week."

For a moment, silence hung in the room like a thick, damp blanket in a small wash room; it took up space and it was obvious.

Evelyn raised her hand, hoping to lighten the mood.

"Yes?"

"What's the worst food you've ever eaten as a missionary?"

Kathleen cracked a grin.

During the relaxed part of the meeting—when people intermingled, conversed, and waited their turn to speak one-on-one with Kathleen—Troy worked his way patiently to the front of the line. He and Walter had agreed that he, Troy, would launch the next offensive.

As his turn approached, Troy felt sweat beading beneath his arms. When he thought no one was looking, he sniffed quickly under his right arm. Good, he didn't smell any body odor. He knew that his sudden concern about repelling Kathleen with unpleasant smells should be the last thing on his mind. He chided himself that it wasn't. But he couldn't help it. When he stood in the lady's presence, he—in a boyish way— didn't want to be thought of as unattractive.

When he was finally next up, he overheard the lady in front of him, a grandmother, asking Kathleen about the malaria that killed her husband. He heard Kathleen answer the lady's curiosity with words like 'pulmonary edema' and 'adult respiratory distress.' Troy wondered again if he wasn't going to be embarrassed intellectually. He was suddenly wary that his high school diploma might just fail him here.

And then, there was no one between him and Kathleen, the object of his and so many other's offense. The last thought that went through his mind before he opened his mouth was; she honestly doesn't look like a church-wide threat.

Kathleen extended her hand first.

Troy wondered if he should accept her hand and even engage in this simplest form of peace offering. But the lady's winsomeness pulled him in. He shook her hand, trying somehow to make the physical contact feel emotionally cold.

"I'm Troy, the deacon who spoke up earlier," he asserted.

Kathleen nodded.

"On behalf of all the deacons," Troy declared without wasting another second, "I just need to let you know that we're all unanimously opposed to what's happening here."

Kathleen kept quiet and let him talk. She didn't shuffle. She didn't drop her shoulders. She didn't display a single hint of nervousness or discomfort.

"I'm assuming you're a Bible believer," Troy bulldozed ahead. "So how is it you can just outright ignore a verse like First Timothy two-twelve that says 'But I suffer not a woman to teach nor to usurp authority over the man, but to be in silence'?"

Troy waited, trying to stay chilled.

Kathleen, with her intoxicating sapphire-blue eyes, looked him straight in the face and asked kindheartedly, "Do you think there was a context for that verse, Troy?"

Troy felt his eyes crisscross. "What do you mean?"

"Do you think Paul wrote that particular verse to a particular person, with a particular reason in mind? Or do you think he wrote the verse in a universal way to a universal audience?

Troy had guessed that he might feel unprepared, and now he did. "I...uh...would believe it's both. It's the Word of God. It's for everybody. Don't you believe that?"

Kathleen looked up at the ceiling and pressed her lips together, then looked back. "When is the last time you kissed a man, Troy?"

Troy felt his face contort into a mass of shock and confusion. What the heck? What kind of question was that? Should he even dignify the asinine question with an answer? What was the lady...?

"The apostle Paul, the same person who wrote First Timothy two-twelve," Kathleen continued her point, "says in Romans sixteen-sixteen, to greet one another with a holy kiss. So, if you are a Bible believer, Troy, why don't you obey that verse? As a matter of fact, I haven't seen a single soul here at Central Baptist, male or female, practice that verse. Why is that?"

Troy felt himself mentally stumble.

"And what about First Corinthians eleven-five?" Kathleen pressed. Her voice and temper remained totally good-natured. "It too was written by the apostle Paul. It says a woman should pray with her head covered. I haven't seen any head coverings here at the church. So, do you guys really not believe the Bible?"

Troy had never thought about the application of these particular verses. And now he was wondering why. "Well, your head is not covered. And I haven't seen you greet anybody with a holy kiss either," he volleyed.

"Exactly," Kathleen stressed, "Paul was highlighting some of the practices that were relevant to those Mediterranean cultures. He is not asking twenty-first-century Christians in America to change the way we greet one another. He's not asking us to stop shaking hands and to start kissing one another's cheeks. He's not asking Asian Christians to stop bowing and to start kissing. He's not asking Bedouin Christians to stop rubbing noses and to start kissing. Is this making any sense?"

Troy really didn't want to concede. He fought inside his head for a legitimate way to keep confronting and opposing. "So, how does all that relate to First Timothy's command about women being silent?"

"Well, we have to look at the context to see what Paul was really saying, and ask if he was focusing on a cultural issue."

"And?"

"And, he was writing to Timothy, a young pastor who was serving a congregation in Ephesus. And at the core of the Ephesian culture was a temple to Artemis, a female goddess. The temple was one of the largest in the ancient world. You can read all about the goddess and her temple in Acts nineteen. And according to historical documents, this pagan temple was serviced, not by men, but by women priests. These female priests served a goddess who claimed authority over all men. Could it be—and I'm just asking—that Paul in this case was saying to the Christian ladies in this community 'I'm urging you to not mimic the position of Artemis by claiming that you are an authority over the men in the church? If you take this stance, then you should not be a teacher; you will only be condescending and hurtful.' Plus, according to Acts nineteen-eighteen, a lot of the women in the Ephesus congregation were converted witches who had probably held positions of destructive influence over men. Therefore, could it be that Paul was simply forbidding female dominance to migrate from the Ephesus culture into the Ephesus church?"

Troy cleared his throat. "But aren't you dominating the men in our church right now?"

Kathleen stared at him thoughtfully. "Have I given you any orders, Troy? Any instructions? Any rules? Have I claimed any authority in your life? Any whatsoever?"

Troy started to shuffle, then caught himself. "No, but...you are here against the will of the deacon board."

"And why actually is the deacon board opposed to me being here? Because of this verse? Because of a long-held southern tradition? Or simply because it looks and feels awkward?"

Troy shook his head and held his ground, "It's because for over two hundred years, it's been the accepted position of the Baptist church in this country; that's why! Obviously there is a Scriptural reason. So that's what I'm going to believe. Period."

Around midnight when Kathleen crawled under the bed covers in the privacy of her residence, she was emotionally spent. The reverse culture shock she was facing, along with her new role, simply wasn't going to be a docile burden.

As she switched off the bedside lamp, she was at least thankful no one had asked questions such as: Why did you leave Africa? How did you get your neck scar? Do you have any children?

As the last question echoed in her mind, she rolled onto her stomach and gripped the cotton bed sheets with both hands. She slowly squeezed with a death grip and then wailed into the mattress.

Eric Sawyer, around the same time, was soaking in a tub of hot water in his Vidalia apartment. As a journalist he had wanted badly to approach Kathleen at the evening meeting, introduce himself, and ask questions for a 'personal interview.' But out of respect he had impulsively chosen for the time being to just listen and observe. He would have other opportunities to meet the lady face to face.

He typed the name 'Nick Rose' into the search engine of his laptop. Nothing that came up looked relevant to a former missionary leader in Africa. He typed 'Nicholas Rose.' Still nothing.

Could the lack of an internet footprint for Nick and Kathleen Rose be attributed to an intentional effort to live below the radar, because of security reasons?

Eric still wondered about the lady's identity.

Something still didn't seem right.

15

Three Days Later - Saturday, April 11
Bamako, Mali - Africa
Sotubu Neighborhood

Medibo, at the age of 45, was the black Imam of the Sotubu Mosque at the far eastern reaches of the Malian capital. Permitted by Islam to have a maximum of four wives, he currently had room and resources for only three.

At the moment, he had his third and youngest wife, only 18, cornered in the main bedroom of their mud house. He angrily raised his hand at her a second time.

Trying to be brave, the young wife bellowed in the Bambara language, "The lady said she's read every page of the Quran and that it doesn't command us to do this thing, that there's no good reason to keep doing it. I've only had problems my whole life because of it. So, I will not put our two-year-old daughter through the same thing. Especially if Allah doesn't demand it."

Medibo again slapped his young wife across the face. He watched her flinch and scream in pain. "Then I will have it done to her without you," he snapped. "I am the Imam. It is our way. So, I will do what is right as an example to our people."

The young wife, catching a second wind of boldness, clutched the plastic hair brush already in her right hand and swung hard, thrashing Medibo across the edge of his face. The firm bristles caught the corner of his eye.

Medibo jerked in excruciating pain. He bent over and placed the heal of his hand into his eye socket and pressed. He yelled in the Bambara language, damning his young wife to eternal punishment. As he grimaced and rubbed vigorously at his eye, he noticed the young wife moving in a panic around his side, trying to escape. He lunged for her and knocked her to the floor. He crawled on top of her and wrangled to keep her arms and hands pinned to her chest. In a fit of rage, he then fisted her so many times on the side of her head that she momentarily went unconscious.

Standing to his feet again and breathing like a lion that had caught its prey, he stared at his wife's still body, blood pooling around her face. "That'll teach you, you fool," he growled.

He then went to their small kitchen to a bucket of water and liberally massaged his face. Still fuming, he hoped he would not lose any sight in his still-hurting and twitching eye. When he finally managed to sit cross-legged on the floor and be still, he closed his eyes and took deep breaths.

His mind, however, continued to race. His young wife had never defied him before. And he was now completely dumbfounded. How could a foreign woman, even a persuasive one, have had such an impact on his young Muslim wife in just one conversation? Or had his wife lied? Had she actually met with the foreigner on more than one occasion?

He strongly inhaled.

Whatever the case, he would teach the illiterate tramp that he was the authority in her life, not some outside voice, especially that of an infidel daughter from the Great Satan.

Still, there was one more thing about his wife's account that confounded him. Her description of the American lady she had conversed with at the market three weeks ago sounded too much like the infamous woman who for years had created havoc all over the country. But that particular woman had been silenced nearly a year ago; hadn't she?

If the lady at the market was not the noted American, then who was it that had told his wife these things? Seriously upset, he knew he had to somehow alert the group that had reportedly dealt with the situation.

Grimacing and rubbing his eye, he decided he would try to reach out to his contact the first thing tomorrow morning.

16

"It's your turn," Troy told Walter when they met at the church parking lot on Sunday morning. It was a glorious spring day. The sweet smell of honeysuckle wafted across the church property. "You need to face off with her now. She needs to hear another voice."

Walter, the youngest of the deacons, had always told himself he was a brave man. And he believed it. He had, for example, never refused a dare, especially a double-dog dare. He was proud of the fact that he was the type who would often make a daring decision even before he was officially dared. "All right, then, let's wait until she's about five minutes into her sermon and we'll march in like we own the place and walk straight down to the front. And after the sermon, I'll be the first one up front. I'll dominate her time and try to make it as unpleasant for her as possible. I'll especially use the verses we've talked about."

Troy gave a thumbs up.

Evelyn, with her black Bible open on her lap, had just finished following along with Kathleen's reading of the sermon text—John 1:1-14—when Troy and Walter came huffing down the center aisle distracting everyone. Projecting the image of provocative juveniles, the men obstinately waved at a couple of people and walked side by side all the way to the communion table where they plunked themselves down on the front pew.

Evelyn turned and looked at Kathleen behind the podium.

Kathleen had stopped talking. She was quietly staring at Troy and Walter. With a lighthearted look, it appeared for a moment she was going to issue a wisecrack remark, perhaps to solicit laughter from the crowd regarding the two men. But she obviously curtailed the notion.

"So, as I was about to say," Kathleen picked up, "the apostle John in these verses is speaking on behalf of the other apostles. This is highlighted when he uses the word 'us' in verse fourteen. And he says...that they, the apostles, came to understand that Jesus, their Rabbi, was God incarnate...God in the flesh, the actual Creator of the universe. So, the question is: when did they come to this realization? Was it before the resurrection? Or after?

"I submit to you that it was before. Here are three quick reasons.

"First, in John ten, the apostles heard Jesus in a public arena declare 'the Father and I are one.' There was no misunderstanding as to what He was saying. They saw the crowd pick up stones and shout 'we are going to stone you because you as a man claim to be God.' It's against all logic to think the apostles didn't bring this up as a matter of discussion later that night.

"Secondly, the apostle Philip in John fourteen approached Jesus and said quite daringly, 'show us the Father.' Jesus replied, 'The one who has seen me has seen the Father.' This was not an ambivalent statement. It was clear, dogmatic, and resolute. And Philip understood it completely.

"And thirdly, in Jesus' lengthy prayer in John seventeen, Jesus says to the Father 'they—the apostles—have known for certain...for certain...that I came from You.'

"For these reasons I believe we can say with a degree of confidence that the apostles, with the exception of Judas, came to recognize Jesus as God incarnate prior to His death. Actually, this is probably the reason they were so derailed when they saw him die on the cross. God can't die! So, had they been scammed? Had they believed a hoax? Had they been so foolish and naive to actually fall for the rabbi's self-delusional charade?

"No wonder they were beyond angry and depressed following His crucifixion. No wonder they cursed when people identified them as His disciples and followers. They had been fools and were now trying to hide from the fact."

Evelyn for the first time in years took notes. She was hungrily digesting all she was hearing.

"And then three days later—as we learned last week—Jesus walked into their presence and said, 'Hello, gentlemen.' And then suddenly, everything they had earlier witnessed Jesus say and do came into focus and made sense. He WAS God! And as God, He had BECOME the sacrificial lamb who takes away the sin of the world, the ultimate sin bearer for all humanity."

Kathleen then went on to explain how at least ten of the apostles, at the decree of the resurrected Lord, left Israel behind in due course and preached the Good News of the Gospel throughout Asia, Africa, and Europe. And how, in the end, they all accepted martyrdom as incessant witnesses of the resurrection of Jesus and of His absolute exclusivity.

"The point I want to make this morning is that the apostles' journey of understanding was not quick and easy. They first acknowledged Jesus only as a rabbi - John, chapter one, verses thirty-five through thirty eight. They later came to understand that He was more than just their rabbi; He was the promised Messiah - Matthew, chapter sixteen, verses thirteen through sixteen. And then finally, they came to understand that He was more than just the promised Messiah; He was God incarnate - the Creator and Savior of the world. And this last step was not achieved without a major upheaval.

"All this information helps us better understand the apostles. But hopefully, it will help us better understand ourselves as well. Our journeys of faith, even in the twenty-first century, are not quick and easy either. Our knowledge of God is constantly growing. And this is okay. Actually it's normal.

"For example, it took me years to understand that God isn't as small as the Baptists' understanding of things. It took me a while longer, but I eventually learned that God isn't as small as America's understanding of things. And then one of the most difficult concessions for me was to admit that God isn't as small as the world's understanding of things.

"And I'm still learning. So, this morning I want to encourage us all. Let's keep our minds open. And let's allow God to reveal Himself to us more and more. Let's eagerly take these progressive steps of understanding. And let's allow our faith to soar."

Walter—sitting speechless on the front pew—suddenly faced a personal conundrum. This was his first time to hear Kathleen teach. And he was not only impressed; he was genuinely touched and inspired. He didn't want to be, but he was. The sermon was honestly thought provoking. Even eye-opening. And when was the last time he could say such a thing about a Sunday sermon? It had actually been a long time. Yet, did this make it right that Kathleen was standing behind the podium as the shepherd of the flock?

Within minutes, Walter had convinced himself that he needed to stop thinking, and just simply act on his upbringing. And on his manly instincts. After all, he knew what was right.

He was so absorbed in rehearsing his planned argument that he missed Kathleen's closing remarks and most of her dismissal prayer. As soon as he heard the word "amen" pass through her lips, though, he refocused on his surroundings and made a beeline to where Kathleen was standing on the platform.

He needed to be assertive. Wanted to be assertive. He thought he would be assertive. Yet, Kathleen—when seeing his determined approach—humbly, but undauntedly turned to face him.

He opened his mouth to launch his first verbal assault when the lady's piercing blue eyes brought him to a brief stand still. Before he could regroup and espouse his condescending judgement, he heard Kathleen say, "Is Nympha a man's name or a woman's name?"

Walter mentally tripped. He looked around to see if a third party had joined the conversation. When he realized Kathleen was talking to him, he did a retake. "Pardon?"

"Is Nympha a man's name or a woman's name?"

Walter shook his head as if to clear his brain. "It's a woman's name, I guess. Why?"

"Paul says in Colossians chapter four, verse fifteen, to give his greetings to Nympha and the church in her home.'"

Before Walter could formulate a response, Kathleen spoke again. "Is Phoebe a man's name or a woman's name?"

Walter didn't answer.

"It's a woman's name," Kathleen explained. "And Paul says in Romans chapter sixteen, verse one, that Phoebe is a minister in the church at Cenchreae. Shall I go on? What about the chosen lady that the apostle John writes to in Second John? She is definitely a church leader of some type."

Walter tried not to get flustered. "Yes, but First Corinthians, chapter fourteen, makes it very clear that women should be silent in all the churches of the saints. That women are not permitted to speak."

Without hesitation, Kathleen replied, "But could 'all the churches' in that verse simply be referring to all the churches in the municipality of Corinth? In other words, could the issue have been a cultural one? And nothing more?"

Walter shook his head. "I think you're twisting the verses to say what you want them to say."

A tranquil look spread across Kathleen's masterpiece of a face. "How long have you personally been a believer?" she countered.

"For about fifteen years," Walter answered, not sure what the point of the question was.

"Fifteen years. I'm assuming and hoping then that you have learned a great deal of Bible truth during that time."

"Enough," Walter touted.

"Good, then since you think I shouldn't be teaching from the pulpit, I'll let you teach next Sunday."

Walter almost choked. "What...I...uh...I'm not a preacher. I can't...I mean I won't..."

"You better be prepared," Kathleen said, looking as if she were masking a grin, "because I will start announcing today that you'll be the key speaker next week."

"I've never preached before. I..."

Kathleen placed a hand on his shoulder and gently squeezed. "Then you're overdue." She then turned to greet others who wanted her attention.

17

On Thursday morning, after serving a breakfast of home-cooked biscuits, eggs, grits, and bacon, Evelyn kissed Ray on the cheek and sent him out to his backyard tractor shop with a pat on the butt.

Evelyn cleaned the kitchen, then sat down to read the latest *Vidalia Times* article about the church. She laid the paper open across the kitchen table.

The Onward March Of
Kathleen Rose At
Lyons Central Baptist

For two Sundays now, Kathleen Rose, the new pastor at Lyons Central Baptist has led the congregation.

The resistance movement, led by the church's four remaining deacons continues at full force. Most of the older male members of the church have stopped attending. And most of the volunteer staff—the pianist, song leader, ushers, and Sunday school teachers—have stopped serving. Yet, the two Sunday services since Pastor Rose's arrival have been full and vibrant.

Young men and women, mainly from Vidalia Technical College, have helped fill the auditorium and have helped serve as amateur ushers and musicians.

Floyd Baxter, the man behind Pastor Rose's Central Baptist appointment, says, "I cannot be more pleased with the way things have developed."

And perhaps Mr. Baxter has a reason to be optimistic. Pastor Rose is now settled in her new house. She is visiting widows, shut-ins, the sick, and is seeing her church filled with young men and women eager to learn and serve.

Evelyn looked up toward the kitchen window and beamed. Old man Baxter had never been one of her favorite people. Yet she now admired the man for his brave and unconventional move. She had no idea what his connection was with Kathleen, but she definitely shared his optimistic view of the lady. Kathleen, against all logic and against all odds, seemed to be the perfect solution to their church's disappointing past. The lady was amazing in every sense of the word.

Evelyn's excitement was hampered only by her husband, Ray's, downcast spirit. Ray still wasn't willing to make any concessions, even a small one, regarding a lady pastor. Or to even consider such. He was so disheartened, actually, that for the first time in their thirty-seven years of marriage he was refusing to attend church anywhere. "I'm just fed up with the whole thing," he had declared to anyone willing to listen, including their nineteen-year-old son, Billy. He had even found it offensive that Walter had been cajoled by the lady pastor to preach for the first time; that Walter had spinelessly surrendered to the lady's wishes. "What a circus!" Ray had derided.

Evelyn stood up and walked over to the kitchen window. She looked out at the steel-and-concrete workshop in the backyard. "Oh, God," she whispered toward the glass, "please take care of my husband. He's a good man. And a strong man. He just needs a little encouragement right now. Can you please give that to him? Please."

When Evelyn started to leave the kitchen she glanced one more time at the open newspaper lying on the table. She suddenly felt impressed to pray for Eric Sawyer, at the *Vidalia Times*, as well. "Lord, you know whether he's a believer or not. As long as he keeps coming to church, and for whatever reason that might be, I pray you will gently hammer away at his heart. And not let up."

*   *   *

On Saturday night, when his wife and two kids were sound asleep in bed, Walter sat fidgeting at his kitchen counter. His cup of coffee, laptop, Bible, pen, and notepad were spread in front of him across the beige laminate surface.

How had he ever agreed to this?

Out of all the deacons, he was the only one who had never preached or led a church service.

A couple of days ago, he had called deacons Jim Manley and Jack Evans and asked if either of them could speak in his place. They had both declined, reiterating they would hold to their commitment to boycott all Central Baptist services until Kathleen Rose had officially stepped down.

He had then called Troy with the same request only to learn that Troy and his family would be away on vacation over the weekend.

As a last resort, he had reached out to a friend in neighboring Emanuel County who for many years had served as a full-time evangelist. "I'm really sorry," the man told him. "But I'm already booked for the weekend."

Walter looked at the kitchen clock. It was already 11:30 PM. He wiped sweat from his brow.

He was secretly ashamed that, with all of his supposed Bible knowledge, he hadn't been able to come up with a simple Bible lesson that he felt would be helpful or appropriate.

He was now looking online at a preprinted sermon based on First Corinthians fourteen, verses thirty-three and thirty-four, 'As in all the churches of the saints, the women should be silent in the churches, for they are not permitted to speak, but should be submissive, as the law also says.'

Should he use the pre-packaged sermon and hammer the verse home?

He felt the urgency to keep fighting in a visible and public way, regardless of what Kathleen Rose believed.

18

Walter looked out at the Sunday morning crowd of nearly two hundred people. He was only five minutes into his sermon and was feeling more and more skittish by the second. The fact that most of the people already looked bored and distracted certainly didn't help his confidence.

"You know what we, the Christians of Lyons and Vidalia, should be ashamed of, don't you?" he asked rhetorically. "Female pastors; that's what the Bible says we should be ashamed of!" He started reading verse thirty-five of the First Corinthians passage, with emphasis.

Before he could complete the verse, he heard the background 'boos.' And then the swell. A whole row of male students suddenly stood and accompanied their ominous boos with a thumbs-down gesture. Other students, both male and female, quickly stood up and joined in.

Walter raised his voice into the mike. "You might say, 'I'm embarrassed over your sermon.' But why is it that you're embarrassed over my sermon, or even the Bible verse, but you're not embarrassed over female preachers? The Bible makes it emphatically clear that this is a shameful matter. The Bible says the man is to lead in the home and in the church, and that the woman's role is to submit to the man's headship."

The boos continued to come in rounds.

Walter tried for another ten minutes to persuade the congregation to see his point. By the time he sat down, he wondered if the whole town was going to hell. What had happened to the Bible-believing church that for decades had occupied these sacred grounds? He almost cried. He definitely felt sick at his stomach.

Emboldened by anger, Walter on his way out of the building stopped to engage Kathleen one more time. He waited until two older ladies finished their exchange with her, then stepped forward.

Kathleen, seeing him approach, issued a smile. Not a haughty smile. But an 'I care for you' smile.

"You're ruining our church," Walter blurted from his heart. "Can't you see that?"

Kathleen, as usual, appeared to weigh her thoughts before she spoke. Eventually she said, "The next time you preach I would encourage you to relax. Try to project the Word in its context above everything else - above personal agenda, above anxiety. Oh...and I would also encourage you not to preach other men's sermons. You are better than that. You need to wrestle with the Scripture in your own heart first. Examine it. Compare it. Sift it. Fight it. Think it. And then share what you think you've learned. And let the people take it or leave it."

Walter placed his hand on his forehead and squeezed. "Next time? What do you...?"

"Of course next time. I want you to teach at least once every six weeks or so."

Walter couldn't believe what he was hearing. Was the lady even listening?

"And you honestly believe that what I preached this morning was wrong?" Walter caught himself starting to breathe heavily.

Kathleen remained composed. "By the way, did you happen to read verse twenty-six in the same chapter you preached from?"

"Verse twenty-six? What? From First Corinthians fourteen?"

"Yes. It says, 'Whenever you come together, each one has a psalm, a teaching, a revelation, another language, or an interpretation. All things must be done for edification.' Is this verse addressing only the men in the church? If not, then Paul is permitting, and even encouraging, the women to speak up in church."

"Are you saying the Bible contradicts itself?"

"No. I'm saying that the discrepancy is not in the passage itself, but rather in our understanding of the passage."

Walter shook his head in frustration.

"And what about the Magnificat of Mary?" Kathleen gently pressed.

Walter raised his eyebrows. "The what?"

"The Magnificat of Mary. It's the song of Mary in Luke one, verses forty-six through fifty-five." Kathleen opened her Bible to the passage, then handed the open pages to Walter. "Take a look."

Walter murmured under his breath. He took the Bible and read the verses. "And?" he said.

"And, do the verses teach us anything about God?"

Walter looked at the passage again. "Yes. Of course the verses teach us some things about God."

"Is Mary—the one speaking—a male or female?"

Walter closed his eyes and puffed. He was really tired of being on the defensive.

"So," Kathleen continued, "Is God contradicting Himself then? Would He use a lady here to teach hundreds of millions of males around the world important truths about Himself, and then turn around and declare that no other lady in any church anywhere in the world under any circumstance at any time can ever open her mouth and teach spiritual truths?"

Walter wanted to pull at his hair. Instead, he handed the Bible back to Kathleen and turned to leave the building.

"Be ready to preach again in six weeks." Kathleen said. The words followed him out of the auditorium.

19

Opposition Leader
Preaches At Lyons Central Baptist

Deacon Walter Johnson, one of the voices opposing the new Central Baptist pastor Kathleen Rose, preached last Sunday morning at Pastor Rose's invitation.

Declaring from the Central Baptist pulpit that female pastors are a disgrace, Mr. Johnson's message was greeted with hisses and boos. It seems the new group of church attendees, mainly elderly women and college students, stand behind the new pastor wholeheartedly and has grown weary of the old guards' opposition. "I love the new pastor; she's the only pastor I've ever liked, who I believe is totally genuine from head to toe," declared one of the female college students.

Pastor Kathleen Rose, following the service, refused to give public comments.

Floyd Baxter, who is personally
paying Pastor Rose's salary, was not
present at the meeting for feedback.

Ray Huxley read the Tuesday morning article alone in his grimy tractor-repair shop. When he finished digesting the words, he picked up a greasy half-inch bolt and threw it hard against one of the concrete walls.

*   *   *

Kathleen parked her white 2013 Toyota Camry, provided by Mr. Baxter, right in front of the E.Z. Grocery Store on the east side of Lyons. It seemed to Kathleen, judging strictly by the customers coming and going, that the store catered primarily to the black community. She needed to restock her refrigerator with milk, eggs, and vegetables, along with some shelf items like fruit and bread. Plus, she was ready to meet some of the local residents of color.

As she got out of her car to enter the store, she heard catcalls coming from a group of young black men standing and talking four or five cars away. She ignored them and went inside.

Within minutes of entering the building and putting a few items in her cart, she reached the bread aisle. There she witnessed a middle-aged black woman pushing an older woman in a wheelchair. She noticed that the wheelchair-bound lady looked to have some kind of muscular dystrophy. The woman pushing the wheelchair was also pulling a grocery buggy behind her and was struggling somewhat with the feat.

"Here, let me help you with that," Kathleen said.

The woman standing behind the wheelchair turned and looked. Her eyes revealed an instantaneous moment of suspicion when she saw that Kathleen was white.

Kathleen pointed to the lady's buggy. "You look like you could use an extra hand. Can I help push the cart for you?"

There was another look of suspicion. The lady quickly looked Kathleen up and down. "Okay," she said slowly, "Sure I can use a little help if you want."

"My name is Kathleen."

"My name is Willow. This is my aunt, Ida Mae."

Kathleen looked at Ida Mae, smiled, and nodded.

Ida Mae, whose body was twisted in an unnatural position, returned the nod with a spastic jerk. The aged black lady was definitely handicapped, but looked bubbly.

"Ida Mae can hear, but she can't talk. She's what they call mute."

"Hi, Ida Mae, my name is Kathleen Rose." Kathleen reached over and softly held Ida Mae's curled-up boney hand.

Ida Mae returned another spastic nod and smiled, then jerked back and forth, as if wanting so badly to reciprocate with a normal handshake.

"Ida Mae's a miracle baby. She lost so much oxygen at birth that she's what they call a 'spastic paralysis' person. The doctors say she shoulda died after only five years or so. But here she is. Seventy-two and still goin' strong."

"I would say she's a miracle baby indeed, then." Kathleen smiled at Ida Mae one more time, then extended her hand to Willow.

Willow shook her hand.

Kathleen took the initiative and took hold of Willow's cart. "All right, well, I'll just leave my buggy here. There are only a couple of items in it anyway. And I'll just push your buggy and follow you around."

"You sure?"

"I'm more than glad to help."

"Who'd you say you are again?"

"My name is Kathleen Rose. I'm the new assistant pastor at Lyons Central Baptist." Kathleen felt the title of assistant pastor might be less off-putting than pastor. Besides, she had reformulated in her mind that she was technically under the wing of Mr. Baxter's authority. Baxter was the deed holder of the church property and was paying her salary at his personal directive.

"So you're the one!" Willow looked absolutely surprised, then looked suddenly pleased. "I done heard about you. Seems like you done stirred up quite a hornets' nest. Or as my mammy would say, 'This here is a two-devil town and you done gone and stirred up both those devils.'" Willow chuckled.

Kathleen couldn't help but smile. "Well, people keep telling me that. But in all honesty, I'm trying to help settle things down at the church. As much as possible anyway."

Willow blinked and grinned her support.

"I don't know if you're a praying woman, Willow," Kathleen continued, "but if you are, pray that God will help me be a source of strength and unity at the church, and here in the town as well. And not a source of discord."

"Well, be honest with you, Miss Kathleen, it's been years since I been anywhere near a church. I just growed tired of pastors yellin' at me and wantin' my money all the time."

"I understand," Kathleen said as they slowly started moving through the store again.

By the time they reached the frozen food section, Kathleen —because of the natural lighthearted banter that occurred— was laughing harder than she had laughed in three years.

At one point Willow placed her hand on Kathleen's shoulder and said, "You done said you wanna be a source of unity here in our town. Well, it's not helpin' that you walkin' around and cuttin' up with me and Ida Mae here. People are already staring at us like we be crazy." She made the observation while holding back another laugh, like they were already cherished friends and couldn't care less what anybody else thought or said.

At the checkout counter, Kathleen wanted to make a statement of sisterhood. She pulled out her wallet and, against Willow's protest, paid for all of Willow and Ida Mae's groceries. She then helped load Ida Mae into the front seat of Willow's car, and helped fold the wheelchair and stow it away in the trunk.

"No white person ever helped me liked this before," Willow said, suddenly becoming serious. "I just wanna say you're real nice. Real nice! I wish all pastors were like you."

Kathleen hugged Willow and wished her a good week, then hugged Ida Mae. An energetic hug was returned by both ladies.

"Maybe we can go for a walk sometime," Kathleen said to Willow as part of their goodbye, "I've heard that Partin Park is a nice place to walk, but I haven't been there yet. Maybe we can go together and walk around, and you can tell me more about the people and the history of the town."

Willow slapped her thigh. "Lordy, Miss Kathleen, let's do it."

The ladies exchanged phone numbers and promised to stay in touch.

20

As Kathleen commenced her Sunday morning sermon to a packed house, she publicly—from the microphone—asked a middle-aged lady sitting at the front of the sanctuary, "Who influenced you to come to Christ?"

The lady sat straighter and leaned forward when she registered what was happening. "My mother," she called out.

"Who influenced your mother to come to Christ?"

"I think it was her mother."

"And who influenced her mother?"

The lady puffed. "I honestly have no idea."

"But somebody did, didn't they? And someone influenced that person. And someone influenced that person. And someone influenced that person."

Kathleen pointed to the male undergraduate student who had just been playing the drums. "Who influenced you to come to Christ?" she asked gently.

"It was a girlfriend."

"And who influenced her?"

"I'm pretty sure it was her youth pastor."

"And who influenced him?"

"Not sure," the young man answered.

"But somebody did," Kathleen drove home the point. "As a matter of fact, if you, I, or any other believer in this room could trace our chain of influence back through history, we would discover that our lineage of faith would eventually lead literally across continents and nations, all the way back to one of the apostles, and then to Christ himself.

"Now turn to Matthew chapter twenty-eight, verses eighteen through twenty."

When Bible pages around the room ceased to ruffle, Kathleen read aloud the three verses.

"As you all know," she said when she finished reading, "these verses are known as the Great Commission. They're called the Great Commission because of the magnitude and scope of the mission.

"When Jesus initially spoke these words, who was he speaking to? Who was his audience? Look at verse sixteen."

"The eleven disciples," a young man with a scraggly goatee shouted.

"Yes," Kathleen volleyed, "The eleven disciples. Minus Judas.

"Does this commission take place before or after the resurrection?"

"After," came a female voice.

"Yes...after the resurrection. So these eleven men knew without any doubts or suspicions at this moment that Jesus was God incarnate. They knew they were looking into the eyes of God.

"And they hear God say to them—and I freely paraphrase —'Three years ago I asked you to be my students. And in so doing you gave up your jobs, your villages, and your other interests. You followed me all over the land. And in so doing, you sacrificed a great deal. But now I'm asking for an even greater sacrifice. I want each of you to leave Israel. You've been trained for itinerate living. You've learned to sleep under the stars. You've learned to sleep in the homes of strangers. You've learned to eat the food of strangers. You've learned to preach in public places. You've learned to interact with small and large groups of people. You've learned to disciple new converts.

"I want you to continue what we've been doing. But now I want you to take my message outside Israel. I want some of you to go into Asia, some into Africa, and some into Europe.

"And you're never coming back.

"As you go, I want you to stop in every village, town, and city. If people will listen, then tell them what you have witnessed. Then teach them all the truths I've taught you over the last three years. If anyone embraces my message. And me. Then publicly baptize them as my followers. If there are multiple converts in the same town, then appoint the most qualified one to be the leader, and help them set up a church. And then move on to the next town.

"Well, did the eleven disciples obey?"

No one offered up an answer.

"We know from the book of Acts," Kathleen pressed onward, "that they did not obey quickly. And we know that James, one of the eleven, was eventually executed by Herod inside Israel. But based on exclusive and oral histories from around the world, we learn that the remaining ten men did in fact leave Israel, never to return.

"History is clear, for example, that Thomas laid a trail across the territories known today as Jordan, Iraq, Iran, Pakistan; all the way to India where he was eventually martyred. Every Christian from India will tell you they can trace their Christian heritage back to the apostle Thomas.

"We know that the apostle John ministered throughout Asia Minor, a part of the world known today as Turkey. Before he was imprisoned on the island of Patmos, he most likely planted most of the churches he addressed in Revelation two and three.

"Peter made it into Europe and was martyred in Rome. It is believed that James the younger also went into Europe, that Simon the Zealot and Matthew went into Africa, that Nathanael, Thaddeus, and Andrew went into Asia, and that Philip went into Greece.

"As these men went out, they turned the world upside down.

"And their converts, as trained, continued to spread the Gospel. John's disciple, Polycarp, for example, carried the Gospel into Asia Minor. It's believed that one of Matthew's converts, King Egippus of Ethiopia, made it possible for his entire African nation to hear God's truth. Titus, one of Paul's many converts, boldly proclaimed the Savior's message through-out the island of Crete. And the stories go on and on in hundreds of directions.

"The point is, the apostles eventually obeyed Christ's commission to take His message to all parts of the world. The individuals they won to Christ took the baton of Christianity and gave it to the next generation. The next generation boldly passed it to the next. The trail of influence rippled from one neighbor to another, from one country to another, from one continent to another.

"Eventually, along that particular trail of influence, you—the Christians here in Lyons, Georgia—were given the baton by the person who influenced you.

"So we learn from Christianity's long history," Kathleen emphatically summarized, "that whenever we influence someone for Christ, our influence will not stop with that one individual. Rather it will ripple forward from that person onward—possibly to a spouse, a child, a grandchild, a neighbor, a friend—to the next generation and the next and the next, until the end of time."

Troy Bingum, sitting in a brown suit and burgundy striped tie at the front of the auditorium, hung his head during Kathleen's dismissal prayer, and wrung his hands. The dilemma unfolding in his mind continued to grow in complexity. He had been so immersed in the latter part of Kathleen's sermon, for example, that he had forgotten he was supposed to be an enemy. He tried to shake the confusion from his head. If Kathleen was so out of place behind the podium, how was it that God was using her so visibly to reach the hearts and minds of the whole congregation, including himself? Like many others, whose opinions he had overheard, he too found Kathleen's teachings to be wholly enlightening, life-touching, and memorable, more so than all bygone sermons he had ever heard preached beneath the Central Baptist Church roof.

He concluded that Jim and Jack, the other two deacons, just didn't understand. They had not witnessed or heard Kathleen in person.

Still, he had to be strong. Didn't he?

Maybe it was good then that he and Walter had already made a commitment to accost Kathleen again, today before she left the church property. Or else he might have bowed out.

Walter, on one of the back pews, sat in admiration. He couldn't help but compare his scant attempt at opening God's Word last Sunday to today's remarkable presentation. He was still somewhat embarrassed by last Sunday's debacle. Yet, he had at least stood up and spoken out. And, regardless of everything else, he still felt that having a lady pastor was wrong. All the pastors he had heard expound on the subject through the years were in agreement. They couldn't all be wrong; could they?

He tried to mentally prepare himself for confronting Kathleen again. He wasn't sure he really wanted to go through with it, but he had already made the promise to Troy.

21

Kathleen, at Troy and Walter's request, sat down on the end of a pew after everyone else had left the building. She sat midway in the auditorium, beneath one of six chandeliers that hung decoratively from the ceiling.

Troy sat on the cushioned pew in front of Kathleen and immediately noticed two things. Number one, the lady's beauty just didn't seem to have an expiration date. He constantly had to fight the physical attraction. Number two, instead of appearing exasperated by him and Walter—the two pests who wouldn't go away—Kathleen actually seemed to welcome them, even with a friendly smile.

"So, how can I help you two?" Kathleen asked, totally at ease.

Troy saw that Walter had chosen not to sit. Instead he was standing in the aisle, hovering over them. Was he just nervous? Or was he hoping to unnerve Kathleen with his posture?

"Look," Troy began, turning to look at Kathleen, "it's obvious that more people are attending church now than before you arrived. And most of those people, for whatever reason, seem to like you and support you. Of course, most of those people are female, along with a few male students who are short-term in the community. But regardless of all the..."

Kathleen raised her hand. "Is it okay if I interrupt?"

Troy stopped, started to say something, then yielded.

Kathleen opened her Bible. "I understand you two gentlemen believe you're fighting for a Biblical cause. Correct?" Kathleen looked at one man, then the other.

"Yes, of course we do; we wouldn't be here otherwise," Walter retorted from his elevated position.

"All right; let's get straight to the point," Kathleen said. "Most Bible verses are clear in their given context. And I know that both of you believe the First Timothy and First Corinthians passages are clear as well. But what if I could show you some progressive interpretations of those verses that Bible scholars are newly considering? Would you let me do that?"

Troy weighed the moment. With a lift of his eyebrows he granted a reluctant nod.

Kathleen turned to the Corinthians passage first. "As you know, it's verses thirty-three, thirty-four, and thirty-five in chapter fourteen that are continually cited to keep women from teaching in the church. Yet in all honesty these verses seem to be out of place. Why? Because in all the verses before and after, Paul is encouraging everyone in the church—both male and female—to contribute to the wellbeing of the body with meaningful and orderly words. In verse five, for example, he says 'I would rather all of you—both male and female—prophesy.' The fact that he's including females is confirmed in chapter eleven, verse five, where he lays a woman should prophesy with her head covered. And 'to prophesy' he explains in chapter fourteen, verse three, is to publicly edify, encourage, and comfort.

"And then in verse twenty-six, he says it is normal to come together as a church and listen to a variety of people—both male and female—share a teaching, a psalm, a revelation.

"So, why then would he turn right around and prohibit women in verses thirty-three, thirty-four, and thirty-five from speaking publicly in church? It doesn't make sense. Again, these verses honestly seem to be out of place when you look at the overall context.

"So, here is what some theologians are now saying.

"In verse thirty-four, Paul refers to a law that forbids women from teaching. Well, we know it's not an Old Testament law. So, what law is it? Some believe it was simply an oral law, or a manmade custom, created by legalistic Judaizers to keep women quiet, and that Paul here is actually mocking the custom. That he is saying, 'some of you believe this custom is of God, but did the laws of God originate with you?' And that Paul is actually challenging them with sarcasm."

Troy extended his hand to take Kathleen's black leather Bible. Kathleen handed it to him. Troy couldn't help but notice how well-worn the Bible was when he held it in his hands. Handwritten notes were everywhere in the margins. Troy wondered if most of the pages in her Bible looked that way. He then refocused and read the First Corinthians passage in silence. He read it a second time. Could it be?

Troy looked up and gave Walter an I'll-talk-to-you-later-in-private look.

Troy turned and looked at Kathleen. "Next."

Kathleen took her Bible and promptly turned to First Timothy, chapter two. "As you know," she began, "it's verses eleven and twelve in the First Timothy passage that are used to ban women from teaching. Again, these words are written by Paul. So, why would he encourage the women in Corinth to prophesy, or teach, in the church, and then tell Timothy to forbid the females in his church from teaching? Is there a contradiction here? If not, how do we explain the apparent discrepancy?

"Again, here's how some theologians are explaining it.

"In verses eleven and twelve, Paul uses the word 'woman,' singular. In all the verses before and after, he uses the word 'women,' plural. Greek scholars say the singular word 'woman,' can rightfully be translated 'wife.' And that the singular word 'man' in the same verse can be rightfully translated 'husband.' If this is the case, then the verse can actually be translated 'A wife should learn in quietness; I do not permit a wife to dominate her husband and attempt to be the teacher in his life; this is contrary to human nature, contrary to the natural order of things.'

"This would be part of the 'good behavior' he talks about for women in verse ten."

This time, Walter gestured for Kathleen's Bible. He took it and looked at the verses. Within fifteen seconds he gave the Bible back to her and said, "It sounds to me like you're just trying to twist the Scriptures to fit your own personal beliefs. And that's the God's honest truth."

Kathleen sighed. "It's not just women—or me—who's promoting these interpretations, Walter. Godly men are pushing them to the forefront as well, men who sincerely revere God, revere His Word, and revere His church. Not wicked people. Not people who are scrambling with some sinister motive to undermine God's authority. Or to destroy His church. But God-honoring people. Devoted people.

"Could it be," Kathleen threw out, "that the old standard interpretations most people hold to are simply old puritan interpretations that centuries ago were wrongly engrained into our church culture? Interpretations that, for whatever reason, we've hesitated to let go?"

Troy wasn't sure what to say. He noticed Walter wasn't saying anything at the moment either.

Before they could regroup and voice their thoughts, Kathleen resumed her critique. "Besides, every church in the Evangelical Baptist Alliance that I'm familiar with allows women to teach Sunday School. And many of those female teachers are leading mixed classes. Plus, all the churches in the Alliance allow women to sing, pray, and testify from the pulpit. They even allow female choir directors and soloists to give devotional snippets to the audience when they're introducing new songs.

"So, where's the consistency?

"If you or any other male leaders insist on holding to the old puritan interpretations of these verses, then you really need to be consistent. You shouldn't allow women to speak, period. You shouldn't allow them to sing, to pray, to testify, to comment, to lead choirs, or to make announcements. Nothing. Signs should be posted on all the church doors, 'Women be silent; No exceptions.'"

Once again Troy gave way to a temporary hush. So did Walter. Troy was amazed that Kathleen could sit there and, whether right or wrong in her insights, face off with two belligerent men and to do so with such remarkable grace and poise. And grit.

"I'm simply saying," Kathleen concluded, "that these verses are not so easy to understand, especially when compared to other Scriptures, and equally so when compared to ministries all around the planet where God is blessing female pastors, missionaries, church planters, Bible translators, evangelists, counselors, and teachers in a way that is inarguable.

"And as I've said before, if it's the title 'pastor' for a woman that bothers you, then I am more than willing to abdicate the title. But if the people insist I have a title, then feel free to title me 'assistant pastor,' 'servant teacher,' 'interim helper,' or whatever you like."

Troy heard Walter totally ignore Kathleen's words and with a frustrated tone say, "Everything I'm hearing sounds…just… so…stretched, and so off the mark. I just don't feel good about any of it." Looking suddenly stern, Walter changed the subject and said, "Why did you agree to come here anyway? Why Lyons, Georgia? What made you leave Africa?"

Troy looked at Kathleen.

Kathleen went abruptly silent, eerily so, like a burglar suddenly trying to hide from the police.

Troy noticed for the first time since he had met her that the lady appeared distinctly unsettled. Walter's question had obviously jolted her. But why?

Kathleen twisted in her seat, started to say something, then stopped. Her eyelids closed, concealing her spectacular blue eyes. She made a second attempt to speak but was simply unable to present a response. She abruptly stood up and shook her head. She cupped her hands over her face and without delay exited the room.

Troy and Walter turned and looked at each other in pure bewilderment.

22

Kathleen had just started her car and was getting ready to back out of a Vidalia Technical College parking space when she heard her phone ring. She had just finished a Tuesday afternoon lunch with a female student, a church attendee, who had sought counsel for coping with the recent and heartbreaking divorce of her parents.

Kathleen looked at the phone screen. The name Evelyn Huxley was displayed. Two Sundays earlier, on the Sunday that Walter had preached, Kathleen had publicly given out her phone number to the congregation. She had invited the people to write down the number or enter it into their cell phones and contact her whenever they needed her or just wanted to talk.

She had been receiving at least two calls a day.

Kathleen switched off the car engine and accepted the call. "Hello, this is Kathleen."

"Kathleen, this is Evelyn Huxley!"

Kathleen detected immediately that something wasn't right. Evelyn's voice was abnormally tense and breathy.

"Evelyn, are you okay?"

Evelyn choked up. "I'm calling from the county jail. Ray didn't want me to call you. But our son, Billy, has been arrested. And he's not doing good. Could you possibly come down and talk to him and see if you can help calm him down! I just don't know what else to do, or who else to call. They're telling me the only people who can see him right now is someone who's an attorney or a clergyman."

Within ten minutes, Kathleen was at the county jail. Outside the main building entrance, an American flag was flying high on a giant flagpole.

Kathleen greeted Evelyn in the small waiting lobby with a giant hug, then quickly signed in through the security window to visit Billy. When she completed the admission forms—signing in as a member of the 'clergy'—she submitted the papers, along with her driver's license and cell phone, to the male officer behind the bulletproof glass.

"Have a seat and we'll call you when we're ready to send you through security," the officer told her over a small intercom.

Kathleen rejoined Evelyn.

"I'm so sorry to bother you," Evelyn muttered in a state of distress when they took a seat. "I just didn't know what else to do."

Kathleen reached over and squeezed Evelyn's hand. "It's okay. I want to be here for you. I want to help."

"I'm just in shock," Evelyn said as she balled her fists in her lap. "I just can't believe what they're saying! Not about my boy! Not about my baby!"

Kathleen tried to keep a steady pulse. "What are they saying?"

"They're saying a policeman stopped him for rolling through a stop sign. And when they pulled him over they found marijuana in his car. So much, they say, that he was arrested on the spot. They've charged him with...with...drug trafficking." Evelyn burst into tears.

"Have you seen him? Have you been able to talk to him?"

"That's why I called you," Evelyn blubbered. "They only gave me thirty minutes to talk to him. And that was through a glass. Then they told me my time was up and I wouldn't be able to see him again till tomorrow." Evelyn wiped at her tears.

"Did he talk to you? What did he say?"

"He just kept saying 'you gotta help me...you gotta get me out of here...it's not what they think.'" Evelyn pulled a handkerchief from her purse and blew her nose. "Like I said, I'm just in shock right now. I'm confused. I just don't know what to believe."

"Has Ray been able to see him?"

Evelyn blew her nose again, and nodded her head yes. "But, he can't go back in till tomorrow either. He just left a few minutes ago to run back to the house and get some toiletries for him."

Kathleen squeezed Evelyn's hand again. "Okay, we at least know Billy's safe. So that's a start." In that instance, Kathleen was unexpectedly slammed with a flashback to Africa. Her own son's face, terrified to the max. The fatal and unforgivable decision. The nightmarish act that no mother in a thousand years should ever have to witness. Kathleen struggled to resist the mental ambush and the complete loss of spirit that always accompanied it. "Let me pray for him," Kathleen insisted as she tried to conceal her own emotional dilemma. "And then when I see him I'll do my best to touch hearts with him and help him settle down and focus."

Evelyn fell into her arms and embraced her.

"If it's okay with you," Kathleen told Floyd Baxter at her kitchen table later that evening, "I would like to change my official title to 'interim helper.'"

Baxter said, "Changing your title isn't going to lessen the controversy. But you're the pastor. So, you do whatever you think is best."

Kathleen didn't offer a response.

"So, what happened today with the Huxley kid?" Baxter forged ahead to a new subject.

"The police found a kilo of marijuana in his car. It seems he had been to Atlanta and was on his way back home when a Toombs County policeman stopped him for a minor traffic violation and smelled a strong odor in the car. The drugs were found in the trunk. He was taken straight to the county jail and charged with drug trafficking. A bond hearing is set for Thursday afternoon at the Superior Court. He was pretty shaken up. I was able to spend about thirty minutes with him. I just prayed with him and promised him that I will stand by him, along with his family, and encourage him in any way I can."

"I guess Ray and Evelyn are in shock."

"Evelyn is. I didn't see Ray. But you might want to call him and let him know you're still on his side."

Baxter cocked his head and looked bemused. "I'm not sure Ray would welcome a phone call from me right now."

Kathleen looked Floyd in the eye. "You never know. Perhaps you should at least try."

23

"Billy Ryan Huxley has no previous criminal record in this county or any other county," the Superior Court judge rambled in the Thursday afternoon bail hearing. "Yet the amount of illegal substance found in the defendant's car is a serious breech of law, and merits the court's full attention. I hereby set the bail at fifty thousand dollars. Can the defendant make bail?"

"The defendant cannot make bail your honor," the court-appointed lawyer, standing at the defendant's table, stated. "But the defendant's parents are ready to meet with a bail agent and post bond."

"All right, well as soon as that is taken care of, the defendant can be released. But on one stipulation. I don't want him to leave the county—not by car, bicycle, foot, train, plane or any other means—not until the trial. Is that understood?"

The public defender explained to Billy, sitting nervously with his hands clinched at the table, that the court date would most likely be eight to twelve months away.

Billy tensely nodded his cooperation.

The public defender turned to the judge. "We accept the conditions, your honor."

"Very well. Return the defendant to the county jail until bond has been posted."

Ray Huxley, sitting with Evelyn directly behind the court-room railing and the defendant's table, let go of Evelyn's hand. He stared at his nineteen-year-old son dressed in an orange prison jump suit. He watched the boy stand and listen to something the public defender whispered in his ear. Ray then saw the court bailiff escort Billy, handcuffed, out the side door.

Ray's heart sank. How could his son have made such an idiotic decision? How long had this drug stuff been going on? As a proud Christian father who had always taught his boy right from wrong, he had almost refused to put up bond. He wondered even now if he shouldn't change his mind and let Billy sit in jail until the trial. The angry side of his soul concluded that it might not be so difficult.

His anger at the moment truly scared him. And it seemed to be growing. He was angry at life. He was angry at his son. He was angry at his church. He was angry at Floyd Baxter. He was angry at God. He was angry at his wife. And he certainly didn't spare any good feelings toward Kathleen Rose who had entered his family's life completely unwelcomed and unwanted. He had even had to put his foot down, insisting the lady not be invited to the bail hearing. Whatever happened to Billy was just none of her dang business.

Ignoring Evelyn's reach to take his hand, Ray turned and walked out of the courtroom.

By the next morning, Floyd Baxter had heard the report of Billy Huxley's bail hearing, along with all the details, through the town's social grapevine. He considered taking heed to

Kathleen's advice and giving Ray Huxley a supportive call. But he couldn't bring himself to do it. Besides, Ray Huxley would never forgive him for railroading Kathleen into the church's pulpit. The man was just too proud. And too set in his ways.

As Baxter sat at the desk in his home office and stared at a potted plant, the phone suddenly rang causing him to flinch.

He picked it up and looked at the caller ID. The call was from one of the secretaries at the Prime Vidalia Onions Enterprise.

"Yeah?" he answered.

"Mr. Baxter, I've got Mr. Ted Higgley on the other line. He is the director of our regional Baptist Alliance. He says he wants to talk to you about what's happening at Lyons Central Baptist."

Baxter went silent for a moment and mulled over the request. "Tell him I'm busy right now and really don't have anything to say to him." Baxter looked out the window of his office, across the gorgeous pond, and grinned. "Let him know, though, that he's welcome to come down and visit the church anytime he wishes."

"Is that all?"

"That's it; nothing more."

"I'll convey the message."

"Thank you, Mable."

*   *   *

"Will you dismiss us in prayer, please," Kathleen said at the conclusion of the Sunday morning service to a lanky male student standing in the third row.

The young man, wearing thick glasses, nodded nervously, then bowed his head along with everyone else in the packed-out auditorium. "Thank you, Lord, for Kathleen's message this morning," the student invoked, raising his voice. "I know I personally needed it. I've never thought about all the different and important things, especially the Old Testament books, that Jesus progressively taught his apostles. I've been encouraged this morning to be a more knowledgeable student of the Bible. I pray that we all have. Don't let any of us be satisfied with a juvenile knowledge of Your Word. Motivate us to study and to study with a new passion in our hearts. Go with us now and help us bring glory to Your name this week. In Jesus' name, Amen."

Walter again was acutely impressed with Kathleen's gift for teaching the Scripture. She consistently seemed to reveal rich and important facts that many pastors overlooked. Yet, after she highlighted the facts, they seemed so obvious.

As people all around him dispersed, Walter looked down at the Bible in his hand. He suddenly wanted to know it better.

And then he looked back at Kathleen, now surrounded by a plethora of college students wanting to talk. He moved to get in line. He really wasn't in the mood for another verbal confrontation, but Jim and Jack, the other two deacons, constantly probed him for updates and pressed him, along with Troy, to continue the emotional, mental, and social assaults.

When he finally waited out the line and stood face to face with his demoralizing opponent, he started to launch his half-hearted offensive when he heard her say, "I just learned last night that there are over a hundred ladies around the country who are ordained pastors in Baptist churches outside the Evangelical Baptist Alliance. I know this still doesn't make it right in your eyes. But just know that in the eyes of plenty of other serious congregations, this isn't a sealed black-and-white issue. It's still open for interpretation."

Walter didn't want to argue, not today. He started to tell her he would look in to it when he heard her add, "Oh, and don't forget, you're on the docket to preach again in four weeks. May thirty-first to be precise."

Walter just shook his head and walked away.

As Kathleen watched Walter depart up the carpeted aisle, she whispered a prayer for him. "Break the chains holding him captive to a Southern-United-States view of the Scriptures," she implored. As she interceded for him, she saw Evelyn approach.

Evelyn grabbed her hands, leaned in to her, and whispered, "After all that's happened I honestly thought Billy would come to church with me this morning. He so much needed to hear your message. I'm still just so heartbroken." Evelyn shook her head like someone mourning at a graveside funeral. "I just don't know what I'm going to do. Would it be too much to ask you to come by the house sometime this week and try to talk to him again?"

Kathleen's image of her own thirteen-year-old son flashed across her mind again for the millionth time. She had failed him in his hour of greatest desperation and greatest torment. How could she now turn her back on another young boy in need, especially when the mother was outright petitioning for help?

"Sure, I'll make time," she promised. "Should I call first?"

"If it doesn't bother you to be totally ignored by Ray, then just drop by whenever you can. Billy should be there."

"All right; I'll make a note on my calendar."

Evelyn, still holding tightly to Kathleen's hands, squeezed them harder. "Thank you, thank you," she said.

Kathleen saw two more ladies, the last people in line, waiting patiently for her attention. She recognized their faces but had not yet memorized their names. Both ladies looked to be in their mid-to-late thirties. As far as Kathleen could remember, both ladies were married and had children. Kathleen waited for the ladies to speak first.

One of the ladies, blonde and full-figured, stepped forward. "We just couldn't leave this morning without saying how much we enjoyed your message." As Evelyn had done, the blonde took Kathleen's hand and squeezed. "You're such an inspiration to us."

The other lady, shorter and thinner with chestnut colored hair, stepped in close beside the blonde. She nodded her concurrence but allowed the blonde to do the talking.

"I can't help but believe your overseas mission work has somehow helped broaden your perspective on life and on the Bible; it's just so obvious," the blonde continued to say to Kathleen. "It seems that it's helped make you, what can I say, a more well-rounded Christian. My friend and I are envious. We can't move overseas, of course, but we've been talking; and wondering if there's anything we could do to get involved in missions right here in our own state. Something that might stretch us a little bit. We're wondering if you can make any suggestions."

Kathleen was humbled by the words of admiration. But she was pleased, thrilled actually, that the two ladies were insightful enough and daring enough to want to attempt something out of the ordinary. "Give me a week to consider some possibilities. And I'll be ready next Sunday to give you an answer."

The two ladies turned and looked at each other. They gave each other a mutual bob of satisfaction and turned back to Kathleen.

"We'll be here," the blonde declared. "And again we just want to say how much you inspire us. We're really, really glad you haven't let the deacons run you off."

Kathleen paused, then nodded her understanding with a gracious smile.

As she watched the ladies walk away, her mind catapulted her to the distinct memory of standing behind a lectern in a high school auditorium in Bamako, the capital of Mali. The lectern was draped beautifully in the Malian flag. Two hundred and fifty African women, ready to listen and learn, sat in folding chairs covered in white slip-ons. The women were all dressed in flowing robe-like dresses, national boubous, that highlighted vibrant blues, greens, golds, and oranges. It was one of the first of many such gatherings that would eventually control her life as a key speaker and crusader, and that would forever change her perception of mankind at myriad levels.

Yes, the Lyons ladies had judged correctly. Living overseas in a foreign culture, and seeing the different ways people interpreted life, definitely broadened ones perspective. On the world. And the Bible.

24

Eric Sawyer sat at his office computer early Monday afternoon and typed several potential headlines for the next article in the ongoing Lyons Central Baptist saga.

He finally settled on one he thought was catchy.

Lyons Central Baptist
Loses New "Pastor"

He gulped a big swig of Dr. Pepper from a large red-and-black UGA Bulldogs cup, then typed the first draft of the article.

Kathleen Rose, pastor of Lyons Central Baptist for just four weeks, attempted on Sunday to lessen the controversy of her role as a female pastor by officially announcing she will forfeit the title "Pastor."

She will maintain her role and function as the primary facilitator and teacher, but now asks to be called "Interim Helper."

A couple of older men in the congregation concurred that the revised title might indeed help remove some of the perceived stigma associated with the words "lady pastor." "No longer do we have a lady pastor," one of the men highlighted. "We now have an Interim Helper who happens to be female."

Several students from Vidalia Technical College and Ailey Bible College who attend the church dismissed the title change as irrelevant. Observed one Ailey Bible College student, "Kathleen Rose, whether she carries the pastor's title or not, essentially serves that role. Nothing has really changed."

Jack Evans, a still-active deacon at the church who has vowed to boycott all church services as long as Kathleen Rose is at the helm said by phone, "This is a first step in taking away her prestige. The deacons will keep fighting until Kathleen Rose is a fading memory."

Eric reread the paragraphs two more times. He wasn't completely satisfied with the flow. But it was a start. He would keep coming back to the draft and tweaking it throughout the afternoon until his five o'clock submission deadline.

* * *

Around eleven o'clock Tuesday morning, Kathleen turned her Toyota Camry onto the gravel driveway at Ray and Evelyn Huxley's residence. She hoped to catch Billy at home and—in keeping her promise to Evelyn—once again offer her friendship and support to the young man. She prayed she could win his ear and, over time, possibly have some kind of positive influence on his life.

The May morning was absolutely intoxicating with its perfect temperature, spectacular blossoms, and the distinct and spicy smell of pine. The warmth of the unobscured sunlight caressed Kathleen's neck and shoulders as she got out of the car and walked across the yard to the front of the house.

Kathleen ascended the few concrete steps to the front porch and knocked on the front door.

"Coming!" she heard Evelyn shout.

When Evelyn opened the door, her face automatically lit up with a huge smile. "Come in, come in," she urged. She then turned, faced the back of the house, and yelled, "Billy, there's someone here to see you!"

As Kathleen waited, along with Evelyn, for Billy to make an appearance, Kathleen couldn't help but notice the eighties decor and furniture that filled the house—brown wall paneling, brown sculptured carpets, and almond kitchen appliances.

When Billy didn't respond within fifteen seconds or so, Evelyn said, "Wait here. I'll be right back." She then headed toward the back of the house shouting Billy's name.

Kathleen saw no sign of Ray anywhere. She then saw Evelyn and Billy appear in the hallway, heading in her direction. Billy looked as if he had just crawled out of bed. His hair was matted and his eyes looked groggy. He made no effort to spruce himself as he got closer.

Before Kathleen could offer any preliminary words, Billy suddenly stopped. He stiffened his back, stared at her with a half-nervous look and said, "Not interested; but thanks." The words were issued with a definite scowl. Billy then turned and disappeared to the back of the house from where he had come.

Evelyn was visibly stunned.

Kathleen quickly assured Evelyn she was not offended in the least. She did think, though, and told Evelyn, that it was probably best for Billy's sake if she didn't hang around. She didn't want her lingering presence in the house to in any way add fuel to his current mood. Or to Ray's.

Evelyn, with tears on her cheeks, apologized profusely. She started to apologize a second time, but Kathleen silenced the attempt.

Within minutes, Kathleen was back in her car.

Kathleen returned to her house and ate a reflective lunch —a turkey sandwich, chips, and iced tea. As she ate, she prayed for Billy. And his dad.

Afterward, she spent an hour in her home office preparing for the first part of her Sunday sermon.

She then picked up her cell phone and called Willow and Ida Mae.

"Hello, is this Willow?"

The response came after a trace of hesitation. "Who is this?"

Kathleen recognized Willow's voice. "Willow, this is Kathleen Rose, the minister at Lyons Central Baptist. We talked at the E.Z. Grocery Store a couple of weeks ago."

"Why, lordy, lordy! Miss Kathleen! Yeah, this is Willow. It sure is good to hear your voice again. What can I do to help you today?"

"We had talked about going for a walk one day at Partin Park. I was wondering if you and Ida Mae might have an interest in going out for a bit this afternoon?"

"Why, that sure is nice of you to remember us." There was a certain pause, as if Willow had to sort in her mind that the important white lady was really wanting to connect with her again. "Yeah, if you sure you wanna do that, I suspect we can be up to it. But I'd need to let Ida Mae get up from her nap first."

"It's one-thirty now. Would you want to meet at the park around three or three-thirty?"

"Yeah, I think three-thirty would be a good time.

"All right, I'll see you then." Kathleen envisioned the park's parking area that she had recently scouted. "I'll park as close to the walking path as I can. I'll be in a white Toyota Camry."

*   *   *

At 3:40 PM, Kathleen—with a few bottles of water and a variety of chocolate bars in a backpack—was giving hugs to Willow and Ida Mae at a handicapped parking space, right next to the paved Partin Park walking trail.

Once Ida Mae was situated in her wheelchair and they were all starting down the asphalt trail, Willow said, "You was serious."

Kathleen wasn't sure if Willow was making a statement or asking a question. She just knew the words were directed at her. So, she replied, "About getting together and going for a walk? Absolutely. I'm just glad you had the time."

Willow, pushing Ida Mae in the wheelchair, stopped for a moment and said, "I'm just curious; why you wanna hang out with two black women?"

"Some of my best friends are black."

Willow punched Kathleen with a hard stare. "You serious, girl?"

Kathleen raised her eyebrows and nodded. "Absolutely serious."

Willow's brown eyes lit up. "And how is that?"

"Because for fifteen years I lived and worked as a missionary in Africa."

"A missionary? In Africa? For fifteen years? So, you really do be as comfortable with black folk as you be with white folk then?"

"Yeah! I am," Kathleen nodded again.

"Willow shook her head in astonishment and emitted a celebratory giggle. "Well, I'll be," she declared. "I knows you were special the first time I saw you."

Kathleen responded only with a smile.

"Was you a pastor in Africa like you are here?" Willow asked as she started moving Ida Mae down the trail again.

Walking again at Willow's side, Kathleen looked straight ahead through the pines at a small gazebo in the distance. A vivid memory shot to the forefront of her thoughts, the memory of being the special guest at President Amadou Toumani Tourés presidential palace in Mali and receiving the <u>Knight of National Order</u> award, one of Mali's highest merits for humanitarian work. Being hailed as a 'teacher of colossal influence who has challenged and educated a generation of Malian women.' Being spoken of as…

Kathleen squinted and interrupted the memory. "No, I didn't serve as a pastor there like I do here." She paused for just a second, expecting to hear a follow-up question about what she did do. But the question never came. So, she happily swept the conversation in a different direction.

*   *   *

That night Kathleen awakened at two in the morning screaming and grabbing at the scar on her neck and swatting at the air. It took her at least forty minutes and a far greater number of tears to go back to sleep.

25

On Sunday morning at five minutes till eleven Kathleen stood in front of her designated chair on the church platform. The crowd was already so large that folding chairs were being set up in the aisles to accommodate the expanding number of worshippers.

Kathleen sat down and briskly reviewed the notes for her morning message.

When the service finally got under way, Kathleen was thrilled to watch an array of new volunteers—primarily college students and a couple of high school students she had helped mobilize—lead the worship songs, play the music, make the announcements, collect the offering, lead the prayers, and serve the Lord's supper.

When it was eventually Kathleen's time to speak, she publicly recognized each of the volunteers by name and thanked them earnestly for their contribution to the service.

"Now," she announced, as she delved into her message, "This morning I want to challenge a traditional assumption that's been part of the American church for way too long. It's regarding the apostle Paul. The assumption is that Paul was an extraordinary human being. A supernatural Christian. A picture-perfect apostle as some would suggest.

"I would like to say to the contrary, and strongly so, that Paul was just an ordinary human being who possessed a depraved nature and struggled in life like every one else on the planet.

"Of course, there are several things that are extremely noteworthy about Paul and should never be undervalued. His devotion to Christ was exceptional; there's no question about it. His labor was outstanding. And his self-discipline was impressive.

"But…I repeat, as a human being, with a fallen nature, he was only ordinary.

"For example, it's clear throughout the New Testament that Paul was constantly surrounded by an entourage of young men on his missionary journeys. It is automatically assumed that Paul was so spiritual that he purposely surrounded himself with these young men in order to train them to become needed pastors, evangelists, and missionaries for the young, fledgling church.

"I suggest to you otherwise.

"I propose to you that Paul was just an ordinary man and that God used Paul's thorn-in-the-flesh—an eyesight impediment—to actually coerce him, as a scholar, into asking young men to go along with him on his journeys to be his eyeglasses, to read for him, and to take dictation for his collection of writings. And that he, by default—and only realizing it later—ended up fulfilling God's plan to disciple a whole new crop of young men as ministers of the Gospel."

Kathleen highlighted a variety of passages from Romans, Corinthians, Galatians, and Colossians to substantiate her points, especially the point about Paul's eyesight impairment.

She added a couple more examples of Paul's humanness, then brought the lesson to a close.

"The gist of the message is this," she spotlighted. "God used an ordinary man in an extraordinary way.

"This means, of course, that God can use you and me—just ordinary people—in an extraordinary way. Just as He used Paul."

Kathleen closed her Bible and put away her notes.

"With this in mind, I would like to conclude with a challenge. Two precious ladies from our congregation approached me last Sunday and asked what they can do to get involved in missions right here in Lyons, Georgia.

"I've thought a lot about their request.

"I'm now going to answer their question. And I want to do it publicly by tying my answer to the summation of today's Bible lesson."

Kathleen intentionally paused until every ear was listening for her next words.

"Here's how you and I as ordinary people can become involved in missions right here in Toombs County, and perhaps make an extraordinary difference.

"I would like for the two ladies who posed the question, along with anyone else who is interested, to accept this specific challenge. I would like for you to take the initiative sometime in the next two to three weeks to reach out to a stranger. To be specific I would like for you to invite a nonwhite family or individual—African American, Asian, Indian, or Hispanic—into your home, your dorm room, or out to a restaurant for a meal. Not just once, but twice. I want your agenda to be simple; to just engage them in conversation about their life, culture, and work. Listen to them. And embrace them as a friend. And then see what happens. Now, I don't want you to make a commitment this week. I want you to go home, discuss it, pray about it. And then next Sunday I will ask for a show of hands, while everyone's eyes are closed, to see how many are willing to accept the challenge."

Kathleen then prayed a dismissal prayer.

During Kathleen's prayer, Floyd Baxter—sitting on the back row—pumped his fist and grinned like a cheshire cat.

The post-service chatter that followed the benediction was noticeably quieter than usual.

*   *   *

The next morning, with bright skies and temperatures in the high seventies, Kathleen got in her car after a hearty breakfast and explored the various residential conclaves of Lyons. She wanted to learn more appropriately the lay of the land.

At some point, as she was riding around on the south side of town, she passed a street named Pecan Drive. Just because she liked the name, she turned around and steered the car up the narrow asphalt lane. The street was short. And quickly came to a dead end. There were only eight or nine residences on the street. And almost all of them were poorly maintained mobile homes. It was definitely a poor section of town, at least by American standards.

Kathleen turned the car around at the end of the lane. She had barely accelerated forward to head back to the main road when ahead on the left she saw two kids, a boy and a girl, running toward the edge of the street. The girl was playfully chasing the boy. The youngsters looked to be about ten or eleven. And they appeared to be Hispanic. At the edge of the yard, the boy swiftly ducked and swerved to avoid the girl's reach, then headed back around to the far side of the mobile home. The girl followed in hot pursuit, her long dark hair bouncing on her shoulders.

On impulse, Kathleen slowed down and turned into the trailer's unpaved driveway. She pulled up to a well-worn spot in the grass near the front door of the trailer and turned off the engine.

At that very moment, the boy—with jet black hair and brown-leather colored skin—came running around the other side of the mobile home. When the boy spotted Kathleen's car he immediately slowed to a wooden walk. The girl promptly stopped and hovered in the boy's shadow.

Kathleen stepped out of the car.

The boy eyed Kathleen scrupulously. When he decided she presented no threat, he moved in her direction. "Can I help you, lady?" he asked in near-perfect English.

"Yes, I'm looking for the lady of the house. Can you tell me if she's here?"

"Okay, I'll get her. I'll be right back," the boy said. He spoke with only a hint of a Latino accent. Immediately he ran to the front door and hurried up the steps inside. The girl was right on his heels.

While Kathleen waited to see if the lady—presumably the children's mother—would make an appearance, she visually took in the yard with its soccer ball, sandbox, frisbee, bicycles, sliding board and broken swing set. The yard wasn't attractive, but at least the kids got some exercise and fresh air.

Kathleen's attention was diverted back to the front door when a short, dark-haired lady, with the boy and girl in tow, stepped outside. Judging by the lady's appearance, she was Hispanic as well.

Kathleen headed up the steps and extended her hand. "Hello, my name is Kathleen Rose."

"Hello," the lady said, cautiously reaching to take Kathleen's hand.

"Do you speak English?" Kathleen asked.

The lady nodded that she did.

"I apologize for bothering you," Kathleen said, "but I'm new in the area. I was recently hired as the assistant pastor at Lyons Central Baptist Church. This morning I'm just riding around, meeting new people, and getting acquainted with the community."

The lady looked dubious, but seemed momentarily awestruck by Kathleen's beauty and stature.

"I'm not trying to convert anyone," Kathleen emphasized. "And I'm not trying to pressure anyone to come to our church.

I'm just riding around and seeing who lives in the community. When I saw your children playing in the front yard, I thought I would stop. I thought I would just ask how long you've lived in Lyons and find out if you've adjusted okay."

The lady once again looked dubious. Nevertheless, the hint of a tear dappled at the corner of her eye, behind a hard-looking exterior. "I...uh...have live here four years, and you're the first guera, white person, to ever ask me that question."

Kathleen winced at the revealing information. "Is it okay if I know your name?"

"Alexa."

"Well, Alexa...on behalf of all the white people who live in the area, and I say this in all sincerity, I want to apologize that no one has ever taken the time to ask about your adjustment. It's probably because most of the white people around here have never lived outside the United States and have no idea what it's like to uproot from their home culture and live as a guest in another country."

"And you?"

Kathleen smiled. "I lived in Africa for fifteen years. Actually I just moved back to the States a little over a month ago. And to be honest, I'm right in the middle of reverse culture shock. And it's not easy."

Alexa nodded as if she suddenly found a white person who understood. "You come in?" she asked.

Kathleen accepted the invitation.

Once inside, she sat on a cheap lopsided couch for nearly an hour and, in a gradually relaxed atmosphere, learned that

Alexa was from Mexico, was Catholic, was a single mom, worked as a custodian from five in the afternoon to eleven at night at the Lyons Upper Elementary School, and that her two kids—the boy and girl who, on a teachers' work day, were now playing in their room—were Marcos and Valery.

She also learned that Alexa's only friends were other Mexicans who lived in the area and that not one white person had ever so much as welcomed her to the United States, to Lyons, or to Pecan Drive.

Kathleen instantly remembered the public challenge she had presented to the Central Baptist congregation the day before. "This might sound really strange to you," she told Alexa, "but not only do I want to welcome you to the United States and to Lyons, but if you'll let me I would like to go one step further. I would like to take you and your kids out for a meal one evening. And I would like to give you a book that talks about the particulars of adjusting to a new culture. It's very insightful. I think it would be a real encouragement to you."

Alexa's nose twitched. "Really? You would want to do that for us?" She still looked slightly suspicious.

"Absolutely. Plus, I want to hear more from your point of view about how the white community can better welcome the Hispanics to our area. I would like to pass your insights along to my people."

Alexa suddenly appeared interested.

"If it's okay with you then," Kathleen suggested, "why don't we go ahead and mark a date on the calendar."

Alexa nodded her consent, but let Kathleen take the lead.

"What about Saturday, two weeks from now?" Kathleen said, "I think that will be...uh...May the twenty-third."

Alexa thought. "The twenty-third is my best friend's birthday," she said a bit nervously. "So it's not possible."

"What about the following Saturday, May thirtieth?"

"Yeah, I think that day will be okay."

"All right; can I pick you guys up here around six that evening?"

Alexa okayed the plan with a congenial nod, and straight-away wrote the time and date on a scrap piece of paper that was lying on a lamp table next to her chair.

Kathleen stood. "Is it okay if I give you a hug before I go?"

Alexa stood and extended her arms. Kathleen, with additional words of support, welcomed Alexa to the community of Lyons with a heartfelt embrace.

Alexa's eyes brightened as if she had inhaled a promising amount of light.

"Also, is it okay if I pray for you before I go?" Kathleen probed. She knew she was being a little forward, but sensed it was okay. Besides, she really wanted to pray aloud for Alexa and be a genuine source of blessing.

"Sure, I guess it's okay," Alexa said, caught a little off guard.

Kathleen closed her eyes. "Dear, God, I thank you that I've been able to meet Alexa, Marcos, and Valery on this beautiful morning. I ask for your forgiveness that no one in the white community, especially the community of believers, has taken the time or energy to make Alexa and her children feel welcomed in our town. I pray that the situation will change. I pray that You will begin to open the eyes of the white people at their school, their bank, their grocery store, their playground, their gas station, and their neighborhood. Prompt the people around them to see a family who has been uprooted, who is trying to adjust, and who can use a little acknowledgement, validation, and friendship. Prompt people to be proactive and to take the first steps toward building these types of friendships. Please, I ask You to smile down on Alexa and her kids in a special way. In the upcoming weeks and months, I pray that You will even sprinkle their lives with a few divine surprises. Do things that will prove to them that You exist and that You love them. I ask it all in Jesus' name. Amen."

When Kathleen finished praying, she hugged Alexa one more time.

Alexa fought back tears. "No one has ever prayed for me and my kids before," she sniveled. "I want to thank you."

Kathleen gently swiped at a fly. "You are more than welcome, Alexa. Thanks for letting me come in and meet you. It's been an honor. It really has. And I'll definitely look forward to seeing you again on the thirtieth."

Alexa called the kids back into the room where everyone said a round of goodbyes.

Back in the car, Kathleen was amazed at how quickly and spontaneously such a bona fide act of ministry could occur in the south.

Feeling a rare fusion of zest, she happily sang her way through a couple of more outlying neighborhoods and then all the way to lunch.

26

Jack Evans called for an emergency deacons' meeting at his home on Tuesday evening.

When Walter pulled up into Jack's driveway—out in the country, eight miles from town—he could still hear the anger in Jack's voice when he got the call earlier in the day. "We've got to meet tonight," Jack had barked without apology. Yet, he had been unwilling to divulge the agenda. "I don't want the subject of our discussion to leak beforehand" had been the expressed reason for the secrecy.

Parking his truck, Walter saw that the acre of green lawn around Jack's four-bedroom brick house had been freshly cut. Walter wondered if his friend had taken out some of his anger on the helpless centipedegrass. He then saw, by the vehicles in the driveway, that he—Walter—was the last one to arrive.

He got out of his truck and went directly to the backdoor, accessible through an attached two-car garage. Jack's wife, Holly—a short, petite blonde—ushered him in. "They're all in Jack's office waiting for you," she told him.

Walter hustled through the kitchen and living room and moved down the carpeted hallway to the office. He found the office door closed. When he opened it and stepped in, the other men—Jack, Jim, and Troy—paused in their conversation and welcomed him.

Ignoring all protocol for a deacons' meeting, Jack quickly took control of the gathering and pounced. "We're all here now. So, I'll go ahead and jump right in." He smashed his fist into his open palm. "As you can tell, I'm a little angry right now. And I don't apologize for it, not for a second. I've been angry ever since Kathleen Rose arrived, but as of this past Sunday, my anger has flat out reached a boiling point." He paused for a split second to catch his breath. "When I heard that Kathleen Rose"—he almost spat the name—"challenged the congregation on Sunday morning to befriend blacks, spics, and Asians, I knew right then that we had to take some serious action. I don't think a black person has ever been in our church, and in my opinion there's no need to start inviting them now." Jack looked around the room to gauge the men's reactions, then continued. "She's already allowed drums and guitars into the church. And now she's opening the doors to all kinds of racial riffraff. It's not good, gentlemen. So, if we want to save our church I think it's time to get serious and try to put a stop to it."

"And?" Walter prompted, definitely feeling the tension in the room.

"And since your and Troy's efforts on the inside of the church," Jack retorted, "and mine and Jim's on the outside all seem to be pretty lame and ineffective, I suggest we try something a little more drastic."

Walter, feeling slightly pinged, slumped his shoulders and just listened. He noticed that Troy and Jim were silent as well.

156

"I want us to file a lawsuit," Jack finally blurted out. "A lawsuit against Floyd Baxter. I want us to sue him for breach of church polity. He's hijacked the church from its appointed administrators and he's taking it down a path that will kill it. Yeah, I know, the auditorium is filled to capacity right now. But seventy percent or more of those people are college students for God's sake. They don't have money to tithe. And there's no longevity there. Most of them will be gone within a year. And then, what'll be left? A lonely female pastor who's down to her last six months. And a stagnant church. The whole two years with her at the helm will have been a monumental waste. And the church's reputation will have gone down the drain." Jack paused for a second, looking as if he would welcome some supportive feedback.

"I second the motion!" Jim quickly hailed, his hefty frame overflowing his cushioned chair.

Walter looked at Troy slouched in a leather armchair. Troy wasn't saying anything. Walter shifted in his seat. He hadn't opened up to Troy in recent days about his thoughts regarding the current state of the church. Nor had Troy opened up to him. But he could tell by the way Troy had been interacting with Kathleen in the past few weeks that he was softening in his opposition. And truth be told, so was he, the very one who in the beginning was the most critical and the most brazen about the whole situation. Walter scratched his scalp. Neither Jack nor Jim, he reminded himself, were eyewitnesses of what was actually transpiring. They weren't hearing the sermons. They weren't seeing the hearts being touched and changed. They weren't seeing all the people—albeit mainly college students—being mobilized. They were just hearing weekly reports that apparently were nothing more to them than sterile data. Walter sighed. Apparently Floyd Baxter had known something all along that they, the deacons, just hadn't known.

"Would that kind of lawsuit even hold up in court?" Walter finally asked.

"That's the reason we're here, Walter," Jack huffed. "I want to know if I can use three thousand dollars of church money to hire a lawyer and find out."

Silence permeated the room again.

Troy finally disturbed the void. "Three thousand dollars? That's a lot of money, don't you think?"

"Of course it's a lot of money," Jack consented. "And we might end up just throwing it all away. But if a lawyer tells us we have a case, we can sue Baxter for a half million dollars, or more, and ask the court to make him pay for all the psychological and emotional damage he's caused. And if we win, we'll have a windfall of cash that we can put away in a protected bank account, money that'll guarantee the church a new start once Kathleen Rose is long gone and forgotten."

Walter didn't say it, but he was already pretty sure Kathleen would not be forgotten, especially not by anyone who was currently sitting under her ministry.

"I'm just curious," Troy reacted from across the room, "I wouldn't think the church had that kind of money to just gamble with. Or do we?"

"I asked Holly earlier this evening to give me a print out of the church financials," Jack specified, acting as if he had anticipated the concern. He then picked up copies of the financials from his desk and distributed them.

Walter knew that Holly, Jack's wife—the church treasurer for six years—would have printed an up-to-the-minute report. He took his copy and scoured the bottom-line numbers.

"As you can see," Jack proclaimed, "there's fourteen thousand in the savings account and three thousand, eight hundred in the checking. And I'm sure you'll be intrigued to know not a penny has been spent out of either account since Baxter started financing the church operations out of his own pocket."

"What about the offering money that's being collected every Sunday?" Troy asked.

"Every cent is being deposited into the church's savings account," Jack pointed out. "As you know, Holly is boycotting the church services. But she and Mary Ann are briefly onsite every Sunday to take control of the money when it's collected."

Walter knew that both Holly and Mary Ann, a single mom acting as Holly's assistant, were totally trustworthy. "And you're saying that Baxter who's authorized to write checks isn't trying to get his hands on any of it?"

"How can he?" Jack asked. "There have to be two signatures on every check issued by the church. And none of the other three people authorized as signees are going to co-sign anything with Floyd Baxter right now."

Walter looked at the numbers again. He rubbed his chin. He no longer carried a sense of certainty about what should be done at the church. He looked at Troy. Troy looked equally as unsettled.

"Well?" Jack pushed.

"Are we within our rights to make this kind of decision without a church vote?" Troy inquired.

Jack was ready. "The Constitution and Bylaws say the Finance Committee will oversee all collections and make sure all bills are paid in a responsible fashion."

"But what about unplanned-for expenses?" Troy pushed back. "Doesn't the Constitution and Bylaws say something to the effect that if the Finance Committee wants to spend more than a thousand dollars on any given item or service, there has to be a congregational vote?"

"Yeah," Jack spouted, "And that the vote has to pass with a fifty-one-percent, or better, show-of-support."

"So?" Troy volleyed.

Jack scooted to the edge of his seat and leaned forward. He exhaled a low-pitched groan. "Look…first of all, if you haven't noticed, the Finance Committee is pretty shot to pieces right now. Ray Huxley has left the church, and his place on the committee hasn't even been filled yet. And Floyd Baxter, I would assume everybody here would agree, is totally out of the picture. So, that leaves Holly…and"

"And Bruce Dickerson," Troy murmured.

"Exactly," Jack said. "And Bruce is one of those members who's boycotting all the meetings right now."

Walter hung his head and moaned in silence. The other men seemed to be speechless as well. Walter then heard Jack speak up again.

"So look," Jack urged. "We have to be realistic. We're deep in unchartered territory here. The Finance Committee is in shambles. And most of the church's full-fledged members are not even attending the services anymore. Honestly, there aren't enough members attending right now to even make up a quorum. So, does this render us useless? Or what? I mean, we are the elected board of deacons for God's sake. I say we get Holly and Bruce to sign the three-thousand-dollar check. And we hire the attorney. I can guarantee you that if all the members of the church were sitting here with us right now, we'd get a unanimous vote to do this."

Walter closed his eyes for a moment. "I suppose you already have an attorney in mind," he said, lifting his head.

"He's just waiting for the check," Jack said, smiling as he said it.

"So," Troy interjected, "we would be paying the attorney to simply review the situation and tell us if there's a case for a probable lawsuit?"

Jack nodded. "That's it."

Walter scratched at his head again. He wanted to say, 'What if old man Baxter, still an active member of the Finance Committee, gets mad and decides to counter sue?,' but decided to keep quiet and not add to the mayhem. He finally sighed. "All right."

Troy lifted a reluctant finger to cast his approval.

Jim said, "Let's do it; absolutely."

"All right, then," Jack said, "It's done."

Early the next morning, Jack took the three-thousand-dollar check, signed by Holly, to Bruce Dickerson's place of work at the Toombs County Board of Education where Bruce quickly and gladly gave the check its second signature.

Fifteen minutes later, Jack delivered the check to the attorney's office in downtown Vidalia.

In return, Jack was given a list of documents that he needed to deliver to the attorney in the next three days—a copy of the church's Constitution and Bylaws; a copy of the original property-agreement between Floyd Baxter, his brother, and the congregation; a copy of the property deed for the church building and the land it sat on; a statement by Jack and the deacon board as to how Floyd Baxter's decision had caused emotional and mental harm to the Central Baptist congregation; and a list of the deacons' names and phone numbers in order to set up interviews.

PART II

27

The sun, glorious and huge-looking, hung low in the west.

Ag Alhabib, a 53-year-old Ansar-Dine leader, squatted in the dirt behind the low mud-walled compound. His indigo tunic, covering his pants, draped onto the dusty earth.

Oumar, a devout Muslim in his late twenties—squatting in the dirt facing Ag Alhabib—tried not to show fear of the older man. Chewing on pistachio nuts, Oumar wanted to prove his worth as the leader of Ansar-Dine's Bamako faction. But he was terrified at the moment.

"Why weren't you ready for me?" Alhabib snarled in the Bambara language from behind huge menacing eyebrows. He had pulled Oumar out of the house and out of the presence of five other men. Spittle now collected on his full black beard. He looked ready to lurch across the dirt and use his knife to inflict punishment.

"We didn't expect you to arrive from the north until tomorrow," Oumar explained. And then added, "Since we've stopped using cell phones, communication in the group is not as efficient. I apologize. Please forgive me. We'll have your quarters and your meal ready in no time."

Alhabib spat on the ground as a dog barked in the distance. "When I'm finished with the meal, we'll gather in the house and have the meeting. Make sure everyone is present."

Oumar nodded. "Of course. Everyone will be here."

Not more than two hours later, Oumar was introducing Alhabib to a group of fifteen seasoned Ansar-Dine fighters. Sitting cross-legged in a circle on colorful hand-woven carpets, most of the men had never met Alhabib face-to-face. All of the men were nervous.

"Ag Alhabib is a hero to all Tuaregs in northern Mali," Oumar echoed common knowledge to the men, trying to display unquestionable homage to their commander. "As our esteemed leader, he led the bloody attack at Aguelhok. He announced on public radio that Sharia law would be enforced in Timbuktu, causing most Christians to flee the city, praise be to Allah. The U.S. State Department has designated him a Global Terrorist. He is our leader and our commander. Under his rule, we will rid our country of Western influences, over-throw our government, and establish Sharia law everywhere."

"Alhabibbb! Warrior of Allah!" the men started shouting. "Alhabibbb! Warrior of Allah! Alhabibbb! Warrior of Allah!"

Oumar sat down and allowed the men to shout until Ag Alhabib himself gestured that it was enough.

With a scarred round face, broad straight shoulders, and intense tea-colored eyes, Alhabib bowed subtly to acknowledge the men's veneration, then motioned for the men to cease.

"I have made my long journey here today," Alhabib declared, still standing, "because I need information. And you are the men who carry this information. There was an infidel lady from the 'Great Satan' who wielded too much influence among our women. You know who I speak of. She went all over our northern regions telling our men, our tribal leaders, even our Imams, and especially our women, that our centuries-old custom of female genital cutting is wrong, unnecessary, and harmful. She spoke in universities, she spoke in villages, and she spoke in market places. She was a voice of Satan. Yet, many of our women listened to her. And believed her words. Her words have now become poison and are creating problems for our men and our religion."

Alhabib squatted and suddenly appeared even more sinister. "I heard rumors that you dealt with her," he whispered tersely, piercing the group of men with his no-nonsense eyes. "Yet, now I hear rumors that she is still alive. So, tell me what you know. And I want to hear only what is true. Do you understand?"

Oumar squirmed to his feet. He pointed to a dull-looking young man to his right. "Drissa can tell you what happened. He was one of the fighters assigned to the mission. He was there."

The young man, Drissa, scampered to his feet. Without pause, he proclaimed, "I stripped her son and castrated him. This is what I know. We held her and made her watch until the boy bled to death. And then while she was still screaming we unclothed her and each had our way with her. Issa was the last in line. When he finished with her, he was the one who killed her." Drissa pointed to a third young man in the circle, a young man wearing a smirk. "Issa plunged his knife all the way into her neck. We all saw it. We saw her collapse in a pool of blood and die."

Alhabib shifted his gaze to Issa. "Did you feel her pulse? Are you sure she was dead?" he demanded to know.

Issa waffled. "We all saw her. She was…"

"Did you feel her pulse!" Alhabib roared.

Issa, still sitting cross-legged, unconsciously dropped his shoulders.

Alhabib stood up and stomped the earthen floor. "Which one of you should I punish!" he roared again, even louder.

Oumar this time could not hide his fear. He cringed. Terror rushed him from head to toe.

"Put out your hand, Issa!" Alhabib abruptly demanded.

Oumar watched Issa physically recoil as the smirk on his face disappeared.

"You know our law," Alhabib hissed, pure disgust frothing from his tongue. "We take the hands of thieves. And you are a thief, Issa. You've stolen from me. You've stolen my certainty. You've stolen my assurance. You've stolen my peace of mind that this matter has been dealt with. Rumors are saying that Christians found this devil woman and saved her, that she's still alive and is being protected somewhere here in Bamako. Other rumors are saying she's fled across the border to Guinea, or that she's even been escorted back to the Great Satan."

Alhabib spat at Issa's feet.

"What I do know," the old warrior continued, "is that her spirit is still alive. And that her spirit is still working like a disease in the hearts of many of our Tuareg women. And I want that spirit to die. I want her to die. So I want you to find her. Spare no resources. Spare no expenses. I want her found. Show me a dead body. And I want proof this time. No excuses. No suspicions. Only proof!"

Alhabib paused as if he wanted his words to sink in. He then picked up his machete lying next to him on the floor. He gestured with unflinching authority for Issa to extend his hand into the circle.

Oumar held his breath. He watched as Issa stepped into the circle and slowly, slowly lifted his hand, trying to be stoic.

Surely Alhabib wouldn't…

But he did.

28

Friday, May 15
Lyons, Georgia

Around 2:00 in the afternoon, Jack—on behalf of the deacon board at Lyons Central Baptist—delivered the requested documents, including the list of deacons' names and phone numbers, to the attorney's office in Vidalia.

"Janet, my secretary will begin this afternoon calling the other deacons and setting up interview appointments," the attorney, Rupert King, declared.

Jack went ahead while he was in the office and arranged his interview for Thursday, May 21.

Kathleen Rose sat alone on a wooden bench overlooking the half-acre flower garden at Ailey Bible College in Ailey, Georgia, fifteen miles west of Lyons.

One of the young female students who had begun attending Sunday services at Central Baptist had invited her for lunch and a tour of the campus. Kathleen had just wrapped up a delightful two hours with the girl, a third year student majoring in Language and Literature. They had shared a pizza and salad in the dining hall, had strolled across an acre or so of the grounds, and had visited a couple of the main buildings, all while asking questions and enjoying one another's stories.

Kathleen had discreetly, however, omitted a lot of the details of her own personal story.

Before the young lady had broken away to attend a mid-afternoon class, she had given Kathleen a copy of the latest edition of the *Vidalia Times* and said, "I don't know if you've read this, but I want you to know you've had a bigger influence on my life in just four weeks than anybody I've ever met. Just watching you and listening to you has given me a new hunger for God. And I want to say thanks."

Kathleen had been humbled by the young lady's sentiments. Touched in a significant way, she had decided to sit in contemplation at the flower garden for a few moments before heading back to Lyons.

She now looked out over an array of purple, white, and yellow blossoms. She had agreed initially to come to Georgia to find a place of refuge and healing. She had never thought she might have a lasting impact on the people here, not in the Bible belt. Yet, it appeared she had perhaps made a wrong assumption.

She unfolded the newspaper and found the article the girl had made reference to. With a cool breeze blowing her hair, she slowly took in the printed words.

Central Baptist Pastor,
Kathleen Rose, Boldly
Stirs Racial Anxiety

Pastor "Interim Helper" Kathleen
Rose issued a public challenge on
Sunday, May 10, to a packed-out
white audience to intentionally start
socializing with Blacks, Hispanics,
Asians, and Indians.

"I challenge you to step out of
your comfort zone, at least for a
moment," Pastor Rose encouraged,
"and see what new discoveries can
be made about yourself, your church,
your faith, and your God."

The church will find out this
weekend how many will pick up the
gauntlet and run with the proposal.
According to one church member,
"segregation" at Central Baptist has
always been an unspoken policy.

Some in the town are asking,
"What else might the new maverick
pastor do to shake up the community?"

Finishing the article, Kathleen realized she probably needed
to speak to the journalist Eric Sawyer. She knew the young
man had been regularly attending the church services since her
arrival. Yet, she had been apprehensive about engaging him in
conversation. She simply did not want to take the risk that he

would start asking questions about her past. She did not want her outright refusal to answer certain questions to provoke him to dig around and uncover information that would eventually expose her true identity.

She looked up into the cloud-speckled sky, "Father, I am a weak, broken vessel. I'm not even sure what I'm doing here."

She sighed, then stood up and headed back to the car. After taking only a few steps, she felt her stride falter and her chest tighten. Once again, she suddenly felt all alone in the world. Utterly and hopelessly alone.

29

The final verses of the final song, before Kathleen's Sunday morning message, were being sung by a capacity audience.

The college musicians—the keyboard player, the guitarist, the bass player, the drummer, and the violinist—were synching wondrously.

The voices of the congregation were projecting without constraint.

Yet, Kathleen was still in the grip of a languorous mood. Sitting on stage in the pastor's chair, she at least mouthed the closing lyrics with her lips.

> You, Jehovah, have stamped Your image
> Across the human race
>
> And fortified our existence with Your
> infinite amazing grace
>
> For all that spoils or hinders -
> pride, prejudice, and race
>
> May it be fought and conquered
> To reveal your glorious face.

Right when she sang the word "race," Kathleen saw two black ladies, Willow and Ida Mae, enter the sanctuary, looking somewhat daunted, assumedly by the all-white and 'sacred' environment. Willow pushed Ida Mae five or six feet up the aisle and stopped.

Kathleen instantly caught herself smiling. Not with a tiny smile. But with a burst of heartfelt and unearthly exuberance. She started to motion for someone to assist the ladies when she saw a tall college basketball player move to help. Within seconds, the young man had asked several people to scoot to the center of the pew to make room for Willow on the end. The student helped position Ida Mae in the aisle right next to Willow, then helped lock down her wheelchair.

Kathleen suddenly noticed, with a pinch of hurt, that a couple of the elderly female members sitting in the rear of the auditorium were staring at Willow and Ida Mae and were wearing an unconscious expression that bordered on nocuous.

Kathleen held her focus on Willow until Willow looked in her direction and made eye contact. Kathleen smiled and nodded.

Willow smiled and nodded back.

Evelyn Huxley was sitting up front in the sanctuary as had become her new custom. She turned in her Bible to the Old Testament book of Jonah after Kathleen moved to the podium and announced that her morning text would be chapter four, verses one, two, and three in the famous minor prophet.

Evelyn's thirst for truth had grown exponentially under Kathleen's tutelage. Never in all her years as a church goer had her mind been exercised with such wonderment and inquisitiveness. She almost felt that her spirit had been reborn. A new twinkle seemed to burn in her eyes. Ready to absorb, hopefully, another thought-provoking lesson from God's Word, she heard Kathleen open with the statement:

"One hundred percent of the human race is prejudiced and racist."

Evelyn was taken aback by the bluntness of the words. She felt a dicey tension fill the room.

She watched Kathleen pause for effect, then follow the unpleasant statement with:

"One hundred precent of whites are prejudiced and racist. One hundred precent of blacks are prejudiced and racist. One hundred precent of Asians are prejudiced and racist. One hundred precent of Hispanics are prejudiced and racist.

"Some people, because of the way they are raised, easily overcome these tendencies. Others fight hard to overcome these tendencies, and do a remarkable job. Others veil their sentiments behind a mask of denial, pretense and political correctness. Others don't hide at all; they simply voice their prejudices and their racist feelings without shame.

"It is a simple fact that most people find it easier to love their own kind. To think their own kind is superior. More lovable. More deserving.

"But…might I echo this morning the most famous Bible verse of all…John three, sixteen…that God so loved…THE WORLD!

"These are the words of the Savior Himself. In the context, Jesus is addressing Nicodemus and all those like him who are self-righteous.

"Nicodemus was a leader of the Pharisees, a man who honestly thought, and believed, he was better than, more deserving than all other people groups on the planet. Not just all other Jews. But all other people, period.

"The text is quite beautiful, really. God, incarnate, looks this man in the eye, a man who is at the religious pinnacle of life, a man who carries a high position of respect, a man who is intelligent and literate…and pretty much tells him…'You're not special in the least, Nicodemus. You are just an ordinary man who needs Me. Why, I love the prostitutes of Jerusalem as much as I love you. I love every lying, scheming tax collector as much as I love you. I even love the Roman suppressors as much as I love you.'"

Evelyn, nearly holding her breath, watched Kathleen turn a page in her notes.

"Here is another statement," Kathleen pressed, "that is not easy to hear or digest. But I feel it must be said. I love our country. But…God is NOT an American! And God does not love Americans 'more than.' He does not love Americans more than North Koreans, Iraqis, Mexicans, or any other people group.

"God loves THE WORLD.

"EVERY human on the planet is the object of the Creator's infinite and unconditional love. No one…not you, not me, not anyone…is special or superior in that regard. In God's eyes, no one is 'more lovable' than any other person.

"In spite of this truth, our world today seems more polarized than ever before. Or perhaps it just seems that way because of all the media attention that is focused on it. But, we have a stark polarization between blacks and whites, between liberals and conservatives, between citizens and migrants, between Christians and Muslims. And on and on. And this polarization has seemingly been used by the forces of darkness to fortify individuals inside bubbles of contempt, even hatred, for those they oppose. And, yes…even Christians are guilty.

"And I am here to tell you this morning that God wants to burst those bubbles. He wants people to learn to love as He loves. He wants people, especially those who claim to be His followers, to demolish their prejudiced and racist outlooks and learn to love…the world."

Evelyn still felt a protracted tension in her shoulders at Kathleen's words. She would have never guessed in two lifetimes that such forthright and masculine-sounding proclamations would come from a woman whose physical beauty eclipsed that of most fashion models.

"We're taught this lesson quite vividly," Evelyn heard Kathleen emphasize, "in God's personal interaction with Jonah. So, let's start at the beginning."

Evelyn took notes as Kathleen, through logical deduction, helped everyone see that Jonah's reason for rebuffing God's mandate to go to Nineveh was not a lack of monetary resources, a lack of courage, a lack of adventurism, or a lack of trust. Or even a personal fear of being killed.

Kathleen pressed home, "It was because he…hated…the Assyrians. And it wasn't that he hated all foreigners. He was willing to die for a ship full of Gentiles. But he did hate the Assyrians. And he didn't want them, not even for one solitary moment, to have the God-given opportunity to repent of their murderous ways and be forgiven. He didn't want them to be on the receiving end of God's grace. He wanted them to be on the receiving end of God's harsh punishment.

"Jonah honestly believed," Kathleen stressed, "that he, as a Jew, was 'better than' or 'more deserving than'."

Evelyn sat entranced as Kathleen concluded the message by explaining that God had put Jonah through this arduous and painful journey, as portrayed in the book's four chapters, in order to burst his bubble of 'hate' and teach him to be like his Creator - abounding in love toward all people, even toward those who 'deserved' to be hated.

"Loving, like God loves, is the mark that can, and should, distinguish a believer from the rest of the world."

When Evelyn heard Kathleen finally make her closing remarks, she exhaled slowly. The message, in its entirety, had been so emotionally intense that it had frozen her in her seat.

Evelyn then grinned. The overall experience, though, had actually been therapeutic, not demoralizing like a hellfire-and-damnation sermon where the preacher sucked air, damned you to hell, and nearly spat in your face.

Evelyn got so caught up in her thoughts, along with a whole new list of questions, that she nearly forgot what was coming next.

30

"All right," Kathleen said, returning to the microphone following a reflective congregational hymn of just one stanza. "How many will accept the challenge put forth last Sunday?"

Kathleen quickly reiterated the proposal, adding a few comments.

Then, in a brief tally, with the congregation's eyes closed, Kathleen counted thirty raised hands out of an approximate two hundred people in attendance. She even saw Evelyn Huxley's hand partially raise, then lower, then raise again. When she counted the thirty hands, Kathleen smiled softly on the inside. She knew the church paradigm was about to change. Even further.

Kathleen closed the service with an encouraging word for those who accepted the challenge, offered a benedictory prayer and blessing, then headed back toward the rear of the auditorium to embrace Willow and Ida Mae.

She was intercepted halfway down the aisle, though, by Troy and Walter. She could tell by the distressed look in their eyes and their sharp gestures toward the rear pews that they wanted to voice their concern and displeasure regarding the two black visitors.

"Do you want to just pamper tradition, gentlemen, and remain static? Or do you want to change lives?" she whispered formidably like an unflinching leader.

Without a lot of patience, she maneuvered her way around them and caught up with her black friends.

On Monday morning Kathleen was awakened out of a deep sleep around 5:00 AM by the abrupt ringing of her cell phone.

She jerked upright, grabbed the phone from a bedside table and groggily mumbled, "Hello."

"It's not a black church, you filthy slut!" a man's voice cut through the night. "Leave now while you can. Or else!" Just as quickly as the call came, it ended.

Kathleen's eyes popped open. She shook her head. Blurry-eyed she looked at her phone. She shook her head a second time. Did she just hallucinate? A tightness rippled all the way up her spine to her neck and shoulders. She stared at the phone, still in her hand.

After four or five seconds, she laid back in bed and tried to relax, hopefully to fall asleep again. But she couldn't. She was now wide awake. Her mind instantly resurrected memories from an evening in Timbuktu when, following one of her highly publicized lectures to women, three men threw her into the back of a filthy van, closed the doors, and beat her. She had never been so frightened or so physically traumatized. Cursing her to hell, the men eventually threw her out of the back of the van and assured her that if she didn't stop her crusade immediately, she would be hunted down and killed.

The recollection only heightened her fear surrounding the newly received threat.

She got out of bed.

Seconds later, she picked up her phone and called Floyd Baxter.

The next night there was a patrol car parked outside Kathleen's West Oglethorpe Avenue address. Floyd Baxter informed her that the police had determined the malicious call had been made from an untraceable burner phone and that they would watch her house closely over the next several weeks.

On Thursday afternoon at 3:15, Jack pulled up to the attorney's building in downtown Vidalia for his interview with Rupert King. The three-story red-brick building, an architectural relic from the 60's, was located a block from the railroad track and, ironically, just around the corner from the First Baptist Church of Vidalia.

Seeing the Vidalia church building just seconds earlier had fueled Jack's sadness and anger. The word was that the Vidalia congregation was thriving. In harmony. In morale. And in reputation. Many of their new members, Jack knew, were spillovers from the Lyons Central Baptist debacle.

Jack squeezed his fist. "Let there be a lawsuit, let there be a lawsuit!" he prayed, feeling his spite ever growing toward old man Baxter. "Our church doesn't deserve this mess; it's not right!" he told God.

He was still fuming when he entered King's office on the second floor. The front-desk assistant, a curvaceous brunette with stylish short hair, dutifully acknowledged his presence, then picked up the desk phone and announced his arrival to Mr. King.

The lady asked Jack to take a seat. "Mr. King will be with you in a moment," she explained.

Jack sat in a cushiony leather chair in the reception area and waited. King's office obviously wasn't suffering financially. The whole interior of the space looked as if it had been newly renovated from top to bottom. The feel was that of traditional elegance.

Jack, continuing to gaze around the room, simmered in his church-related frustration for only about five minutes before King came out and ushered him into a back conference room furnished with a grand wooden table and black leather chairs.

"Is it okay if I record this on audio?" King apprised more than asked.

Jack nodded and took a seat at the huge table.

Before King commenced the interview, he summoned a female assistant to sit in on the session and take notes.

Once the lady, a thirtyish-looking librarian type, was in place, the interview officially began.

For about forty-five minutes, Jack answered what seemed like a hundred questions or more.

Name? Address? Two previous employers? Number of years with each employer? Place of birth? Number of years residing in Lyons, GA? Number of years attending church? Name and address of two previous churches before Lyons Central Baptist? Number of years attending Lyons Central Baptist? Number of years as a member? Number of years as a deacon? Number of years knowing Floyd Baxter? Followed by a whole cadre of personal questions regarding his experiences, opinions, and speculations surrounding the current church situation.

When Jack left the office, he felt mentally tapped out. At the same time he felt morally justified. And equally optimistic. He was confident that King's investigation would be worth every penny of the three thousand dollar service fee.

When Jack got into his car, he looked at his watch. It was 4:30. He had been instructed by King to not disclose the contents of the interview with the other three deacons. He was fine with that request. He would only have to stifle his urgency-to-talk for about twenty-four hours. Troy's interview would take place in the next hour. Walter's and Jim's interviews were scheduled as back to back sessions early tomorrow afternoon.

On Saturday night, Kathleen was sitting alone in her study going over her final sermon notes for Sunday morning when her cell phone rang. As she had done the last four nights when her phone rang she looked at the caller ID with faint breaths.

This time she gently smiled.

"Hello, Walter, how can I help you this evening?"

"Are you still expecting me to preach on the thirty-first?" Walter asked bluntly without any pleasantries.

"It's being announced in tomorrow's bulletin. Yes, you're still on the calendar."

There was a heavy pause.

Walter exhaled into the phone. "Do you have any suggestions for a sermon topic?" The query came with a half-humble note.

Kathleen smiled again. "I'd suggest first of all that you avoid preaching anyone else's outline or printed sermon."

On the other end of the line, Walter faltered again in silence. Walking alone across his back yard in the dark he stopped and closed his eyes. Before he could respond to Kathleen's advice he heard her say, "What's a subject that's been weighing on your heart and mind personally these days, a subject that can be inspirational, meaningful, and interesting for the people?"

Walter opened his eyes and smirked. He understood that the latter part of the question was an indirect way of saying 'you need to address a subject other than female-teachers-in-the church.' Of course, female teachers in the church, especially a female who was the prominent teacher, was still a sore issue for him. But to be honest, and it definitely wasn't easy for him in this case, he was no longer a hundred percent convinced that female-teachers-in-the-church was a scriptural issue more than a cultural one. He had spent hours researching the matter online, in commentaries, and one-on-one with friends in the ministry. Yet, somehow Kathleen always managed to artfully dismantle the arguments he dug up, arguments that initially sounded so substantial. So, was she a voice of Satan that mastered in deception? Or was she a voice of God that shattered lies and defended truth? At least for the moment, he was not convinced she was a mask of the enemy. The enemy, he was almost certain, would never under any guise drive people to God and to His Word like Kathleen had been doing.

"I'll answer the question with a question," he told her.

"All right."

"What about the hundred-plus college students attending the services?"

"What about them?"

"Are you sure they're all Christians?"

"No…I'm not absolutely sure, but…"

"Well I just know that many of them don't look like it. I mean…with the long hair, tattoos, piercings. And such."

Walter thought he heard a sigh on the other end of the phone. He started to ask if anything was wrong when he heard Kathleen say, "Walter, I think a clear presentation of the Gospel would be a great idea. Which verses would you use as your text?"

"Well…I uh…last Sunday you made reference to John three, sixteen. So, I guess I could elaborate on that verse. And go into it with a little more detail."

"Sounds good. Is it okay if I give you some suggestions?"

Walter realized that as a public speaker he would need all the help he could get. "I'm listening," he said, trying to sound a little indifferent.

"C.W.I."

Walter started slowly walking again. "I'm sorry. I don't understand."

"C.W.I.," Kathleen repeated. "C - context. W- words. I - illustrations. Concentrate on those three points."

Walter kept walking. He listened as Kathleen elaborated.

"First of all," she exhorted, "look again carefully at the context. Who is talking? And who is he talking to? Then look closely at the meaning of each word. You might want to explain the meaning of the words to the congregation. And then use experiences from your own life to illustrate some of your points. You might, for example, want to use some of your experiences as a self-employed electrician to illustrate the word 'whosoever' or 'believe'."

"Okay," Walter said, lengthening the word.

"Oh…and one more thing," Kathleen pressed. "Use resources like a good expository dictionary and an exhaustive concordance. Try to avoid commentaries. Don't just echo the thoughts and conclusions of other men. Don't get into that practice. Rather, study the verse yourself in a raw kind of way. Dissect it from all possible angles. Meditate on it over and over. Then frame the truth of the verse in your words. Not someone else's."

In that moment Walter felt something inexplicably lighten in his spirit. "Okay, I got it. I'll follow your suggestions," he promised.

When he ended the call, he huffed. He wondered if he had sounded too dependent. Too compliant. He kicked the grass. "Wuss," he declared to himself.

Maybe it really didn't matter, though. For the first time ever, the idea of preaching actually started to excite him.

31

The next morning was overcast and drizzly. Kathleen arrived early at the church to unlock doors and open up the building. The man who normally did the job, one of Floyd Baxter's hired hands, was sick and in bed with some kind of stomach virus.

Needing no more preparation time for her sermon, Kathleen took advantage of the spare moments and stood at the big white doors of the foyer and welcomed people with hugs and encouraging words as they stepped inside out of the rain.

Beneath her umbrella Evelyn Huxley rounded the sidewalk and approached the main entrance to the sanctuary, all while skirting rain puddles. She was in an exceptionally good mood, despite the weather.

When she entered the foyer and collapsed her umbrella, she saw Kathleen standing in the area talking with Walter. At that instant, she saw Kathleen warmly pat Walter on the shoulder, say another word or two to him, then turn in her direction.

"Good morning, Evelyn."

Evelyn, as always, was taken in by Kathleen's engaging manner. "Good morning," Evelyn replied.

"You look full of life today," Kathleen said.

"I feel full of life."

Kathleen pulled Evelyn into an infectious hug.

Evelyn closed her eyes, simply appreciating Kathleen's presence in her life.

"So how are Ray and Billy these days?" Kathleen asked, retreating slightly from the embrace.

"Well, Ray is still sulking. Especially around all his buddies," she chuckled. "But I keep telling him you're my favorite pastor of all time and I'm not going to cater to any of his bad feelings about you. And Billy…he's working with his dad in the repair shop nearly every day, and is quieter than he's ever been. But other than that…life is wonderful."

Kathleen squeezed Evelyn's shoulder and gave her a supportive sigh. "I saw that you raised your hand last week, accepting the missions challenge. Do you think that will go over at home okay? Or…?" Kathleen raised her eyebrows.

Evelyn felt a tinge of apprehension. "I really don't know. I… uh…it's something I'm praying will somehow just fall into place. If you don't mind, pray that God will help me figure out a way to keep the promise without adding any more aggravation to Ray's plate."

"I'll do it," Kathleen assured her with a sisterly wink.

Before turning to greet someone else who scampered in, Kathleen hugged Evelyn one more time and added, "I appreciate you. And don't forget; I'm here when you need me."

Kathleen had greeted and interacted with more than two dozen people when she heard the youth band inside the auditorium begin to run through one of their worship songs.

Hearing the keyboard play, Kathleen understood she should start moving toward the stage and gearing up for the service.

Just as she began to shift in that direction, she saw Willow and Ida Mae unexpectedly come through the front door. Kathleen's lips spread into an earnest smile. She promptly stepped toward the ladies with open arms. "Ladies! Ladies! It's so good to see you again!"

"Pastor Rose," Willow responded with a nod and a smile, taking her hands off Ida Mae's wheelchair and receiving Kathleen's hug.

Kathleen chuckled softly. "Now, girl. I've already told you not to call me pastor…that you should just call me Kathleen."

"In front of all your people?" Willow mildly retorted, leaning into Kathleen's embrace. She then whispered into Kathleen's ear, "Girl, you are the pastor. And a dang good one. And you need to wear that title proudly."

Kathleen still smiling, lifted her eyebrows in a friendly concession. Letting go of the hug, she chuckled again and said, "I want you to know that your presence here means more to me than you know."

"Well…," Willow said, looking around, "It is a bit crazy; I gonna tell you." She winked. "But you're why we're here. It's the first time I've wanted to come to church since I don't know how long."

Kathleen playfully rolled her eyes.

"And," Willow added, "because of you I done started readin' my Bible again. Can't say that I understand a lot of it. But at least it feels good to be doin' it."

Kathleen felt her heart leap. "I'll tell you what; I'll be glad to meet with you any time to try to help you make sense of it and to try to answer any questions you might have."

Willow cocked her head. "You'd do that?"

Kathleen initiated a soft high-five. "Absolutely, it would be an honor." Not waiting for Willow to throw more accolades her way, Kathleen then gave Ida Mae a hug and saw the lady's head rock stiffly from side to side, grunting joyously and displaying one of the most exuberant smiles Kathleen had seen in a long time.

Kathleen then grabbed the handlebars of the wheelchair and proudly pushed the old black lady into the auditorium, with Willow just a half step behind.

* * *

Around 10:00 on Tuesday morning, Evelyn Huxley was returning home from a trip to the grocery store. Before Ray and Billy had left earlier in the morning to go fishing for the day, Ray had asked if they could have pork chops, cabbage, black-eyed peas, and an apple cobbler when they returned for dinner around 6:00 PM. Evelyn knew it was one of Ray's favorite meals, and was glad to cook it for him, but after checking her kitchen had realized she did not have Granny Smith apples or ground cinnamon for the cobbler.

Approaching her house, with groceries in tow, she prayed for both Billy and Ray. It had been awhile since the two of them had done anything fun together. She was just thankful Ray could take the day off and spend time with their son. "Lord, please, somehow speak to my boys out on the lake today. Let 'em know you're still there and that you're still a good God. Keep trying to draw them back to you. Please, whatever you do, don't give up on them."

Slowing to turn into the driveway, she was interrupted in her prayer when she noticed a truck of some type parked on their property, just right down the road in the grass, off the shoulder of the highway. Was someone lost? What were they doing there? A smidgen of uneasiness touched her stomach. She came to a full stop at the entry of the driveway and took a closer look, then realized to her comfort that it was a work truck from the tree-removal service Ray had talked to a week or so ago about taking down the large pine in that part of the yard. The tree, Ray had decided, was leaning too precariously toward the main power line.

She then proceeded up the driveway and parked. She took her bag of groceries and headed toward the house. At the front door, as she fiddled with the house key, she heard what sounded like a car door slam. She looked in the direction of the work truck fifty yards away. She saw two Mexican-looking men walking toward the base of the big pine. They waved at her. She nodded to acknowledge their presence on her property, then went inside.

But the moment she stepped inside, she froze. Her thoughts, like colorful pieces of a jigsaw puzzle, speedily assembled into an obvious-looking image. The nonwhite men in her yard. The pledge she had made in church a week and a half ago. The prayer for God to open a door of opportunity to help her fulfill the pledge.

She slowly moved to the kitchen and sat her grocery bag on the table. All the while, her mind was strumming, softly but relentlessly, like someone with a tic disorder tapping their index finger.

Her breathing slightly accelerated. Should she dare? Considering she was home alone, was it irresponsible to even entertain the notion? What if she invited them in and they actually accepted; how would Ray react if he ever found out? And he probably would.

She removed the groceries from the bag and placed them on the kitchen counter. She pulled a pot from the cabinet, filled it with cold water, and dumped in the black-eyed peas to soak for a few hours.

But her spirit wouldn't be silenced.

She walked to the front living room window and looked out. The two tree cutters were already at work. They were lowering the outriggers around the truck in preparation for using the lift bucket.

She squeezed her eyes shut and stood motionless. "All right," she finally mumbled to herself and to God, 'I'll do it, I'll do it."

She took a deep breath, straightened her dress, and walked outside.

"I'm doing this for you," she reminded God as she walked across the grass toward the men, trying not to be nervous.

She soon saw one of the men notice her and look up. He motioned to the other man. Both of them stood to see what she needed or wanted.

To Evelyn's eyes, both men were definitely Hispanic - short, with brown skin and black hair. "Hello," she greeted them, "Do you speak English?"

One of the men, probably the boss, answered from the side of the truck. "Yes, I speak English. We are here to cut the tree down for Mr. Huxley. He told us to come by when we had time. Are you his wife?"

"I am. My name is Evelyn." She stepped forward and shook the man's hand. "I'm just curious; how long do you think you'll be here?"

"Oh…it will take a couple of hours just to cut the tree to the ground and grind up the stump. And then we'll have to stack up all the wood and clean up the yard…all the branches and pine cones."

"Okay," Evelyn replied, bobbing her head. Was she really going to do this? She was suddenly emboldened. "Well, since you're going to be here at noon, why don't I prepare a lunch for you? That's just another way Ray and I can say 'thank you' for your help."

The man for a split second seemed uncertain. Or maybe just surprised. He eventually looked at the other man and said something in Spanish. He waited until the other man responded.

"Okay," the lead man finally answered. "That'll be fine. When you bring it out, will it be okay if we sit and eat in the shade of the oak tree over there?" He pointed to a tree in the middle of the front yard.

"Oh, no, no," Evelyn clarified. "I want you to come inside and sit down at the table where it's cool and comfortable."

The man looked surprised all over again. He spoke again in Spanish to his partner.

Evelyn watched the men exchange a few words and a few awkward looks.

"Are you sure?" the chief guy finally turned and asked Evelyn. "We'll be dirty and sweaty."

"Absolutely," Evelyn assured him. "That'll not be a problem."

The man shrugged his shoulders. "Okay, we'll just knock on the door when we're ready then."

"I'll be ready whenever you are," Evelyn told him. She returned to the house and immediately brainstormed about what she could serve. She looked in the refrigerator. She saw she had a full dozen eggs. That was it; she could make her famous egg salad sandwiches that everybody always raved about. She could also serve chips and iced tea. Plus, she had some coconut cake leftover from Sunday's lunch.

She was soon dancing around the kitchen, with a spoon in her hand, on a spiritual high.

Around 12:20 Evelyn heard the men knock at the front porch.

"Lord, I remind you again that I'm doing this for you," she whispered as she headed for the door.

"Come on in. Lunch is on the table," she told the men when she opened the door and greeted them. "If you want to wash up, or use the bathroom, it's right down the hall on the right. Just make yourself at home."

"Thank you, ma'am," the lead guy said softly. "We don't want to get anything dirty, so we will wash our hands first."

"Wash rags are hanging over the bathroom sink. So just come to the kitchen when you're ready."

The guy nodded.

Both men, one after the other, quietly utilized the bathroom, then showed up at the kitchen table together.

"Welcome to my home," Evelyn said. "Please! Have a seat." She motioned to the boss-apparent and said, "You can sit there." She put him at the head of the table. "And you can sit here," she told the other man, and pointed to the chair just around the corner from his partner.

Evelyn had set a place for herself across from the partner.

"Do you drink iced tea?" Evelyn asked when the men took their seats.

"We do. That would be nice," said the talkative one.

"What are your names?" Evelyn inquired, still standing, as she poured tea into ice-filled glasses.

"My name is Carlos. I am from Mexico. My helper is Felipe. He is from Guatemala. He speaks no English."

Evelyn made a point to remember the names. Carlos was the English speaker; the boss. "My name is Evelyn. I'm Ray's wife," she said and shook their hands. She started to explain that Ray was out of town for the day, but decided that giving out that information was probably not wise. She chose instead not to highlight Ray's absence at all. She took her seat at the table, smiled, and said, "All right; let's eat. Just help yourself."

Carlos translated for Felipe. And the two men, with utmost manners, dived right in.

Within thirty minutes or so, Evelyn was pleasantly astonished. She had learned that Carlos was married. Had four children, ages 12, 11, 9, and 6. Had lived in the US for thirteen years. Had lived in Georgia for eleven of those years. Had started working in the tree cutting business ten years ago. And, on the side, was currently helping his wife, an eighth-grade dropout, get her GED diploma - in English.

Evelyn felt true admiration for the wife after hearing details of how diligently the mother-of-four had worked to make headway in her studies. And she definitely appreciated that Carlos, as a husband, was willing to sacrifice to help tutor his wife and enable her to make such wonderful progress.

In addition, she had learned that Felipe was 28 years old and single. Had only been in the States for four years. Had lived in Georgia for only six months. And had been Carlos' helper for four months.

The men had even seemed proud to answer her questions.

And not once during the busy conversation had she felt tense or uncomfortable in the men's presence.

Both men had been total gentlemen. And, judging by their smiles and occasional laugher, they too had felt relaxed.

Carlos had even sung the praises of her egg salad and had asked if he could have the recipe for his wife. Felipe had asked, through translation, if he could get the coconut cake recipe, and kept rubbing his stomach as a sign of goodness. Evelyn had happily obliged them both.

As Carlos finished his last bites of cake, Evelyn noticed that he—almost tentative like—finally ventured out to ask a few personal-information questions himself.

"Have you lived here in Georgia a long time?" he quizzed.

Evelyn nodded an affirmative. "I've lived here in Georgia all my life. I was born about seventy miles down the road in Fitzgerald."

She followed by answering questions about Ray, about his tractor-repair business, about their son Billy, and about the extent of their out-of-state or out-of-country ventures.

Evelyn thought Carlos somehow looked dumbfounded or disappointed when she told him she had never traveled outside the five-state area of Georgia, Florida, Alabama, South Carolina, and Tennessee. She wondered fleetingly if her lack of exposure to other parts of the country, or to other cultures, had somehow been to her disadvantage. As a contented homebody and a proud Georgia girl, she had always assumed she had been exceptionally blessed.

All too soon, it seemed, the men were getting up to go back outside to finish their cleanup.

"Thank you very much," Carlos asserted in a soft meaningful tone, shaking Evelyn's hand. "We really appreciate your kindness.

No one has ever invited us in for lunch on a job site. This was very special."

Felipe thanked her equally with a jovial handshake and a glowing smile.

Evelyn's heart leapt. "You are more than welcome. It was my pleasure."

As Evelyn walked the gentlemen to the door, she wondered why she had never initiated contact like this before with people outside the white community.

She started to write them a check for the day's work. But then thought of a way to get them to come back. "Is it okay if you stop by tomorrow or the next day and pick up your money? Ray will be here and will take care of that for you."

"No problem," Carlos said.

Waving them out into the yard, Evelyn retreated to the dining room. She stood at the table and consciously inhaled a deep breath. Then exhaled. She suddenly felt alive.

32

Floyd Baxter was sitting in his Prime Vidalia Onions office on Wednesday morning, scrutinizing some financials, when his no-nonsense secretary stuck her head into the room and said, "Excuse me. Mr. Ted Higgley, the director of the regional Baptist Alliance, is here to see you. He knows he doesn't have an appointment. But he insists he should talk to you."

Floyd set a few papers down and looked up from the desk. He squeezed his forehead and sighed. "Okay, send him in."

When the secretary vanished from the doorway, Floyd huffed, then mumbled to himself, "We might as well go ahead and nip this in the bud and get it over with." He rolled back a few inches in his stately leather chair and sat more upright. Then perversely waited.

Fifteen seconds later the secretary ushered in a tall spindly man dressed conservatively in a white shirt, black suit, and gray tie. For some reason the man almost looked out of place in a suit. He reminded Floyd of a commercial painter he once knew.

"Welcome Mr. Higgley. Have a seat." Floyd directed the man to one of the chairs facing his desk.

"Thank you," Higgley said as he sat down. "I won't take up much of your time."

"Then how can I help you, sir?"

Higgley shifted uncomfortably in his seat. "Well, after hearing rumors and then reading all the newspaper articles about your church, I decided as the director of the regional Baptist Alliance to attend a service at your church last Sunday and see for myself what is going on. And I've got to tell you, Mr. Baxter, that out of the fifty churches in our Alliance, spread out over four counties, the Central Baptist Church of Lyons is completely out of line and out of place."

"Because?"

"Because? Because your preacher, your pastor, your leader is a lady. That's why. And a lady pastor is strictly forbidden according to Baptist Alliance beliefs and practices." Higgley reached into his suit pocket and extracted a folded sheet of paper. "In case you're not familiar with it, here is a copy of the Evangelical Baptist Alliance Confession. It's a registry of beliefs and policies that was officially reaffirmed at the national convention in 2006. Every EBA church in the nation, without exception—in order to maintain their membership status— has to agree to abide by these words. And I've circled the paragraph here that's pertinent to the situation." Higgley unfolded the sheet and handed it to Baxter across the desk.

Baxter took the copy. His eyes zeroed in on the paragraph circled by a yellow marker. The paragraph was titled 'Section V, The Local Church.' One solitary line in the section had been highlighted with the same yellow marker. Baxter read the mandate: 'While we believe that every believer is gifted by God for ministry in the church, we believe the role of pastor, as dictated by Scripture, is limited exclusively to qualified men.' The statement was followed by a list of Bible verses.

Baxter looked up. "So?" He felt the emotional heat in his one-word question.

Higgley leaned forward in his seat. "So, if Lyons Central Baptist doesn't reverse its decision, the credential's committee in our Alliance will assess the situation and will predictably make a motion at our annual meeting in October to suspend the church from membership. The motion, once it is explained, will be seconded and passed."

Baxter truly wanted to shout at the man and say, 'What difference will it make; the lady pastor we have now is three times the teacher and leader as the two previous jerks that ruled our pulpit!' At the same time, he wanted to temper himself. He still believed that the Evangelical Baptist Alliance network as a whole was one of the true pylons of truth undergirding the country. Why, even he had become a Christian as a teenager because of their influence. And he had been a loyal member and supporter ever since. He knew their far-reaching influence. But now, for Lyons Central Baptist, maybe it just didn't matter anymore if the church was embraced by the fold.

Baxter stood up and handed the document back to Higgley. "Well, sir, I guess you've got to do what you've got to do."

Higgley followed suit and stood as well. "Aren't you even going to take this before the congregation and let them decide?" he nearly scoffed.

For a fleeting moment, Baxter realized he probably should. But then he remembered Kathleen. Her distant past. Her recent past. And her present. His bond and connection with her was simply far greater than his bond with the Alliance. "No sir, I'm not, Mr. Higgley. The decision stands. Now, if you don't mind…"

*   *   *

Kathleen sat barefoot at the desk in her private home office trying to finish several thank-you notes before lunch. Since her arrival in Lyons eight weeks ago, a number of wives in the church had brought her fresh-cut flowers, home-cooked meals, and a good supply of household items - dry foods, paper towels, body lotions, laundry detergents, ink pens, stationery, and such.

She took her eyes off the computer screen for a moment and looked out the window. It was another lovely day. She massaged her feet across the carpet and stretched.

She suddenly wondered how the missionary couple, acting as her interims in Mali, were coping. She badly wanted to call them and get an updated report. But she would abide by the agreement and not contact them. They did not know exactly where she was residing in the states and, therefore, could not slip up and reveal her location to anyone.

And for security reasons not many people in Mali knew the identity of the couple. The work they were doing on her behalf was restricted to correspondence and administration, just enough to keep the organization alive until she returned.

Peering out the window again, she saw a vibrant red cardinal land and perch on a limb just a few feet away. She was being pulled into its exquisite beauty when she heard her cell phone ring. The caller was identified on the screen as Floyd Baxter.

"Morning," she answered.

"Have you seen today's paper?" Floyd jumped right in.

"No, not yet. Why?"

"Can I read to you the latest article about you and the church?"

Kathleen's insides were gently pinged. "Okay, go ahead." She leaned back in her chair and stretched her legs forward.

"It's titled <u>The Changing Face Of Lyons Central Baptist</u>." Floyd cleared his throat. "The article reads: In just two months time, Lyons Central Baptist—to the chagrin of many and the praise of others—has overturned one hundred years of steadfast traditions, beliefs, and practices. The deed holder of the church's land and building, Floyd Baxter of Prime Vidalia Onions, unilaterally installed the church's first female pastor, enabled that pastor to replace the organ and piano with drums, keyboards, and electric guitars, allowed that pastor to replace hymns with contemporary worship songs, and has himself remained silent while the pastor has encouraged ethnic groups to now attend the historically all-white church. In this day of fast-pace change, Lyons Central Baptist has definitely been reborn overnight with a new face. Says one new attendee, 'Exceptional teaching. Inspiring music. Great fellowship. What more can we ask for? It's the first time in years I've actually wanted to go to church. I love it.'"

Baxter finished the article, then paused.

It sounded to Kathleen like Baxter was on the verge of adding commentary or saying something he felt was important.

Yet, Baxter continued to pause.

"But you're okay with the changes that have taken place; correct?" Kathleen punctuated.

"Are you kidding? I just want to say 'attagirl.' Actually, I couldn't be more thrilled. I'm looking forward to going to church for the first time in years as well. Besides it was Jack's and Jim's decision to call for all the church workers to boycott the services that opened up the positions for new musicians and such. If anyone's upset about the music, they should blame the music director, pianist, and organist who stepped down and left a vacuum. And if they're distraught by a few black people showing up, then maybe it's best they move along anyway. All I can say is, we are way overdue for all these changes. And I couldn't be happier."

Kathleen suspected all along that Baxter had approved the church's spontaneous and ongoing evolution regarding music and attendance-makeup. She still felt bad, though, that her presence as a female had repelled most of the church's middle-aged and older men. She was pleased, however, that Troy and Walter, despite their initial attitude and behavior, had remained faithful in their attendance. Whatever their original goals or intentions, they were seemingly experiencing a gradual change of heart. They were being less argumentative and combative.

Last Sunday she had even seen Troy for the first time laughing and carrying on a conversation with some of the new college students. She had high hopes for both men.

"Then, if you will," Kathleen emphasized in her response to Baxter, "just pray that God will help me navigate any additional changes in a way that will offend the least number of people. That's my heart's desire."

"I have prayed for you, Angela…oops, sorry…Kathleen," Baxter informed her. "And I'll continue to do so. That's my promise."

Kathleen ended the call with a buoyed heart.

33

On Wednesday evening, Ray and Evelyn were finishing their last bites of supper. Billy had already retreated to his room.

Evelyn heard what sounded like a truck door slam in the front yard. She looked at Ray, with a bit of pecan pie on his cheek, and raised her eyebrows.

Ray had heard the sound as well. He shrugged in response. He pushed himself from the table to move toward the front door.

Evelyn stood up, wiped the crumb off Ray's face and carried plates of left over mashed potatoes and fried okra to the kitchen. She was getting ready to return to the table to fetch other food dishes when she heard Ray at the front door.

"Hon, can you bring the checkbook? It's the tree man."

Evelyn stopped in her tracks. She had told Ray yesterday evening that she had given food to the "tree cutter and his partner" for lunch when they had shown up and done their work. She had briefly mentioned the fact in passing, but had given no details. Ray, to her relief, had seemingly let the statement go in one ear and out the other. He had been focused at the time on a tractor-related problem.

She sidetracked to the bedroom, retrieved the checkbook from a drawer and took it to Ray at the front door.

As soon as she walked into Carlos' sight, the man's eyes brightened.

"Mrs. Huxley," Carlos said, acknowledging Evelyn with a smile.

Evelyn wanted badly to greet Carlos by name and invite him inside. Instead she looked the man in the face and presented a cheery "Good evening" as she handed the checkbook to Ray.

"All right, do I make the check out to you or to your company," Ray asked Carlos.

Carlos told Ray the dollar amount, then spelled out the name of his company.

Ray filled out the check and handed it over.

"Thank you, sir," Carlos said. "And please keep me in mind if you ever need more trees taken down."

"I'll do it," Ray promised.

"And I want to thank you for the lunch yesterday," Carlos added, looking over at Evelyn. "It was really, really good."

"You are absolutely more than welcome," she told him, refraining from looking at Ray at that precise moment.

"Do you mind if my wife asks you a question about the egg salad recipe? She's out in the truck."

Evelyn cringed on the inside, afraid of Ray's reaction if he started asking questions and discovered she had fed the two strange men inside at the dining room table. "Well sure," she finally blurted. "Let me go out and meet her." Evelyn tried not to sound nervous. But the pitch of her voice went higher as she uttered her compliance.

Still skirting eye contact with Ray, she stepped around him and walked with Carlos to his truck.

Moving toward the truck, Evelyn could see the wife peering through the windshield from the passenger's seat. It looked as if she was sitting alone in the truck, without the kids.

Evelyn recalled Ray's frequent remarks about the way Hispanics were popping up everywhere "like too many flies that ruin a picnic." He didn't hesitate to use them for cheap labor, though, when he found himself in a pinch; that was for sure.

Evelyn then reflected on how much time and effort Carlos' wife was investing to learn English and earn a GED. The lady, bless her heart, was trying to fit in.

Evelyn saw the lady lower the passenger window. Without waiting for Carlos to make an introduction, Evelyn walked right up to the window and extended her hand. "Hello, my name is Evelyn."

"My name is Margarita," the lady said slowly and shyly, shaking Evelyn's hand. "It is nice to…meet you."

"It's nice to meet you too," Evelyn said with a bit of nervous excitement, now fully committed to her plan even if Ray pitched a fit about it.

Pint sized, but bosomy, Margarita raked her fingers through her dark hair. "Carlos say you…you are lady…that makes best egg salad."

Evelyn noticed the lady had a meek, but beautiful smile. "Yeah, it's a family recipe passed down from my grandmother.

The secret to the taste is the combination of sauces and peppers, along with steaming the eggs instead of boiling them."

Margarita suddenly looked lost.

Evelyn backtracked. "I could write it all down for you, but you might not be able to read my handwriting. So…maybe you can come back to the house in the next day or two, and I can show you in my kitchen how it's made. We can make it together. And you can write the recipe down in Spanish."

"Me come to your house?" Margarita repeated.

"Yeah, if it's okay with your husband. Do you have a car? Do you drive?"

Margarita's face immediately showed chagrin. "No," she said, scrunching her shoulders. "I do not have driver's certificate. We have only one truck. And Carlos…how do I say…must use every day for work."

"Well, do you live far away? Perhaps I can come and get you." Evelyn forced a smile and tried to look natural. Ray would definitely be mad now if he found out what she was doing.

"We live out in Collins. I don't know…maybe…maybe it is too far away for you," Margarita declared. The young lady suddenly looked a little disappointed as if Evelyn might indeed abandon the invitation.

Evelyn knew that Collins was a poor little town about thirteen miles to the east. She tried to think quickly. To drive to Collins and back two times in one morning or afternoon would not be a problem. But…

211

Before Evelyn could jump back in and maintain the conversation's initiative, she heard Margarita say:

"Maybe you can just come to my house and use my kitchen."

Evelyn's mind reeled. She had never been inside the home of a nonwhite American, not of any color. She couldn't help but think of Ray. He would fuss at her like there was no tomorrow if he found out she had been in a Mexican's home as the only white person. Evelyn turned her head and looked back toward the house. The front door was standing wide open. Ray was nowhere to be seen.

"All right," Evelyn said gently. "Let's do it. Today's Wednesday. Should I come tomorrow or Friday?"

Margarita took a few seconds to consult the calendar on her smartphone. "Friday will be good."

"Around eleven-thirty?"

Margarita nodded, emitting a pleasing smile. "Eleven-thirty is good."

Carlos, who had been standing off to Evelyn's side listening to the conversation, moved around toward the driver's side of the truck.

Within a minute or so, Evelyn was heading back toward the house with Margarita's address and phone number clutched in her hand on a small piece of paper. She turned and waved goodbye as the truck pulled out of the yard.

*   *   *

Later, in bed, with Ray snuggled up behind her breathing across the back of her neck, Evelyn found it difficult to quieten her thoughts. Thankfully, Ray had not asked a single question about the evening's encounter. He seemed clueless. But could she keep him in the dark? Or should she even try? What if he questioned her on Friday morning when she was preparing to leave for the all-day excursion to Collins? Or would he possibly be so absorbed out in the workshop that he wouldn't even be aware of her absence?

She suddenly felt as anxious as she did on the night she snuck out of her parents' house at the age of sixteen and ran off to the "forbidden school party" - as her parents had deemed it. She was grounded for two whole weeks when her father learned what she had done. The silver lining, though, was the fact that she had enjoyed her first conversation and first dance with Ray at that party. He had been a senior. She had been a sophomore.

Engrossed in the memories she finally started to doze, a spontaneous smile wrapped across her face.

34

Friday morning was the worst morning of Evelyn's life.

She was sitting in her car, still parked in her yard, and was wiping a deluge of tears from her face. She was a nervous wreck. Her knee was jackhammering up and down and she couldn't even stop it.

The reoccurring image of Ray's raised hand, poised to slap her, was rocking her to the core. It was the first time in their life that Ray had threatened her with physical harm.

After that commotion, he had stormed out the back door shouting "I hate that damn woman!" He had slammed the door so hard it had made her shudder.

She had earlier in the morning written a note to leave on the kitchen table, explaining she would be gone for awhile and that lunch was in the refrigerator. She had hoped the morning and early afternoon would pass without Ray stepping inside the house. And that he would never even register her absence.

But, contrary to her hopes, Ray had made an appearance inside the house right as she was getting ready to leave. He noticed when she immediately became nervous.

"What's happening, hon?" he had asked softly.

She had wanted to be evasive. But her conscience, and especially her nerves, wouldn't let her play the game anymore.

The inner persuasion to be completely honest and trustworthy slowly took over.

So, she made her decision; she divulged everything - her acceptance of Kathleen's challenge to eat two meals with non-whites, her first meal with the tree cutters inside the house with no one else around, and her latest commitment to visit the tree cutter's wife today, alone in Collins.

At first Ray had become inordinately quiet.

And then abruptly, and in a condescending voice, he said, "And did it ever occur to you that having those two men inside the house might have been a little bit dangerous?"

Before she could answer, he erupted again.

"You have no idea who those men are! You don't know them for heaven's sake! They could have easily overpowered you and hurt you; don't you understand that?"

While she was scrambling to find words to help calm him down, she saw him suddenly shake his head and then slam the table with his fist.

"I don't want you to ever do anything like that again! Do you hear me?"

She paused.

"I said, do you hear me?" he barked.

"Ray," she pleaded, lowering her shoulders and trying not to add fuel to his seemingly off-the-scale behavior. "Have you considered that God might want to…"

Ray hit the table again. "What I've considered is that God has made me the head of this household, of this family, of this marriage. And I'm telling you, I WILL make the decisions about my family's safety - not Kathleen Rose!"

Evelyn suddenly saw it. It was Ray's pride that was in play. It was almost as if he was jealous. "Ray," she said, this time even softer, "I don't want you to think…"

Ray immediately raised an open palm to signal silence. He took a couple of deep breaths, like a wild animal claiming his ground. "Right now," he hissed, "I don't really care what you want, or don't want, in the matter. I just want you to promise me you will submit to my authority."

The sudden clarity of what was happening helped Evelyn relax deep in her spirit. "So, are you saying you do not want me to go to Collins this morning? That you want me to go back on my word?"

"That is exactly what I'm saying," Ray shot forth. "I don't want you to go today, or any other day. I want you to give up this idea of trying to satisfy some lady pastor who wants you to intermingle with people you have no business intermingling with. What she did in Africa was her business. But her ideas don't fit here. Our church has always functioned just fine without them. And always will."

Evelyn's swirling thoughts quickly morphed into a few clear questions. But before she dared even think about voicing those questions, Ray continued his barrage.

"So, are you going to promise to do what I say, or not?"

She had wanted to say, and intended to say, *Of course I'll submit to your authority; we'll get through this.* But the questions in the forefront of her heart had caused her to pause for too long.

It was at that moment Ray had snapped.

Maybe he had seen the questions in her eyes.

That's when he had raised his fist to hit her. She couldn't shake the image of his fist twitching over her like a rabid dog. He had seriously wanted to hit her. After too many seconds of wanting to do it, he had then turned and trounced out the back door cursing Pastor Rose with a vengeance. Hurt pride or not, his reaction had gone too far.

From behind the steering wheel, Evelyn held out her hand. She was still shaking.

She opened her purse and pulled out her mobile phone and the sheet of paper with Margarita's address and phone number. She needed to call her and tell her she wouldn't be coming.

With myriad feelings entangling her like kudzu, she desperately laid her forehead against the steering wheel to pray. To pray for some kind of calm. But the only words that would come out were, "Help us; please help us!"

Not knowing what else to do, she started the car, backed out the driveway, and headed for a private place to make the call.

After the unwanted and bumbling phone conversation with Margarita, Evelyn was in no emotional state to return home. Feeling completely adrift for the first time in life, she came close to calling Pastor Rose and pleading for comfort, shelter, and advice. But somehow the explosive scene that had taken place back at the house was too ugly and too personal to talk about.

She finally decided, for the sake of last-ditch direction, to visit a sick cousin who was hospitalized thirty miles away in Swainsboro, Georgia. She knew immediately that it was not a logical decision, but the trip would give her some alone time to catch her breath and to sort through everything.

So, she turned the car toward Georgia Highway 1 and headed north.

Ray could later believe her, or not, regarding her afternoon and evening whereabouts. She really didn't care at the moment.

35

At 5:45 on Saturday evening, May 30, Kathleen pulled out of her driveway to go to Pecan Drive and pick up Alexa, Marcos, and Valery—the Mexican family—for the evening meal.

She had spent a couple of hours earlier in the afternoon shopping in Vidalia for three small gifts. She wanted Alexa and the kids to feel as if they were being honored in a simple, non-overbearing way.

She was pleased with her selection - a porcelain horse figurine wearing a name-tag necklace engraved with the name *Valery*; a beautiful handcrafted leather belt with *Marcos* engraved on the buckle; and a pleasure-pampering bath set with body lotion, body butter, bubble bath, shower gel, and a pink loofa for Alexa. In addition, for Alexa, was the highly insightful book *Cross-Cultural Survival* that Kathleen had promised, written by an American executive who had moved his family to seven different countries over a period of just sixteen years.

With the gifts wrapped and sitting in the seat beside her, she tapped the car radio to a Gospel music station and sang along all the way to Pecan Drive.

She had told Alexa in advance that she would take them to some place nice. So, she wasn't surprised when she greeted Alexa and the two kids at their front door and saw them each dressed in a set of spiffy clothes. Even Marcus was wearing a collared shirt and khaki pants.

Kathleen could see excitement, fused with modesty and gratitude, radiating across Alexa's face.

Kathleen felt excited herself. She could be way off the mark, but she suspected it had probably been a long time since Alexa and the children had enjoyed a fine-dining experience.

"Before we pile in the car," Kathleen said, with the family of three staring at her with spellbound eyes and listening for her instructions, "I want you to know again why I'm doing this."

Alexa, Marcus, and Valery were the perfect audience.

"I know what it's like," Kathleen reemphasized, "to be a resident in a foreign country and to try hard to fit in and be accepted. And then to feel the serious disappointment when many of the citizens in that country seem to ignore you, or even look down on you. So," Kathleen stressed, scanning the eyes of the three individuals, "I want to do this as a gesture of human kindness and decency. I want to say, welcome to America, welcome to Lyons. And I want to say a special thanks to you, Alexa, for contributing to the Toombs County labor force and for fighting for your family while figuring out a new and different culture."

Alexa and the kids just stood there, speechless. A new tear teased Alexa's cheek.

"And," Kathleen continued, "I've brought a few welcoming gifts." As she reached inside her gift bag, she chuckled, "If I were a sovereign ruler, I would make it a policy that every new citizen in my land, regardless of their background, would be thrown a small party where they would be given cultural information, helpful advice, gifts, and a list of business contacts relevant to their skill set.

"But I'm not. And I can't. But I can encourage one guest and one guest-family at a time."

Kathleen handed the gift-wrapped horse to Valery first.

Valery's eyes hesitated momentarily, then flared with excitement. She took the present with unbelievable gentleness. "Can I open it, mommy?"

Alexa looked to Kathleen.

Kathleen nodded.

"Sure, Mi Sol."

In less than a minute Valery was squeezing the personalized figurine to her chest, begging her mom to let her take it with her for the evening. At the same time she was scooting up against Kathleen's leg.

Kathleen couldn't help but smile. It was amazing how a simple gift could instantly build an emotional bridge.

Marcos showed an equal amount of appreciation when he opened his gift. He immediately unstrapped his old belt and replaced it with the new one. He then stood in front of a mirror near the front door and admired the image looking back at him. He gave Kathleen a side-to-side one-armed hug around her waist.

When Alexa opened her bath set, she was as moved as the children. She leaned in and gave Kathleen a tentative, but serious, hug of her own. "The gifts are wonderful," she said softly.

"Thank you. And as I say before, this is first time anything like this has happened to our family in the US."

"It's long overdue then," Kathleen declared as she headed her three guests to the car.

Kathleen drove them to downtown Lyons. The restaurant she had selected, and where she had made reservations, was the modern-industrial Elements Bistro and Grill on Broad Street. The milieu was a beautiful brick-exterior, brick-interior renovated old corner building with windows from floor to ceiling, highlighted with foliage inside and out.

The maître d', a young lady dressed in a white blouse and black pants, led them to their table. Piano music was playing in the background.

When they were seated—with linen napkins, polished silverware, and glasses of iced water— Kathleen looked at each of her three Hispanic guests and said, "Well, let's relax and have a fun evening."

And have a fun evening, they did.

Valery and Marcos enjoyed Smokehouse Burgers, all while Valery tiptoed her horse around the section of table immediately in front of her and lost herself in a world of fantasy.

Kathleen and Alexa indulged in Filet Mignons.

Afterward, everyone shared a couple of desserts - small portions of blackberry cobbler, sprinkled with cinnamon crumble and topped with vanilla ice cream.

Throughout the evening, in the backdrop of the kids' perfect behavior, Kathleen closed the gap between two cultures and two lives with heart-to-heart conversation.

Her interest in Alexa's family simply compounded as she learned that Alexa was a lone child raised in the metropolis of Monterrey; had lost her first husband—a law enforcement officer—in a drug cartel shooting; had lost her parents to the same cartel; had sought refuge and safety for her and the kids in the US with a legalized Mexican who she met online; had married the man in Valdosta, Georgia six years ago; had been abandoned by the man two years into the marriage; and had relocated to Lyons shortly thereafter to start over in life.

Kathleen at one point reached for, and held Alexa's hand. "I am not allowed to give details about my own personal circumstances, but please know I feel a certain connection with you. I too am an only child, have experienced the premature loss of a husband, and have relocated to the states for a safe, fresh restart."

Alexa's eyes reacted to Kathleen's similarities. "I would never have guessed," she said quietly. "How is it then that you seem so strong...so positive?"

Kathleen chuckled lightly. "*Seem* is maybe the operative word there. Sometime I do feel strong, and that's only because of God's help. At other times I just want to hide in the house and cry."

Alexa nodded her understanding and struggled to hold back sudden tears of her own. "So, tell me how God helps you," she abruptly wanted to know.

For fifteen minutes or more, Kathleen tenderly but valiantly shared God's message of redemption. When she finally wrapped up her answer, she said, "So, it's His continuous presence and accessibility that enables me to keep standing, to keep breathing, to keep putting one foot in front of the other."

Alexa sighed with envy. "My Catholic upbringing never explained it that way. But you make it sound so beautiful."

"It is beautiful, Alexa. But it's more than beautiful; it's life changing."

"And is this what you teach in your church?"

"It is."

Alexa dabbed at the tear that finally seeped from the corner of her eye. "Is it okay if I bring the children and visit one Sunday?"

"Alexa," Kathleen grinned, "you are more than welcome to visit anytime you want."

Marcos, who had been busy doodling on paper that the server had given him, suddenly pulled his mother close and whispered in her ear.

"Marcos wants to know if we can come this Sunday," Alexa relayed to Kathleen.

Kathleen's heart reveled. Then she remembered that Walter was scheduled to speak on Sunday. She almost proposed to Alexa that they wait and visit the following week. She impulsively changed her mind, though. "We will have a guest speaker this Sunday, but, yes, absolutely. I can personally meet you at the front door around 10:45 if you'd like."

"Shall we?" Alexa asked her kids.

Both Marcos and Valery nodded with a big grin on their face.

"All right then, we'll do it," Alexa promised.

Before they gave up their table, Kathleen raised one final subject. "I still want to find out if you have any advice on how the white community, including my congregation, can effectively welcome the Hispanics to our county and make them feel part of the area?"

Alexa closed her eyes for a moment, then reopened them with a glimmer of hope. "I do have advice. Tell the white community to follow your example. For some reason we are shy around white Americans. So, tell the white community to take the first step. Tell them to acknowledge our presence with eye contact, a wave, a smile. Tell them to carry on a conversation with us and to ask us questions. Tell them to listen to our stories. If they will do that, we will respond. We will become the friendliest and best neighbors they will ever have."

Kathleen felt her face light up as she stood and gave Alexa a hug.

The kids were beaming as well.

36

Walter was ten minutes into his Sunday morning sermon.

Sitting on the third row in one of the overflow chairs, Kathleen was starting to relax. She had met with Walter twice in recent days to help him prepare for today's message. Plus, she had talked to him briefly right before the service had begun.

As agreed upon, he was using John 3:16 as his text. And as she had coached him, he was highlighting and explaining the central words throughout the verse. But in a unique twist, which Kathleen liked, he was focusing on the words in reverse order. He had begun with the words *eternal life*. He had now worked his way backward to the word *whoever*.

Kathleen stared at him for a moment. He was different than the man she had first met eight weeks ago. He was not wearing new clothes. He was not sporting a different haircut. He hadn't lost or gained weight. Physically, he looked the same. But his spirit was clearly being reshaped. He was no longer belligerent toward her. He was no longer obstinate. Rather, he was carrying a hunger, an excitement, in his eyes regarding his faith. He was asking more questions.

Even his demeanor today as a teacher was more self-effacing and respectful.

Kathleen grinned on the inside. *There is hope for you yet, Walter Johnson.*

Walter was taking extra measures—because of the presence of the Hispanic family in the crowd and because of Kathleen's desire to accommodate them—to enunciate his words clearly. Out of the corner of his eye he saw Kathleen give him a subtle thumbs-up from the shadow of her lap.

That one gesture alone helped him catch a second breath. He was just relieved that no one was trying to *boo* him off the platform this time.

"As we look at the word *whoever*," he said into the microphone, "I want to illustrate the dimension of the word by using my own trade as an electrician. Everybody will understand when I say that *whoever* pays the power company for electricity will receive electricity, whether that customer is a city councilman, an average citizen, or a serial killer. The power company doesn't discriminate. *Whoever* pays receives. The *whoever*, in the power-company context, shows the limitless dimension. No one is barred from receiving electricity, for example, because of a criminal record, because of an unstable mind, because of a lack of education, not even because of being irresponsible with electricity. *Whoever* pays receives.

"The word *whoever* here in John three, sixteen carries the same limitless dimension. *Whoever* believes in the Son receives eternal life. We've already defined the word *believe*. So again, whoever believes in the Son—regardless of sex, education, skin color, or character—receives eternal life. God is barring no one, not the most immoral person in the world, not the most prideful person in the world, from this extraordinary invitation. *Whoever* believes receives."

Walter paused and looked down at his notes.

Sticking to his outline, he took the next fifteen minutes and finished underlining the final five words - *Son, gave, world, love, and God.*

He concluded the sermon with his personal story of trusting Christ and receiving eternal life when he was in his early thirties.

And then on impulse he decided to do something he had not planned. All former pastors of the church—during the years he had been a member anyway—had regularly given nonChristians in the audience the opportunity to come to the front of the church at the end of the sermon and publicly say "yes" to God's offer of salvation. Kathleen, for some unspoken reason, had not given a public altar call at the church.

Walter felt that to not give a public invitation today would be a missed opportunity, especially in light of the declared salvation message along with the number of college students in the sanctuary whose spiritual status was unknown.

"Before I turn the service back over to Kathleen," he stated in a hushed tone, "I would like to ask the pianist to come to the keyboard and play a soft instrumental in the background."

Walter waited while a young man moved to the front.

"Will everyone stand, please," Walter asked.

He waited until everyone was on their feet.

"If you are here today and you have never trusted God's only begotten Son for your salvation, then today is the day that God is inviting you with open arms—no matter who you are—to receive His eternal forgiveness. This forgiveness, as we've learned today, only comes through God's Son. If you are here today and you've never given your soul to Jesus, but would like to do so, then I encourage you, while the music is playing, to come to the front. Kathleen will be here to pray with you and to answer any questions you might have. I will ask Deacon Troy to come and stand here as well."

There was a moment of heavy pause while Kathleen and Troy absorbed what was happening and adjusted to the sudden redirection.

Kathleen moved first.

Troy followed.

They stood at the front, facing the crowd, as requested.

Walter signaled the keyboard player to commence playing. The young man immediately brought a sense of calm to the room with his heavenly rendition of a slow contemporary song from Australia called 'I Surrender.'

"All right," Walter said tenderly into the microphone, "if you would like to receive God's gift of eternal life, then come. Come now. Don't wait. Today is the day of salvation."

Walter motioned with his arms for someone, anyone, to step forward.

"Kathleen and Troy will greet you and will help walk you through the decision," he emphasized again.

Walter then waited as the music touched emotional cords across the room.

Kathleen was out of sync with this element of the southern-church culture. Standing there, she felt a little awkward. Was this something everyone was comfortable with? What about the millennials?

She decided if Walter tried to pressure the people she would simply intervene and bring the service to a close.

She would give him about a minute.

Out of curiosity she looked at Alexa, seven or eight rows back, to see if she was okay or if she was totally confused.

Exactly at that moment Alexa—with a perplexed look on her face—grabbed Valery's hand and scooted in front of a few people as she worked her way toward the aisle. Marcos was right behind her.

Kathleen immediately wondered if she had been frightened? She was nearly ready to go after her to explain the situation.

But...

When Alexa stepped into the aisle she didn't turn toward the foyer. Rather she stood for a split second facing the platform and looked at Kathleen with an expression of longing in her eyes. She nodded at Kathleen as if seeking permission to approach.

Kathleen, unsure of what was happening, nodded back.

A host of college students were now singing to the music. Their voices filled the room with a hushed and sweet spirit.

With her eyes locked on Kathleen, Alexa walked steadily to the front. Marcos and Valery followed.

Kathleen opened her arms.

Alexa walked into her embrace.

"I would like eternal life," Alexa said softly, tears beginning to wet her face. "I want to believe. Like you do. And like the man does."

Kathleen's heartbeat accelerated. She gripped Alexa's hand. "Here, let's take a seat." Kathleen led the family of three to an empty spot on the front pew. She sat next to Alexa and faced her. She could still feel her heart pulsing. She looked Alexa in the eyes. "So, you want to accept God's forgiveness, and become His child?" Right when Kathleen asked the question, she saw out of her peripheral vision a young college couple approach Troy at the front. She could hardly believe it. She never took her focus from Alexa, though.

"Yes, I need Him," Alexa responded with a raw intensity. "I want to believe."

Kathleen felt tears spill from her own eyes now. She ran her hand through her hair. "Pardon me. I'm just over thrilled; that's all." She took Alexa's hands again. "All right. Let's pray together. Just in your own words, tell God you want to believe. And He WILL respond."

Kathleen bowed her head.

"And He will hear me?" Alexa interrupted.

Kathleen looked up again. She took her Bible and turned to the first chapter of John, zeroing in on verses twelve and thirteen. She pointed to the words for Alexa to see. "These words are written by the same apostle who wrote John three-sixteen. The apostle says, *The person who receives Jesus, who believes in His name, is given the right to become a child of God—a spiritual child— not born of physical birth, but born of God.* So, the answer is 'yes,' He will hear you when you tell Him you want to receive His Son. And he will give you new life. It will be a new birth. A spiritual birth."

"And this is free?" Alexa's eyes quizzed as much as her voice.

"Free to you and me and every other individual, yes. But like I explained at the restaurant last night, it cost Jesus a sacrificial death, a death where he suffered in our place."

"Because He loved us? Like the man said in the sermon. And like you said at the restaurant."

"Yes," Kathleen nodded, "because he loved us." Kathleen could have sworn she saw some kind of enlightenment occur in Alexa's understanding at that precise moment.

Alexa, without wasting time, gripped Kathleen's hands again and bowed her head. "Heavenly Father," her voice quavered, "I believe." There was a long pause while she tried to catch her breath. And then, "I don't know how you could love me. Or die for me. But I believe! I believe!"

When the building finally cleared, Kathleen, Troy, and Walter were left standing alone in each other's company. For a moment they looked at each other in silence. They all knew something extraordinary had just happened. It permeated the air.

"Both the boy and the girl trusted Christ," Troy said reverently. "And they both want to be baptized."

Kathleen beckoned both men to walk toward her. She reached out, took their hands, and pulled them into a circle. "Father, I want to thank you for these men. Thank you for what happened today. Thank you for Walter's clear presentation of the Gospel. Thank you that you're using your Word to make a difference. In our church. In our community." She halted, then added, "In Troy's life. In Walter's life. And in my life as well."

After celebrating collectively with a few more remarks and observations, they each collected their items to leave the property.

"Oh," Kathleen injected to Walter right before she walked out the back door, "July the twelfth. That's the next time you're up."

Walter stared at her with a look of humble gratitude.

Kathleen smiled. "If you don't mind, present the Gospel again. From John chapter one, for instance."

Walter slowly nodded.

37

On Monday morning, Kathleen typed out a partial "to do" list for the week.

* This afternoon - buy groceries and office supplies.
* Tuesday morning - call Evelyn Huxley. How is she? How is Billy?
* Tuesday afternoon at 1:30 - meet with Alexa and explain what has transpired in her life.
* Wednesday morning - select a day for a baptismal service - Sunday June 28?
* Wednesday afternoon - visit church members in the hospital and work on Sunday sermon.
* Thursday morning - call Willow and set up a time for our first Bible study.
* Thursday evening at 7:00 - Lead Bible study with girls at Vidalia Tech campus
* Friday - spend the day alone.

When Kathleen finished the list, she printed herself a hardcopy. She then returned to the keyboard and compiled a grocery inventory and office-supply list for her afternoon shopping spree. She added "Spanish Bible" as a last-minute item.

*　*　*

Late Tuesday afternoon, attorney Rupert King looked across his desk at the four men - Jack Evans, Jim Manley, Walter Johnson, and Troy Bingum.

"Gentlemen," he acknowledged, "Everyone's here. So let's get started." The investigative file was already open, lying in front of him on the desk.

"I've carefully examined every document that was given to me." He pointed to the papers in his folder. "Plus, I've done a little extra digging on the side. And as you know, I've interviewed each of you at length. I've given you the freedom to tell me anything and everything on your mind pertinent to the inquiry.

"So, I know you've been waiting patiently for my summation." He cleared his throat and lifted papers from the folder.

"Well, here you go; here's a copy for each of you.

"Feel free to look it over," he said when the men took hold of their sheets. "You are welcome to ask any and all questions. But unfortunately," he announced as he leaned back in his chair, "it is my professional assessment that there is no case here."

Rupert especially took notice of Jack's reaction when he made the pronouncement. He saw the man instantly freeze. Hope seemed to momentarily leak from the man's countenance, only to be replaced instantly with what looked like exasperation.

Rupert pushed onward. "The primary document—the original property agreement—was signed by two trustees, now deceased, and notarized. It is a binding document. And the document makes it clear that as long as Floyd Baxter lives he will be the deed holder to the land and the building. Upon his death, the deed of ownership will at that time pass to the governing body of Lyons Central Baptist Church."

Rupert gave the men a chance to jump in. They remained silent.

"In addition to my interviews with the four of you, I interviewed five other active attendees of the church. I met with those individuals separately and privately. I asked for their personal evaluation of the church's health and morale. The names of those five people have been omitted from my summation. I promised I would keep their identities confidential. But based on their independent testimonies it is quite evident that most of the people attending the church from week to week under the current pastor's leadership are absolutely elated. The church is growing numerically and the group spirit has reputedly never been better. And you gentlemen are in control of all the monetary collections."

Rupert chose to not dance around his honest opinion. It was the least he could do for his fee of three thousand dollars.

"Actually, no one, except for the four of you, has lodged any official complaints. Of course, I understand you are the governing body. And you say your leadership role has been undercut by Mr. Floyd Baxter's unilateral decision to hire the lady pastor. You say you've been emotionally traumatized and damaged as a result of that move. But to be quite honest—" Rupert pointed to Troy and Walter. "—your testimonies especially weren't that convincing."

Rupert saw all the men look at each other with unspoken questions.

"I personally don't know a sitting judge in this county who would award you any damages. I mean, the church is a nonprofit entity. You have no financial investment in the church, absolutely none. It is understood that every dollar you've given through the years has been a voluntary donation. Even your time and service have been volunteered."

"Yes, but…," Jack finally spoke up, his face a flush red.

Rupert held up his hand. "Do you own a house, Mr. Evans?"

Jack offered an obligatory nod.

"Is it paid for?"

Jack huffed. "Yes, it's paid for."

"So you hold the deed to the property?"

Jack nodded again.

"Let's pretend for a moment that you've used the services of two maids who have volunteered, without pay, to work for you three days a week, every week, for the last fifteen years. They have voluntarily cleaned your house. They've cooked your meals. They've watched your kids, et cetera. And let's say you decide one day to sell the house without including the maids in the decision making process. Would there be a viable lawsuit, do you think, if those two maids said, 'You have caused us emotional damage by selling the house. We've worked here for fifteen years. We've made important day-to-day decisions regarding the house and the kids. We feel secure here. We are comfortable here. You're taking away our identity, our work.'"

Jack closed his eyes and nervously rubbed his thigh.

"I think you get my point," Rupert concluded. "It's my expert opinion that if you file a class action lawsuit and take it to court, you will lose. And you will pay anywhere from thirty thousand to eighty thousand dollars for the process."

The men looked at each other with expressions of shock.

Jack sighed in annoyance, clinched his fists, then finally grunted, "Can you somehow invalidate the property agreement in question if I pay extra money, a lot of extra money, out of my own pocket?"

Troy and Walter raised unbelieving eyebrows at the outright attempt at bribery.

Rupert stood to his feet. "I think this meeting just ended, gentlemen."

38

Early Wednesday morning, Ted Higgley—director of the regional Baptist Alliance—sat down in his spacious office in Metter, Georgia, twenty-four miles northeast of Lyons. At his request, a copy of the Tuesday edition of the *Vidalia Times* was already lying on his desk.

He had been told about the article, but he wanted to read it for himself.

He found it on page two. The title leapt out at him - *Lyons Central Baptist, Mundane to Memorable*.

He wasted no time reading what followed:

> My name is Eric Sawyer. I'm twenty-eight. I have worked as a journalist for the *Vidalia Times* for three years. For the last two months I have written weekly articles about the controversial transition taking place at Lyons Central Baptist. My key source of information has been my own personal observation. I have attended the Sunday morning church service every week for the last eight weeks. I have watched. I have listened.

I have taken notes. I have tried to be
purely objective in my reporting.
But it is becoming more and more
difficult. This is the first time I have
attended church since I was thirteen.
I have always considered church
to be boring and irrelevant. But
hearing Pastor Rose for the last
two months has been…different.
I have been emotionally, and I would
even say spiritually, touched. After
I wrote the initial article about
the newly commissioned female
pastor, I attended the church for the
first time to collect eyewitness information for a follow-up piece. I thought I
would be attending just the one time.
But what I saw and heard intrigued
me as a reporter. My curiosity about
the emotionally charged story compelled me to return from week to
week to write new articles. Eventually
I realized I was attending for reasons
other than collecting facts for a
series of newspaper columns. I was
attending because I was being
nourished, inspired, and challenged
by the very figure at the center of

the undying controversy - Pastor Kathleen Rose. I am not a Bible scholar by any means and cannot offer a theological thesis on the rightness or wrongness of female pastors. But I can say I have never heard a pastor or teacher who has provoked me to think quite like Kathleen Rose. I have never heard a theologian who has reached my heart like Kathleen Rose. So, I will continue in the foreseeable future to attend the Sunday services and report on the unfolding saga. Just forgive me if my journalism in upcoming features is overcome by personal commentary. I will try to remain objective, but again it's becoming more and more difficult. Regardless of the divisive debate, I for one want to say "thank you, Kathleen Rose, for coming to Lyons, Georgia. You have blessed us with a breath of fresh air."

"Great," Ted whispered in disgust. "This will only drive a whole new horde of people to the lap of the beast."

He lifted the phone on his desk and dialed an extension. "Julian, this is Ted. I need for you to contact everyone on the credentials committee and nail down a date for the group to visit Lyons Central Baptist. I want this visit to take place as quickly as possible." Ted looked at the calendar on his desk. "Today is the third. Just go ahead and set it up for Sunday, June 28. That'll give everyone three weeks to work it into their schedule. And, Julian? I want everyone there."

By Thursday evening, Jack Evans had dropped the lawsuit action, and his and Jim's friendships with Troy and Walter were at a breaking point.

Jack called Troy and Walter "traitors."

Jim called them "compromisers who had bowed at the feet of Satan."

Troy and Walter tried to defend themselves and save face, but finally conceded they were now at a different place in their understanding of things.

Troy at one point turned on his two attackers with a raised voice and said, "We've heard interpretations of Scripture that are actually in her favor, interpretations that make sense! If you had an open mind, you'd at least listen to the arguments!"

Walter jumped in with equal heat. "Plus, we're hearing and seeing things every week that have God's fingerprints all over them! It would be crazy for us to deny them! So, to be honest, we're not sure where we stand on the issue anymore. And until we do, we've decided to start giving her the benefit of the doubt!"

Jack threw up his hands and cursed under his breath. "When the church sinks, then you'll be the ones to blame! I hope you're ready to give an answer to God for it!"

Jim spat on the ground to show his contempt.

The deacon board was now in shambles.

39

Bamako, Mali

It had taken three weeks, but Oumar had successfully gathered the information the Ansar-Dine leader, Alhabib, had demanded. Hopefully, the report would salvage the reputation of the capital city's Ansar-Dine's faction.

As planned, Oumar arrived at the nondescript hookah bar at 3:30 on Friday afternoon. The lounge was in an extremely poor section of north-central Bamako known as *the forgotten Africa*. The streets were unpaved. The shops were tin-roof-laden shacks that were shoddy and filthy. It was an ideal place in the capital city for the leader of a major terrorist group to keep "out of sight" while in public.

When Oumar entered the cafe, it took him a few seconds to adjust to the dark and the smoke. He didn't see Alhabib anywhere, so he secured a small table in the back and waited.

He waited anxiously for about ten minutes before Alhabib appeared suddenly in the haze of smoke, followed by three men, presumably assistants or body guards.

Oumar stood to his feet and subtly bowed his head, enough to show reverence, but not enough to draw attention from anyone else in the room.

Alhabib wasted no time with pleasant greetings. He promptly sat down in a cushioned chair across from Oumar and said quietly, but sternly, "Tell me what you know."

Oumar took his seat. "I have an acquaintance whose brother works at the airport in the international terminal. I arranged a private meeting with this brother and showed him a picture of Angela Carter. With a thousand U.S. dollars I bribed him to use his airport security and connections to find out if Mrs. Carter has been on any flights out of Mali during the last six months."

"And?" Alhabib snapped, his brown eyes as sharp as daggers.

Oumar removed a stapled set of papers from his tunic and laid them face-up on the small rickety table.

Alhabib questioned with his eyes.

"It's a passenger manifest," Oumar clarified. "It shows that on March the thirtieth, Angela Carter flew from Bamako to Paris, and from Paris to Atlanta, Georgia."

"And from there?"

"The trail goes dead there."

Alhabib picked up the stapled sheets of paper and held them close to his face. He studied the pages carefully, scrutinizing Mrs. Carter's information above anything else. When he finished, he put the manifest back on the table and closed his eyes. He breathed deeply, lost in thought for several seconds. When he opened his eyes, he issued his order. "Contact all our affiliates in the U.S. Send them a copy of the whore's picture. I want her found. I want her dead. And I want verification."

Oumar, instantly burdened with a new round of anxiety, nodded.

As mysteriously as Alhabib had appeared, he stood up, faded into the smokey haze with his group of men, and was gone.

40

At seven minutes till eleven on Sunday morning, Kathleen looked out over the now-familiar auditorium from her designated seat on the platform.

Despite her occasional feelings of "what am I doing here" and the on-again off-again annoyance of reverse culture shock, Lyons was feeling more and more like home, at least a temporary one. She was still amazed at how quickly most people in the south would welcome a new person—especially a person with a professional title—into their lives.

She inserted her sermon notes into her Bible and just let her gaze drift around the room for a moment.

She noticed that Evelyn Huxley, sitting on the front pew as usual, looked somewhat downcast this morning. She had tried to call her a couple of times over the last week but had received no answer. She would try to speak with her today and find out if she was okay.

Willow and Ida Mae were present for the fourth Sunday in a row. Ida Mae was bobbing her head and smiling at every one who looked her way. Kathleen was excited about the appointment to meet with Willow for a one-on-one Bible question-and-answer session on Tuesday afternoon. She was especially excited that Willow had mildly pressed for the session.

Walter and Troy were sitting in the front-row section. They were engaged, it seemed, in some kind of lighthearted conversation. Both men looked less tense than normal, or was it just her imagination? "Continue to minister to their hearts, Lord," she pleaded under her breath.

She saw the young, blonde journalist, Eric Sawyer sitting about midway back. It appeared he already had his notepad and pencil in his lap. She had still not engaged the man in a one-on-one conversation. She continued to be fearful that he might start asking personal questions that she didn't want to answer. She definitely didn't want certain bits of information showing up in a public newspaper, information that could be easily uncovered in a computer search.

She observed Floyd Baxter sitting alone at the end of one of the pews. It appeared he was doing business on his smartphone. The old man was still a mystery to her. She still wanted to know why the man had started supporting her when she was just a foster child and had continued to support her through her college years and missionary years. It was irritating to the max that he would not talk about it. But she never ceased to be appreciative for the man's utmost generosity. She wondered how many others there might be on the receiving end of the man's benevolent kindness.

She started to bow her head and pray for everyone when she suddenly saw Alexa, Marcos, and Valery stroll into the sanctuary. Her heart instantly lit up. She bunched her lips with gratitude. The Bible study she had conducted with Alexa last Tuesday had lifted her spirit at an absolute crucial moment.

Before the Bible study that morning she had reached another low point of self-hate and gloom, a point where she had nearly —like many times in Africa—lost her will to keep breathing. She had gone to the Bible study wanting to curl up in a secret place and fade away into oblivion. It had been the energy and hunger of Alexa's transformed heart that had persuaded her to keep inhaling that day.

She caught the eye of Alexa and her kids and nodded to them with a heartfelt smile.

And then, her heart leapt again. Right behind Alexa and the children appeared three young ladies, college-looking, who were definitely Asian. Kathleen was sure the ladies were first-time visitors. This was encouraging. Kathleen wondered who in the church, if anyone, had invited them.

"Oh, Father," she closed her eyes and whispered inside her own world, "What a joyous moment. All of these people are hungry." She dropped her head even further. "They're looking; they're searching; they're expecting; they're hoping." Flashes of terror from her past lunged at her again out of nowhere. "Life is hard. Everyone in this room needs you. I beg you; don't let our gathering this morning be a waste. Please! Use me! Use us! Enlighten us! Teach us! Correct us! Encourage us! Help us! Inspire us! Please…" She slowly tapered her prayer, exhaled, and opened her eyes.

She zeroed in on the clock hanging on the back wall of the auditorium. It showed two minutes till eleven. She saw the musicians making their way to the front.

She glanced again toward the foyer as people kept coming in.

And then her eyes froze. And time seemed to morph into slow motion. She was suddenly looking at a strange man who captured her gaze. She tried to look elsewhere, but couldn't. It was odd. Only once or twice in her life had her eyes ever been kidnapped by the presence of a man. One of the times had been by the man who had become her husband. The man corralling her sight now was walking slowly down the aisle looking for a seat. What was it about the man that drew her attention? His height? His head full of dark hair? His handsome, rugged physique? His expensive, tailored-looking clothes? His aura of masculinity? His air of confidence?

She quickly averted the image from her head and readied herself to welcome everyone to the morning worship service.

When all the worship songs had been sung, Kathleen stepped to the podium. She first announced the baptismal service planned for June 28, three Sundays away. She gave a brief explanation. And then when it was time to teach, she found herself just staring down at her notes, and then at the vase of gorgeous white roses positioned on the communion table. The people waited in silence for her to introduce her message. On impulse she lifted her head and asked out loud if anyone wanted to share a testimony.

There were about twenty seconds of dead air.

A long-time female member who had chosen from the beginning to not boycott any of the services and had continued to serve as a teacher in the children's Sunday school department stood to her feet near the rear of the auditorium.

"Yeah, I can share something." The lady, in her fifties, but energetic, took a deep breath and said, "I've been a member here at the church for eight years. I've been a kids' Sunday school teacher for five of those years. And I hope I'm not speaking out of turn when I say the last two months here have been…the…the most interesting, the most exciting, the most unforgettable months I've ever experienced, not only in this church, but in any church, period. Of course, I've had to drastically readjust my thinking," the lady said soberly with a grin, "but the experience has been worth every late-night tear, every late-night prayer. And I just want to say, I'm glad to be here. Honestly, at this point you couldn't pull me away with a room full of interventionists."

The lady sat back down in the backdrop of responsive laughter, followed by a totally unexpected and impromptu burst of applause.

Before the clapping subsided, a second person—a young female college student with visible tattoos, body piercings, and dyed black hair—stood up. "I just want to say I gave up church when I was thirteen. I did attend church one time when I was sixteen, and I was quickly reminded why I gave up church at thirteen." The girl was halted in her story as a few people laughed, as well, in harmony with her remark. "I came here," she continued with emphasis, "for the first time five weeks ago. And I only came because of the invitation of a girlfriend who kept pressuring me. Plus, I thought it would be novel to hear a lady preacher. Well, I have come back for the last four Sundays completely of my own free will. And I plan to keep coming. The reason is two-fold. The first reason is you, Pastor Rose. I love your teaching. I mean the Bible message two weeks ago on *justification*, for example, was something that was so powerful. Yet, I had never heard it explained, or even talked about, in Christian circles before. You're a very gifted communicator. You've challenged me more than you know. The second reason I've come back is that everyone here has made me feel accepted. Just like I am. As you can imagine, I probably wouldn't be accepted in most churches here in the south. Anyway, that's what I wanted to say."

As the girl plopped down, another wave of applause swept the packed-out building.

Kathleen sensed a clear and collective eagerness for further interaction.

"Anyone else?" she invited.

There was another.

And another.

And another.

As the meeting unfurled, there were in the end fifteen people who stood and voiced their thanks, their excitement, their thoughts, their stories, and their prayer requests. It was an-hour-and-fifteen-minute experience that reached even beyond Kathleen's expectations.

Kathleen was finally getting ready to bring the meeting to a close when she saw a belated hand go up.

She curiously felt faint-hearted. "Yes," she said, nodding toward the tall man who had captured her attention at the beginning of the assembly.

"Hi, my name is Ian Corley," the man stated in a nice clear voice as he rose to his feet, stretching upward to six feet and some-odd inches.

Kathleen noticed that everyone turned and stared.

"I'm en route from Atlanta back to my home in Savannah. As you can tell by my strange accent, I'm not a native of the U.S. I'm from South Africa. And I've only lived in your country for about two years. But I'm one of the redeemed and am an active member of a fellowship in Savannah. I recently heard about your church and just wanted to stop and see what the controversy is about." The man looked full of contemplation, as if he wanted to expound on his reasoning, but instead chose to temper himself. "After sitting and listening for an hour or more, I would really encourage you as a congregation to totally ignore your critics and keep pushing onward. And I just want to say to Pastor Rose; keep it up, you're doing a great job. God's Spirit is definitely using you in this place."

A new and brisk round of clapping occurred as the man sat down.

"Thank you," Kathleen said, looking straight at the man. Her soul was momentarily buoyed. Outside of Floyd Baxter and a couple of male college students, this was the only adult male who had publicly affirmed her ministry in Lyons, Georgia. And it felt…noteworthy. She instantly felt an attraction to the man.

"Well," she said to the audience, "I guess it's time to bring the meeting to a close." But even as she made the statement, she sensed a collective desire to prolong the feel-good moment. She sighed. "So, why don't we do this. Let's all come and gather around the platform. You can kneel. You can stand. You can sit. But let's pray together as a family."

Everyone immediately moved toward the front.

"I needed that prayer time more than you know," Evelyn confided to Kathleen immediately after the people had been dismissed.

"I tried to call you last week. Is everything okay?" Kathleen asked, placing a hand on Evelyn's arm.

Evelyn squinched up her face and squeezed her forehead. Her graying hair somehow looked tired. "Well, I can say life has certainly been easier. And a lot more pleasant. So it was helpful when I heard a couple of people praying for me this morning."

Kathleen could feel the lady's burden. "Let me pray for you too." Gently gripping Evelyn's shoulder, Kathleen heartily petitioned God there on the spot to grant Evelyn special wisdom, insight, and understanding. And comfort. After praying, she said, "Would you like to come by the church office one day this week and talk?"

"Yeah…that might be a good idea; let me do that," Evelyn said as she wiped a tear from her eye. "Let me go home first and look at my schedule. And then I'll call and set up a time."

"Good, I'll be expecting the call."

As Evelyn turned to walk toward the rear exit, Kathleen pivoted and headed through the crowd and made her way to

Willow and Ida Mae before they left the building. When she reached them, she had to wait a few seconds until they finished talking to a middle-aged wife, a physically handicapped lady who was dependent on a walker.

When Kathleen finally got Willow's attention, she said, "I just want to confirm our meeting at your house on Tuesday afternoon at one-thirty."

"Lord, Mrs. Kathleen, I wouldn't forget that for anything. I've already started making myself a list of questions."

Kathleen couldn't help but smile. The lady always seemed to bring out the sunshine and laughter whenever she was around her. Kathleen gave her a hug. "Good. I'm looking forward to it. I really am."

Willow gave a robust wink. "I'll be ready for you."

Kathleen was almost immediately pulled into a new conversation with a group of three female undergraduate students. Out of the corner of her eye, she saw four or five other people waiting to talk to her. One was Alexa. Another was…the visitor, Ian Corley. She suddenly felt herself breathing heavier.

Glimpsing the man in the immediate background, she had a tough time focusing on the conversations that followed. Even with Alexa. Even when Alexa asked a serious question about baptism. Thankfully, she managed to clear her head and thoroughly answer the question.

And then, after a brief exchange with a jovial female college professor, Ian Corley approached.

41

When Kathleen pulled her Toyota into Willow's driveway on Tuesday afternoon, she felt like she had traveled back in time to her own childhood, to the early 80's in rural north Georgia.

The small clapboard house she was staring at was unpainted and had darkened with age. The unscreened and uneven front porch was furnished with a worn fabric couch and a couple of weathered rockers. The sandy-gray yard looked as if it had lost its grass decades ago. Three or four large oak trees shadowed the property from direct sunlight. A couple of abandoned and tireless vehicles—a rusty car and pickup truck —sat at the side of the house.

A large brown dog was lying next to the useless truck. It started wagging its tail on the dirt when Kathleen drove up.

The house and the setting gave her flashbacks of the neighborhood where she had grown up as a foster child in Chatsworth, Georgia, near the Tennessee state line.

She quickly shook the memories when Willow stepped out of the house and beckoned her with a hearty welcome from the front porch.

"Come on in here, girl!" Willow beamed.

Kathleen got out of the car, Bible in hand, and headed toward the house.

"Lordy," Willow nearly laughed, "I never thought I'd see the day when a white pastor would come and have a conversation with me in my own house." She paused, and then added, "Ain't that something!"

Kathleen returned the chuckle. "I got a feeling that the white pastors have just missed out; that's all."

"Don't you know it," Willow giggled as she gave Kathleen a hug at the top of the porch steps. "Come on in. I got ice tea and chocolate cake for us while we talk. And I done put Ida Mae down for an afternoon nap. So, we can talk without nobody botherin' us."

And talk, they did.

Kathleen spent an hour at Willow's kitchen table, with Bibles open, answering a handful of questions that had been lingering in Willow's head for years—questions about forgiveness of past sins, eternal security, drinking a little beer every now and then, holding grudges, the trinity, and baptism.

By the time Kathleen got up to leave, Willow's eyes were pregnant with tears. "I wish someone woulda taught me like that when I was young. You done answered all my questions and done it in a way that makes me understand. Teaching this here book is a mighty special gift. And you certainly got that gift, Pastor Kathleen Rose; I don't care what no man say." Willow emphasized the word 'pastor' with staunch satisfaction.

"You're a gem of a lady, Miss Willow. Don't ever doubt it. Oh…and whatever happens in life, never stop asking questions."

Both ladies cracked up.

When Kathleen got back on the road, she retrieved her smartphone from the car-door pocket and checked it for messages and missed calls. Her lungs nearly skipped a breath when she saw a missed call from "Savannah, GA." She was on a section of road with no other residential properties in sight, so she pulled off onto the grassy shoulder of the road and stopped. She saw that the caller had left a voice message. Kathleen pressed the play button and held the phone to her ear.

"Hi, Pastor Rose. This is Ian Corley. I am calling from Savannah. I'm the man from South Africa who visited your church on Sunday. I talked to you briefly following the service. If you don't mind, I would like to visit the church again next Sunday. And I would even like to take you out to lunch, if you're available, to find out more about your story."

Kathleen awkwardly grinned and dug deep in her thoughts. Her verbal exchange at the church with Mr. Corley had lasted no more than five minutes. Yet, she had felt an attraction, a tension, a chemistry, in the man's presence in those few short minutes that she couldn't explain. The feeling was totally out of the ordinary for her. And she wasn't sure she was comfortable with it.

Had he felt something similar? Had he seen something in her eyes that gratified him? Was that why he was calling? Was that why he was presuming she might be free for lunch? Was he wanting to return eighty miles to Lyons and learn 'more about her story' as an excuse to pursue an attraction? For personal interests only?

Or was his motive entirely professional? Was he involved in ministry, in journalism, in cultural studies perhaps? Was he wanting to learn about her story at Central Baptist as part of legitimate research?

Should she call him back?

She swept her hands through both sides of her hair and tied her hair into a ponytail.

Before she pulled back onto the asphalt, she decided to reply with a simple text. She typed *Not available for lunch, but available to speak at the church for fifteen to twenty minutes after the service.* She reread the message for clarity, then pressed 'send.'

She had driven no more than two miles when her phone signaled a reply. The message said, *See you on Sunday.*

She sighed. This was already sounding too friendly.

She was still feeling tense about the circumstance when she pulled into her driveway on West Oglethorpe Avenue. She had no sooner killed the ignition in front of her house when her phone rang. She jumped. Surely it wasn't...

She was relieved to see the incoming call was from Evelyn Huxley.

"Hello, Evelyn," she answered.

She ended up sitting in the car for thirty minutes or more, listening, counseling, and praying—instead of meeting at the church office in person as they had earlier talked about—with her dear church member and supporter.

42

Kathleen asked every one with a Bible on Sunday morning to turn to the Old Testament text, Numbers 25:3-5.

After fifteen seconds or so, she read the verses unhurriedly into the microphone, "Israel aligned itself with Baal of Peor and the Lord's anger burned against Israel. The Lord said to Moses, 'Take all the leaders of the people and execute them in broad daylight before the Lord so that His burning anger may turn away from Israel.' So Moses told Israel's judges, 'Kill each of the men who aligned themselves with Baal of Peor.'"

Kathleen gave the people a second or two to absorb the words. "A great number of people in the world," she began, "who oppose God, and who grow angry just by thinking about Him, often refer to Old Testament stories like this—and there are several—where God kills large numbers of people seemingly without heart and without discrimination. And they say, 'This is a mean and hateful God, and I want nothing to do with Him.'

"Even Christians struggle with these stories.

"So…how do we explain this dark side of God? How do we explain this seeming discrepancy between God's loving side and God's killing side?

"Well, shortly after man's fall, God revealed He would implement a plan to provide a Savior for all mankind.

"God then handcrafted a nation through which He would unfold that plan, and at the appointed time bring the Savior into the world.

"This plan, beginning with Abraham, unfolded step-by-step through Israel over a two thousand year period. Along the way, God established His name through direct revelations. He established His power and authority through unparalleled miracles. He established His morality through His commandments. He established His wisdom through the Old Testament Scriptures. He established His trustworthiness through hundreds of fulfilled prophecies. He established His majesty through a system of awe-inspiring worship that included priests, sacrifices, feasts and a magnificent temple. He established His love through His undying patience with the Israeli people.

"And it all culminated with the incarnation - when God stepped into human skin and revealed Himself as the promised Messiah who would be sacrificed for the sins of the world.

"Again, God unfolded this plan through a legitimate, visible, and distinct people group.

"Now, follow my thoughts here.

"If Israel had at any point during this two thousand year period been disabled, dismantled, or destroyed—from within or without—there would have been no ongoing revelation of God, no Savior, and no redemption. If Israel had gone down, so would have God's plan of redemption for the whole world.

"So…was Israel at any point leading up to the incarnation ever threatened or compromised? Yes. Many times. From outside. And from within. Therefore, in order to unfold His plan all the way to fruition, God was forced to protect Israel at every juncture.

"Look at it this way: Israel's two thousand year history, from Abraham to the incarnation, was a pregnancy. And God was going to protect that pregnancy at any and all cost. Even if He had to kill large groups of people to do it.

"In order to bring salvation to the billions, He was willing to kill the thousands who endangered the pregnancy.

"Had God, for example, not stepped in—here in Numbers twenty-five—and killed all the leaders of this *false god* movement, Israel would have conceivably slid into paganism and permanently walked away from God all together. And then, the pregnancy—his plan to bring redemption to the world—would have been aborted or ended in a still birth.

"So…these mass killings in the Old Testament are not the random acts of a mean, bored, or highly volatile God. Rather, they show God's passion to provide redemption to every individual born to the human race.

"He killed, because He loved. Actually, God could not have said 'I love you' in any greater way."

"The sermon this morning was a masterpiece," Ian Corley declared with enthusiasm when he and Kathleen sat down together after the service. "It actually answered another Scriptural dilemma that no one has ever been able to answer to my satisfaction."

Kathleen had just finished a round of Sunday post-sermon exchanges and was keeping her promise to sit with Ian for fifteen to twenty minutes to hear what was on his mind. They were sitting near the foyer. She was sitting at the end of a pew, beneath the center beam of the sanctuary. He was sitting sideways on the pew just in front of her, facing her at an angle, with his arm stretched over the back of the wooden bench. There were still pockets of conversation ongoing throughout the room. She was glad she wasn't alone with Ian. She was already nervous enough.

"And what dilemma is that?" she asked.

Ian turned even more to face her. He didn't shy away when talking to her like many people. He looked directly at her. "It pertains to the one hundred and thirty-sixth Psalm. The Psalm proclaims twenty-six times that God's love endures forever. The proclamation is made at the closing of each verse."

Kathleen nodded. She knew the chapter.

Ian opened his Bible to the chapter. His eyes scanned the verses. "Here," he showed her. "read verses ten, seventeen, and eighteen."

She took his Bible and read: *He struck the firstborn of the Egyptians, His love endures forever. He struck down great kings, His love endures forever. And slaughtered great kings, His love endures forever.*

She returned the Bible and, with a gesture of her eyes, welcomed him to continue.

He cleared his throat. "To me, these verses have always been self-contradictory. I mean, how does killing Egyptian babies show God's love? How does killing famous and mighty kings show His love?"

Kathleen didn't respond. She chose to wait and hear the man elaborate.

"I've pondered this for years. And I've never understood it. And in just thirty minutes, you solved the mystery for me."

The man was obviously thrilled. It was written all over him. Kathleen subtly smiled, but still didn't say anything. She was more than curious to hear his next words.

"In each of these cases, God killed, quite evidently, to protect Israel or, as you say, to protect the pregnancy from outside danger. To repeat your words this morning: He killed because He loved." Ian closed his eyes. "So…God slaughtered great kings…to protect Israel from their threatening armies; His love endures forever. God killed the firstborn of Egypt, because it was the one measure that would convince Pharaoh to release Israel from Egypt's savage abuse and from the influence of Egypt's false gods. Thus, God's love endures forever. It all makes sense now." Ian opened his eyes. They were gleaming with enlightenment. "I owe you a gigantic thanks. I really do."

Kathleen was taken aback by the excitement of intellectual stimulation showing on the man's face.

"You're welcome," she replied, trying to act and sound somewhat aloof. Yet, the truth was, the man had made a beautiful connection that probably would have passed her by forever had he not verbalized it in her presence. She couldn't help but be impressed with his thinking skills. "So, what brings you to the States? Or, particularly, to Savannah?" she asked.

Ian ran his fingers through his thick hair. "I work for a company called LabVance Incorporated. I serve as the Vice

President of Pharmacy Services. I was headhunted from a comparable company in South Africa."

Kathleen was sure she looked clueless. She slightly turned her head and lifted her eyebrows as if to say, 'And…'

Ian read the signal. He smiled. "I'm a glorified manager for drug distribution services. I interface with physicians, nurses, and pharmacists all over the country. I sell our company's delivery systems and manage the sales."

Kathleen asked a few additional questions about the work.

She then answered several questions that Ian threw her way about her controversial ministry in Lyons. As always, she steered away from giving details about her life and work in Africa.

The fifteen-minute conversation was definitely pleasurable enough. And the chemistry between them didn't languish. She could still feel her breath shorten whenever he paused and stared at her.

She knew intuitively that he wanted to push for further contact and to undertake another attempt at a dinner engagement.

Just when she decided it was time to stand up and bring the dialogue to a close, Walter suddenly appeared, looking almost jealous, and said, "If it's okay, I need to go ahead and lock up."

Kathleen glanced around and noticed for the first time that everyone else had already left the building. "Of course," she said, actually grateful for the interruption, "I was just getting ready to leave."

*   *   *

That afternoon, when she laid down on the couch in the privacy of her study, she told herself with absolute certainty that she wasn't ready for a new male-female relationship. And she understood why. She wasn't emotionally capable of such a connection at the moment. Not in the slightest. She was just too messed up on the inside.

For a brief second, it was a nice thought, though. She grinned as she closed her eyes for a nap, right before pain and grief once again reclaimed preeminence in her soul.

43

Kathleen was sitting in her car, idling in the parking lot at the Marathon gas station at I-16 and Georgia Highway 1. She kept staring toward the east-bound ramp onto I-16. It was Friday afternoon, June 26.

Over the past ten days Ian Corley had talked to her five more times by phone. His calls usually came in the evening after he had settled in to his Savannah condo for the night.

The first call was to simply say an extra thanks for the "killing-side of God" sermon. He still appreciated the insight more than he could express.

The subsequent calls all began with fresh theological questions and discussions, but ended up centering around his and Kathleen's range of cross-cultural struggles in Africa and the United States. The "African connection" created a natural sense of empathy between them.

She learned, for example, that he was the oldest of three siblings who had been raised on a two-thousand-acre maize farm that his parents owned outside Johannesburg. His parents had been married for forty-seven years and still managed the farm. His two sisters were married, had children, and still lived on the farmstead. He himself, though, no matter how hard he had tried, had never adapted to farm life and had moved into the city of Johannesburg at the age of twenty to pursue a college education and a career in chemistry. It was that substantial career that had eventually landed him his job inside the United States and still got him out of bed every day.

Kathleen really enjoyed their conversations, especially hearing snippets of his history.

She had taken his last two calls while sitting in bed sipping hot tea. The setting and time of day had given those two particular calls an air of intimacy, an air Kathleen had found both pleasant and relaxing.

And God knew she needed such moments.

In his last call, two nights ago, Ian had invited her to drive over to Savannah this evening and enjoy the Friday-night atmosphere of open-air restaurants and live music in the downtown walking district. He would be her host for the evening. "The getaway will do wonders for you," he assured her.

She had told him she would think about it.

"Take all the time you need. There's no pressure. You can even let me know at the last minute if you want to, or need to," he told her.

And now, here she was. Wanting to go. But knowing deep in her soul it probably wasn't what she should do.

She still had not answered any of his questions, at least not in detail, about her former family and former work. Thankfully, though, he had respectfully not pressed for the information.

She closed her eyes and tapped the steering wheel.

"Oh, God," she whispered. "He doesn't even know my real name." She pulled a Kleenex from her purse and dabbed at her eyes. "What am I doing?" she whispered. She squeezed the steering wheel and rocked her head back and forth in silence. "I'm not fit to be loved," she finally driveled. "I know that. You know that. I'm just not worthy. I think what I really want," she groaned, imagining God's presence, "is just to come on home. Is that okay?" She sniffed, then punchily wiped her eyes. "I just want to see my husband and my son again! Is that too much to ask!"

She started sobbing uncontrollably. And lost all track of time.

At some point, she heard someone knocking at her car window. It was an older man.

She wiped at her face and lowered the glass. She knew she probably looked like a basket case. But at the moment she didn't care.

"Are you okay, ma'am?" the old gentleman asked. "Do you need a doctor? Or do you need for someone to make a call for you?"

Kathleen couldn't speak. She sniveled and just shook her head from side to side.

"Are you sure?" the man gently asked.

Kathleen bounced her head up and down. "I'm sure," she finally managed to squeak.

An hour later, she was curled up under the covers of her bed, and was still squalling.

* * *

With her hair tied up in a bun, Kathleen stood waist-deep in water in the church baptistry. Below the waterline, her white baptismal robe faintly bobbed with every move she made.

In the last thirteen minutes or so, she had baptized nine people. The atmosphere throughout the church was absolutely joyous. Ovations had followed each of the baptisms.

Five more individuals were waiting their turn at the edge of the pool.

Kathleen looked over at the top of the baptistry. Alexa was next in line. Already emotionally volatile, Kathleen broke down. She fought tears as she reached up, took Alexa's hand, and helped her descend the baptistry steps. The smile across Alexa's face was one of the most glorious and memorable expressions Kathleen had ever witnessed.

Alexa, usually mellow and a tidbit shy, moved to the center of the water—in view of two hundred and fifty people—without a hesitant bone in her body.

Kathleen helped position her so that she was standing perpendicular to the audience.

Kathleen looked out at the crowd past Alexa's glowing countenance. She placed her left hand on the back of Alexa's neck. She raised her right hand to shoulder height and nodded for Alexa to clasp her wrist. She then spoke directly toward the mic mounted at the edge of the pool. "Watching God change a life in front of your very eyes is one of the most beautiful experiences of the Christian journey." Kathleen looked at Alexa and smiled. "And I have been honored to watch such a supernatural change take place in Alexa's life." Kathleen paused to fight back another push of tears. "Alexa, do you confess that Jesus is the only begotten son of God, crucified for the sins of the world, and resurrected to live forever as our righteous mediator?"

Alexa turned and looked at Kathleen. "I do," she proclaimed.

"And do you trust Him as your personal Lord and Savior?"

"I do."

"And you want to be baptized to proclaim your new faith to the world?"

"I do."

Kathleen cupped Alexa's nose as Alexa held tightly to Kathleen's wrist.

"Then I baptize you, my sister," Kathleen declared, "in the name of the Father, the Son, and the Holy Spirit." Kathleen lowered Alexa beneath the water, then raised her upright, soaked in baptismal splendor.

Alexa gasped with an ethereal joy.

Kathleen truly wanted to pause and savor the moment, but there was no time. There were four more people to baptize. Three of those people—two college students and a farmer's wife—had made their decision to enter the baptismal waters less than thirty minutes ago, at the end of Kathleen's exegetical sermon on 'baptism.'

Kathleen, with a full heart, gave Alexa an enormous hug, helped her up the baptistry steps, then received the next person.

"I'm absolutely flabbergasted. I never thought we would see this in our Alliance. I'm just ..."

Al Simpson, a long-time member of the credentials committee for the state Evangelical Baptist Alliance, didn't finish his sentence.

Standing outside the Lyons Central Baptist church building with five other members of the committee, he just shook his head in disbelief.

Julian Meed, the secretary of the committee rubbed the back of his neck, "I guess Ted was right. It looks pretty much like a lost cause."

The group, comprised of five men and one lady, had just sat through the entire morning service, including the baptismal service. Director Ted Higgley had briefed them over a week ago on all the details related to the situation: Floyd Baxter's ownership of the property; his unilateral authority in the matter; his refusal to admit any wrongdoing; and his unbending refusal to consider a compromise.

"Well," Al asserted, "If things don't change quickly, and I'm assuming they won't, then I don't see that we have any other choice but to oust the church from the Alliance." He shook his head again.

"Let's at least give them till October when we have our annual review meeting," one of the other men inserted. "That'll at least give them four months or so to change their mind."

The other members, still somewhat in shock, voiced their concurrence.

In the backdrop of the four or five seconds of silence that followed, the lady on the team spoke up and said, "Were those baptisms even valid? With a lady doing the baptizing?"

"Absolutely not," Julian declared, shaking his head. "There's no such thing in the Scriptures."

"God help us," Al muttered as they headed toward their van. "I still can't believe it."

*   *   *

On Monday morning, Eric Sawyer spent more than an hour trying again to find an internet footprint for Kathleen Rose and her former husband, Nicholas Rose.

He dug through layers of websites. Especially mission-related websites pertaining to Africa. He searched every conceivable connection he could think of. But found nothing. Not their names. Not their photos. Not their bios. Not a single report. Not a single article. Not a single blog. Nothing.

Maybe he should just outright ask Kathleen face-to-face for an interview and try to learn more about her than what he, and everybody else, was seeing and hearing at church.

He tap-tap-tapped his pencil on his desk.

He couldn't do it next Sunday. He would be away for that fourth of July weekend. But maybe he should try the following week, July 12.

He tapped the pencil again. He nodded. *It's time*, he told himself.

44

Near the intersection of Hull and East 11th on the south side of Richmond, Virginia, Yacoob Ghaly looked over his desk, out the window of his third-story apartment. He stared blankly for a second or two at the old two-story brick building, undergoing renovation, across the street.

He looked back at his laptop screen.

His parents, both natives of Mali, Africa, had been granted asylum in the United States twenty-three years ago, when he was only one.

He himself had visited Mali only three times in his life. The last time had been two years ago. During that three-month visit, without his parents, he had learned one night in a dingy Timbuktu nightclub, in the backdrop of loud music and booze, that the cousin he was drinking guava with had become a member of the terrorist group Ansar Dine.

Yacoob, as a devout Muslim, had listened with fascination to his cousin's narrative about the group's size, actions, and noble cause to impose Sharia law all across Mali. Yacoob had been absolutely intrigued by the thought of his cousin's higher purpose. He even liked the name of the group: Ansar Dine, defenders of the faith.

During his stay, Yacoob had carefully probed for answers about the organization's make up, requirements for membership, and average age.

In the end he had casually, yet seriously, mentioned to his cousin that if the group ever needed a set of eyes and ears inside the U.S. to contact him.

And two days ago, they did.

Yacoob stared at Angela Carter's photo, along with the article, on his laptop screen. It was his task now to read all about the lady and find out, if possible, where she was residing in the States.

He was definitely curious as to why a group such as Ansar Dine was interested in a middle-aged white lady residing in America.

He noticed immediately that the article showing on the screen had been written by a professor of sociology at the University of Bamako a little over a year and a half ago. The write-up was in Bambara, the secondary language of Mali, a language he—Yacoob—had grown up with in the home of his parents. It was a language he knew well.

He scratched an itch on the side of his neck and read.

Angela Carter, a Christian missionary from America, was a guest speaker at this year's annual UB "cultural diversity" conference. Her presentation was titled "The Culture At Odds With Society." Mrs. Carter, the wife of the former American educator Scott Nicholas Carter, spoke passionately about the dangers of holding on to cultural traditions with blind allegiance and reverence, especially when such traditions threaten the health of society. She then talked about her ongoing campaign to educate Malian women regarding the dangers of female genital cutting and to encourage them, along with their village leaders, to revisit this age-old custom and ask, "Is it worth the sexual dysfunction, the psychological scarring, the urination complications, and the unnecessary pain to cut off a precious part of the female body which God Himself designed, simply because the previous generation of elders said it should be done?" In recent years, Mrs. Carter has visited more than forty Malian villages, has spoken to more than five thousand women and a hundred village elders, and has been aired on multiple radio programs, endeavoring to expose the 'myths' associated with female cutting. Her visits and declarations have been condemned by most village leaders. Some of the elders, she claims, have

even threatened her. Mrs. Carter
blames the complacency of Mali's
educated community for the perpetuation of this custom. She insists the
educated leaders of Mali should use
all available avenues and resources
to snuff out this tribal practice and
restore God's natural order to Malian
women.

Yacoob read a couple of more paragraphs. He made notes
on a piece of paper.

He then shifted in his seat and clicked on another article.
The article, he saw, had been featured in the L'Essor newspaper,
one of Mali's premiere periodicals. It was in French, Mali's
national language. Yacoob stared at the text for a moment. His
French was not as good as his Bambara. But it was good
enough to decipher the newspaper article.

The article, he noticed, was a little over a year old.

American Honored
At Presidential Palace
For Herculean Campaign
Against Female Genital
Mutilation

Before a private audience of two
hundred political and humanitarian

dignitaries, American Angela Carter, renowned educator, was presented the prestigious Knight Of National Order of Merit award by President Amadou Toumani Touré.

Carter was chosen for the award because of *"her tireless and heroic efforts to educate Malian women about the dangers of FGM."*

Carter's prolific and self-funded campaign, having reached all corners of the country, has won her the hatred of many, but the respect and admiration of others, including President Touré.

Carter, in her ceremonial speech, heralded her reminder that *"eighty-five percent of Malian women from ages 15 to 50 are current victims of this age-old custom."*

The government of Mali in 2002 launched a State program to discourage FGM, a custom many believe to be a religious requirement. But it has been individuals like Carter who, in the words of President Touré *"who, resisting all opposition and threats, inspire our own State officials to keep driving our national campaign forward. Carter's unquenchable voice has empowered our women every-*

where to rise up against the tyranny of tradition."
Carter is only the second American
to ever receive Mali's National Order
of Merit.

The article was accompanied by a photo of President Touré
presenting the award to Mrs. Carter. Another photo, a closeup
of Carter, revealed she was a stunning woman with an
unmistakeable look of intelligence.

Yacoob looked out the window again and pondered. He
was not told *why* Ansar Dine wanted to know the lady's location.
He had assumed the woman was somehow construed as an
enemy of the organization. And now a snapshot began to take
shape in his head. The lady most likely had persuaded Malian
women in large numbers to stand up and oppose their God-
ordained authorities regarding FGM and had thus created
significant havoc within Muslim families and communities.

And it made sense; if Ansar Dine was the protector of
Mali's Muslim culture, why wouldn't they use their resources to
stop this American woman from continually marching in and
imposing her contrarian views?

Yacoob turned back to the computer and carefully browsed
through six more articles about the lady and her antagonistic
work. The lady was hailed as a hero by many in the Western
world and by the few liberal Malians who had developed a
western, anti-fundamentalist mindset.

By the time he stood up and stepped away from his desk
to get a drink of water, he had compiled several pages of

handwritten notes. He felt it was safer to keep his file in a handwritten form rather than on a computer which could be potentially reviewed at a later date by law enforcement agencies.

He knew from other research that the United States government had added Ansar Dine to its list of foreign terrorist groups. He had even discovered on his own that Ansar Dine was allied with Al Qaeda. Therefore, he didn't want to leave an internet trail that would connect him in any way with the group. He especially didn't want to engage in any additional dialogue with his cousin via email or Skype. If his cousin happened to be on an international "watch list," Yacoob didn't want to alert American intelligence agencies—who would be snooping around on the web—to his personal connection. He would communicate with his cousin from now on by public pay phone. He knew the location of one at a nearby AMF bowling center. He definitely wanted his association with his Malian cousin to stay below the radar.

In his small apartment kitchen he gulped down a glass of water. Now, how was he going to help track down the lady? She was an educator and an activist. He had seen in several of the online articles that she had spoken at multiple universities across Mali.

He returned to his desk and picked up a clean sheet of paper and a pen. He sat down and wrote "Universities" across the top of his paper.

Ansar Dine was convinced the lady was back in America. She had apparently flown into Atlanta, a transportation gateway to the whole country. And there they had lost her trail. So, if the lady was indeed back in the States, she would most likely —based on her profile—surface somewhere in the world of academia.

Later in the evening he would submerse himself into the world-wide-web and scour university websites. He would look at staff photos, calendars, blogs, and online campus newspapers. He would search the various universities state by state. He would begin with his own state, Virginia. He would then work his way digitally up and down the eastern seaboard. If his hunt came up empty handed, he would then turn westward.

He was sure he had a good chance of finding the lady.

He was pleased. He was convinced his cousin would be too.

45

On Sunday morning, July 12, Evelyn Huxley stood at the mirror in the lady's restroom at the church. She had ten minutes before the service started.

She was already perspiring from the sweltering and humid morning heat, and her hair was starting to frizz. She took a brush out of her purse and ran it carefully around her head, trying to make sure every hair was in place.

While she was standing there tidying up, she saw Willow —the black lady—come in and disappear into one of the stalls.

Evelyn half smiled. The blacks, Asians, and Hispanics that had started attending the church in the last two months seemed to be growing in number by the week.

Evelyn closed her eyes in a moment of nostalgia. She understood that the "old" Central Baptist—with its all-white congregation, its old-fashion hymns, and its hellfire-and-damnation preaching—would probably never show its face again. She knew there would be times when she would actually miss it. But deep down, she knew the changes—even the changes in the composition of the crowd—were for the good. Even though she was still a bit uncomfortable with the interracial mix, she was convinced the integration was a healthy sign of God's providence in action. She was even jealous to some extent that others in the church had the freedom to invite their nonwhite acquaintances and neighbors. She still carried a trace of resentment that Ray continued to block her every time she tried to get together with the Mexican tree cutter's wife.

Evelyn sighed.

What a season the last three months had been!

She put away her hair brush, then reapplied her lipstick.

Kathleen Rose. Evelyn whispered the name. The lady had brought change to everything. Evelyn returned the lipstick to her purse and looked up to the ceiling, as if looking all the way to heaven. She sighed again, then smiled.

At that instant, Willow walked up to the adjoining sink to wash her hands.

Evelyn watched Willow's reflection in the mirror for two or three seconds, then saw Willow suddenly notice the gaze.

Evelyn turned and faced her. "Hi, my name is Evelyn; Evelyn Huxley," she said boldly and intentionally, extending her hand.

Deacon Troy was sitting five rows from the front, with his eyes closed, in an aura of solitude when he felt a tap on his shoulder.

"Will you come to the back and pray with me," Walter petitioned him. There was a look of mild anxiety written across Walter's face.

Troy knew that Walter was scheduled within the hour to deliver the morning sermon. "Are you okay?" he asked calmly.

"Yeah, yeah, but I would just feel better if someone prayed with me."

Troy nodded, then followed Walter to the hallway behind the platform.

Once they were in the hallway, Troy placed a hand on Walter's shoulder and interceded in a quiet, somber tone. "Dear God," he prayed, "I thank you for my brother, Walter. Please help him when he stands up to preach this morning. Give him a special boldness. Let him call to mind everything he's studied. Use Your Word to touch hearts." Troy squeezed Walter's shoulder. "And when he steps down from the pulpit today, may he know with certainty that you were with Him. I ask it in Jesus' name. Amen." Troy smiled when he opened his eyes. "Just relax," he told Walter, "You're going to be fine."

Floyd Baxter, sitting midway in the auditorium, could hardly believe it when—halfway through Walter's sermon from John chapter one—he caught himself thinking *This isn't half bad; the fella's actually doing a pretty good job.*

Floyd looked at the open Bible lying on his lap. He followed Walter's voice as the next verses were read from the podium: "Yet to all who received him, to those who believed in his name, he gave the right to become children of God—children born not of natural descent, nor of human decision or a husband's will, but born of God."

As Floyd listened to Walter expound on the "born of God" phrase, he slowly looked around at all the faces—nearly three hundred he guessed—in the packed out auditorium. The room was filled everywhere with overflow chairs. He noticed five or six African Americans, about the same number of Hispanics, and a dozen or more Asians. He sighed a good sigh. He couldn't be happier for the church.

He then looked at the back of Kathleen's head where she was sitting way up on the front pew. He stared at her for a few seconds, then thought, *If she only knew.*

Kathleen was once again pleased with Walter's presentation. The progress he had made as a public speaker in just three turns at the pulpit was impressive. He had listened well to all her advice. Even though the contents of his sermon were still rudimentary, nothing had been said that violated the context of the verses. And to Kathleen's great pleasure, Walter was not regurgitating another preacher's outline or echoing the overview of a commentary. Admirably, he was doing his best to be original. Kathleen smiled on the inside. Surprisingly, she felt that inner smile seep through to her whole face. "Keep shaping him into someone special," she prayed in her heart.

Eric Sawyer was sitting in the back corner of the sanctuary. As always he was holding a pen and pad of paper. As Walter, the deacon, began his conclusion, Eric scribbled a note to potentially use in one of his newspaper articles: *Contrary deacon slowly becomes an ally. Quite amazing. Just shows the inside, one-on-one, power of a strong and intelligent woman like Kathleen Rose.*

After he penned a few more thoughts, he put his pen and paper away and readied himself mentally to speak to Kathleen face-to-face for the first time. There were a couple of questions he definitely wanted to ask her.

Kathleen had not encouraged or discouraged Walter from extending another invitation for people to come to the front and make a public decision to follow Jesus. As a matter of fact, she hadn't mentioned the subject to him at all. She had decided to let him exercise his own discernment. So, she really wasn't surprised when, following his closing remarks, he called for their young pianist to come and play a soft rendition of "Just As I Am," asked her and Troy to stand down front as counselors, and then invited people to come forward.

She WAS surprised, however, when—standing at the foot of the platform—she saw five or six people making their way to the front.

Two or three of those individuals simply knelt at the front to pray.

Two elderly ladies, she noticed, lined up to speak to Troy.

Two young Asian men came to her.

"I need a spiritual birth," the first young man declared to her in a hushed tone, almost with bent shoulders. Kathleen was touched by the juxtaposition of the bold and overt move made by such a timid spirit.

Kathleen quickly motioned for the guitar player, a young American strong in his faith, to talk with the other Asian. She then turned and gave her full attention to the first Asian guy.

"Let's sit and talk," she told him.

For several minutes, sitting on the front pew, she carried on a dialogue with him to ascertain his grasp of the Gospel. When she was convinced he was being drawn by God's Spirit, she prayed with him as he opened his heart and humbly confessed Jesus as his Creator, Lord, and Redeemer.

When all those who had come to the front had been listened to, counseled with, and prayed with, Walter dismissed the Sunday morning gathering with a short and exuberant benediction.

Immediately following the "Amen," the throng of three hundred worshippers broke apart, like mercury, into myriad beads of interconnection. Small groups here. One-on-one there. Short exchanges. Lengthy exchanges. Most people lingered and enjoyed the fluid motion of mass fellowship.

Kathleen was wrapping up her dialogue with the young Asian man she had prayed with when she saw two people draw near to speak with her. One was the newest member of the worship team, a female vocalist. The other was Eric Sawyer, the journalist from the *Vidalia Times*. The sight of Eric getting in line to speak with her was not alarming, but it was definitely distracting. As a voice reaching thousands of people in the county, was he wanting to talk face-to-face with her for the first time to simply offer a few pleasantries, to share some feedback, or—God forbid—to probe with out-of-bound questions? And was he planning to use their conversation as the basis for a new *Vidalia Times* article?

Kathleen arranged to meet with the Asian later in the week to follow up and enlighten him further about his life-changing decision.

She then turned and gave attention to the young female singer. The girl, a short brunette with a flicker of excitement in her eyes, just wanted to say 'thanks' that she was permitted to sing on the worship team. "I've wanted to do something like this for a long, long time," she declared, giving Kathleen a colossal hug. "You'll never know what this means to me."

Kathleen assured her that her participation on stage was a win-win for everybody. "You've got that rare type of voice that people can listen to all day. It would be a shame if you didn't have a public platform."

As the girl walked away with a huge smile, along with another "thank you," Kathleen took a deep breath and braced herself for the next person in line - Eric Sawyer.

Eric tried to relax as he stepped forward. He extended his hand. "Eric Sawyer," he announced. "Reporter for the Vidalia Times."

Kathleen shook his hand warmly as if he had been any good ole' boy.

Eric had predetermined to not be distracted by her beauty. He purposely focused on her face. Even still, the glamour of her eyes, lips, and hair all combined presented an image that was hard not to gaze at with manly appreciation. "I guess you've seen the series of articles I've written about the church?" he said.

"I have indeed," she replied. She didn't smile. She didn't frown. She actually looked cool and collected.

"And as you've no doubt noticed, I've attended your Sunday services for several months now. I actually never intended to become a regular visitor. But I've got to say that the caliber of your teaching and the exciting atmosphere you've created, not to mention the surrounding controversy, has continued to pull me back week after week. Until now, I've intentionally kept a distance. Each week I've come in late. And I've exited early. I've tried to remain uninvolved. I've tried to be objective in my reporting. That's one of the reasons I've never taken time to talk to you one-on-one. But…"

"But…?" Kathleen cocked her head.

"But…I'm not sure I can be objective anymore. Subconsciously I think I've already taken sides." He smiled. "So, I think I need the input of a new and fresh perspective. And…it just dawned on me a week or so ago that the voice that's missing in this whole ongoing narrative is yours. So…"

Eric was not certain if eyes could cringe. But if they could, then that's what he saw in Kathleen's eyes. And it immediately put him on the defensive.

"So…if possible," he said slowly, "I would be more than honored if you would let me ask a few questions. If not today, then whenever it's convenient." Before he gave Kathleen a chance to respond, he broke his own journalistic rule and added, "I'll let you proof anything I use from the interview."

Kathleen closed her eyes for a moment.

Eric could see that, for some reason, the lady was not jumping at the opportunity. Perhaps she didn't have any interest.

"All right," Kathleen finally mumbled. "What's your first question?"

Eric smiled. "Well, first of all, I would like to hear a little bit about your past. Where in Africa did you live? And what kind of missionary work did you do?" Eric started to additionally ask why she appeared to have no internet presence. But before he could say another word, he saw the lady close her eyes again, then slightly lift her hand for him to stop.

"Can we make an appointment to speak in private," she asked. The tone of her voice was almost cold.

Eric wondered why she was immediately so cautious. His mind went into overdrive. Was she actually trying to hide something? His curiosity was now peaked more than ever. "Sure," he answered respectfully. "Can I call you tomorrow when you're close to your calendar? And you can give me a day, a time, and a place."

Eric assumed there would be a verbal response. But all he got was a half-hearted nod and an expression that seemingly said *Thanks; you've just ruined my day.*

As he walked away, his journalistic mind spun out of control with a dozen new questions.

46

Four days later, on a splendid Thursday afternoon, Eric met Kathleen for lunch at the Cross-Eyed Cricket Sports Bar, west of Lyons, just off Vidalia Road.

Eric selected a table near the front of the cafe, a table that was bathed in sunlight.

He let Kathleen sit first.

Then he sat.

Kathleen was dressed casually in a pair of jeans and a lavender t-shirt. It was the first time Eric had seen her dressed in a laid-back style. And it was ridiculously obvious; her beauty just wasn't going to be masked—not even with the most informal attire. Her eyes alone, with their brilliant blue, were just too mesmerizing to be muted by anything she wore. She was absolutely stunning.

For a brief moment, Eric fantasized about her. He had never been attracted to older women at any point in his life. But this lady could definitely be an exception. His fantasy, of course, was beyond reason and practicality. So, he quickly returned to reality.

"Everything is on me," he told Kathleen as a server approached their table.

Kathleen ordered water with lemon.

Eric ordered a Coke.

As the waiter left to prepare their drinks, Eric conveyed his appreciation to Kathleen for being willing to meet with him.

Kathleen offered a minuscule nod and sighed. "I've thought long and hard about the questions you asked me at church, and how I can respond. And I'll just go ahead and tell you that you're going to be disappointed with how I've decided to answer."

Eric felt his shoulders slump. He quizzed Kathleen with questioning eyes.

Kathleen carried on. "You asked me where I lived in Africa and what I did there." She sighed again. "I've decided I can't answer those questions, Eric. All I can say is—my decision to withhold that information is for security reasons. And I can't even tell you why. You'll just have to take my word for it."

Eric started to respond.

But Kathleen quickly added another surprising twist. "And I would ask that you not mention any of this in any of your newspaper articles. Or to anyone in any verbal conversations."

"But…"

"Please, Eric. You've got to trust me."

For a moment, Eric, with his journalistic ego, wanted to resist such a concession. To the contrary, he was strongly tempted to badger the lady for just some small morsels of information that she was intent on hiding. But he suppressed his natural instinct and capitulated. At least for the moment.

"All right," he said, "I'm a little puzzled by all the secrecy, but I'll agree. What you just told me is off the record." He scratched his forehead and looked her in the eye. "So then, what info…"

"What information can I give you about my past?"

"Yeah, what can you talk about?"

Kathleen opened her mouth to reply when the server returned with their drinks and to take their food order.

Two hours later, Eric was sitting at his cluttered desk at the *Times* office. His fingers were poised on his desktop keyboard. He typed:

Lyons Central Baptist
Pastor Rose's Troubled Past

Eric gazed at the title for a second. The words were definitely a hook that would grab a reader's attention.

He continued typing:

> It has been reported by many in the community that despite her beauty and intelligence, an aura of brokenness and self-depreciation hovers around Pastor Rose's character. If these reports hold any validity, perhaps it's because Pastor Rose was orphaned at the age of four when her parents were killed in a motorcycle accident involving a drunk driver while crossing Fort Mountain west of Ellijay in 1978.
>
> "My childhood was lived in the

shadows of unmitigated sadness," Rose
recently revealed.

Plus, her husband of twelve years
died three years ago—during their
missionary work in Africa—from
cerebral malaria. "I still miss him
every day of my life," Rose asserts.

Eric halted.

He had wanted to include a current photo of Kathleen
with the article. During his interview, he had pulled out his
cellphone and asked if he could take a picture to accompany
the story.

"Absolutely not, please," she had quietly replied. "Again, it's
for security reasons," she told him.

He had asked if she could somehow elaborate.

She had looked at him with eyes that begged for understanding and said she couldn't.

And for the last two hours now, he had entertained one
wild theory after another. Was she a CIA operative who had
worked undercover in Africa as a "missionary" wife and had
now been retired or put on leave? Was she running from an
African government or law enforcement agency because of a
crime she had knowingly or accidentally been involved in?
Was she an eyewitness to an international incident of some
kind and was now being secretly hidden away in a witness
protection program? Or was all the secrecy for a reason that
was far more simple?

He had wanted to ask if "Kathleen Rose" was even her real name. But he was pretty sure by now it wasn't. And that would, of course, explain her invisibility on the worldwide web. Most likely, Nick wasn't her husband's real name either. And nobody had even asked, as far as he knew, if she had any children. Parenthood was a subject she had never mentioned.

Eric slapped the stapler on top of his desk and wondered how much about her past Floyd Baxter knew. The old man obviously knew something.

Eric huffed. His journalistic mind wanted answers, if for no other reason than to satisfy his own burning curiosity. He closed his eyes and for a moment pushed the questions aside. He returned his attention to the keyboard and continued the article.

> In the face of her losses, Pastor Rose bravely pushes forward in life and—though a relative newcomer to our community—has already become one of the most influential pastors in Toombs County.

Eric went on to expound on Kathleen's growing impact, especially among undergraduate students.

He read and reread the piece, edited and re-edited. He then saved it for the *Times* upcoming edition.

That evening, Kathleen was sitting in the study at her house preparing for Sunday's sermon when her phone rang.

She was already a little distracted, wondering if her interview with Eric would only provoke him to ramp up his questions and dig deeper to uncover the answers he wanted. Or if he would be content to leave matters as they were and not chase them any further.

She reached for the phone. "Hello," she said. "Kathleen speaking."

"Kathleen. This is Ian calling from Savannah."

Kathleen gulped slightly for extra air. "Hi, Ian. How are you? How was your business trip to Miami?"

Ian offered a minor chuckle. "To be honest, it was a bit frustrating. And that's why I'm calling actually. I need to decompress and think about something more positive for awhile. I need to smile and laugh and have a little fun. So, I'm wondering…" He allowed his words to fade into an amusing fill-in-the-blank.

Kathleen could envision him grinning childishly on the other end.

"Yes, Ian—what exactly are you wondering?"

Ian cleared his throat. "I'm wondering if there's anything I can say or do to entice you to join me in Savannah tomorrow evening for a stroll around town, for a great meal, and for some enjoyable conversation. I'll even drive over and pick you up if that will make a difference."

"So, you're not giving up, huh….?" Kathleen said in a playful tone.

"Not until you look me in the eye and tell me to go away."

Kathleen paused for a few seconds. "I'll tell you what," she finally said in a moment of weakness. "There are a couple of items I need to take care of during the day tomorrow. But if I can mark those things off my list by three or four o'clock, I'll…"

"Yes?" Ian probed as Kathleen went mute.

"I'll…uh…go ahead and get in my car and head that way." Even as she said the words, Kathleen wondered about the rightness of her decision. She had bailed on him the first time. Why not again? What was she doing? The relationship realistically couldn't go anywhere, could it? She fought her inner demons. Why couldn't she simply enjoy an innocent evening out with a kind, intelligent, and interesting person of the opposite sex?

"Wow!" Ian's elation-filled voice sang out through the cellular connection. "I'm absolutely honored. Thrilled actually. If it's okay, then I'll go ahead and make dinner reservations on the river front. I can always cancel them if I need to."

Kathleen's hesitation was suddenly baptized in a responsive smile. "All right; sounds good. I'll keep you updated as to where I am throughout the day tomorrow."

47

As Ian watched Kathleen approach their rendezvous spot on the river front around 6:00 p.m.—in front of the Steamship Memorial fountain—he involuntarily gulped.

If he had ever seen a more staggeringly beautiful woman, he honestly couldn't remember. He noticed that she turned the head of every man around her.

Dressed in a form-fitting black evening dress and a white-pearl necklace, she looked like the masterpiece of a renowned sculptor who had spent a lifetime painstakingly creating the ideal female figure.

Ian took a deep, deep breath, waved in her direction, and smiled.

Kathleen quickly spotted him and smiled back.

Ian saw instantly, though, that her smile was not one of abandonment, but was instead one of restraint, maybe even apprehension. But for him, that was okay. He didn't have any farfetched expectations for the evening. He would be fully delighted to just sit in the divine creature's company for a few hours.

*   *   *

Alexa, in her strong Mexican accent, read nervously from her script as she stood at the microphone in her best dress and faced the Sunday morning audience of three hundred people.

"Pastor Rose asked me to take some minutes and tell you my thoughts about how the people of Lyons can help my Hispanic community know they are welcome to live here."

Evelyn Huxley, sitting near the front of the auditorium as usual, was already locked in to Alexa's words, especially after hearing Kathleen introduce the lady and reiterate the young mother's story of running into the arms of the Savior six weeks ago for personal redemption.

"First of all," Alexa continued to read, "Please know my people are really shy around you and will never take the first step to meet you. We are shy because of our poor language skills, because of our poor standard of living, and because of our poor education. We automatically think you will not like us. I, for example, am only here today because Pastor Rose took the first step to talk to me and be a friend to me. If you will do the same, the Hispanic people will respond with much thankfulness. And second, please know my people really, really want you to see them, talk to them, and be a friend to them. That is what they hope for when they move to America."

Evelyn Huxley's thoughts went straight to the morning she had initiated the conversation with the tree cutters and witnessed how quickly and gratefully the men had responded, exactly the way Alexa was explaining.

Evelyn slightly squeezed the pew cushion. If only Ray had let her follow through with the tree cutter's wife.

"Dear God," she prayed silently, "Please open Ray's heart to the good things outside his comfort zone. Please, I beg You. Don't let him get stuck in the obstinate place he's in right now. Not for his sake. My sake. Or Your sake. Please!"

On Sunday afternoon, Yacoob Ghaly sat staring at the laptop screen in his Richmond, Virginia bedroom.

He then looked down at his handwritten notes. In the last two weeks, he had scoured the websites of colleges and universities throughout Virginia, Florida, Georgia, Alabama, Tennessee, and South Carolina. He had previewed the names and photos of every faculty member, guest lecturer, and administrative staff member listed on the sites.

Neither the name Angela Carter nor her picture had shown up on any of the hundreds of digital pages.

But he would keep looking until, if necessary, he had checked off every university in every state of the union. He was determined to find the devil-lady. He would make his cousin proud.

Plus, at a recent mosque gathering, his Imam had declared "A sacrifice for Allah is the greatest sacrifice of all."

Yacoob was resolved to make such a sacrifice and to please the one and only god. His god.

Allah would surely reward him.

* * *

Three days later, Angela Carter's full-colored photo, under the name Kathleen Rose, appeared—without Kathleen's knowledge—in the one and only summer edition of The Vidalia Tech newspaper called *The VTC Aristocrat*.

The image of Kathleen's countenance had been taken by an undergrad student right before a Sunday morning service when Kathleen was engaged in a conversation with the church drummer. The picture, captured by a digital zoom on a smartphone, showed a closeup of Kathleen smiling in response to something said by the young man.

The photo was accompanied by a short article touting Pastor Rose's rising influence on many of the college's male and female students - the students enrolled in summer classes as well as those who lived locally and were still attending the church during summer break.

Five hours after the newspaper's physical distribution, a full digital copy—including the color photograph of Kathleen—was uploaded to the internet.

PART III

48

October

As Troy sauntered across the parking lot toward the church building on Thursday evening, October 1, he couldn't have been in a more jovial mood. The weather was a perfect 75 degrees, a reprieve from the sweltering 95-plus degree weather of previous weeks, and the agenda for the deacons' meeting was certainly going to be another turning point for the church, in a good way.

He started whistling. Six months ago, he would have never imagined that his Christian walk could be completely turned upside down and revolutionized by a lady pastor.

"By a lady pastor," he mumbled out loud. He then chuckled.

Yesterday evening, he had made a written inventory of the ways his attitudes, beliefs, and ideas had been completely recast because of Kathleen's influence.

Moving leisurely and enjoying the evening sunshine, he mentally went over the list. He wanted to be prepared to share the items in a few minutes at the start of the meeting. And he wanted his memory to be clear and sharp.

The first thing on his list was the fact that, for the first time in his spiritual journey, he was experiencing an insatiable hunger to know God's Word and to know it well. Kathleen's yearning for truth had been, and was still, genuinely contagious. He had dialogued with her about so many of his own recent thoughts and discoveries that she had even asked him to teach a couple of times during the last two months. "I want others to feel your enthusiasm," she had told him.

The second item on his list, and he could hardly believe it, was the certainty that he was now welcoming Blacks, Hispanics, Indians, Asians—and all other ethnic groups—into the fabric of the church's membership. He had slowly come to understand, after hearing several international students testify up front, that the body of Christ was bigger than just the community's middle-and-upper-class white American Republicans. His eyes first started to open when he heard a female exchange student from Germany, sporting dreads, piercings, tattoos, and ear gauges—expressions that six months ago would have led him to judge the girl as a lost soul—share a passion for Jesus so deep and so raw that it put him to shame.

The third major thing was coming to understand how important it was for church leaders to involve and mobilize as many people as possible in the life of the congregation. He had watched Kathleen transform the church simply by asking and gently nudging dozens and dozens of young adults from multiple ethnic backgrounds to share their stories of faith, play in the band, sing up front, write music for the congregation, lead Bible studies, facilitate small groups, usher, make announcements, develop specialized ministries, and recruit volunteers for those ministries. This mobilization, he saw, had given people a sense of ownership, along with an energized passion for church. Consequently, the church's Sunday morning service could no longer seat everyone. So, a Sunday PM gathering had been added as a second service. The evening service was now averaging over a hundred people.

Troy looked upward into the clear sky. "Thank you, Father," he said. And chuckled again.

Right before he climbed the three steps to the building's side entrance, he saw Walter pull into the asphalt parking lot.

Troy smiled and waved.

Walter stuck up his thumb from the driver's seat.

Troy nodded.

Walter had been equally influenced by Kathleen, maybe even more so. '*Amazing,*' as a descriptive word, fell short of describing just how much Walter—in such a short period of time—had matured in his character and in his preaching AND in his direction in life. As a self-employed electrician, with a work schedule he could control, Walter had recently enrolled at Ailey Bible College—the private Christian college, fifteen miles away—where he was attending classes three mornings a week, majoring in Christian Studies and taking classes in Old and New Testament Survey, Church History, and Pastoral Ministry. And at Kathleen's persuasion, he was now filling the pulpit every four weeks. And he was thriving.

With buoyancy in his gait, Troy proceeded inside to Kathleen's church office.

Inside the office, when they were all seated—Troy, Walter, Kathleen, and Floyd Baxter—Kathleen officially commenced the meeting.

Kathleen led in prayer and then announced, "As you know, this is going to be a very important and extremely controversial decision. So I've invited Floyd to sit with us and act as an eyewitness to what is said and done."

Troy nodded his understanding. Walter did as well.

"All right, then," Kathleen went on, "I know Troy wants to put forth the motion. So I'll turn the floor over to him."

Troy cleared his throat as everyone turned and gave him their attention. He saw Walter offer a subtle thumbs-up.

"Thank you, Kathleen," Troy said. "Before I make the motion, I want to take a minute or so and offer an apology to Floyd." Troy cast his gaze toward the older man and said with a coy smile, "As everyone here knows, I was livid six months ago when you stood in the pulpit and announced brazenly that you were bringing a lady pastor to the church and that there was nothing anybody could do about it."

Every one either smiled or chuckled.

"Anyway," Troy continued, "I've obviously reversed my position on the matter. I now actually want to thank you, Floyd, for your out-of-the-box decision. Your decision has been life changing for the church. And it's especially been life changing for me." Troy's tone softened to the point of humility as he looked at Floyd's aged face. "So, please forgive me for my initial obstinance."

Floyd graciously bobbed his head.

To underscore his gratitude, Troy went on to pinpoint the three significant ways Kathleen's leadership had reshaped his perception of church. "So again, Floyd, I want to say a giant thanks," he finally concluded. "Thanks for riding out the opposition. Thanks for doing what you thought would be best for the community."

Floyd again graciously nodded.

"All right," Troy rolled onward, "Let's…uh…now do what we came here to do." He looked at Walter. "Mr. Johnson," he toyed with a grin, "will you read aloud the portions of our church constitution that we're about to enact?"

"Yes I will, Mr. Bingum," Walter volleyed with a feel-good smile of his own. He held up stapled pages, folded to the relevant section, and read in an emphatic tone. "Article four. Paragraph three. Dismissal of Officers. Any elected officer— deacon, treasurer, church clerk, church trustee, or financial committee member—who is unable or *unwilling* to fulfill the duties of his/her office shall graciously submit his/her resignation in writing to the Pastor and deacon board. If he/ she refuses to subscribe to the Articles of Faith or constitution, his/her resignation shall be requested. If said resignation is not received within a reasonable time, the office shall be declared vacant by vote of the Church, and a replacement secured."

Walter paused to flip a page.

Troy seized the moment and interjected. "And what are the duties of our deacons?" he asked.

Walter—his eyes scanning the constitution—picked up at another paragraph. "Article Four. Paragraph Two," he raised his voice. "The tasks of the Deacons shall include, but not be limited to: (A) To care for all church members and, to the best of their ability, establish and maintain personal fraternal relations with the general membership; (B) To be zealous to guard the unity of the spirit within the church in the bonds of peace; (C) To serve as a council of advisors in conference with the Senior Pastor and the ministerial staff members in all matters pertaining to the welfare and work of the Church; (D) To assist the Senior Pastor in observance of The Lord's Supper and in administering the Ordinance of Baptism."

Troy cleared his throat again. "Over the last six months, have Deacon Jim Manley and Deacon Jack Evans fulfilled these duties, even marginally, to which they were elected?"

"No," Walter responded.

Troy looked at Kathleen.

"No," Kathleen said softly.

"No," Floyd Baxter inserted harshly.

"Have Deacon Jim Manley and Deacon Jack Evans," Troy entreated, "been asked to submit letters of resignation due to their dereliction of duty?"

"They have," Walter answered. "And they have both refused outright to offer such a resignation, either verbally or in writing."

"Then, by allowance of the church constitution," Troy pressed onward, "I make a motion we bring a vote to the church floor to remove both men from the deacon board."

"I second the motion," Walter declared.

"All in favor?" Troy queried.

Every one raised their hand.

Troy shifted slightly in his seat. "Any discussion?"

Every one shook their head negatively.

"So carried," Troy proudly stated. "I make a motion then," Troy continued almost without taking a breath, "that we announce this Sunday that a vote will take place on Sunday morning, two weeks away."

"I second the motion," Walter heralded.

Troy's smile grew subconsciously bigger. "All in favor?"

Again, every one raised their hand.

"Any discussion?"

There was none.

"So carried," Troy stated, making the decision official. With eagerness in his voice, he quickly pounced again. "Next item; has treasurer Holly Evans fulfilled the duties to which she was elected?"

Autumn sunlight was filtering pleasantly through the sanctuary windows when Troy faced the congregation the following Sunday morning, October 4.

Kathleen had called him to the platform, as prearranged, a few minutes before the benediction.

"As some of you know," Troy spoke somberly into the microphone, "two of the deacons on our deacon board—Jim Manley and Jack Evans—have not supported the pastor or the congregation with their attendance or with any kind of administrative or financial help since Pastor Rose's arrival. They have chosen to be completely absent and nonfunctional for the last six months. According to the church constitution they can, therefore—for the welfare of the church—be rightfully removed from the deacon board and replaced. But this can only be done through a church-wide vote."

Troy read aloud the constitutional provision.

And then, as graciously as possible, he went on to call out Holly Evans the church treasurer and Bruce Dickerson the chairman of the finance committee as being in the same "absent" and "non-supportive" category.

"So, two weeks from now, on Sunday morning October 18, we will take a vote among the church members who are present. The will of the majority will determine the outcome. If the church votes to remove the four officers who have been named, then on the same Sunday we'll take nominations for possible replacements. The individuals nominated will be interviewed and considered. When qualified nominees have been selected, hopefully within the next month or so, they will be brought before the church for another vote."

As Troy wrapped up the announcement, he asked everyone to bow their heads for the benediction.

When heads were bowed, Troy started to pray when he suddenly caught sight of Holly Evans, the absentee treasurer, standing out in the foyer staring at him. He was sure her eyes were filled with blazing hostility. Her fists were even clinched.

Late in the afternoon, Floyd Baxter was at home watching a few minutes of cable news when his phone rang. The caller ID showed the caller was Jack Evans.

Floyd smirked, then answered the call from his recliner. "Hello."

"Floyd, this is Jack Evans."

Immediately Floyd could hear the blustering anger. He wasn't surprised, though. Not a bit. "Yes?" he said flatly.

"I don't know what kind of game you, Walter, Troy and your lady friend think you're playing, but I'm prepared to fight you on this!"

Floyd felt his head slightly nod. "Okay." His voice remained emotionless.

"If I have to, I'll file a lawsuit!" The threat was spouted with palpable tension.

"Okay." Floyd's lips cracked a smile.

Jack then spewed with accusatory disdain, "You're destroying the church; you know that!"

Floyd remained silent.

"All right, then," Jack erupted, "expect to hear from my attorney!"

Floyd almost prolonged his silence. But then added, "Jack, you might want to save your money. Even if you can find a lawyer who'll take your case, you know and I know you don't have a winter's chance in hades to win the suit. Besides, I have access to the best attorneys in Georgia. And I don't lack the resources to hire them."

There was a thick moment of silence. And then.

"God spare your soul from hell, old man!" Jack thundered. "You'll definitely be hearing from me again!" He then hung up.

49

On the Sunday morning of the big vote, Evelyn Huxley was sitting up front in her regular place. She had just closed her thick, leather Bible. Her mind was still mesmerized by the thought-provoking exposé of Satan that Kathleen had presented. Evelyn had never heard the subject analyzed in such detail. And as important as the subject matter was—as she was now realizing—she wondered why.

She couldn't thank God enough for her pastor. By far, Kathleen was her favorite pastor and Bible teacher of all time.

As Evelyn watched Kathleen turn the podium over to Walter to conduct the congregational vote, she again whispered a prayer of gratitude that Kathleen had come to Lyons. And, as always, she couldn't help but humbly grin.

"All right, the hour has finally arrived for our church members to cast their vote," Walter's voice suddenly boomed through the sound system. "If you haven't been here in awhile, the vote we're about to take has been announced from the pulpit for the last two Sundays. It's also been announced in the church bulletin and in a massive email send-out."

Walter started to go over the purpose of the vote when a man's voice, out of nowhere, erupted from the back of the auditorium.

Evelyn jerked and felt her shoulders cringe.

"What is wrong with you people!" The words were delivered in an uncontrolled shout.

Evelyn turned and saw that the disruption was coming from Jack Evans. She saw him marching up the aisle. His face was red. Veins appeared to be bulging from his neck.

"Can't you see that this witch, this devilish woman," he bellowed, pointing at Kathleen, "has led you all astray! Can't you see she has you under a spell!"

Evelyn nearly panicked. Jack was a quarter way up the aisle, looking as if he was going to tromp up onto the stage and take over the pulpit, maybe even confront Kathleen nose to nose.

"She is destroying this church!" Jack continued his tirade as he proceeded toward the front. "She is in direct violation of God's Word! She knows it! I know it! Those who've left the church know it!"

Everyone was momentarily frozen in place by the unexpected breech of everything normal. Out of the blue, though, Evelyn saw Ian Corley—the South African who had visited several times—suddenly jump up from his second row seat and rush to the middle aisle to block Jack's path.

Jack seemed to be taken aback when a man much taller than himself deliberately obstructed the way to the pulpit.

Jack—clad in a suit and tie as if he were a respectable deacon serving communion—stopped in his tracks. Appearing as if he might actually raise a fist, he gave a complete sigh of confusion when six or seven college guys quickly joined Ian's side to form a solid barricade.

Evelyn noticed that Kathleen, who was sitting in her chair on the stage, immediately bowed her head as if beseeching God for wisdom and intervention.

"I'm sorry, sir," Ian barked at Jack with impressive composure, "But you're completely out of line here. So, if you don't mind, I—we—would like to ask you to calm down and step away."

Jack looked around with menacing eyes. He started to offer some kind of retort when Ian said, "Now please."

Jack raised clinched fists. "This church has a rich history! It's been a beacon in this community for over a hundred years! And you," he hissed, pointing at Kathleen, "have nearly destroyed it all in just a few short months! And you," he declared, pointing around the room to Floyd Baxter, Walter, and Troy, "are responsible for letting it happen! I'm ashamed of each of you! Against everything you know to be true, you've encouraged it all!" Jack shook his head. "If you go through with this vote, then there's no going back! It's over! Absolutely over! Is that what you want?" He ceased his shouting and waited for an answer.

There was none.

"All right," Ian said, "Let's move along now." He placed a hand on Jack's shoulder to guide him back down the aisle.

Jack roared, "Take your hand off me!"

At that moment, the group of college jocks who had been standing at Ian's side closed in on Jack. Their move looked absolutely threatening and intimidating.

"God have mercy on your souls!" Jack lambasted. He reluctantly pivoted, then strode toward the foyer and out the building.

Tension lingered all throughout the room.

Evelyn suddenly realized she had stopped breathing. She inhaled deeply.

There was instant movement all throughout the sanctuary as if everyone else had been holding their breath as well. Pockets of mumbling erupted everywhere.

"All right, all right, give me your attention," Walter instructed from the microphone. "Let's get things back under control."

Within a second or two, the chatter around the room gave way to attentiveness.

"First of all; thank you, Ian," Walter asserted, nodding at the South African, "for helping temper the disruption there. And thanks to all the young men who stood with you. You helped divert a potentially bad situation." Walter took a visible breath. "I guess I need to explain," he said, motioning toward Jack's exit path, "that this particular man is one of the long-standing church members and long-time deacons who's at the center of the vote we're about to take. He's one of the two deacons who has purposely not attended the church in over six months and who's knowingly not supported our pastor according to the requirements of the church constitution. The second deacon at the center of the vote has been singled out for the same reasons. And the same is true for the church treasurer and the chairman of the finance committee who are on the list."

Evelyn noticed that the atmosphere in the hall morphed straightaway from an uncertain confusion to an urgent seriousness.

Walter, without wasting any time, explained all the ground rules for the vote. He then said, "Can I have three or four young men who are not members of the church, and who'll not be voting, to secure the doors for us please. We want to prevent any further disturbances from the outside while we're taking the votes."

Several young men jumped up and fanned out to cover the various exit doors.

Walter thanked them.

In the ten minutes that followed, motions were made and seconded—with no discussion wanted—to remove deacons Jack Evans and Jim Manley, treasurer Holly Evans, and the finance committee chairman Bruce Dickerson from their respected offices.

The votes were taken by a show of hands.

Each vote garnered a unanimous decision.

A few additional minutes were then taken to accept nominees as potential replacements. A list of the nominees was recorded for follow-ups and interviews.

The meeting was then dismissed.

Activity and conversation spread everywhere throughout the room.

Evelyn started to stand up when an unexpected release of tension occurred throughout her entire body and spirit. She sat back in the pew and cupped her face with both hands. A feeling of optimism swept over her. The feeling was almost euphoric. She emitted a muted laugh. What a life-changing six months! In all that had happened at the church, it had transpired in the face of persistent opposition, especially from the four people whose voices had just been silenced.

Those four people had for years been part of her spiritual family. She stared at the pulpit. Maybe she should feel sad. But the importance of church traditions and time-honored relations—just for the sake of 'the good ole days'—had started to fade weeks ago. As of right now, that element of importance seemed to vanish altogether.

Oblivious to anybody watching, Evelyn raised her hands in the air and squinted to hold back tears. "Thank you, Jesus," she whispered.

She eventually got up, feeling as if she were walking on air.

That afternoon, Walter sat at his computer and typed out an email:

Jack, Jim, Holly, and Bruce

Portended by a full two-week notice, motions were made this morning, October 18, 2015, and seconded to dismiss each of you from your official positions as deacons, treasurer, and chairman of the finance committee.

The votes today were officiated in a

transparent and proper manner and
carried out among members, and only
members, of the church. Each of the
four votes—without any undue influence
—brought a unanimous decision by show
of hands.

This email, which will be sent in
letter form to each of your home addresses,
is to inform you that as of today, October
18, 2015 at 12:20 P.M., you no longer
hold offices at Lyons Central Baptist.

Walter started to make it clear that, starting tomorrow, he
would begin the process of removing Holly's and Bruce's
names from the church bank account and transferring all the
church savings to a new and different account. But he changed
his mind. He didn't want to tempt the group of four to try
anything vindictive over the next twenty-four hours with the
current account.

Your church membership, however,
is still in place unless, or until, you
request a transference of your church
letter.

The church and church leadership
team want to thank each of you for your
faithful and valuable service through
the years.

We earnestly regret that the events of the last six months have created a personal dilemma for you that has eventually led to today's decision.

Sincerely,
Walter, Troy, Floyd, and Kathleen

After reading the paragraphs several times and making an edit or two, he forwarded the digital letter to Kathleen, Troy, and Floyd for their feedback and/or approval.

Kathleen was thirty-two miles northeast of Lyons, in Twin City, Georgia, when her phone signaled her about the incoming email. She and Ian were walking along an asphalt pathway at George L. Smith Park, by the edge of Watson Pond. For several minutes they had been holding hands and strolling in silence - smiling and enjoying the feel of autumn in the air. They were feeling good. It was just pleasant to be in each other's company.

"Excuse me," Kathleen said softly, offering an apologetic lift of the eyebrows, "Let me see if this is the email I've been expecting." She let go of Ian's hand and checked her phone. "I think this is it," she told him. "If you don't mind just give me a moment to read through it."

Ian looked her in the eye and grinned. "Of course. Take all the time you need." He turned to gaze out over the pond to give her privacy.

Kathleen tried quickly to assess the letter composed by Walter that would be sent out on behalf of the church's entire leadership team. But due to the relaxed and intimate moment with Ian, she had to force herself to concentrate. It took three attempts before her mind adequately absorbed and registered Walter's six paragraphs. Had she been alone in her office, she would have totally immersed herself in each paragraph for a more in-depth judgment. As it was, the surface reading convinced her the letter was fine. It seemed to cover all the necessary points. She clicked 'reply' and sent Walter her approval.

She then put the phone away and turned to give her attention back to Ian.

When she spun, she slightly flinched.

Ian was staring at her with eyes of consummate desire. He stepped forward until there were only inches between them, then pulled her into a full-mouth kiss. His hands slid beneath her hair and gently enveloped her face and neck.

She moaned as her lips surrendered to his.

50

"I can't," Kathleen nearly cried as she eventually broke off the kiss. "I'm sorry...I uh..."

Ian tenderly grabbed her chin and held her face. "I have fallen in love with you, Kathleen," he said, looking directly at her. "I know you have feelings for me as well. I'm just perplexed that every time I try to hold you or kiss you, you put up a wall. What is it that's going on? Just give me an explanation and I'll try to understand."

Kathleen closed her eyes. Yes, she did have feelings for him. She had felt she was falling in love as well. Their times together over the last several weeks—walking on the beach at Tybee Island, sailing on the Atlantic Ocean, touring the Coca Cola museum in Atlanta, enjoying an outdoor festival in Macon— had been nothing short of blissful.

She had felt her heart wanting more and more to be entrusted to this magnificent man. She wanted to be held by him. Kissed by him. But...

She opened her eyes. "Can we sit down somewhere?" she asked in a jittery tone.

Ian found them an old bench. It was extremely weathered, but stable. He wiped off a layer of pine straw. They sat and faced each other at an angle.

Kathleen dropped her eyelids again. How much should she tell him? What would be safe? She squeezed the fabric of her pants. *Oh God, help me here!* she pleaded inside her head.

She took a giant breath, opened her eyes, and said nervously, "Okay, I'll tell you what I can. I'll try to help you understand."

Ian shifted. His facial expression was one that was serious, one that wanted to comprehend, one that wanted to protect.

"First of all," she forced the words, "Kathleen Rose is not my real name."

The expression on Ian's face changed instantly to one of mental confusion and upheaval as if he had been viciously yanked out of bed from a deep sleep by a loved one and thrown across a bedroom.

Kathleen inhaled deeply. "I'll explain that later," she uttered. "But first, I should tell you about my past. You've probed several times and I've always evaded and stonewalled."

She hung her head.

"This isn't easy." She blew a puff of air. "I…uh…was orphaned at the age of four. My parents were killed one evening in a motorcycle accident on Fort Mountain in north Georgia back in nineteen-seventy-eight. A drunk driver veered into their lane and hit them head on. Without any relatives to take me in, I was sent to a foster home in Chatsworth, Georgia. That was my home for the next fourteen years, until I turned eighteen."

Kathleen felt tears crest in her eyes.

"I can't begin to tell you how lonely those years were for me. I hated life and often wanted to give up. As irrational as it was, I blamed my parents for abandoning me. As an adult, I've honestly tried to bury all those memories."

She squinted, almost in physical pain. "Anyway, I moved out of the home at eighteen and moved to Greenville, South Carolina where I spent the next four years in college. Through an on-campus ministry I became a believer in my sophomore year. The group that introduced me to the Gospel loved on me and discipled me. I knew within six months of my new birth that I wanted to devote my life to Christ. I had never felt such love. And I wanted to spread that love to the whole world."

Ian brushed at a bug on his neck.

Kathleen gave him a moment.

"I'm sorry," he told her with near flatness in his voice. "Keep going."

Kathleen compressed her lips and nodded. "After earning a Bachelor of Education, I decided to go to seminary and earn a degree in Theology, to prepare for a ministry of some kind. I ended up at Gordon-Conwell in Massachusetts."

Kathleen paused and swallowed hard.

"A month from graduating, I met the man of my life. I was twenty-four. He was thirty-two. He was a guest speaker at one of our school's final chapel services that year. He was the Vice President of a small Bible college in Chesapeake, Virginia. He was intelligent. He was humble. He was sensitive. He was handsome. And he was focused passionately on God's kingdom."

A Quiet Roar

Kathleen hung her head in silence for a moment. She wanted to tell Ian that he possessed many of the same qualities, and that's the reason she had been attracted to him. But for reasons she still didn't understand, she demurred.

"Are you okay?" she asked almost sheepishly. "Shall I go on?"

Ian nodded. "Please."

"We immediately fell in love. I know it sounds crazy, but following my graduation a few weeks later, I promptly moved to Chesapeake to be near him. Our courtship was fast and intense, and filled with nonstop talking and planning. In our heart-to-heart talks he shared with me his vision of one day planting a Bible college in Africa. He had been strongly influenced by a group of young African men who had studied at the college there in Chesapeake. I totally supported his dream. Not just his dream, but him. And within three months we were married. A year and half later, we were in Africa as full-time missionaries. In record time, it seemed, he founded the Bible college and…"

"Which country in Africa?" Ian asked. He had asked the question before in other non-related conversations, but Kathleen had always been intentionally vague in her answer.

Kathleen halted and sighed. "It's…it's Mali," she confessed, actually feeling frightened that she had identified the place still posing a threat to her life. She looked up. Ian hadn't diverted his focus. He was still with her. "I'll explain in a few minutes why I haven't revealed that country to another living soul here in the States. Only Floyd Baxter knows. But he's always known. And he'll take that information to his grave if I ask him to."

Ian, totally serious, stiffened his jaws, trying to absorb and process everything he was hearing.

"Anyway, during the first days of the Bible college classes, we learned I was pregnant. In May of 2001, I struggled in labor for twelve hours to give birth to our…son."

Kathleen fought to stay composed.

"He was the most beautiful creature I had ever seen. I promised God that day that I would never abandon my son like my parents abandoned me. That I would always be there for him."

Failing her attempt at composure, she started weeping.

"When he was about four years old I made a decision that unknowingly would change the course of my life. And my son's. Forever."

She paused and sniffed, stood up, then sat back down.

"I had learned about the ritual of female genital mutilation all throughout the country. The more I learned about it, and just how destructive it was to a young girl's well-being, the more concerned I became and the more angry I became with the practice. After a few women confided in me about the lifetime negative effects of the custom, I decided to take action. After interviewing twenty to thirty women and doing extensive research, I finally put together a three-day FGM conference at our new school, both for male and female students. At the conference, I highlighted the alarming percentage of young girls across the country who were forced to undergo the procedure, and then asked *WHY*. I explained that none of the stated reasons for the practice were well-founded or beneficial. That it was all a total waste. I explained that 'tradition' for tradition's sake was a pathetic reason."

Ian shifted on the wooden bench, but never stopped focusing on Kathleen's words.

"All the females who attended the seminar," Kathleen continued, "begged me afterward to take the seminar on the road, from suburb to suburb, village to village, town to town, city to city. At first, I took their recommendation as just an inflated compliment. But, in the end, I couldn't shake the idea. I actually spent hours dreaming about such an undertaking and what it would look like and what it could achieve. I regularly talked to my husband about it. I guess I lit up every time I discussed it with him. He eventually looked at me one night and said, 'Go for it; I'll support you every step of the way.'"

Ian looked as if he wanted to interrupt with a question or statement, but immediately backed down.

Kathleen continued the outpouring. "I knew, of course, that the seminar wouldn't be welcomed in public places if I called it something like 'The Horrors of Female Genital Mutilation.' So I added different components to the material —components about marriage and the family—and called it 'The Well-Being of Muslim Women.' I felt, with this name, that the men would not keep their wives and daughters away. I held the first public seminar in our capital city at a huge community center. Over one hundred women attended. I only talked about the mutilation issue during our final hours together. The seminar, especially the FGM element, proved to be more meaningful to the ladies than I could've ever imagined. After the official closing, I spent four hours answering questions, listening to tearful stories, and just being an encourager and advice giver. I knew then that I had to take the message to as many Malian women as I possibly could."

Kathleen paused to catch her breath.

Ian gently swiped at another bug, but was still fully engaged.

"Over time I ended up speaking all across the country - in cities, small villages, universities, even on the radio. The seminar took on a life of its own. At some point, the ripple effect gave me national recognition. And that gave me an even bigger platform. I became one of the major voices calling for nationwide legislation to outlaw the cuttings."

Kathleen puffed and looked heavenward.

"At some point," she said, lightly massaging one of her forearms, "I started receiving threats from angry men - husbands, village leaders, Imams, even local politicians. Since my main office was at the Bible college facility, my husband hired several security guards to stand at the school's entry ways during school hours. But then one day, when I finished speaking in Timbuktu at a highly promoted gathering, I was accosted by three men who put me in the back of a dark van. They bashed me around and told me if I didn't immediately stop my crusade, they would kill me. My husband insisted at that juncture that I stop making public appearances, that if I wanted to continue to get out my message, I should do it through radio. So I started broadcasting every two weeks from the Bible college. Since faces couldn't be seen, wives, daughters, and mothers started coming onto the program as anonymous guests. We talked about many things, but we primarily talked about genital cutting and its horrors. Bags of mail from appreciative women starting arriving at the school every week. Not that I wanted it, but I was constantly recognized and honored by the liberal voices in government. I was even honored by the Malian president himself."

A faint smile finally broke across Ian's serious face. It was a smile that said, 'why should I be surprised?'

"I was six and a half years into my push for new legislation," Kathleen stated, "when my husband was diagnosed with cerebral malaria. He was gone within eight weeks. That was just three and a half years ago."

Kathleen squeezed the bridge of her nose.

"My whole world collapsed. The Malian Bible college staff took over the school. I shut down my radio program. I could barely even function as a mother to my then eleven-year-old son. It took me a full year to get back on my feet. I eventually restarted the radio broadcast. And almost immediately, threatening letters started arriving at the school. This time they were from…a terrorist group called Ansar Dine, a group tied to Al-Qaeda."

Kathleen hung her head.

"I…uh…didn't know what to do at that point. My colleagues at the Bible college advised me to immediately cease all activities in that field. And I almost did until I received a letter a couple of days later from a twelve-year-old girl. The girl explained that seven years earlier she had been scheduled to go under the knife on her fifth birthday. But a few days before the cutting, her mother had attended one of my seminars, and that the information given out at the conference changed her mother's mind. Her mother explained to her that there wasn't a single health benefit derived from the practice and that it would only produce a lot of unnecessary pain and problems. In her twelve-year-old way, the girl thanked me profusely. She declared she was taking the information to all the new mothers in her village. And that two young mothers had already decided to spare their daughters from the knife. 'I want to be like you,' she said. 'I want to help as many women as I can.' She closed her letter, saying, 'Whatever happens, please don't ever stop teaching my Malian sisters.'"

Kathleen stopped and closed her eyes. "So, right or wrong, wise or unwise, I decided to keep speaking out." She opened her eyes. "I continued the radio broadcast. I even went on to produce a TV special. A couple of American gynecologists were in the country doing charitable work at the time, so they agreed to be part of the TV program. As experts in the field, they explained in detail all the lifelong problems that can, and often do, follow FGM. They highlighted the urinary problems, the infections, the childbirth complications, the sexual discomfort, the psychological scars, and a host of other difficulties. The program was one of the most watched on Malian television that year. It received so much attention that it compelled a few government officials to step up and call for a ban on the ritual."

Kathleen felt her shoulders rise and fall with a deep breath.

"I knew I was treading a dangerous path. It never dawned on me, though, that…that…"

Kathleen suddenly felt lightheaded and wobbly.

Ian started to reach out to help her, but she quickly managed to steady herself.

"…that my son could be in danger because of what I was doing."

Kathleen suddenly went still. It took half a minute before she could speak again.

"I picked him up at school one day and was driving him outside the city to his cello lesson. He had just turned thirteen. We were within four or five miles of our destination when we rounded a bend and saw a young Muslim boy in the middle of the road, just on the other side of a low bridge, stooping over a dead goat."

Kathleen slowly closed her eyes.

"We didn't know it was a trap."

Kathleen struggled as she told the story for the first time in nearly a year.

"My son wanted to get out and help. It looked like a safe place. So I stopped the car. He got out and helped the boy lift the animal. The boy motioned for them to walk the goat down the embankment beside the bridge. So they disappeared down the bank."

Kathleen tried to loosen her shoulders, but they stiffened like bags of wet concrete.

"I always carried a pistol in my vehicle. I already had the gun in my hand when I heard the nightmarish scream. It was my son crying for help. In a panic I chambered a round, jumped out of the car, and raced down the embankment."

Kathleen bent over from the waist.

"It all happened so quickly," she wept, planting her face in her palms.

Ian reached out and took her arm in an effort to give comfort. She pulled away. She tried to sit erect again. She verbally paused for so long she eventually heard Ian say, "It's okay. You don't have to finish. You can…"

"No!" she groaned. She held up a hand to indicate she needed another second or two. When she spoke again, her voice was strained. "There were eight or nine men under the bridge. Three of them were…holding my boy. He was… stripped from the waist down. A machete was pressed to his neck. I aimed the gun at the man holding the machete and shouted, 'let him go!.' The man looked like he had no soul. He yelled, 'drop the gun or I'll cut his throat.' I suddenly saw three rifles pointed at me. Everybody shouted for me to put the gun down."

Kathleen felt like she might hyperventilate. She took several deep breaths.

"I had fifteen rounds in the magazine. I came close to…" She closed her eyes again. "I should've…I could've…" She stopped herself short and opened her eyes. "I hesitated too long. In the commotion, one of the men grabbed the gun. I fired a shot, but I don't know if I hit anything. The gun was yanked out of my hand and I was grabbed from all directions. My hands were tied behind my back. And I was gagged. My head was gripped and held steady, facing my son. He was crying. He was...so afraid."

Kathleen felt like her head might explode. She again went silent. And then the remainder of the story spilled out, along with a hundred tears.

"While they held me, they made me watch as they... castrated my boy...with the machete. They held me and made me watch until he bled to death." She paused as she rocked back and forth. "There was ...nothing I could do. When he was lying limp on the ground, they threw me down beside him and raped me. I don't know how many men were on top of me. When they were finished, they made it known they were members of the terrorist group that had warned me to stop my crusade. At that point, one of the men held up a knife and plunged it into my neck. They left me for dead. I was found less than an hour later by a man on a scooter. I had somehow managed to crawl from beneath the bridge to a place visible from the road. The man used a cell phone to call a nearby friend who had a truck. I was taken to a hospital. I was barely alive."

Ian started to lean in and move toward her. She put out a hand for him to keep his distance.

"Don't you understand? There's something in me that died that day. I will never be whole again. Never. There are parts of me—in my heart, soul, conscience—that will *NEVER* heal! Every single day, every single hour, I regret I was rescued from that ditch. I cry myself to sleep every night. I constantly hear my son's screams. I will have to live with those screams for the rest of my life. I killed my thirteen-year-old son, Ian. I'm…I'm not fit to…"

In less than a second, Ian had her wrapped in his arms.

Kathleen felt her head fall to his shoulder as she bawled.

With tears now streaming down his own face, Ian whispered into her ear, "I'm so sorry. I can't even conceive of…"

"Just hold me," she pleaded.

Ian squeezed her tighter. After minutes of feeling each other's face-to-face tears, Ian whispered longingly, "What's your real name? Who's the broken lady I've lost my heart to?"

Kathleen just shook her head.

Ian shifted and looked her in the eye. "Whoever you are, I *WANT* to love you. Do you hear me? I want to love you in all your pain, your brokenness, your grief! I want to love the parts of you that are still alive. I want to care for you. I want to…"

"They know I survived, Ian!" she added. "They're looking for me as we speak. And they'll never stop till they find me. If my real name is ever leaked and accidentally ends up on the internet in connection with Lyons or the people of Lyons, they'll send someone."

"Then I'll protect you," he assured her as he strengthened his embrace.

"It's a terrorist group, Ian! They blow people up! They are murderers funded by a gold mining industry! They will just keep sending people once they know my location. And, at that point, I'll be putting all those around me in danger - including you."

Ian held her quietly for a few seconds. He then slowly nodded his head. "After hearing everything you told me, my heart loves you even more. I'm strong-willed, so I'll just keep loving you and caring for you for as long as you let me in. Even if you never tell me your real name. And even if being with you puts me at risk."

Kathleen broke into a new round of tears.

*   *   *

Later that afternoon, Walter—with Kathleen, Troy, and Floyd's stamp of approval—sent out the email to Jack, Holly, Jim, and Bruce, officially notifying them of their dismissal from the service of the church.

51

South of Columbia, South Carolina on I-26, Ian was clipping along in his Audi A5, headed for a Monday afternoon meeting in Charlotte, North Carolina at the Presbyterian Medical Center.

He was scheduled to meet with the hospital pharmacist and his staff at 2:00 to present LabVance's cutting edge delivery system.

He had been trying for fifteen minutes to rehearse his presentation, but was distracted. He couldn't get Kathleen off his mind. Her story was absolutely mind boggling and continued to weigh heavily on his soul.

His heart ached as he ruminated about her immense grief and overwhelming guilt. How could anyone emotionally survive something so unspeakable? Could a seasoned grief counselor even begin to assuage the pain?

He squeezed the steering wheel. "Oh, God," he prayed. "I can't perceive that time alone can even begin to heal something of this magnitude. It's just too brutal. It's more than anyone should have to bear." He squeezed the steering wheel harder. "You are the Sovereign physician of the Universe, not only of the physical realm, but of the emotional and mental as well. So I'm asking You right now at this very moment to hold Kathleen in your arms. She's your daughter. Console her,

PLEASE, with a divine reassurance that she will one day feel hopeful again. Please, will you do that for her? I beg You in the name of your Almighty Son. Amen!"

Ian wiped his brow. He wondered if Kathleen would be willing to meet with a grief specialist if he could find the right person and cover all the costs. To provide that kind of connection would be the least he could do. He already cared too much to just sit idly by. He audibly recorded the task on his iPhone. He would start researching this evening. He smiled. He felt good about the proposition.

His thoughts were suddenly interrupted when he saw an exit sign for the small town of Orangeburg where there was a gas station. He moved to the outside lane and started slowing down. The Audi needed to be refueled.

* * *

Kathleen had just pulled into the Walmart parking lot to buy groceries for the week when her cell phone started ringing. She looked at the caller ID to see if it was Ian. All morning long she had been thinking about their time together yesterday afternoon. Her heart sank a little when she saw the call wasn't from him. It was from Evelyn Huxley.

She pulled into an outlying parking slot close to the Murphy gas station and idled the car.

"Hello," she answered.

"Kathleen, this is Evelyn. Do you have a moment?"

"Sure, Evelyn, I have a moment. Go ahead."

"Well, it's official," Evelyn declared, breathing a little heavier than normal. "We received a letter in the mail today from the Superior Court saying Billy's trial is set for Tuesday, December 8. Please keep the date in mind. And please keep praying for Billy. He seems to be totally lost in his own world and has no spiritual interests whatsoever. He gets really angry whenever I try to talk to him about the Lord. It seems that Ray's bitterness continues to rub off on him by the day." Evelyn vented a heavy sigh. "I'm just heartbroken. But, I wanted to call and let you know about the date."

"My heart goes out to you, Evelyn. I know it's not easy to carry a burden like this. If it's okay, I would like to go ahead and pray for you."

"Please," Evelyn nearly begged.

Kathleen, oblivious to her parking-lot surroundings, bowed her head. She prayed aloud, first for Billy - for his spiritual, emotional, and mental well-being; for his present and his future. She then prayed for Ray. And then for Evelyn. In her prayer for Evelyn, she petitioned God to help carry her sister's maternal burden and to help the older woman sense His strong presence every hour of every day throughout the whole ordeal.

"All right," Kathleen promised when she finished praying, "I'll mark December the eighth on my phone calendar. And I'll be sure to keep praying for you and the family."

On the other end of the connection, Evelyn blew her nose. "Thank you," she said, choking up. "This means more to me than you know."

337

Within minutes of the phone call, Kathleen parked closer to the Walmart building and approached the designated "Market" entryway.

She was already thinking about Ian again.

* * *

Floyd Baxter—at Kathleen, Troy, and Walter's request—walked into the Southern Federal Bank on Vidalia's East First Street to carry out some needed business. He had just finished lunch. He was holding a manila folder and a cash pouch.

"I'm here for my appointment with Paul Miller," Floyd said to the greeter.

"Go ahead and have a seat, Mr. Baxter, and I'll see if he's ready for you."

Floyd sat in a leather chair. He only had to wait for a minute or two before the greeter, a middle-aged lady dressed in a navy blue suit, returned and said, "Follow me, Mr. Baxter." The lady turned and ushered him down a short hallway to the bank manager's office.

When Floyd entered Miller's office, Miller stood and said, "I've been expecting you, Floyd. How are you doing these days?"

The two men shook hands. They had known each other for over thirty years.

"Doing good, Paul. How are Lorene and the kids?"

Miller chuckled. "Lorene is as busy as ever. She's involved in just about every community activity there is. She never sits still, that woman. Paul Jr. is still doing his chiropractic work in

Atlanta. And Marcie and her family are still in Macon. She was recently elected to the city council. She's hoping she and the other dozen or so councilmen can put some new policies in place that will help bring businesses back to the downtown area. But…" Miller threw up his hand. "…you're not here to talk about those issues. So, have a seat and tell me how I can help you today."

Floyd sat in a wooden chair with an inserted fabric cushion.

Miller sat down behind his desk in an age-old executive chair.

"I'm not here to check on my personal money, Paul," Floyd explained. "Rather, I'm here to make a change in the church accounts, both the savings and the checking. And I thought I would just come straight to you."

"A change?" Miller looked concerned.

"We're not moving the money," Floyd quickly stressed to put Miller at ease, "but we need to close down the existing accounts and open new accounts with new authorized users. As you know, there have been some major changes at our church in recent months. And those changes haven't settled well with some of the longtime members. A couple of those individuals are Holly Evans, the church treasurer, and Bruce Dickerson, the chairman of the finance committee. You're aware, of course, that both Holly and Bruce have been authorized users of the church's accounts for years. But they both stopped supporting the church when the new pastor arrived. And yesterday morning, the church voted to remove them both from their respected offices."

Floyd opened the manila folder and pulled out a sheet of paper.

"Here are the minutes of yesterday's official church-wide business meeting." He handed the sheet to Miller. "And, as you can see, it's even notarized by Nora Mae. She was there as an eyewitness."

Miller looked carefully at the document typed on Central Baptist stationery.

When Miller finally looked up, Floyd added, "It spells out quite clearly that Holly and Bruce no longer hold offices at the church. Yet, they still have checks in their possession for the checking account. Instead of trying to retrieve those bank documents from them, I thought it would just be easier to annul both the savings and checking accounts and transfer all the money to brand new accounts - with new account numbers, new checks, and a new list of authorized users.

Miller thoughtfully nodded. "You're the primary user on both accounts, Floyd. The document looks in order. If you don't mind, though, give me a minute to make a quick call to Nora Mae. Officially, I just need to cover my bases; you understand."

Floyd nodded his understanding. He and Miller had both known Nora Mae for years. Nora's secretarial role at Vidalia's Board of Public Service had earned her a stellar reputation for playing by the rules. She was a no-nonsense kind of gal.

"I'll just step out while you make the call," Floyd said.

Miller was already reaching for the phone as Floyd left the room.

Within five minutes Floyd was called back into the office.

"All is good," Miller declared.

In less than thirty minutes, the church funds—including the cash deposit Floyd carried in the pouch from yesterday's offering—were set up in new accounts with Floyd, Kathleen, and Walter listed temporarily as the sole authorized users. "The names will change when we elect a new treasurer and finance-committee chairman," Floyd underlined.

"Understood," Miller replied.

"What are the account balances at the moment, including today's deposit?" Floyd queried.

Miller looked again at his computer screen. "The current balance for the savings account is twenty thousand, three hundred and five. The balance for the checking account, including today's deposit, is nine thousand, seven hundred and two."

"Is there anything else pending besides today's deposit?"

"No, sir; that's it."

"Thank you, thank you," Floyd concluded.

The next morning, Holly Evans picked up a copy of the *Vidalia Times* at a convenience store and added it to her Ibuprofen and soft-drink purchase. She was en route to visit the wife of Jim Manley, the other deacon who had been forcibly dismissed from his position at the church. Both ladies needed a time of sympathetic sharing, venting, and commiserating.

341

She, herself, was still in a state of absolute shock at how callously the church had voted her and her husband, Jack, out of their long-time offices. She never would have believed it was possible. She felt truly violated. And she was sure she wouldn't be able to get over it anytime soon.

When she returned to her car and adjusted herself behind the wheel, she flipped the folded newspaper onto the passenger seat. Her eyes glanced at the paper when it landed, then did a retake. She quickly picked up the paper again. Across the bottom righthand corner was the byline - "Have The Old Guards Seen Their Final Days At Lyons Central Baptist? questions journalist Eric Sawyer - p 4."

Holly, sucking in her next breath, immediately turned to page four. Sitting in her car in the convenience-store parking lot, she read the words:

Old Guards' Final Days?

> For the last six months, since the arrival of Pastor Kathleen Rose, several key office holders at Lyons Central Baptist—two deacons, the treasurer, and the finance-committee chairman— have led a nonstop opposition movement to cripple the church's operation under Pastor Rose's leadership.
>
> Two weeks ago, however, an announcement was made from the

pulpit that a church-wide vote would
be taken on October 18 to hopefully
oust the opposition group from their
church offices, and their positions of
influence, once and for all, calling on
a clause in the church's constitution that
says, *"Any elected officer—deacon,
treasurer, church clerk, or financial
committee member—who is unable
or <u>unwilling</u> to fulfill the duties of his/
her office shall graciously submit his/
her resignation in writing to the Pastor
and deacon board. If said resignation
is not received within a reasonable
time, the office shall be declared
vacant by vote of the church, and a
replacement secured."*

At the time of this publication, the
church vote will have already taken place.

Ironically, for the first time in the
history of Lyons Central Baptist, African
Americans, Hispanics, and Asians—new
members in the church—will have the
opportunity to cast influential votes.

Whatever the outcome, Pastor
Kathleen Rose, throughout the surrounding months-long controversy,
has refrained from voicing a single word
of denunciation against those who have

fought against her. She has remained
steady, professional, and unpresuming.
And she has won the hearts of many.

Still gripping the newspaper, Holly closed her eyes. She had never met Kathleen Rose face to face. She had only seen her from a distance whenever she went to the church building late on Sunday mornings to take possession of the offerings. Yet, she hated the lady. Hated her for disrupting something that had been good and beautiful, something that had been part of the community fabric for decades.

She also hated Floyd Baxter. The humiliation he had now brought on her and her family sprouted feelings of vindictiveness in her heart that actually frightened her. She almost wished the man had died years ago, before the idea of bringing in a lady pastor had ever taken root in his mind.

And she would never, never forgive Troy and Walter for their abandonment of all that was right and honorable. Their conversion to Floyd and Kathleen's side was a putrid reflection of their weakness. They had now left a stain on the church's history that could never be washed away and that would never be forgotten.

Holly, with her eyes still closed, wadded up the newspaper and threw it on the floorboard. Then broke into a muted sob.

52

"There's a call for you on line two," Floyd Baxter's secretary informed him on the main line. "It's Mr. Higgley, the director of the regional Baptist Alliance."

Floyd rolled his eyes. He looked at the clock on his office wall. It was 11:45 Friday morning. He had just been getting ready to end his work week and top if off with an enjoyable steak lunch at the Steeplechase Grill. The last eleven days of dealing with the community fallout following the church decision to unseat Jack, Jim, Bruce, and Holly had left him feeling less than energetic. At the moment, he was just tired of people. He just wanted to eat a nice meal and go home and hibernate for a day or two.

"Thank you, Mable. Go ahead and connect me."

When Floyd heard the click in the line and knew the connection was made, he said, "Hello, this is Floyd Baxter." He knew the tone of his voice didn't sound very inviting. He didn't intend for it to.

"Mr. Baxter, this is Ted Higgley from the regional Baptist Alliance."

"Yes, sir," Floyd replied flatly.

"As the director overseeing the credentials committee, I've been asked to give you this last-chance call. The committee met last night for their annual action meeting. And in that meeting, they decided that time has run out for Lyons Central Baptist to fall into sync with the guidelines forbidding female pastors. The members of the committee voted unanimously to expel Lyons Central Baptist from the state Evangelical Baptist Alliance, and thus the nationwide Alliance, pending your response to this call. If you can give me a promise in good faith that you and the deacon board will begin taking immediate steps to resign Pastor Rose, then we will keep the church tentatively listed on the EBA roster and will plan another on-site assessment as soon as possible. Otherwise…"

"Excuse me, Mr. Higgley," Floyd interrupted. "There's no way in hades that I or anybody else at Central Baptist is going to ask Kathleen Rose to step down from her pastoral role. The church is more alive now under her leadership than it's been in the last fifty years. Period." Floyd paused to take a breath. "So, I guess our affiliation with the Evangelical Baptist Alliance has just ended."

Ted Higgley cleared his throat in apparent shock. "Okay, well, all I can say then is that an official letter announcing our decision will be in the mail tomorrow. I'm sorry it's had to come to this."

"Oh, don't feel sorry, Mr. Higgley. God's at work here. I think you should be rejoicing instead of feeling sorry. Anyway, thanks for the years of camaraderie. It was appreciated while it lasted."

When Floyd ended the call, he realized that a hundred years of history for the Central Baptist Church of Lyons had just been capped. And that a new and uncertain history would now commence. And he hoped he had made the right decision.

Later that evening, Floyd called Walter and Troy with the news. Like him, both men confessed there was really no other choice, but expressed an initial trepidation that the church would be left "all alone" without the undergirding of a strong and resourceful brotherhood. In Troy's words, it was like "being twenty-one and kicked out of the house, told by the parents they never wanted to see you again."

Floyd did not call Kathleen. She would receive the official letter soon enough. He would simply spare her a day or so of taking the blame.

The authorized letter from the credentials committee arrived at Floyd's office the following Monday, November 2. He learned, when he received a call from Kathleen an hour later, that a copy had arrived at the church office as well. The letter could not have looked more official. It was printed on the Evangelical Baptist Alliance stationery, branding the logo of the statewide network—the silhouette of a Bible emblazoned across a peach-colored map of Georgia.

Floyd read the letter at least three times.

> Dear Floyd Baxter, Troy Bingham,
> and Walter Johnson, the recognized
> leadership team at Lyons Central Baptist
> in Lyons Georgia.

On this 29th day of October, in the year 2015, it is the solemn duty of the credentials committee of the state Evangelical Baptist Alliance to inform you that the committee has voted unanimously—in light of your congregation's continued violation of the 2006 EBA Confession, Section V, forbidding females from holding the office of senior pastor—to permanently suspend the church's membership in the Evangelical Baptist Alliance. As of today, Lyons Central Baptist, as a church entity, will be removed from the state and national EBA membership roster. This decision comes only after multiple warnings.

Please take immediate action to disassociate your congregation from both the statewide Evangelical Baptist Alliance and the national Evangelical Baptist Alliance - with all office materials, congregational materials, and promotional materials.

Sincerely,
Ted Higgley - EBA Regional Director
Patrick Moore - EBA State Director

Floyd lifted his eyebrows. Well, what was done, was done. Knowing the news would eventually leak to the public, he would go ahead and read the letter to the church family on Sunday. The older members of the church would just have to step up and push forward with an upbeat attitude. The younger people, he was sure, wouldn't care a naked iota about the expulsion. If anything, they might even consider it a badge of honor.

His main concern was Kathleen. He didn't want her to feel culpable, not in the least, for what had just happened. He lightheartedly even joked with himself that perhaps the church should change its name to Rose Memorial Baptist. Now that would be a kicker, wouldn't it? He smiled at the very notion.

53

At the conclusion of her sermon on Sunday morning, Kathleen informed the packed-out crowd that Floyd Baxter had an important announcement to make before everyone was dismissed.

Floyd, dressed in a crew-neck sweater and casual trousers, ascended the steps to the pulpit. He was holding the Evangelical Baptist Alliance letter folded in his hand. He unfolded the document and laid it face-up on the wooden lectern and leaned slightly toward the microphone. It was the first time he had stood behind the pulpit since the first week of Kathleen's arrival. The sea of faces, from the platform perspective, was breathtaking to his eighty-one-year-old heart.

He smiled to the audience and said, "I've been a member of this church for fifty years. And I think this is one of the most beautiful crowds I've ever seen sitting under this roof." He grinned again, then almost shed a nostalgic tear. He just couldn't help it. "Well, I know you're ready to head out for lunch. But give me just a moment to read an important letter to you. I'll read it first without any preface. And then I'll quickly answer any questions you might want to throw my way."

Floyd cleared his throat, picked up the paper, and started reading. He enunciated the words clearly and slowly.

Kathleen, still sitting on the stage, watched the faces of the people as Floyd delivered the Baptist Alliance's judgment. Some of the facial expressions quickly revealed concern and confusion. Kathleen sighed on the inside. She was the centerpiece of the story and, therefore, by default felt guilty. Yet, Floyd Baxter had already looked her in the eyes two or three times and reminded her that he was the one who had repeatedly said "no" to the Alliance's demands. Kathleen then saw Ian, sitting on the third row, forming a circle with his index finger and thumb, signaling her not to worry, that "everything was going to be okay."

When Floyd finished reading, he raised the document in the air and said, "When we're dismissed, I'll give this letter to deacon Walter Johnson to file away in the church records as part of our history. Now, before you erupt with questions, let me just say I'm the one who invited Kathleen to be our pastor. I'm the one who didn't give the older congregation a choice about the decision. Up until last Sunday, I'm the one who has paid Pastor Rose's salary every month. I'm the one who has persistently said 'no' to the Alliance's credentials committee when they've instructed me to remove Pastor Rose from the role of senior pastor. And forgive me if you need to, but I'm the one who chose not to bring this decision to the church floor for a congregational vote. Yes, I know I've made a lot of unilateral decisions here, but I've done it for the welfare of the church. And for those of you who don't know, I'm the one who holds the deed to this property and these buildings. That's why I've taken so many liberties. But...but...you can rest assured that I've only made unilateral decisions when it has involved Pastor Rose. Now that the offerings are back in the hands of the active members, however, and now that the church will be paying Pastor Rose's salary, I will fade into the background. And I'll let you, the members of the church, make all future decisions as a congregation." Floyd paused, then quickly added, "The one exception is that Pastor Rose will unequivocally be allowed to stay in place through April 2017, the two-year mark of her arrival. At that point, as I promised when I brought her in, you can vote to let her stay or let her go. Any questions?"

Kathleen was amazed at Floyd's bluntness. She wondered how the people would respond.

At first, there was an awkward silence that hovered over the room. Then an older lady, one who had been around for decades, raised her hand near the center of the sanctuary.

Floyd pointed to the lady. "Yes, Imogene?"

The lady rose to her feet. "Floyd, I can't say I'm thrilled with the way you've forced some of your decisions down our throat," she proclaimed without any show of nerves. "But I trust you will keep the promise you just made and not do it anymore." The lady, with her eyes locked on Floyd's, paused until she saw him nod his understanding. "Now with that said, I'm not sure I'm comfortable with our church being kicked out of the Alliance. So, are you telling us there was no way to keep Pastor Rose as our pastor and make a few changes that would have satisfied the credentials committee?"

Floyd didn't hesitate with his reply. "That's exactly what I'm telling you, Imogene. The only way for us to have stayed in the Alliance, according to the credentials committee, was to remove Kathleen as our pastor."

"What do we stand to lose if we're no longer part of the EBA then?"

Floyd scratched at his partially bald head. "We'll lose our label, our network, some of our resources, and, of course, our church vote pertaining to Evangelical Baptist Alliance issues and policies."

"And you're confident the church will be okay on its own?" There was a faint sound of uncertainty in the question.

"Imogene, what can I say? It's not like the EBA has paid our bills, planned our church services, or visited our sick. If anything, we've helped pay their operating bills through the winter and spring Helping-Hands mission offerings every year." Floyd shook his head. "I think we're going to be just fine. To be honest with you, we've always been on our own anyway. We've always been self-governing and self-supporting. It's just that now, we'll not carry the Evangelical Baptist Alliance label; that's all."

"I guess I'll get use to it, then. But for the moment I'm still a little shaken." After saying her piece, Imogene sat down.

"Any other questions?" Floyd asked the audience.

A young college boy raised his hand.

"Yes," Floyd acknowledged the young man.

"Does this mean the church will have to change its name?"

"Nope; I've already looked into that," Floyd explained. "The EBA doesn't have a trademark on the name 'Central Baptist.' So we're fine."

There were a few more questions, but very minor ones. And then the meeting was brought to a close. The news of the transition had been abrupt. But it was now complete. The pieces of the aftermath would just have to fall where they may.

*   *   *

Lyons Central Baptist
Forced Out Of
Evangelical Baptist Alliance

There had been very few times in life when Ray Huxley had used profanity, but the *Vidalia Times* headline alone, along with the uncertainty of the long-term implications, left him reeling. He spontaneously filled his workshop with enough expletives and flying tools to scare an innocent bystander. The following article only exacerbated his feelings.

Nearly a hundred years of history for Lyons Central Baptist has just been archived. A new history for the church has now begun as the Evangelical Baptist Alliance on November 2 announced that Lyons Central Baptist has been severed from all ties with the state and national networks of the EBA member churches.

Floyd Baxter, deed-holder to the church property, has refused to yield to the demand of the regional Alliance director that Pastor Kathleen Rose be forced to step down in accordance with the '2006 Evangelical Baptist Alliance Confession,' stating in Section V that - "While we believe that every believer is gifted by God for ministry in the church, we believe the role of pastor, as dictated in the Scripture, is limited exclusively to qualified men."

The regional Alliance has offered Floyd Baxter no other concession.

While most Baptist churches are in decline, losing members and cultural relevancy, Lyons Central Baptist has seen a massive resurgence in both attendance and impact. The conservative Evangelical Baptist Alliance, though, will not acknowledge the value of this revival, being that a lady is at the helm.

In the midst of the final ruling, many are wondering who will actually lose out here.

PART IV

54

On Tuesday, December 8, at 2:36 p.m. Billy Huxley was found guilty of "drug trafficking" by a jury of his peers. The trial, in an overheated and stuffy courtroom, had begun that morning and had lasted two hours and fifteen minutes. The jury deliberated the case's evidence for only fifty-three minutes before returning a "guilty" verdict.

Evelyn wept openly in the courtroom when the jury foreman delivered the verdict. Ray stood ramrod straight and fumed silently on the inside.

Two weeks later, on December 21, the Superior Court judge, presiding over Billy Huxley's case, sat sternly at his bench during the sentencing phase.

"Please stand, Mr. Huxley," the judge ordered.

Billy stood. His public defense attorney, a nerdy looking man in his mid-forties with silver hair, stood with him.

Ray Huxley, sitting in the public section right behind Billy, saw that his son was breathing short breaths. It was obvious he was frightened. As a father, Ray could feel his own hopefulness quickly melting away. He took a deep breath and held it as he waited for the judge's next words.

"I've given a lot of thought to your case," the judge stated. "I've looked carefully at the mitigating circumstances. Number one; your mother and father have been outstanding citizens in our county for over thirty years. I can't see that either of them has ever so much as received a speeding ticket. Number two; up until you were stopped with an illegal substance in your vehicle on Tuesday, April twenty-eight, you had a clean slate as well. No criminal record. You weren't on any law department's 'watch' list. You were totally clean.

"Yet, overnight you went from being a law-abiding citizen to being a felon." The judge took a breath of exasperation. "And this is beyond serious." The judge took another noticeable breath. "I could easily sentence you to ten years behind bars. But under the circumstances, I'm going to go out on a limb here. I'm going to give you only twenty-four months of jail time, followed by a full year of probation. And if I ever see you in this courtroom again, I promise you there will be no further tolerances. Not an ounce. Do you understand, Mr. Huxley?"

Billy, still shaking from the significant punch of the judge's decision, closed his eyes and hung his head.

Ray winced under the load of his own emotional hit. He even felt his shoulders give way under the weight of it all. He hardly even noticed Evelyn who was sobbing into her palms.

"You will be handcuffed at this point and taken to the county jail," the judge explained to Billy. "In the next week or so, you will be sent to the diagnostic center in Jackson. From there you will be transferred to a designated facility where you will spend the duration of your sentence. Any questions?"

With his head still hanging, Billy shook his head.

"All right, Bailiff," the judge said coldly, "handcuff Mr. Huxley and take him away."

It was three days before Christmas, and Ian was overjoyed. Kathleen had just finished her initial therapy session with an exceptionally recognized grief counselor. He ushered Kathleen out of the specialist's private office in downtown Savannah.

"You were right; I admit it," Kathleen conceded as they exited the building and headed for Ian's car. "I should have done this a long time ago. Thanks for pushing me. I'm still absorbing everything that was said. But I am appreciative. I really am."

With plans to eat lunch with Kathleen at the Frali Gourmet restaurant on West Liberty Street, Ian could not have been happier. It had taken him over six weeks to convince Kathleen to see the therapist—at his expense, and gladly so—but he had finally succeeded. He had promised her if the first session was helpful he would pay for as many ongoing sessions as were needed. He just wanted her to experience as much emotional healing as possible. She deserved it.

He helplessly smiled at her as he opened the Audi door and let her in on the passenger side. Since hearing her story eight weeks ago, his mind had been relentlessly preoccupied with her wellbeing. Thoughts and visions of her seemed to dominate his life, to the point of actually interfering with his focus at work. She was like an overpowering magnet that attracted, and held captive, every part of his body and soul. He had never met another woman like her, not anywhere. He could not stop hungering for her company, her conversation, and her touch. Every minute he spent with her was like a fantastic dream come true.

"I love you more than ever," he avowed when he settled in behind the steering wheel. Then added, "I know, I know; you're not quite there yet. And I'm not asking for a response. I just want you to know I'm totally on your side. And I'm cheering you on. I'm just so glad you've taken this step. And I'm really praying you'll find some of the healing you deserve."

Kathleen leaned over and gave him a tender peck on the cheek.

Ian nearly swooned from the feel and smell of her hair.

"You're a kind and gracious man, Ian," Kathleen said softly, still sounding a bit preoccupied with thoughts of the counseling session. "Your support, your prayers, your love mean more to me than you'll ever know. Just don't stop praying for me. Please."

At the restaurant, Kathleen sat back in her seat and stared straight ahead. She didn't tell Ian that just last night she had been vanquished by such a fierce bout of depression that she had begged God to terminate her life.

Over a nice lunch of turkey paninis, she did tell him, "Dr. Blitz seemed to be especially sympathetic to my story. After listening, he went over the different stages of grief, especially the stage where I seem to be stuck at the moment—the stage where grief unpredictably ambushes a person and lays them waste." She wiped at her mouth with a napkin. "He explained that one of the ways to weaken the ambush is to personally share with a friend what's going on, to talk it out." She stopped eating for a moment and looked Ian in the eye. "But, because of my circumstances, it's something I've just not done. And, I'm sure it's been to my own detriment. So, if you don't mind… now that you know my story…"

"Any time, any place," Ian broke in and assured her. "All you have to do is give me a call and I'll stop whatever I'm doing. I'll give you all the time you need."

Kathleen felt her heart sigh. She wanted to kiss the man fully on his lips and bask in his love right then and there. But now wasn't the time.

Maybe someday, though.

55

Dressed in a pale-silver blouse, an elegant gray cardigan, and a red skirt, Kathleen stood up to speak on Christmas eve. The auditorium on the celebrated evening was illuminated only by candlelight, creating a warm and intimate ambiance.

Kathleen sensed the sacredness of the moment. She stood behind a portable podium that had been positioned out in front of the platform, at floor level.

Being that the room was only half full, she asked everyone to move forward and bunch together in the front pews.

The attendees freely cooperated. The mood all around was one of special gladness.

Kathleen looked at her sermon notes. A small podium light gave visibility to her written pages.

"As we focus on the Christmas story," Kathleen began when everyone was settled, "I want to call your attention to one of the main characters of this remarkable narrative, and how God lovingly watched over, protected, and nurtured that main character. That person is Mary.

"I want us to see in the person of Mary that God does not just stand by and passively watch his people from afar, and then let bygones be bygones. Yes, it might seem that He sometimes does. But, according to His track record through Scripture—of which Mary is just one example—He does not.

He has always been intimately involved in His plan to redeem the nations. He passionately protects that plan. And He protects the people who are vital to that plan. He is a hands-on Lord and Savior.

"I want you to note first of all how God protected Mary socially and emotionally when she was carrying the Savior. God lovingly moved her far away from the hurtful gossip surrounding her pregnancy to the safe environment of her older cousin, Elizabeth, who lived near Jerusalem."

Kathleen elaborated on the point for three or four minutes.

"Secondly," she proceeded, "notice that God provided Mary with a comforting role model and mentor during her pregnancy. Elizabeth was an adult cousin who was also the recipient of a miracle and could thus understand and support Mary's situation, a cousin who was six months pregnant ahead of Mary and could model for her all the specifics of a pregnancy. Mary most likely witnessed, and learned from, the birth of John the Baptist. She could have even received lessons on how to breast feed.

"Thirdly, God did not leave Mary clueless about the Old Testament prophecies related to her forthcoming son. Remember, Mary was in the house of a sympathetic cousin who was married to a *priest*. I'll say that again; a *priest*. It is illogical to think that Zachariah, though mute at the time, did not teach Mary—via writing, via Elizabeth, or via another priest—all the messianic prophecies such as the virgin birth, the place of the birth, and the type of death Jesus would die.

Zachariah definitely knew the prophecies according to Luke one, verses sixty-eight through seventy-nine. It is no wonder then—in light of the conjecture that Zachariah indoctrinated Mary in all the Messianic prophecies—that Mary was willing to make the eighty mile journey to Bethlehem on a donkey during the final month of her pregnancy. She knew the prophecy about the place of the birth. She, therefore, knew that God would protect her and the baby, regardless of the difficulty of the trip. Otherwise, it is not logical to believe she would have risked her treasured pregnancy for such an arduous journey.

"God, in other words, did not leave Mary as a young teenager confused and uncertain as to what was happening. Since she was part of His plan, He protected her socially, mentally, spiritually, and physically. Plus, He enlightened her every step of the way. He even used Joseph, Elizabeth, Zachariah, the shepherds, the magi, Simeon, and Anna to directly reaffirm to her that she was not crazy, that her child was indeed the promised Messiah, the son of God."

Kathleen, according to the program, sat down at that point while one of the pianists moved to the Baby Grand and accompanied a female vocalist as she sang a tune composed from the words of Simeon, one of Mary's affirmers, in Luke 2:29-32.

The solo was almost mystical sounding in the backdrop of the candlelight.

The rendition, solemnly sung, emphasized Simeon's heartfelt proclamation - *Now, Lord, You can let me, Your servant, die*

*in peace as You promised. I have seen Your salvation with my
own eyes. You prepared Him before all people. He is a light
for the Gentiles and glory to your people Israel.*

At the completion of the song, Kathleen returned to the
podium.

"As you remember," she picked up, "God then protected
the Christ child from the hands of Herod by sending Mary,
Joseph, and the child across the border to Egypt, out of Herod's
reach.

"Of course, Mary and Joseph had not planned, when they
left Nazareth, to be away indefinitely. They had not packed
provisions for such a lengthy cross-cultural trip. So, how would
Joseph provide for his family's needs as they headed into a
foreign country? As the head of the household, he would have
certainly been thinking about this issue. Well, God stepped in
and provided for them in an unexpected way—by the hands
of the magi. With the gold. The frankincense. And the myrrh.

"In addition to the gold, the value of which you can easily
understand, the myrrh at this time in history was used
primarily by Egyptians as the principal ingredient for the
embalming of the dead. In Egypt, especially in Egypt, the
myrrh would be worth its weight in gold. Plus, and this is not
an insignificant point, myrrh was a natural antiseptic that was
used to clean wounds, prevent infections, and to clean teeth.
Thus, Mary and Joseph had their own first aid and dental
hygiene kit.

"And then there was the frankincense. Harvested in Oman
at the southern tip of Saudi Arabia it was exported by camel

primarily to Egypt where it was used regularly in religious ceremonies. About the time Joseph and Mary were headed to Egypt with their stash of frankincense, Caesar Augustus was reportedly sending ten thousand troops to invade the Oman area to find the source of frankincense and to control its production. So, frankincense, as well, was a big-ticket commodity.

"So, rest assured during this memorial season that God—as we so plainly see in the Christmas story—intricately and protectively encompasses His plan and His people. This is His track record. Thus, we can say with assurance that the church, the entity through which God broadcasts His plan of redemption to the world, will never be shut down or destroyed. Despite what is transpiring in our culture, God will always have a remnant of people. And He will always protect His mission."

In the shadows of the candlelight, Kathleen again took a seat.

Walter, who had recently been elected chairman of the new group of deacons, stepped to the podium. He thanked Kathleen for the inspiring message, then, as planned, called the people to come and kneel at the front of the sanctuary for a time of group prayer.

The people quietly spilled out of the pews and filled the area around the platform, backfilling the aisles as well. Some people knelt. Some sat. Some laid prostrate.

In the quietude that followed, God's Spirit seemed to usher the hearts of the people into a rare moment of mutual reflection.

Walter prayed first, earnestly thanking God for the way He had used Kathleen's influence to transform Lyons Central Baptist from a stagnant and sterile flock into a vibrant community where life change was occurring every week. He ended his prayer in tears.

For the next twenty minutes, individuals prayed aloud, one following the other. Most of the prayers were praises. Some were confessions. Some were pleas. A few were intercessions.

Someone, at that point, started extinguishing the dangerously low-burning candles.

And then, as if all distractions and time pressures were miraculously unfettered from life, pockets of prayer spontaneously broke out all over the moonlit room. Two or three started praying together here. Three or four praying together there.

To Kathleen, who was kneeling at the platform steps, it sounded like voices of prayer were rising up from literally everywhere across the assembly. She heard people praying for the town, for the church, for each other, for each other's families. She heard people sniffling and weeping. She even heard a few people quietly laughing with pure unadulterated joy. The overall phenomenon was unlike any prayer gathering she had ever experienced.

A few people slipped in beside her and prayed for her as well. She prayed for them with equal fervency.

Caught up blissfully in the Almighty's aura, she let the whole event unfold for another thirty minutes or so.

She then stood and invited everyone to stand with her. As much as she could distinguish in the minimal light, there didn't seem to be a dry eye in the building.

Without music accompaniment, she led the Christmas-eve crowd in a closing hymn - 'O Holy Night.'

Upon finishing the last note, everyone lingered for a few seconds of breathless silence.

When people finally started to disperse, there were hugs all around, quiet conversations, and smiles. Lots of smiles.

Kathleen spent the night alone. As she lay in bed, she thought again about Mary, the mother of Christ, and the way God had cared for her. In light of that particular Bible lesson, Kathleen thought again about her own life. She thanked God for helping sustain her through the love and kindness of people like Floyd, Ian, and all the supportive members at the church.

She hazily looked at the time on her bedside clock. As she faded, she whispered a prayer for Ian who had left nearly thirty hours ago for South Africa to spend Christmas day and New-Years week with his parents and sisters.

Kathleen enjoyed Christmas-day lunch with Floyd and some of his extended family.

She then went home and did some "grief-therapy" reading, in accordance with directives her therapist had given her.

56

On Monday afternoon, following the Christmas weekend, Kathleen—while working in her home office—received a call from Evelyn Huxley.

"We just found out," Evelyn declared with a still-heavy heart, "that Billy is being transferred to Coastal State Prison, just outside Savannah. From what we can understand, that's where he's going to stay while he serves his time."

Before Kathleen could respond, she heard Evelyn say, "Can you pray for us, pastor?"

"I'll be glad to, Evelyn." Right over the phone, Kathleen beseeched the Heavenly Father to somehow step unquestionably into Evelyn's circumstances and reassure her of His goodness. She prayed for Ray and for Billy as well. "When are the visiting hours?" Kathleen asked after she prayed.

"What I'm hearing at the moment is that visitation hours are only on Saturdays and Sundays."

"Okay, let me know when you have an address. Also, let me know if clergy have any special visitation rights."

"I'll call you as soon as I get the information. And thank you. Your role as my pastor, as I've told you over and over again, means more to me than you can imagine."

* * *

On Saturday morning, January 9, Kathleen sat across from Dr. Blitz in his downtown Savannah office. Dr. Blitz, in his fifties, was wearing his long, graying hair in a ponytail. His matching gray beard, nicely trimmed, gave him the look of a hip professor at a laid-back university.

"Were you able to read the compilation of stories I gave you?" Blitz asked.

"I did," Kathleen said. The stories replayed in her head. The dad who had accidentally shot, and permanently paralyzed, his sixteen-year-old son on a hunting trip. The mother who had lost her triplets— her only children, after thirteen years of trying to get pregnant—to pneumonia ten months following a healthy delivery. The military wife who had lost her husband of three years, the love of her life, in an IED accident in Afghanistan during his last day on tour. The fifteen-year-old son who had watched his single mom lose the use of both legs due to a white-water rafting accident.

"And?" the grief counselor asked.

Kathleen blinked. "The stories resurrected my own grief at first. And then, ironically, my grief seemed to dissipate as I took all the focus off my own story and began to see the pain of others. To know there are others out there who carry an unspeakable amount of grief, and to read those stories in detail, somehow gives me a weird sense of hope."

"Let's don't label it weird," Blitz countered. "Let's call it 'grief shouldering.' People help carry one another's grief just by the sheer fact that, due to their own angst, they feel the burden and the pain of the other person's load, right alongside them.

When we're hurting and we're around others who are hurting, especially those who are transparent, we feed off one another's determination to keep putting one foot in front of the other, to take one more breath, to survive one more day. We understand that we're not alone."

Kathleen squinted, then broke into tears. She nodded her understanding.

"Tears are good," Blitz assured her, handing her some Kleenex. "Let it flow."

And she did.

For a good five minutes, she sobbed, groaned, and blew her nose. "Will the pain ever stop?" she asked.

"Not completely," Blitz told her as he handed over more Kleenex. "Grief is like an endless succession of ocean waves. At the onset, when the storm first hits, the waves are monstrous and overwhelming, coming in one right after the other. You think you're going to drown as they knock you down and keep you under. But over time, as life starts to calm down, the waves spread out. At some point, like on a still sea, they grow weaker and come less frequently. It's pretty much the way it stays, except for the giant rogue wave that shows up occasionally and knocks you off your feet. Usually those waves are seasonal - for example, on the anniversary date of your loss, or on the days you pull out photographs and remind yourself of what life was once like."

Kathleen, with a full heart, asked several more questions.

Blitz answered each question thoroughly and frankly, with notable empathy. Kathleen learned that the Dr. himself had, eleven years earlier, lost his youngest brother, his closest sibling, in a drowning accident. Dr. Blitz knew the language of grief.

At the end of their hour together, Blitz gave her another compilation of stories to take home and read. "One day I'll ask you to write down your own story. Just as these stories will give you a small bit of hope, your story will one day give hope to others."

On her way out the door, Kathleen heard the Dr. add, "Oh, by the way, there is no right way to grieve. And no right emotion. Everybody grieves in his, or her, own way. And any way is okay, as long as it's not destructive to you or those around you."

Kathleen again nodded her reception of the counselor's words.

Skipping lunch, she used the GPS on her smartphone and drove straight to Coastal State Prison, about twelve miles north, on the periphery of Savannah, to see if she could visit Billy Huxley.

She had never been inside an American prison before. When she turned onto the state property, she was suddenly seized with a heavy sense of foreboding. The access road ran parallel to empty train tracks. And then, in the clearing beyond a slew of pine trees, the facility came into view. A fence that looked twenty feet high, topped with large coils of razor wire, tightly surrounded the buildings.

She promptly followed signs to the visitor's parking area, then headed on foot across the lot to the small brick building that stood out by default as the first checkpoint. A strong wind blew across the property and blew through her hair. The wind somehow enhanced her perception of isolation.

She walked up the ramp to the door and found it locked. She peeked through the door window, saw a uniformed officer, and knocked. The officer, a short bulky African American male, opened the door.

"I'm here to visit an inmate," she told him.

"I'm assuming you're on the inmate's approved visitor's list," the officer interjected.

"I don't know," Kathleen backtracked. "My name is Kathleen Rose. How can I find out if I'm on the list?"

"What's the inmate's name?"

"Billy Huxley."

"Stand here and I'll check."

The officer went into an adjacent office.

He reappeared a couple of minutes later. "I'm sorry, but you're not an approved visitor for that inmate."

"Then, how can I add my name to the list?"

"The inmate has to mail an application form for you to fill out."

Kathleen closed her eyes for a second. "Does it matter if I'm a member of the clergy?"

The officer looked her up and down and eyeballed her with suspicion, as if to say, *You…You are a minister; I've never seen a minister that looks anything like you.* When he opened his mouth, though, he said, "It doesn't matter who you are; you can't visit an inmate unless the inmate adds you to his list of approved visitors."

"No exceptions?"

"Only for attorneys."

Kathleen nodded her acknowledgement of the policy, thanked the officer, and left.

Back in the car and on the road, she found her thoughts whirling as she accessed I-95 to head back to Lyons. Her reflections bounced from the therapy session to the phone call she would need to make to Evelyn explaining her first attempt to visit Billy. Her thoughts then shifted to Ian. She would have very much enjoyed hanging out with him for the afternoon to just...talk. But he was currently in the air, flying back from South Africa. The faintest of smiles crossed her lips; she would at least get to talk to him by phone tomorrow evening or Monday morning when he was back in Savannah.

As she merged westward onto I-16, her thoughts turned to the worship service tomorrow morning. Walter was scheduled to speak. She knew he had something out of the ordinary planned. Perhaps she should give him a call and talk through the order of service.

* * *

For the final worship song, right before Walter approached the rostrum to preach to a packed-out building, all the members of the music team, at Walter's signal, swapped places with one another.

The lead guitarist sat down at the drums. The drummer picked up the guitar. The bass player switched instruments with the key board player. The lead vocalist picked up the violin while the violinist stood behind the singer's microphone. The backup singer traded places with the flutist.

With no public explanation, the musicians, at the thumb snap of the "new" lead guitarist, broke into a rendition of 'A Mighty Fortress Is Our God.'

Walter, sitting on the front pew, turned and purposefully watched the reaction of the crowd.

The instruments were immediately off key, off beat, and out of sync, and not by intention. The vocals sounded equally dreadful. The group sounded like a middle-school marching band rehearsing for the first time.

Walter could tell the attendees were confused, wondering if this was supposed to be serious, or some kind of joke.

After a minute and a half of torturing everyone's ears, the music team faded their volume and then halted in mid stride. Each of the musicians, without smiling, slowly left the platform and took their reserved seats in the audience.

Walter moved to the podium microphone.

"That was a horrible way to enter into the new year, two-thousand-sixteen, wasn't it?" He spread out his notes. "This is what happens when you marshal people to serve in areas where they are not gifted or experienced. As you turn your Bibles to First Corinthians chapter twelve—the chapter that spotlights the mix of spiritual gifts—I want to say a special thanks to Pastor Rose and to my professors at Ailey Bible College for teaching by word and by example that a local church functions more smoothly, more joyously, and more productively when those who are serving are serving in areas where they are gifted. We have all seen this exemplified right here at Central Baptist over the last six months. And what an absolute pleasure it's been. After witnessing the transformation of this church, and now understanding one of the reasons why, I'm wondering why pastors all over the nation insist on forcing their personal church-wide agendas on people when the people are not gifted, experienced, or interested in those agendas. The results are never pretty. No wonder pastors are frustrated. No wonder churchgoers are frustrated. Why can't pastors just let the gifts, experiences, and passions of their people dictate the direction of their churches?"

With that question hanging in the air, Walter launched into a simple verse-by-verse overview of First Corinthians twelve.

At the conclusion of the message, Walter asked the new deacons, the new treasurer, and the new finance committee members—all recently elected with their giftedness and passions in mind—to come to the front for a planned prayer of dedication.

Walter asked Troy to offer up a prayer for each of the people by name.

Upon dismissal, several people—young and old—offered Walter words of affirmation, telling him his upfront demeanor was improving with each turn at the pulpit. Willow, pushing Ida Mae in the wheel chair, was one of those encouragers.

Walking alone in his yard later that afternoon, Walter wept with gratitude at how much his life had changed in the last half year. Even his wife was thrilled with his new growth. Walter couldn't thank God enough for Kathleen and the impact she had made on his perception of things. For one of the first times he could remember, he was actually exhilarated about the future. Both for himself. And for the church.

57

Over the next eight months of 2016, as public interest surrounding Pastor Rose and Central Baptist waned, Eric's articles in the *Vidalia Times* about the church appeared less and less.

In late August, though, Eric felt compelled to write a new article in light of a significant update.

Bent over his keyboard on a sweltering Thursday afternoon, with the AC unit in the building temporarily down, he typed:

Lyons Central Baptist
Name Change

Lyons Central Baptist voted last week to officially reconstitute as the International Baptist Church of Toombs County, or IBC according to the abbreviated version.

Under Pastor Kathleen Rose's leadership, the Sunday attendance has grown over the last sixteen months from 80 to nearly 500, with two Sunday morning services, two Sunday night services, and

eight home groups that meet throughout
the week. Over 12 nationalities now
hold membership in the church.

Walter Johnson, chairman of the
deacon board, led the motion to
reorganize "in order to better reflect our
new heart and our current church body."

Floyd Baxter, deed holder to the
church property and CEO of Prime
Vidalia Onions, who installed Rose as
pastor in April 2015, says, "I totally
support the name change and the
reshaping of our church body. These last
months at Central Baptist have been the
greatest months of my Christian life,
bar none."

Eric saved the document and forwarded it to the graphics
department to be accompanied by a photo he had taken a few
weeks earlier - a photo of a packed out auditorium with an
African American couple, an Asian woman, a latino teenager
and two white adult males all getting ready to distribute
communion juice together.

Eric leaned his head back and smiled. He agreed with old
man Baxter. The last few months had been the most invigorating
months of his Christian life as well. He had gone so far as to
rededicate his life publicly to his Creator and Redeemer in a

recent Sunday evening service. And he couldn't have felt more joyous. Or more complete.

* * *

On Saturday morning, August 27, Kathleen sat silently for a second or two to compose herself. She looked at the young lady across from her. She then looked at Dr. Blitz.

Blitz, sitting in his regular office chair, offered her a gentle nod.

Kathleen had done this once before when Blitz had brought in a grieving father—grieving the loss of his eight-year-old son who had fallen off the back of a four-wheeler and broken his neck, a four-wheeler the father had been driving—and asked her to tell the man her story of watching her son being castrated and murdered. That experience of sharing with the grieving stranger, though excruciatingly painful, had somehow been cathartic—even if in a minor fashion—for both her and the father, as they sobbed together and released built-up guilt and agony.

It had been only the fifth time she had told the story of her son's death—once to the Malian police, once to Floyd Baxter, once to Ian, once to Dr. Blitz, and once to the grieving dad. Sharing with the father had been, in Blitz's words, "agony bearing the burden with agony," or "grief shouldering" as he had repeatedly labeled it.

Blitz was now asking her to share her rape story with the young woman—twenty-two and single—who had been gang raped while drunk and on spring break in Florida several months ago.

Kathleen stared quietly at the young female for a few seconds. The girl, looking irretrievably lost in an emotional dark hole, was about the age of many of the young ladies in her church. The girl was pretty, but was delicate looking. Kathleen suddenly wanted to help her.

Kathleen tried to open her mouth, but only managed to slightly inhale. She tried again, only with the same results. She closed her eyes. "Okay," she finally managed to say as she lifted her eyes.

Back in the car, she broke down and wept. The young girl, before they had left Blitz's office, had fallen into her arms and clung to her like a child, sobbing, leaking tears all over her neck and shoulder.

"How have you survived?" the girl, gasping and wheezing, had wanted to know.

Kathleen had spent the last fifteen minutes of the session, with shared tears, just holding the girl and telling her she was going to be okay, that God AND people like Dr. Blitz would help her find healing, even if it was one small bit at a time.

The girl had thanked her profusely for sharing her African story and for encouraging her.

Staring through the windshield of her parked Toyota, Kathleen suddenly knew for the first time that her pain would never be wasted. The insight gave her a tiny slice of hope in an often hopeless-feeling world.

She smoothed out her dress, then used the rearview mirror to brush her hair. She then started the car and drove to the northern part of town where she once again pulled her Camry onto the access road at Coastal State Prison.

"Give me special wisdom," she petitioned the Heavenly Father as she drove through the pine trees that flanked both sides of the road.

She had sent letters to Billy five different times since his incarceration asking him to consider adding her name to his selected-visitor's list.

Billy had completely ignored her written communications. And then, out of the blue five weeks ago, she had received an envelope from him. Inside had been a visitor's application - no letter, no explanation, just the blank form to be filled out.

She had filled out the document with all the pertinent and personal information required and promptly mailed it back to the prison. She had received a reply last week from the prison office notifying her that she had been approved as one of Billy Huxley's accepted guests, and would remain on the list as long as Billy Huxley sanctioned her visits.

When she parked in the visitor's section, she turned off the engine and mentally ran through the visitation rules - no purse could be taken inside, no gifts could be taken in; only her car keys and ID that would be left up front with the security guard.

Before she entered the check-point building, she had to stand in line outside and fill out a form requiring the name of the inmate she was visiting, her own name, street address, tag number, employer, and check-in time. When she was called inside the tiny building, she was asked to submit her driver's license and car keys to an official behind a window and was given a numbered chip that she would use to retrieve her keys and license on the way out. She then walked through an upright scanner. An officer at that point used a wand to check her again for any contraband. She was then sent out the backside of the building to follow a concrete path to a huge metal gate. Whoever was monitoring the camera that was focused on the gate electronically unlocked the portal for her to pass through into a huge metal cage. The gate relocked behind her. She walked to the other side of the cage to face another locked gate. It too was electronically opened, then relocked as she passed through. She followed the pathway to the front of the main building. Guided by "Visitors" signs, she turned right once inside. She passed through another cage, this one with concrete walls and steel doors, and finally exited to a stairway that led down to the visitor's room.

Entering the visitation room, she saw dozens of people sitting at short tables, across from inmates they were visiting.

She was stopped by a black female officer. "Who are you here to see?" the officer asked brusquely.

"Billy Huxley," she told the woman.

"All right, have a seat at the table in the back corner, and we'll call him up."

Kathleen proceeded to the table the woman had singled out.

When she sat down, she slowly gazed around the small cafeteria-like room and tried to relax. She saw several men staring at her, momentarily ignoring their own visitors. She intentionally avoided eye contact with them.

Nevertheless, she anxiously studied the room. Fifteen or so inmates, she guessed, had been brought up to sit with their visitors. Nearly every one was engaged in serious dialogue. Guards stood attentively at their posts around the confined area. The inmates were all wearing white cotton shirts and pants. Blue stripes cascaded down the front and center of the blue-collared shirts. Blue stripes ran down the sides of the pants. '*Dept. of Corrections*' was imprinted in bold black letters across the back of the shirts.

As she waited for Billy to be brought in, she decided she wouldn't bring up the subjects of church, theology, or his criminal case—unless he mentioned the subjects first. Otherwise, she would talk about…

And then she saw him enter the room from a side door. He immediately glanced around, looking for her.

She subtly waved until he spotted her.

With a look of listlessness dominating his countenance and posture, he came straight to the table and sat down.

He nodded and, as if embarrassed, mumbled a jittery "thank you for coming."

She noticed his dark hair had been buzzed. And he had lost a significant amount of weight. She didn't know if they were allowed to shake hands, so she kept her hands in her lap.

"Hi, Billy," she said.

There were a few awkward seconds before they settled into a semi-comfortable exchange of words about his ongoing endeavor to adjust, the prison food, his cell and cellmate, and his daily routine.

She asked most of the questions. He answered with minimal words.

When they reached another moment of awkward silence and she realized he wasn't going to initiate questions of his own, she decided she would attempt, for a few minutes at least, to take his mind off his surroundings.

"I understand from your mom that you like to fish."

"Yeah," he said, looking as if he wondered where the conversation was suddenly going.

"You want to hear a good fish story?"

"I guess," he said quietly.

"Well, I don't know if you remember it being mentioned, but I lived in Africa before I moved to Lyons. One day several years ago, before my husband died, he went fishing alone in a big river not far from our house. He was using a huge net hoop. It was tied at the bottom end and opened at the top end with a square wooden frame. It was a device the Africans used. Anyway, he waded into a shallow part of the river until he was waist deep, then submersed the net and started scooping. The water was murky, so he scooped in the blind for about thirty minutes without any luck. Didn't catch a single fish. And then, when he was about to give up and call it a day, he put the hoop in the water one more time and suddenly pulled up a huge catfish that started fighting. He struggled to get it to shore. He thought he was going to lose it. When he finally got it out of the water, he couldn't believe it. He estimated the fish weighed at least fifteen pounds. It was a record for him. And he was close with his estimate. The scale at our house showed the fish weighed just shy of fourteen pounds."

Kathleen registered only a hint of life in Billy's eyes. Maybe she was boring him. He was so lethargic, it was hard to tell.

"When he cleaned the fish in the backyard," she continued, "he was shocked all over again when he found a half-pound perch inside the catfish. But the biggest surprise came when he found a pebble stuck in the perch's gills. And it wasn't just an ordinary pebble."

Kathleen waited at that point for Billy to say something, or to at least signal with his eyes to please finish the story.

His eyes finally flickered with a nominal amount of curiosity.

"Before I tell you what the pebble was, I guess I should tell you that the country where we were living is a major exporter of gold."

Kathleen paused again till Billy's eyes said, *go on.*

"And yep," she revealed, "it was a gold nugget, a gold nugget that he sold for two hundred dollars." Kathleen snickered. "I persuaded him to buy some proper fishing gear with the money. And he did. And you know what?" Kathleen smiled. "He fished with that professional rod and reel and all his special flies for several years before he died. And... ironically, with all that expert equipment, he never caught a fish again that weighed more than a pound or two."

"How did he die?" Billy asked, showing little, if any, interest in the fish story.

Kathleen sighed inwardly. She felt she had flopped in her effort to engage the young man in any kind of pleasurable dialogue. "He died from cerebral malaria," she told him, choosing not to explain.

Billy just nodded.

Kathleen, after only forty minutes, elected to wrap up her visit. As she stood to leave, she asked, "Is there any news I can pass along to your mom?

Billy appeared to ruminate over the question, then replied with a simple, "No, I guess not."

Kathleen wondered if her visit had been a waste.

As she said goodbye and turned to leave, she heard Billy say, "Can you please visit again?"

She turned, curious if she had heard correctly.

"Can you visit again?" he inquired a second time. The expression on his face was one of a child asking a parent for comfort.

"Sure…sure, I'll come and see you again."

Billy thanked her with a modest nod.

At 5:30 PM, Kathleen was sitting at the Noble Fare restaurant in downtown Savannah with Ian. Fresh cut flowers and lighted candles topped a beautiful white linen tablecloth. Soft piano music was playing in the background. The coziness of the small dining area, with its classy decor, provided a quintessential milieu for a romantic outing.

After a day with the therapist, and then with Billy Huxley inside prison walls, Kathleen basked in the relaxing atmosphere.

Her conversation with Ian, over a meal of Herb Roasted Chicken and Crispy Duck Breast, was so easy and enjoyable. They talked about politics, Ian's work, the Lyons church, Kathleen's therapy session, and a movie they had seen recently on television. They even laughed to the point of nearly embarrassing themselves.

"Thanks for an amazing evening," Kathleen told him during dessert. "I really needed this."

Ian reacted with a beautiful smile. Then suddenly he turned serious. He cleared his throat and leaned in over the table. He inhaled. "I've been thinking. I…uh…I just love every moment I'm with you. I'm constantly thinking about you; I can't help it. I'm even miserable when you're not around. You're absolutely magic to me. You've affected me like no other woman ever has." His eyes narrowed. "I've said it before, and I'll say it again; I love you, Kathleen. My mind loves you. My heart loves you. My eyes love you. I…" His baby browns instantly portrayed his utmost sincerity. "So…I…I want to marry you."

Kathleen's mind instantly stumbled, not because of the question, but because of its timing. She closed her eyes to absorb the moment.

Ian carried on, his voice devoured with passion. "I want to marry you more than anything in the whole world."

Kathleen slowly opened her eyes. Ian had pulled out a diamond ring. Kathleen felt her face squint with emotion. Her eyes watered. She reached over and grasped his hand. "Can we go outside and talk?" Before Ian could respond, Kathleen saw disappointment blitz his eyes. Her heart sank. "I need to tell you something," she added. The weight of the extra words unfurled more confusion across Ian's face.

Out on Jefferson Street, with their bill paid, she took his hand and started walking.

"I'm sorry, Ian; but I'm not staying," she broke the news, her voice quivering.

Ian stopped dead in his tracks and looked at her with total bewilderment. He let go of her hand.

Kathleen said, "I haven't told Floyd Baxter yet, but in April —at the end of my two-year commitment—I'm moving back to Africa."

"Moving back to Africa!" Ian shook his head. "For a month? Two months? What does moving back…"

"Indefinitely."

"What?"

Kathleen took the ring and looked at it. It was a platinum ring with a thin, tapered shank with set diamonds sparkling halfway down each side. The center stone was brilliant. It was the most beautiful engagement ring Kathleen had ever seen. She lifted and tenderly kissed Ian's hand. "I love you. More than you'll ever know. And if I've somehow brought magic into your life, then know you've brought twice as much into mine. You've taught me how to love again, and to be loved. And through the gift of Dr. Blitz, you've helped bring more healing into my life than I ever thought possible."

"Then why?"

She choked up. "I can't explain it other than it's a decision

I…I have felt God pressing me to make over the last couple of months."

Ian stood speechless.

Kathleen gently placed the ring back in Ian's hand and continued, "I can't shake the feeling. I've tried. I've looked at it from every angle." Kathleen massaged her hands. More tears appeared beneath her eyes. "I'll go back to carry on my work with Malian women. And to honor the sacrifice of my husband and son."

Ian stared at her in disbelief, then said somberly, "Kathleen! You are one of the most rational women I've ever met. I say that in all seriousness. But what I'm hearing right now just doesn't make sense. It doesn't even sound like you. I mean…look around you in Lyons. A large part of the community has been changed because of you. Because of what you've done. Because of what you're currently doing. And you're honestly just going to walk away? I mean…are you sure this is God's voice you're hearing? Or is this…"

Kathleen held up her hand. "Please don't."

"Please don't what?"

"Please don't make this any more difficult than it already is." Kathleen ran her fingers intensely through her hair. She could see Ian struggling to remain calm.

Ian took a moment of silence. His face twisted as he lowered his head and pinched the bridge of his nose. "All right," he finally conveyed, looking her in the eye, "The decision is absolutely beyond my understanding." He puffed. "It's a shocker actually. So…I'll…uh…I'll just wait and see if you change your mind over the next few months. In the meantime I'll pray that God will give you extraordinary wisdom and clarity as you weigh your plans."

"Thank you. I…"

"And, of course, I'll hold this in confidence," he mumbled in a dispirited voice, still in shock.

Kathleen nodded her gratitude.

For a few seconds, Ian simply stood and tempered his breathing. "And if you weren't thinking of moving back overseas?" He rolled the engagement ring around in his fingers.

Kathleen looked at the ring. "Then I would say, give me a few more months of healing and ask me again."

Ian accepted the answer with a look of fragile hopefulness. He reached out and took her hand. For a long time they walked along the downtown sidewalk in silence, valuing each other's presence.

After a block or two, Ian finally broke the muteness. "If you go through with the plan to move back to Africa, then I'll wait for you. Even if I have to wait three, four, or five years."

58

Saturday AM, November 12, 2016

At Coastal State Prison, Billy Huxley stepped into the small room adjacent to the visitation area. He held up his arms as he was patted down and searched. When he was cleared, he stepped through the metal doorway into the hall where the visitors were seated.

He spotted Kathleen in no time. As difficult as it would be, he was determined to somehow thank her today. Besides his mom and dad, Kathleen was the only other person from the outside—despite the multiple visitation forms he had mailed out ten months ago to friends and relatives—who had taken time to visit him. And he would never be able to adequately explain just how much those visits had meant to him. In addition to her initial visit, Kathleen had returned to see him twice in September, twice in October, and now on this bright Saturday morning in November. Each of the previous two-to-three-hour visits had lifted him out of his caged reality and transported him mentally and emotionally into a world that was normal. The sessions had been like a permissible prison break, if only for a few minutes.

He still didn't fully understand why the lady would spend the time and energy to go out of her way—after he had snubbed her in civilian life so many times—and give him so much support and encouragement. Whatever the reason, though, he didn't care. He was just grateful. And deeply affected. More than any free person could ever comprehend.

In downtown Richmond, Virginia, Yacoob was en route on Saturday evening to hang out with a couple of his Muslim buddies for a fun night of computer games and billiards.

A couple of miles before reaching his destination at a house in East End, he stopped at a convenience store to purchase a pack of Chesterfield Blues. When he stood at the checkout counter and told the Indian-looking clerk what he wanted, the man said, "I'll need to see some ID."

Yacoob pulled out his wallet and showed his driver's license.

The clerk examined the ID, nodded his head, and turned to retrieve the Chesterfields from a plastic rack.

While waiting, Yacoob haphazardly glanced at the photo on his license. His mind was suddenly and unexpectedly held spellbound. He looked back at his license. Why had he not thought of this before? He was still gaping when the clerk said, "That'll be five, seventy-five."

Yacoob paid with cash, put the wallet back in his jeans pocket, took the Chesterfields and returned to his car.

Inside his well-worn and cluttered SUV, he sat silently for a few seconds. He slapped the steering wheel. The first thing tomorrow morning, he would try to find Angela Carter's stateside address by searching online for her driver's license information. All his attempts over the last sixteen months at trying to find her via university and college websites had proven absolutely futile.

And in his latest conversation with his cousin in Mali—by pay phone—his cousin had expressed a newfound urgency for Yacoob to try to find the woman's location as soon as possible.

Yacoob had agreed to intensify his efforts.

He had wondered all along, though, if there were other Ansar Dine associates in the States who were actively searching for the lady as well. Or if he was the sole hunter. He had once broached the subject, but his cousin had outright evaded the question.

The next morning, with the sun well above the horizon, Yacoob, still sleepy-eyed, slid into the chair at his bedroom desk. He booted up his laptop. He rubbed his eyes, then typed *'Angela Carter's driver's license information'* into the search engine.

A plethora of data-collection websites appeared up and down the screen.

One of the sites was called MoleData. The name alone garnered his attention. On impulse, he clicked the link. The homepage that popped up presented empty slots for entering the first and last name of the person being searched for. The page also required the input of a selected state. Yacoob typed in Angela Carter's name. He, of course, had no idea which state she was residing in. But just to see what would happen, he clicked on the first state that was listed - Alabama. He waited while the site made it known that it was searching state and county records. And then finally, before the site revealed any information it had collected, it required the user's email address. Yacoob backed out of the system immediately. He definitely wasn't going to submit an email address.

He tried another website called Public Records Port. Again the homepage offered blank slots to type in the first and last name of the person of interest. But this particular website gave the option of selecting "any state" as the desired location. Yacoob typed Angela's name, then clicked "any state."

As the website searched national data bases, a half dozen questions popped up, one after the other, for Yacoob to answer, such as "Has Angela Carter ever lived in Texas, Arkansas, or Missouri?" "Has Angela Carter ever been convicted of a felony?" "Is Angela Carter related to Scott Nicholas Carter?"

Yacoob answered "I don't know" to all the questions except two. To the question about Angela Carter's possible kinship with Scott Nicholas, Yacoob answered "yes." And to the question, "Is Angela Carter over 30 years old?," he answered "yes."

Finally, a list of more than one hundred Angela Carters' emerged on the screen. The "BEST RESULT," though—topping the list—was the Angela Carter related to a Scott Nicholas Carter.

Bingo!

Yacoob's nervous system was both stunned and adrenalized. He quickly clicked on the tab that said, "Open Report."

A page opened where Yacoob had to "acknowledge" that the following report might reveal embarrassing facts and comments regarding Angela Carter's life. When he ticked the "acknowledgement" box, a page opened requiring the input of his name in order to proceed further.

He stopped and contemplated. He eventually entered a bogus name and hit the return key, wondering if the digital footprint could still be traced back to his computer.

And then...

A window popped up saying he had to purchase the data for $9.99. A credit card would be required, thus obliging him to give his real name and credit card number.

He stared at the screen and cursed. This would leave a digital trail, visible to all law enforcement agencies, leading right to his bedroom. He just wasn't willing to take the risk, especially knowing that Angela Carter would probably be eliminated as soon as he told the "Defenders of the Faith" her whereabouts. He snorted and threw a Bic pen across the room.

He exhaled slowly and pushed air through pursed lips. What now?

Feeling anxious, he returned to the bed and laid on his back, staring upward at the ceiling. After awhile, he closed his eyes and willed himself to fall into an unknotted rhythm of breathing.

In almost no time, he got out of bed again and returned to the laptop. He patiently explored a few of the other listed sites, all of which required a credit card payment to procure data. Feeling his patience being tested, he at some point carelessly abandoned the string of websites and simply typed Angela's name into the search engine. He crossed his arms and stared at the screen. He then added the words "Christian missionary in Africa" following Angela's name, something he had not done since the first days of his search.

A new batch of links appeared. Ignoring them, Yacoob nonchalantly clicked "images" on the menu bar. He had scoured the images of Angela Carter multiple times before. But all the posted photos that had shown up on previous searches—and there were many—had been taken during her years in Mali.

His eyes quickly scanned the remembered pictures from the last year. He scrolled down the page.

And then…

He did a quick inhale. Something different stood out in the pattern of photos.

He did a visual retake.

And then…wait…was it…?

It was. There, far down on the page of images, was a photo of Angela Carter he had not seen before.

He immediately clicked on the photograph. And then clicked on the website link where the photo was featured.

The digital connection landed him on a webpage of the Vidalia Technical College in…Vidalia…Georgia. It appeared that the photo of Angela headed some type of school article. Yacoob drew his next breath slowly and started reading.

A New Role Model In Town
by Heather Blankenship
(A junior)

If you're wondering where VTC students are hanging out these days, well, many of them, believe it or not, are hanging out at Lyons Central Baptist, especially on the weekends. And "Why?" you might ask, are young millennials so enamored with an organized church? The answer is the "pastor." Or should I say "Pastorine." That's right; the pastor is a lady. And not just any lady. Her name is Kathleen Rose, and she is one extraordinary individual. She's passionate; she's smart; she's beautiful; and she has a heart for young people. For the last three months she has opened her arms and encouraged Christian students from VTC and Ailey Bible College to step up and let their voices and talents be heard in the Lyon's Sunday morning services. Drawn in by Rose's wonderful personality, sharp mind, and strong leadership, dozens and dozens of students have joyously embraced her welcome. Students—both male and female—are now sharing testimonies from the pulpit and are leading the worship sessions with their vocal and music skills. An unusually high number of students are even hanging out at her home on Saturday evenings, at her request, for meals, games, and serious Bible studies. And no subject has been off limits in the roundtable conversations that arise. Oh, did I mention that the lady has a Masters in Theology? And that she served as a missionary in Africa for more than a decade? As a result of her local influence—through teaching, listening, advising, leading, mobilizing, caring, and exemplifying—guys and girls alike are taking their faith more seriously. Inspired by the lady's total package, many students are even respecting the role of the "clergy" again in a day when the profession has seemingly lost its nationwide relevancy. Kathleen Rose has definitely become a new role model for the younger generation in Toombs County. Thank you, Kathleen Rose. You are appreciated more than you know.

Yacoob winced as he tried to temper his breathing. He scrutinized the photo one more time. This was a photo of Angela Carter wasn't it? Yet, the article identified the woman as Kathleen Rose. Could Angela Carter possibly have a twin sister?

Or could the angle of the lighting and the odd angle of the photo be misleading? Was it just someone who looked nearly identical to Angela Carter?

Yacoob tried to think clearly.

The "Kathleen Rose" highlighted in the article had spent a significant amount of time as a missionary in Africa. It had to be Angela Carter. So, was Angela living under an alias?

Yacoob looked at the date of the article - July 2015. That was well over a year ago. The date certainly fit the timeline of Angela's escape back to America. But why had he not seen the photo before? And why would the photo, if connected to the name Kathleen Rose, now show up under a search for Angela Carter? Yacoob shook his head as if attempting to shake out the utter puzzlement. He could only guess the accidental find had something to do with the words "missionary in Africa" used in the accompanying article, the exact words he had typed into the search engine. He swiftly accessed Google maps. He learned that Vidalia and Lyons, side-by-side towns in Georgia, were 550 miles from his location in Richmond, a road trip of approximately ten hours. He lightly gripped his hair. Should he plan to drive there next weekend and establish visible contact, and make some inquiries, just for confirmation?

He ultimately decided—in order to maintain innocence in the eye of the law—to simply call his cousin and dutifully pass along information per the original request. Nothing more. Nothing less. Perhaps that alone would be pleasing enough to both the Ansar Dine organization and to Allah.

59

Kathleen took a bite of the carrot cake and looked again at the program lying on the conference-room table.

Wednesday, November 30, 2016
"Town Influencers" Annual Luncheon
Hampton Inn Vidalia

Founder, Host, and Moderator Floyd Baxter
CEO Prime Vidalia Onions

Lunch
Grilled Chicken Breast
Roasted carrots and peppers
Macaroni and Cheese
Cranberry, Cheese, Sweet-Potato-Chip Salad
Carrot Cake

POST-LUNCH SPEAKERS - 5-MIN EACH

Jacob Reed
Mayor, Vidalia

Charles Fisher
Board of Education Director
Toombs County

Aaron Young
Chief of Police, Vidalia

Kathleen Rose
Pastor, International Baptist Church
(Formerly Lyons Central Baptist)

Abigail Waters
City Council Chairman, Vidalia

Christopher Daily
President, Coastal-Plain Bank

Oliver Hatch
CEO, B&B Construction

Daniel Brown
Rotary Club President, Vidalia

There were four more movers and shakers listed on the program. A superior court judge. Another bank president. And two more CEOs of prominent businesses.

When Kathleen looked up and took another bite of cake, she saw Floyd now standing at the miked podium, momentarily carrying on a whispered conversation with an assistant. It looked as if he was preparing to introduce the first speaker.

Kathleen was intrigued by the character of the small, intimate closed-door gathering. She was equally intrigued by what each of the speakers might say. She had overheard Floyd on a couple of occasions in the past mention the luncheon and refer to it as a "shot-in-the-arm, power-networking lunch." And then, two months ago, Floyd had invited her to participate in this year's program.

It was, of course, her first time to attend. And she felt honored. But, she secretly wondered if Floyd now regretted inviting her to be one of the speakers. He had not been pleased, not in the least, when she revealed to him two days ago that she was planning to return to Africa sometime in the upcoming spring. He had huffed, complained stridently under his breath, and made her swear she wouldn't spill that particular information at the "town influencers'" luncheon. She had, of course, promised. But the old long-time supporter had been unusually aloof ever since.

In some ways, she felt truly guilty. She knew Floyd had dearly hoped she would choose to become a long-term, if not permanent, resident of Toombs County and continue to serve indefinitely at the church. And there were parts of her that wanted to do just that. The thought of marrying Ian, building a secure nest, and serving God in the ever-changing milieu of the International Baptist Church was frankly comforting, even pleasing. But for reasons she couldn't clearly identify, the urgency to return to Africa and carry on her work with Malian women was starting to trump everything else in life. Maybe the reason was to perpetuate the legacy of her husband. Maybe it was because she had learned from the counselor over the last eleven months how to face her grief and actually capitalize on it. Maybe it was because there were so few laborers in Mali who were willing to fight for the welfare of the millions of

Malian females, and yet so many who could take the reins of the church in Lyons. Maybe it was because it was God's unspoken priority for her at this season in her life. Maybe it was a combination of all those reasons. Or none of those reasons. Maybe it was...

"All right, let's get started," Floyd's voice suddenly emanated over the sound system.

Kathleen shifted in her seat.

Everyone turned and gave Floyd their attention.

"I trust you enjoyed your lunch and your conversations," the old CEO said, "but it's time now to...to..."

Floyd suddenly went silent as a look of scary confusion spread across his face. Almost immediately, his expression was replaced with one of acute pain. Floyd immediately bent over and grabbed his stomach. He emitted a spine-tingling groan. He tried to stand upright again, but fell to his knees.

The two men sitting at the table closest to him leapt out of their seats and grabbed his arms. They attempted to lift him to his feet. But he pushed them away and remained scrunched over, groaning and rocking in discomfort.

Mild panic blanketed the room. Was he having a heart attack? A stroke?

"Somebody call 911," a man's voice demanded.

Kathleen saw three or four men pull out their phones and start punching numbers.

Up front, Floyd laid down on the floor and curled up into a fetal position. His groans intensified. The men around him were trying to assess what should be done until paramedics

404

arrived. One held his head and tried verbally to keep him engaged. Another gave him a sip of water.

"Paramedics are on their way," someone shouted.

Kathleen, tense to the max, felt even more guilty now. As she watched Floyd breathing erratically, laid out on the cold tile, she wondered fleetingly if her private announcement of leaving in the spring had in some way added undue stress to his aged system.

She stood up and moved in Floyd's direction. She felt her own chest now heaving.

60

"All right, Mr. Baxter," the oncologist reported, his shoulders somewhat slumped. "the pathology report is one no one welcomes." The doctor blinked uneasily. "All the reports show you have stage-four pancreatic cancer. And that it's metastasized to the liver."

Floyd, lying in a private room at the Provincial Medical Center where he had been for six days, stoically nodded his understanding. The oncologist had already forewarned him of a likely diagnosis. Floyd looked beyond the doctor, down the hallway to the nurses' station where a Christmas tree heralded the upcoming holiday season.

Floyd closed his eyes. "How many days, weeks, months do I have?"

"My best estimate is two to five months." The doctor's voice was solemn.

"So, eight, fifteen, twenty weeks," Floyd rephrased as he slowly opened his eyes.

The oncologist nodded a slight, but heavy confirmation.

"So, no possible treatment that might give me a little extra time?" Floyd questioned softly. But he was pretty sure he already knew the answer.

"You told me during our tests that you've had stomach pains, vomiting, and irregular stools on and off for the past several months. I don't know; had you come in earlier, there might have been a chance. But now; I just don't…"

"No experimental treatments that might be available in Canada or Mexico?"

The cancer specialist shook his head. "There are always alternative treatments, but there aren't any legitimate ones that have a convincing track record. In my opinion, they would just be a wild shot in the dark." The doctor started to say something, then looked as if he changed his mind to say something different. "To be honest, in all my years of practice I've only known two people who walked away from pancreatic cancer that had aggressively metastasized and then lived to tell about it. And in both cases, the cancer was not nearly as advanced as yours. So, I…"

"So, I just go home to die." The words were more a statement than a question.

"You can always opt for chemo, but I think it would just add to your stress and discomfort and never even come close to eradicating the tumors. Look…at the moment, you're mobile. You're in your right mind. I would say go home and get your house in order. Bring closure to things—your work, your finances, your relationships—with a certain element of dignity. You'll have meds to manage your pain and nausea. And a hospice nurse will be there when it's time for round-the-clock help."

Floyd looked over at the hospital window, and closed his eyes again. He had been sick very seldom throughout the course of his eighty-two years. Should he fight now for a few extra months or years, and be miserable doing it? He slowly blew a puff of air. He had lived a rich, full life. Even his last seven years as a widower had been blessed. Why not go out, as the doctor said, in a state of dignity?

He squeezed his forehead with his fingers. He definitely had not seen any of this coming, but it appeared his time was up. In spite of his millions, he would now go the way of all men.

He shifted his eyes to the bedside chair and table. Both were laden with cards, flowers, and chocolates. There was even a new holiday sweater that Kathleen had given him. He was, without dispute, surrounded by co-workers, employees, neighbors, and friends who loved him. What more could a dying man want?

And if he had learned anything in life, he had learned from Kathleen in the last twenty months that living with ruthless pain didn't have to produce a victim mentality. One could still be a giver and an inspiration to those around him. As a man of faith, he would likewise—with God's help—refuse to bellyache, beg, and whine. Rather, he would accept his fate with strength and grace.

As the example of Kathleen stuck in his mind, an additional thought quickly surfaced. He decided he couldn't withhold the information any longer. He had to tell her.

If he was going to be brave, then he needed to be brave in every regard.

Whether he was ready or not.

It was time.

61

On Sunday morning, two weeks before Christmas, Kathleen—attired in an elegant rose-colored sweater—sat in her platform chair with her head bowed and listened to Troy conclude the public prayer for Floyd Baxter. Minutes earlier at the start of the service, she had informed the congregation of Floyd's diagnosis and prognosis and had called for a special time of intercession for the old patriarch. Several people had prayed out loud, one after the other, for the influential senior. Troy, now a lead deacon, was bringing the outpouring of public supplication to a close.

Kathleen wished Floyd were present to hear the heartfelt prayers of the people. But she knew he was too proud to be pitied and doted on in a public Sunday morning setting. He had explained he would make his next church appearance in a week or two once the news about his situation had become "old hat."

When Troy sat down and the musicians launched into a contemporary rendition of "The First Noel," Kathleen started to weep. With her furtive plans to return to Africa, and with Floyd's terminal illness now looming as an imminent fact of life, she could feel change in the air. And the sensation toyed with her emotions. She would not only be losing Floyd, her lifelong secret supporter. She would be walking away from a congregation that loved her. She would be saying goodbye to so many new friends. And perhaps foremost, she would be leaving Ian and possibly a grand new start to life. She missed him dearly, even now as he was away on another business trip. She could hardly imagine the ache of potentially never seeing him again.

But the internal pull to re-enter Mali and pick up the work she had left behind had become relentless, despite the potential risk she would be taking. The unyielding pull would not let her relax, no matter the precariousness of the plan. She had determined, though, to defer her departure until Floyd had succumbed to his deadly cancer. This was only ethical in light of all the generous things the man had done for her through the years. In the meantime, she would start grooming Walter openly to succeed her as pastor, and hope and pray the church would follow her lead.

As she stood at the commencement of the next song, and wiped at a lone tear, her thoughts were unexpectedly sidetracked when she saw Evelyn Huxley enter the sanctuary…with her husband, Ray, at her side.

Kathleen did a visual retake.

And another.

When she quickly saw that Ray's demeanor was one of meekness and humility, and not one of ill intent, she felt a giant smile unroll across her face, along with new tears. Why…the man was even holding Evelyn's hand.

Kathleen closed her eyes and whispered inside her private world, "Thank you, Jesus! I don't know what's happening, but thank you for answering the countless prayers that have been offered up for this man. Thank you, thank you, thank you!" She then heard herself emit an inescapable feel-good chuckle. At that point, she couldn't help but repeatedly cast her sights at the couple. She saw one of the young ushers lead them to some of the only available seats in the room - seats next to an Indian family.

The look in Ray's eyes, once he was seated, reflected an understanding that things had changed on a far-reaching scale. And, for whatever reason, it looked as if he were finally willing of his own accord to at least test the reshaped paradigm.

All through the subsequent songs, readings, testimonies, and announcements, Kathleen's thoughts and questions regarding Ray Huxley danced in and out of her head.

And then in a quick span, it seemed, it was her time to stand up and teach.

At the microphone, she thanked several people by name for their part in the service. She then jumped right in to her message.

"Our text this morning," she announced, "is the Gospel of John, chapter one, verses one through thirteen." She waited as Bible pages rumpled across the room. When she was content that most of the people had found the passage, she read the verses aloud without interruption.

She then said, "The focus of our message this morning is 'Why is Faith Necessary?' We are, of course, entering the Christmas season where the Christian community worldwide highlights the incarnation, the one-and-only God, the Creator of the universe, taking human form. Many people across the globe examine the evidence for this teaching—the eyewitness testimonies, the array of stupendous miracles, the claims of Jesus Himself, the bodily resurrection that the enemies of Jesus could neither explain nor refute, and the post-resurrection appearances—and say 'yes, I believe.' Others look at the same evidence and say, 'no, I don't believe.'

"As a matter of fact, verse ten in our text says, when He came into the world, the world in general at that time did not recognize Him. The Greek word for recognize means to perceive. They looked at the evidence right in front of them and said, 'no, I don't interpret it to be legit; I don't believe.'

"On the other hand, many according to verse twelve, who saw the same miracles and heard the same words did perceive Him to be God incarnate, the Savior of the world. And they embraced Him.

"With that said, I want us to focus for a few minutes on the word *perception*. Perception is our understanding and interpretation of things; our mental impression. And I submit to you that no two people share the same perception about everything in life. Everyone's perception is absolutely and totally unique. That's because each person's perception is balanced atop his or her own unique combination of personal temperament, upbringing, education, presumptions, preferences, philosophies, fears, dislikes, experiences, and a host of other variables.

"Plus, by default, everyone's perception has limitations. That's because their experiences and intellect are limited and their preferences are typically selfish to the point of self-deception. So, no single person, no matter how experienced or educated, has a full and accurate perception about all things, especially about the ethereal things of God.

"Therefore, a final step of faith is always required in order to trust the teachings and revelations of the triune God. God has made sure there's enough evidence to nudge us in His direction. But the final leap into His arms must always be taken by faith.

"If you are waiting for every detail of the Gospel message to make absolute sense, then you will never, never settle things between you and God.

"Even the apostle Paul, a magnificent scholar, admitted, 'I only see through a glass dimly.' He acknowledged that his perception was deficient. Faith was required for him as well."

Kathleen directed everyone's attention to a few additional verses that emphasized 'faith' as a prerequisite for salvation. She then closed her Bible.

"At this point," she said, "I've asked Li Chung, a fourth year Environmental-Technology major at Vidalia Technical College, to come to the platform and share his journey from atheism to skepticism to belief. His story will illustrate the essence of my message."

Kathleen took a seat.

Li Chung—looking a little nervous, but excited—made his way from the front pew to the podium. Dressed in a black suit and gray tie, he looked utterly serious about what he was going to say. He pulled the microphone downward to accommodate his shorter stature.

"My name is Li Chung. I was born in Shanghai, China. I moved to this country, to the state of California, with my parents when I was fourteen. I never thought about God when I was growing up in China. Only when I moved to America was I exposed to Christianity. And much of that initial exposure was on TV. And to be truthful, most of what I saw seemed like playacting and not authentic at all. To me, Christianity at the time honestly didn't seem like a serious worldview for someone who was formally educated."

Li Chung adjusted the mike again.

"But…in my first year of college in California I met a couple of Christian professors who caused me to take a new look at the Christian faith. Both men had doctorates. They answered my questions about Christianity in a way that incorporated science, history, and logic. For me, they gave the Christian tenet an air of credibility. Because of their influence, I looked at Christianity for the first time without dismissing it as western mythology. I gradually transitioned from atheism to skepticism. And then I moved with my family to Vidalia.

"During the summer break before I enrolled at Vidalia Tech, a Chinese girl I met invited me to attend a four-day Christian apologetics conference called Truth For Skeptics. It was held at a big church in Macon. I decided to go with her for three reasons. Number one, I was new in the area and it would give me something interesting to do. Number two, the girl was really pretty."

A hearty laughter undulated through the crowd.

Li Chung grinned in response.

"And number three, I was really curious. If there really was a Jehovah God who created all things and then died for the sins of the world, I wanted to hear more of the persuasive arguments. And boy, did I. The apologist, over the course of the four days, gave reasonable answers for the existence of God, for creation, the validity of the Scriptures, the historicity of Jesus, and the resurrection of Jesus.

"I didn't immediately convert to Christianity, but the apologist's presentations created a hunger inside me to know more. It was a hunger unlike anything I had ever experienced. I went out and immediately devoured six books that presented the different facets of apologetics. I listened to dozens of Christian-versus-Atheist debates on the internet. I read numerous testimonies and biographies of former atheists and agnostics who eventually confessed that Jesus is Lord. And about eight months ago, when I perceived that the evidence for Christ was too overwhelming to deny, I took that final step of faith that Pastor Rose just talked about. I humbly trusted Jesus as my Creator and Savior."

A chorus of enthusiastic ovations swept the room.

"The relationship I now have with God has changed my life forever."

Another round of ovations pierced the air.

"Going back to the pastor's message," Li concluded, "it's obvious that some people need to perceive only a small bit of evidence and are immediately content to take a huge, huge leap of faith. Others, like me, need to perceive a lot of evidence. And only then are we content to take what we consider a minute step of faith. Nevertheless, in the end, faith—whether great or small—is required to connect with the Creator."

Li lowered his voice and with utmost passion pleaded, "If you are sitting here this morning as a doubter, I encourage you with all my heart to continue to look at Christianity with an open mind. The historical evidence, the philosophical evidence, the scientific evidence, and the life-change evidence will one day convince you too that Christianity is not, and cannot be, a myth or man-made religion, but rather the flawless plan of a loving God who longs to take you into His Almighty arms and restore you to a place of wholeness. Please know that I'm willing to talk to you after the service if you have an interest."

Li meekly nodded toward the audience, then exited the platform.

A few people applauded.

Kathleen, as planned beforehand, promptly turned the podium over to Walter.

Walter wasted no time. He gave a public invitation as he loved to do. It was an invitation to anyone and everyone to come forward during the reflective music to ask questions, to seek prayer, to join the membership of the church, to request baptism, or to take that final step of faith, acknowledging Jesus as Creator, Lord, and Savior.

During the keyboard player's soft rendition of 'I Surrender All,' eight people made their way to the front.

Kathleen, Troy, and three of the new deacons were there to welcome and interact.

Within ten minutes, two of those who stepped forward—an Asian girl and an American boy—knelt and, with daring faith, reached upward to their Maker for life-changing reconciliation.

Kathleen remained standing at the front of the auditorium when the congregation was dismissed. Within a minute or so, a dozen or more people had lined up to talk to her.

Her first exchange was with an African American lady who expressed a grand "thank you" for the worship service. The lady had recently become a member of the church and was basking in the freshness of the community spirit. The lady had been invited months ago to the church by Willow and Ida Mae and couldn't be more excited.

Kathleen was enjoying the one-on-one chat when she randomly noticed Ray Huxley out of the corner of her eye. He was lingering in the crowd, immersing himself in what appeared to be a friendly conversation with one of the church's longtime members.

As Kathleen greeted the other people in the queue and carried on brief exchanges, she saw that Ray continued to hang around. She got the impression he maybe wanted to speak to her when she was free. And indeed, when she finished talking to the last person in line, Ray, who had prolonged his mingling, immediately excused himself from his company and headed her way.

Kathleen inhaled slowly.

As Ray approached, he made no gesture to shake her hand or offer a hug. He simply walked up, peered at her, and said, "I was wrong about you." He paused for an awkward amount of time as he looked her in the eye. The gears of his thoughts were plainly turning. "And I want to apologize."

Kathleen's emotions were instantly flushed with adrenalin and she didn't know why. At the same time, her mind brimmed with a dozen thoughts. She wanted to say, 'And…what's brought about the sudden change of heart?' Instead, she issued a gentle nod and waited.

"It's my son," he told her. "The changes I've seen in him over the last month are…" Ray choked up. "are…almost unbelievable. And he says it's because of you."

Kathleen again wanted to jump in and talk, but refrained and let the man continue.

"Outside the family, you're the only one who's taken the time to visit him. And it's not because others haven't been approved. And they know it."

Kathleen kept silent.

"And I just want you to know that your visits—and whatever the two of you have talked about—have touched his heart in a way that I, even as his dad, could never have imagined. Every time I see him now, he's talking about the new thing he's learning in the Bible, things that are changing his attitude, his outlook, his behavior. It's…it's amazing actually. And I just want to say thank you."

Kathleen didn't know what to say.

"By the way," Ray added, "when the two-year vote comes up in April to keep you or let you go, I'm going to stand up in the meeting and encourage everyone to vote to let you stay."

Kathleen now felt tears seeping from her eyes. In the moment, she wasn't going to dare tell him she would soon be moving back to Africa.

"Oh…and one more thing," Ray said. "Evelyn has been right all along; you're a fantastic teacher. I'm the one who's missed out by not being here. And I'm really sorry about that."

Kathleen felt all the air go out of her. Choked up, all she could manage to do was reach out and give the man an emotional hug.

62

On Monday morning, Eric Sawyer sat in a window seat at the Huddle House, sipping coffee. He had just devoured a plate of bacon, grits, two fried eggs, and a pecan waffle. He was staring at a piece of lined notebook paper.

With his mind deliberating, he set down his cup of coffee and picked up a pen. He began jotting down the first draft of his next article.

Lyons Central Baptist
(Now International Baptist)
Losing "Guardian Of The Vote"

Floyd Baxter—CEO of Prime Vidalia
Onions, and the man responsible for
bringing Pastor Kathleen Rose to
International Baptist—was recently
diagnosed with terminal cancer. Mr.
Baxter, as the deed holder of the
International Baptist Church property,
installed Rose as pastor in April 2015.
The controversial move was accompanied
by a mandate that Rose would stay
uncontested as pastor for two years at

which time the congregation would be
allowed to conduct a church-wide vote
to keep Rose or demand she step down.

The question now arises: If Mr.
Baxter does not survive until the two-
year mark, will the congregation honor
the "two-year" rule.

Eric put down his pen and looked out the window. He
stared for a moment at the traffic whizzing by on the four
lane. He looked back at what he had written. After serious
contemplation, he asked himself if he really wanted to draw
attention to Floyd Baxter's terminal illness, solely for the sake
of gossip and intrigue. Yes, Pastor Rose and the leadership
team of the church had yesterday morning publicly announced
Baxter's diagnosis to the congregation. But that particular
announcement had been issued in a spirit of sensitivity, for the
purpose of rallying the people to help and to pray.

Eric sipped more coffee.

His thoughts continued to stack up. His fondness and
appreciation for the old man had grown immensely over the
last year. The old gentleman possessed a type of moxie that was
good for society, but that was missing in abundance all around
the country. In truth, the man should be honored, not simply
used as a cheap journalistic prop.

Eric's hand crept closer and closer to the handwritten draft.
He eventually crumpled up the paper and, on his way out,
tossed it in the garbage bin.

* * *

On Friday afternoon, nine days before Christmas, a stateside undercover operative for Ansar Dine entered the city limits of Vidalia, driving a nondescript rented Honda Accord. He had driven down from New Jersey. He was a thirty-one-year-old second generation black Muslim American from Malian heritage. His mission was to simply find and visually identify Angela Carter. If Angela's identity could be confirmed in this small town in the southeastern United States, a hired hitman would be sent in the next month or so to eliminate the target and provide proof of his work.

The man drove the Honda slowly through Vidalia. He noticed there were quite a few black people in the area. He observed them pumping gas, entering and exiting restaurants, and driving vehicles. Good, maybe his presence as a strange black man wouldn't immediately arouse curiosity or suspicion. Regardless, he didn't plan to talk to anyone anyway. He definitely wasn't going to leave behind a trail of people who had been asked the whereabouts of Angela Carter or "Kathleen Rose."

Using his phone's GPS app, he followed directions to the Lyons Central Baptist Church address on Broad Street.

The name International Baptist Church featured on the property's roadside marquee, however, confused him. But when he saw the name of the pastor listed as Kathleen Rose, he brushed off the bafflement. Obviously there was a simple explanation. And, at the moment, that bit of information was useless to him.

Beneath Rose's name, he noted, was the time of the Sunday morning church service. He committed it to memory.

For the ensuing fifteen minutes or so, he scouted the surrounding area in his car, then proceeded to the town of Claxton, twenty-five miles eastward, where he checked in to a hotel.

On Saturday, he spent a lot of time carefully reviewing everything in the "Angela Carter" dossier that had been given to him - a disclosure of her physical characteristics (her height, estimated weight, build, eye color, hair color, and age), a stack of photos of her that had been taken in Africa, a collection of Malian newspaper and magazine articles highlighting her and her work with Malian women, and a lengthy report of the failed murder attempt with all the specifics.

Sitting in his hotel room, he then went online and read all the archived articles from the *Vidalia Times* about "Kathleen Rose" and the Lyons Central Baptist Church.

When he felt he was fully prepared for his reconnaissance, he put away the folder and its contents and went for an afternoon walk.

Around 12:20 PM on Sunday, with only seven days left till Christmas, Walter finished up a sermon from Psalm 119 on the critical importance of studying, contemplating, and memorizing God's Word. He tied his presentation to the holiday message that the 'Word became flesh and dwelt among us.'

"God's Word, in living form or written form, has no equal when it comes to truth, influence, and power," he concluded.

Kathleen, down on the front pew, couldn't help but be tickled. Walter's confidence, poise, and clarity of teaching seemed to improve each time he stood behind the podium. Her investment in his life, along with the weighty influence of the Bible college and professors, was shaping the man into a far more meritorious individual than she, or anyone, could have ever hoped.

At that instant, Walter looked down at Kathleen.

At Walter's request, Kathleen, along with three of the deacons, stood and faced the crowd and prepared to receive anyone who might come forward during the public invitation.

And indeed, several people moved to the aisles and headed toward the front when the invitational hymn commenced.

Kathleen spent five minutes with one young lady alone, a Hispanic who wanted to know how to actually study the Scriptures. Kathleen in a quick overview told her about character studies, word studies, and book studies. She then agreed to link up with the girl in the upcoming week or two and walk her through a sample exercise. The lady, with anticipation in her eyes, thanked her profusely.

Kathleen received one other person, an American teenager who asked Kathleen to pray he would find strength to apply God's Word to a situation at home with his father. By the time Kathleen finished praying aloud for him, the service had come to an end.

Walter dismissed the crowd with a quote from John Quincy Adams, one of America's founding fathers: "'The Bible is of all books in the world that which contributes to make men good, wise, and happy.' Now go," Walter exhorted, "Immerse yourself in God's Word and be better, smarter, and happier. It's the greatest gift you can give to yourself this Christmas season. Blessings. And have a great week."

Kathleen remained standing at the front. As usual, following a Sunday morning meeting, people flocked to talk to her. And she enjoyed it. Always had. She felt that to be accessible as a pastor, even in a cursory context, was vitally important.

The first to approach her was a middle-aged couple who had visited three or four times before. They were the parents of the young drummer who served on the church's worship team.

"We just want to thank you again for asking Jayden to be part of the band," the husband told her. "It's made a huge difference in his life. Not only is he in church every Sunday, but he's…what shall I say…a lot more spiritually aware. And we couldn't be more thrilled."

Kathleen affirmed the dad's observation and bragged on the boy even a little further. She then offered a brief prayer with them for the ongoing spiritual growth of their son.

Evelyn Huxley then stepped up to speak with her. Evelyn's heart was simply overflowing with praise at how Ray was more and more finding peace with God, with himself, and with life. And she had to share it.

"It's almost like I can breathe again inside my own house," Evelyn chuckled. "Why, the man's even apologized for all the tension he brought into the home. And he's promised he's going to do better. I mean…look at him over there with Troy. He's even grinning and laughing."

Kathleen smiled. "I'm seriously proud of both of you," Kathleen told her. The two ladies hugged in earnest, then exchanged a few more words of rejoicing.

When Kathleen saw the next person in line, she was momentarily dazzled by the big bold smile from the visiting black man.

He was confident he could execute the move without arousing any suspicion. He knew he didn't have a Malian accent. He sounded purely American. And if the need arose, he was entrenched in all the facts and data to back up the lies he was about to tell.

He reached out and shook the lady's hand. "Hi, my name is George. I guess you're Pastor Rose."

Kathleen nodded. "I am."

"I'm just passing through, but I stopped by this morning as a favor to my grandmother. She lives in Warner Robins, but she used to live in Vidalia. She still subscribes to the *Vidalia Times*. And she's been following your story here at the church. She says you were a missionary in Africa for quite a few years. Anyway, she just wanted me to come by on her behalf and say thanks for your heart for the black man, not only in Africa, but here in Georgia as well. She's been inspired by the strength you've shown to integrate the Christian community here. As a second generation Nigerian American, she's grown up with a lot of racial abuse here in the south. And not many white people are able to win her respect anymore. But you have, and she just wanted you to know. So, I promised her I would stop by and tell you."

The lady's dynamic blue eyes, he noted, tried to stay zeroed in on his. But she blinked involuntarily, almost nervously, when he mentioned Nigeria, just two countries away from Mali.

He let his eyes divert for a second or two to her neck. He was looking for a possible scar.

"Well," Rose replied, "tell your grandmother I'm both humbled and honored that she would send you by to convey her sentiment."

He let his eyes scan her neck one more time. And there. Was it…? Yes, he was sure of it. It was indeed a scar. His glimpse was quick, but he was positive his eyes hadn't deceived him.

"I'll do it; I'll tell her." He then acted as if he were going to step away, but stopped. "Would it be okay if I took a picture of us?" he asked, trying to sound sheepish. "I think it would thrill her."

The question caused her to stumble unexpectedly in her response. "Maybe another time," she finally managed to say. "There are other people waiting to talk to me right now."

He could tell immediately by the shift in her tone and composure that she did not want to be photographed. And he was certain he understood why. He started to persist, but felt that abject pushiness might shatter his cover.

He smiled again. "I understand. Perhaps another time, then." He shook her hand one more time. "All right, well…

thanks for all you're doing." At that point, he casually walked out of the building, exchanging friendly "hellos" with a couple of other people. He promptly made his way to the rental car he had parked strategically in the rear parking lot, across the street from the church.

He waited until nearly all the vehicles had left the lot. He then positioned his car parallel to a row of tall hedges that lined the property of a small single-family house. He pointed the car toward the back of the sanctuary where he guessed Rose would exit the building. He pulled a high-powered camera from a cardboard box and wrapped it in a bulky winter coat and set it on the dash, pointing it toward the building. He put on a cap to confuse anyone who had earlier registered his appearance and might still be around. He looked into the camera's viewfinder and adjusted the focus to bring the church's back door into a clear and precise image. He then waited with his car running.

When there were only three cars left in the parking lot, parked just outside the building, he finally saw Rose step out into the December sunlight. She was talking to one of the ladies in the church. He quickly leaned over, focused the camera on her and clicked off ten to fifteen pictures.

He quickly moved the camera to the seat, shifted his car into drive, and made an immediate lefthand turn out of Rose's sight.

He drove directly back to his hotel in Claxton.

Within minutes of entering the room, he edited his photos. He then one more time watched a portion of a 45-minute video that had been forwarded to him from Ansar Dine. The footage showed Angela Carter speaking to a group of Malian women in Africa. He compared the video footage of Angela Carter with his newly taken photos and his fresh visualizations.

He clinched his fist and pumped it several times in celebration. There was absolutely no doubt. Angela Carter was living under the alias Kathleen Rose. And she was residing in Lyons, Georgia.

He would track her over the next two or three days to locate the address of her residence. He would then submit his full report, along with photos, to Ansar Dine.

When Kathleen left the church parking lot, she pointed her car toward Floyd Baxter's. She had agreed to have lunch with him today. When he extended the invitation four days ago, he had sounded unusually serious, even somewhat anxious. She suspected he wanted to talk further about his final days. She offered up a heartfelt prayer for him.

She then called Ian in Savannah where he had been scheduled to teach a Sunday school class at a community church. He answered within two or three rings.

"Hi, how did it go?" she asked gingerly. She eventually pulled the car into the outskirts of a shopping center parking lot so she could concentrate on the call and not frustrate other drivers.

She and Ian talked for a solid ten minutes about the Sunday school experience - the lesson, the preparation, the people, the classroom interaction, and the post-class conversations.

"Your teaching has elevated my teaching to a whole new level," he told her with excitement. "I'm no longer content to be just an okay and nominal teacher."

She blushed. "Are you still planning to head this way for the evening?" she asked, partly to change the subject.

"I'll be leaving Savannah around two-thirty, right after I eat lunch and talk to my parents in Johannesburg."

"I'm looking forward to the visit," she assured him. "Oh… and when you get here, remind me to tell you about the black man who visited the church this morning. The visit actually frightened me for a few minutes. But I'll tell you all about it when you get here."

63

As Kathleen entered through the massive gateway at Floyd's estate, she knew he was not having a good day. He had already hired three home-care nurses to take shifts and be available for him around the clock. The nurse serving on the day shift had called Kathleen earlier that morning, at Floyd's behest, and explained that Floyd's prior plan to attend church today had been changed and he would not be showing up after all. He just felt too weak. Kathleen had asked if the lunch appointment should be cancelled.

"No, it's of the utmost importance that you visit today," the nurse stressed, passing along Floyd's response word for word.

Wondering what was going on, Kathleen parked in the driveway and walked up to the door.

The nurse—a slightly overweight middle-aged black woman—answered the doorbell. It was a nurse Kathleen had met a week ago. Kathleen greeted her with a nod.

"Oh…I'm so glad you're here," the nurse declared, sounding relieved. "Mr. Baxter seems desperate to see you."

Kathleen followed the caregiver through the carpeted house to Baxter's bedside.

When Kathleen entered the room and saw Floyd lying in the bed, she was shocked. She had recently talked to Floyd two or three times on the phone. But the last time she had seen him was six days ago. And she could hardly believe her eyes. His face was drawn and gaunt. As a thin man by nature, he now looked frail, as if he had lost an additional fifteen to twenty pounds. He was a proud man who now looked nearly helpless. She had never seen a person physically decline so rapidly.

"I know. It's not a pretty sight," Floyd said in a strained whisper. "I think the doctor's prognosis of two to five months was a little too optimistic." Floyd pointed to the chair beside his bed. "Please, take a seat."

Kathleen, still in shock, sat down.

In a slow, strenuous movement, Floyd shifted in his bed. "There's a letter there," he said, pointing to the mahogany night-stand beside Kathleen's chair. "It's an apology." He immediately choked up. "And it's long, long overdue. I had intended to stand up in church next week and read it publicly, but I think I've waited too late. So, I would like for you to read it now in private and next Sunday in public." Floyd cleared his throat and started to weep. "And then I want you to give a copy to Eric Sawyer at the Times and tell him to publish it so that it will stand permanently on the record books."

Kathleen could feel her countenance growing utterly solemn and forecasting a dozen questions.

"Please. Just read it," Floyd said. "All your questions will be answered. I've left nothing out."

Kathleen slowly lifted the envelope from the nightstand and removed a collection of folded pages. She thumbed through the paper - eleven handwritten pages.

Floyd motioned for the nurse to be dismissed.

When the nurse left the room and closed the door, Kathleen leaned back in the chair and started reading at page one.

Three or four minutes into the pages, she threw her hand over her mouth and gasped. She looked at Floyd, an eruption of tears flowing from her eyes.

He returned the tears.

She continued to read. But did so through unrestrained sobbing, sniveling, and face wiping.

When she finished the letter, she couldn't talk.

She stood up and continued to wipe at the stream of wetness on her face. A part of her wanted to run out of the room. Another part wanted to drop to her knees and grasp Floyd's hands. But the wild and explosive emotions surging through her body made her feel physically paralyzed and held her in place. She just stared at Floyd and tried to bring her breathing under control.

"And all this is true?" she eventually gasped.

Floyd offered an intense half-nod. "Please forgive me." The plea sounded as if he didn't really believe she would forgive, or that she even could. It was simply a desperate move so she could at least hear the words uttered from his lips before he died.

Kathleen continued to stare, her thoughts and feelings now flying, like uncontrolled shrapnel, in a thousand directions.

Kathleen canceled Ian's planned afternoon visit. That evening, she could not stop pacing the floor of her house. Her array of emotions was peaking off the chart. She didn't fall asleep until four o'clock the next morning.

* * *

The following Sunday, Christmas Day, Kathleen arrived late at church. She had notified Walter earlier in the week that she would be rushing in and rushing out. When she took her seat on the platform, she was inhaling and exhaling in short breaths. She was plainly nervous and had no idea what to expect as a result of what she was about to do.

She looked out over the auditorium. As her eyes slowly scanned the room, she spotlighted certain individuals, along with all the memories wrapped up in their lives.

Sitting near the front were Ray and Evelyn Huxley. Ray's arm was placed around his wife. Gazing at them, Kathleen felt her heart sigh with both contentment and pensive heaviness.

Alexa, Marcos, and Valery, along with eight or nine other Mexicans who they had introduced to the church a year ago, were sitting as a group in the middle of the audience. They were all smiling.

Willow and Ida Mae were sitting at the edge of the aisle as usual, with Ida Mae in her wheelchair. There were several other black families scattered throughout the crowd, primarily because of Willow's unabashed support throughout the community of her pastor.

Kathleen fixed her eyes on all the young college students who had become, in many ways, the backbone of the church. There was an absorbing story connected with so many of their faces. Dipping into those memories, Kathleen clutched her brow with shaky fingers.

This wasn't going to be easy.

She spotted several new converts, highlighting them one by one. "Oh God," she prayed, "Watch over them; please!"

Her feelings especially spun off the rails when she looked at Walter and Troy. Those precious, precious men—with their monumental transformations, sacrifices, and alliances—would never be forgotten.

And right before she was expected at the podium, she stared down at Ian on the front row. He was the only person, other than Floyd Baxter and Eric Sawyer, who knew what was coming. Ian's facial features expressed a thousand versions of heartache and sadness.

And then suddenly, the music ended. The musicians descended the stage. It was time for her to approach the microphone.

At the big podium, she grasped the wooden edges to hold herself steady. She sniffled, then leaned toward the mike.

"Good morning," she said softly.

"Good morning," hundreds of voices replied.

She took a deep breath. She could suddenly see all the eyes staring back at her, eyes filled with questions about her uncertain demeanor.

"As you all know," she finally managed to say, "Floyd Baxter—the one who built these facilities with his own personal money and who still holds the deed to the property—has been diagnosed with pancreatic cancer and is dying. It appears as of today he might have only a few weeks left, if that. He had intended to stand here this Christmas morning and read a personal letter to you. But he is now bedridden and is unable to be here anymore. So, he has asked me to read the letter in his place."

She paused and nearly choked up. She hesitated until she could breathe again.

"Following the letter, I will tell you a story. And then I will say goodbye."

She closed her eyes to squeeze away the tears.

A palpable and monstrous silence instantly overtook the audience. It seemed as if literally everyone stopped breathing.

"Today—this morning and tonight—will most likely be my last time to stand on this platform. I will ask Walter to step up, starting tomorrow, and serve as your interim pastor. And I would like to recommend that you even vote him in as your full-time pastor. He's capable. He's got a servant's heart. He loves the Scriptures. He loves the God of the Scriptures. He loves you. He loves this church. And he loves this community."

People from wall to wall, it seemed, were still locked in an airless stupor.

Kathleen lifted the pages of Floyd's letter. She could feel her hands shaking. "I will first read Mr. Baxter's letter, and then in closing I will share with you a personal story." She took a long, deep breath and began reading.

"*In 1954 I was a junior at Georgia Tech. I was 19 years old. And for the first and only time in my life I fell head over heels in love. She was a student at Georgia State, a school a few city* blocks from Tech. I met her for the first time at The Varsity. It was a beautiful fall Saturday afternoon in late November. I was sitting alone eating my lunch and studying for my semester exams. And suddenly she entered my area of the restaurant. She was holding a tray of food, looking for a place to sit. As she stood there looking around, I realized I was holding my breath. She was about five-foot-six and was the most magnificent creature I had ever seen. Everything about her mesmerized me — her posture, her long gorgeous hair, her bright eyes, her face, her lips, her arms, her profile from head to toe. She held my eyes captive. I literally couldn't stop staring. Even when she found a seat and sat down, I couldn't stop staring. I was even impressed by the graceful way she ate. I fell in love with her right then and there, and I didn't even know her. I wanted so badly to rush over and introduce myself. But what could I say? I certainly didn't want to come across as a bumbling idiot. So I just sat and stared and longed to look her in the eye and tell her what kind of impact she was having on me.

And then it happened. When she finished her meal and got up to leave, I saw she had forgotten her scarf, still lying in one of the chairs. So, I jumped up, went over and grabbed the scarf, and caught up with her. At that point, she had exited one of the side doors and was standing outside. She was already looking for the scarf - in her coat pocket, in her satchel. When I walked up to her and held out the scarf, I found that I couldn't even speak. All I could do was stand there and appreciate the beauty staring me in the face.

She looked at the scarf in my hand, then looked at me and smiled. It was a smile that could have been the source of a hundred poems, a smile that only a divine creator could fashion. 'Are you okay?' she asked. Even her voice was exquisite.

I just gently shook my head.

She laughed and said, 'Usually boys talk to me when they approach me.'

I melted. 'Can I walk you to wherever you're going?' I asked her, suddenly emboldened.

'It might be way out of your way,' she said.

'No problem. Can I take your books for you?'

She cocked her head. 'Are you sure about this - a white boy walking side by side through the streets of Atlanta with a black girl?'

'I'll hold my head high,' I assured her.

She laughed and said, 'I like you,' then handed me her satchel. She put her arm through mine and we started walking.

And for the next four months we were inseparable. Her name was Bernadette. We talked endlessly, about anything and everything. We laughed together. We cried together. We studied together. We went to concerts together, went to movies together, hiked together, partied together, and sometimes just sat in silence together. Our bond became so intense that I could hardly concentrate on anything else. I just barely passed my classes. And then in March, we learned she was pregnant. And contrary to what might have been expected, we were elated. At that point, I was so madly in love that I was ready to drop out of school, get a job, and raise a family. There was no one else on earth who I wanted to spend the rest of my life with. In the very minutes she told me she was pregnant, I asked her to marry me.

She wept and said 'yes' and hugged me with such passion that I can still remember the embrace as I write this letter over sixty years later.

Up until my proposal, we had both kept the relationship concealed from our parents. Her father was a pastor of a thriving church in Birmingham, Alabama. My father was a city councilman in Macon, Georgia and was preparing to run for governor of the state. We suspected that neither of them would be thrilled when they learned that their kid was headed into an interracial marriage. After all, such a marriage could easily jeopardize their images as civil leaders. Their careers, career dreams, and positions of influence could be tainted, maybe beyond repair.

We underestimated their response. They weren't just non-supportive; they were both explosive in their outrage. They demanded an immediate breakup.

When they discovered we were not complying with their mandate, Bernadette's father promptly moved her back to Alabama. My dad threatened to cut off all my support - for school, automobile insurance, food, for everything if I didn't 'grow up and exercise some damn common sense.'

Our worlds collapsed. As youngsters, we felt completely overpowered and outnumbered.

Believing I had no other recourse, I backed out of the engagement. I allowed the people in my life, the culture, and the circumstances to take from me everything I counted dear.

I've wished every day since then that I had been a man and told my dad 'hell no.' But I didn't. And I've hated myself for it. Even till this very day.

As for Bernadette, she fought to keep the baby. Even though her mother and father were disgraced that their daughter was having a mixed-race baby out of wedlock, an illegal abortion in a back alleyway was totally out of the question due to her father and mother's religious convictions.

In September of that year, Bernadette gave birth to a healthy baby girl. She named her Ella. Bernadette missed several years of college in order to raise her. Yet, with resolve and determination, she was eventually able to go back to school and earn her Bachelor's degree. She carried on with life and became very successful. But she chose to never marry. In one of our secretive phone conversations, she said to me, 'You will always be the man of my life. I'm content to have no other.'

I became a basket case. No matter how much I wanted it, circumstances never allowed me to know Ella, my own daughter. And it tore my heart out. I only heard reports about her the few times Bernadette and I were able to talk by phone.

Ella, I learned, married at the age of eighteen, right as she was graduating from high school. She married a white man from Dalton, Georgia who had grown up in a broken home where his parents cared very little for him. The man's name was Robert Mixon. A year after the marriage, Ella and Robert had their one and only child, a baby girl who they named Angela - Angela Marie Mixon."

At that point in the reading, Kathleen had to halt everything and fight to compose herself. She knew that the people in the congregation didn't yet understand the connection. But in a few minutes, they would.

She closed her eyes, opened them, and carried on with the recitation.

"Bernadette was only able to enjoy her granddaughter for a couple of months. Bernadette was soon thereafter found dead in a mysterious house fire. A year prior to her death, she had established the Atlanta headquarters for the National Conference of Black Mayors and had become a leading voice for civil rights. Many believed her death was a racially-motivated murder. Yet, no one was ever indicted for criminal involvement.

Anyway, something deep inside me died the day I heard about her passing.

And then when Angela, my granddaughter, was four years old, her parents—my daughter Ella and her husband Robert— were killed in a motorcycle accident on Fort Mountain, outside Chatsworth, Georgia. Angela, I discovered later, was sent to a foster home in Chatsworth.

I should have immediately gone to the courts and fought for custody when I learned of her situation. But, by that time, I was already married to Barb and had established a promising business here in Vidalia. And like a coward, I couldn't bring myself to sit down with Barb and come clean about my past. She had no idea that I had had a daughter, plus a granddaughter.

And then one day, when I couldn't bear the guilt any longer, I went for a long walk with Barb and told her everything. Everything. She listened in cold silence. I told her I wanted us to take legal custody of the young girl. Barb, a woman very much given to social status, looked at me with an expression of utter contempt and betrayal. She put her finger across her lips and said, 'You will never bring this up again. Never. It's over. If you

441

ever talk about it again, I will file for divorce. And I will expose you publicly. As a southern gentleman, respected and trusted by everyone who thinks they know you - you will be left in ruins. I'll take everything.'

From that day onward, mine and Barb's relationship was soured with an element of emotional detachment. No matter how hard I tried, I could never win her totally back. At the same time, I gave up the dream of meeting my granddaughter. I hated myself for being weak, for not doing what was right, regardless of the consequences.

To compensate for my lack of freedom to bring Angela into my home, I established a secret fund to help support her in life. Not even my accountants knew about the fund.

As an anonymous supporter, I assisted the foster home where she lived. I paid for her prom. I paid for her college. I paid for her first car. I financed her all through life, even as an adult. And even after she married. I've continued to keep track of her through all the years. And I've continued to support her. I can say today that I am so ridiculously proud of her. She has beaten her circumstances in life. She has survived so much loneliness and pain. She has risen to the top. She has become a person that's far more influential than I have ever been. So, I've made an important decision. And nobody at this point in my life is going to deter me or hold me back from doing what's right. To hell with the consequences."

Kathleen paused. She felt her shoulders stiffen as she approached the final paragraph. She tried to brace herself for what was to come by pretending she was meshed in a dream that would speedily fade. She gripped the pages harder and continued.

"*As most of you know, Barb and I never had children together. That's because she was barren. So, as I'm lying here in my bed dying I have no living children, or surviving siblings, to be the beneficiaries of my will. But I do have a living grand-daughter. And to help make up for my many regretful decisions, and failures, as a father and grandfather, I'm leaving everything to her, my sole heir - Angela Carter.*

Or as she is known here in Lyons, Georgia - Kathleen Rose."

64

When Kathleen finished reading the last sentence of Floyd's letter, it was as if a shock wave from an exploding bomb had ripped through the Christmas-Day crowd. The initial quietness in the aftermath was so heavy it rendered people physically immobile.

And then the expressions of chaotic confusion—via words, grunts, and gasps—erupted from all quarters of the room. What had just been revealed could never again be contained or controlled. It was the type of small-town news that would become legendary gossip. And would be talked about repeatedly for years to come.

And it wasn't over.

"Yes," Kathleen said as she laid the letter back down on the podium, "My real name is Angela Carter. And I am Floyd Baxter's granddaughter. And like you, I am equally dazed by everything this letter reveals."

Kathleen blew her nose into a handkerchief.

"I learned only a few years ago, for example, that Floyd is the individual who has secretly supported me through the years. And I just met him for the first time face to face when I flew into Atlanta at his invitation about twenty months ago. I had assumed all along that I had just been one of Floyd's charity projects. I honestly didn't know until last Sunday evening when

Floyd asked me to read this letter in private that he was my biological grandfather. I was stunned to say the least. My initial response was one of absolute exasperation and even anger. How could he have left me to grow up in the foster system when he had the resources to place me under his care? It was a question that ran through my mind a thousand times. It took me several sleepless nights over the past week to put myself in his shoes thirty-five years ago and attempt to understand. It took me a few more sleepless nights to bring myself to forgive him."

Kathleen closed her eyes, squinted, and pounded one of her fists lightly on the lectern.

"But with God's help, I have…I have forgiven him."

She started weeping.

"And now that I know who my grandfather is, I find out he's dying."

She wiped at her eyes.

"We've had a lot to talk about the last few days. And we still have a lot more to talk about. But to acknowledge him in his final hours, I've consented to his dying wish of allowing this letter to be published, in full, in the Vidalia Times so that he can die with a clean conscience and be transparent before the world."

Kathleen pointed to Eric Sawyer sitting near the front.

"Eric Sawyer who works for the Times was given a copy of the letter yesterday. He says the Times will run the letter this coming Tuesday."

Kathleen sighed.

"Since Floyd is known around the nation because of his company, and since my presence here at the church has been so controversial at a local level and at a state level, it's safe to predict that Floyd's letter, once it's published, will be picked up as fodder for widespread gossip around the state and maybe even around the country, especially online."

She bowed her head for a second.

"So, this brings me to another bit of news that will take some of you aback."

She took a deep breath and tried to stand straight.

"I will stay around and be close to my grandfather until he passes. After his funeral, as I stated earlier, I'll be leaving."

Eyes and expressions everywhere burst into a plethora of outright denial. People forcefully shook their heads as if they could immediately squelch the announcement and make it go away. Others blurted "No!" as if their spoken desire could possibly override the situation. Some raised their hands to catapult questions and proclaim sentiments.

Kathleen clenched her eyes, then waved her hand to quieten the crowd. "It's for your safety," she told them with emotion. "In order to understand my decision, you need to know that I'm…"

A full ten seconds of silence passed before she could muster the next words.

"…I'm a hunted woman."

If silence could be stacked upon silence, instantly there were multiple layers of it pressing down on the room. The auditorium was so quiet, the wind could suddenly and eerily be heard blowing outside.

Kathleen finally broke the stillness. She took twenty more minutes and told the people about her nine-year-long crusade in Mali to help stem the practice of female genital mutilation which was rampant throughout the country, and how that crusade had made her an object of hate, especially among Muslim men, and more so among those who were willing to die to protect every aspect of their Muslim culture such as the militant group Ansar Dine.

She told about the constant threats on her life by Ansar Dine during that season of her ministry. She told about the ambush and attempted assassination, along with the brutal murder of her thirteen-year-old son. She revealed that the assassination attempt where she was left for dead was the source of the jagged scar she bore on her neck.

"Floyd wanted to protect me following my recovery," she explained. "So, he urged me to leave Africa for a while and come here to Lyons and live under an alias. And though it was a difficult decision to follow through with, it was a life-changing decision for me. Here in middle Georgia I was able to hide. At the same time, I somehow managed to find rest, healing, strength, and love. And I will be forever grateful. To God. To Floyd. To each of you."

She was certain, she went on to explain, that her survival had become common knowledge inside Mali and that Ansar Dine was most likely looking for her even now as she spoke. She made it clear that the group had an international reach and was thoroughly financed by Mali's exorbitant gold industry.

And that they would never stop searching for her. No matter the cost.

"And so," she insisted, "when Floyd's letter hits the internet in two or three days from now, they will have no problem tracking me to Lyons. And if they find me here, they will not hesitate to take me out with a car bomb, a suicide bomber, or a church shooter."

She made it clear that for the safety of everyone in the church that she wasn't going to wait around for something like that to happen. She wasn't going to risk the life of a single person in her congregation.

But, she and Floyd had talked about it and concluded that the publication of the letter could actually play to her advantage. She had been planning at the end of her second year in Lyons, coming up in April, to return to Africa anyway to carry on her work with the Malian women. Floyd's letter and its contents would undoubtedly divert Ansar Dine's search to Georgia. It would, therefore, give her a strong chance—while Ansar Dine was focused on Georgia—to make her way back into Africa, via a lengthy and elaborate route, without being easily detected. And for the first time, because of what she stood to inherit from Floyd, she would have the resources inside Mali to hire a team of full-time bodyguards.

Plus, a portion of the forthcoming inheritance—and, yes, Floyd had already given his approval—would help her build a large, legal, effective organization inside Mali that could perpetuate the campaign of stemming female genital mutilation and thereby improving the lives of thousands, maybe hundreds of thousands, of precious Malian girls. And possibly have a ripple effect for decades and generations to come.

At that point, Kathleen had laid everything out in the open. And she told them so. She suddenly felt her shoulders slump. She was exhausted, both mentally and emotionally.

The faces of the people looked like a patchwork of embellished shock, gloom and grief.

Kathleen announced she would try to answer three or four questions, then she wanted to rush back to Floyd's side.

A man, without wasting a second, sprung to his feet. "Is there anything we can do, or promise to do, that would possibly persuade you to change your mind?"

Kathleen assured him, and all the others who wanted to hear the answer, that her decision was firm and that it was in no way indicative of any personal disappointment with the church or the town. It was a decision she felt God had been continuously prodding her to make over the past few months. Floyd's letter would simply help her pick up her pace.

"Will you ever come back and be our pastor again?" asked a young girl who looked to be twelve or thirteen.

Kathleen felt her heart melt at the longing of the question. She sighed again for what seemed like the hundredth time that morning. "My initial plan is to go back and build my organization so that it becomes so big, so effective, and so lawfully recognized that terrorist groups like Ansar Dine will have a hard time stopping it. At that juncture, maybe I'll sense the freedom to give the reins of the organization over to competent nationals and walk away. Will that take two years, three years, ten years?" Kathleen shrugged her shoulders. "But at some point, I'm sure I'll move back to the States. Will it be to Lyons? I don't know. I'll never say never."

There were three or four more questions: What would happen to the college ministries she had started? Could she possibly teach a few more times before she stepped down? Would she lead the congregation in a church-wide vote to install Walter as the new pastor before she left?

Kathleen answered the questions the best she could, offering no hard and fast promises.

There were a couple of more pleas for her to change her mind. Didn't she know how many hearts would be broken if she left?

And then a hand was raised that caused Kathleen a mild shock. It was Willow who suddenly wanted to say something. As fatigued as Kathleen was, she smiled on the inside. Willow had never, not once, spoken publicly in a congregational setting. Kathleen gladly acknowledged her.

"Miss Rose, did I hear Mr. Floyd's letter rightly say that your grandmother was a full-blooded negro who was a civil rights leader?"

For the umpteenth time, the congregation went silent.

For the first time that morning, Kathleen felt a slight grin raise the corners of her mouth. "That's right, Willow, you heard correctly."

"So, you're telling us that the Central Baptist Church of Lyons has not only been pastored by a lady, but by a lady with negro blood in her?"

The question highlighted an obvious fact that had been momentarily buried beneath the immense down-heartedness.

Kathleen smiled humbly. "Yes ma'am, it does. And…" Kathleen quickly remembered the words of her grandfather. "as a lady of mixed race…I hold my head up high."

"I knowed I liked you the first time I met you," Willow responded loud enough for everyone to hear. "Yes'm. You are special. Special indeed. And," she added, choking up. "Over the last year or so, you changed my life. And I just want to say it in front of God and everybody." She sniffled. "And I think I'm goin' miss you more than anybody else in this room."

And with that, followed by a closing Christmas song and a dismissal prayer by Troy, the Christmas Day service was over.

Kathleen explained that she would not linger. She really wanted to get back to Floyd's side.

As the crowd dispersed, awash in a cloud of uncertain wariness, everyone realized it was a Christmas day service they would never forget.

Those throughout the community who had been opposed to Kathleen's pastorate were absolutely flabbergasted when they learned the woman was partly African American. Their heated feelings over the whole Kathleen-as-pastor issue were only compounded by the mixed-race revelation. And as might have been predicted, rabid gossip reignited all over the county with more than a bit of ugliness.

65

On Tuesday afternoon, Kathleen placed a copy of the *Vidalia Times* on Floyd's nightstand. The weather outside was rainy and chilly. Kathleen sat down in the bedside chair and for a few minutes watched as her grandfather slept.

Floyd had insisted she move into his house right away for her own personal safety. In addition to hiring an array of nurses who were working multiple shifts to manage his blood pressure, nausea, and pain with a potpourri of medications, he had also hired a bevy of security guards who were keeping an eye on the property day and night.

As she sat and stared at Floyd's elderly features, she was still trying to absorb the reality that this man was her mother's biological dad, and more so that she had just learned that fact a measly ten days ago. She was still grappling with some resentment. How would her life have been different had Floyd spared her the lonely foster-home years of her youth? She just kept reminding herself that Floyd had grown up in an era when southerners didn't extend a lot of grace or mercy to neighbors, politicians, clergymen, or businessmen who fell short of all the pious expectations placed on them. And so by default, the Silent Generation, of which Floyd was a part, had typically hidden their problems out of sight, only to fight their inner demons alone - sometimes for decades, sometimes for a lifetime.

Kathleen leaned back in the chair. By sheer discipline she forced herself to thank God again that Floyd had decided to talk. He could have easily taken his secrets to the grave.

She slowly dozed off into a light sleep.

She was awakened at some point when a nurse entered the room and gave Floyd another round of meds.

After swallowing four different pills, Floyd—who was now slightly sitting up—looked over at Kathleen. A joyless expression consumed his countenance.

When the nurse left the room, Kathleen silently handed Floyd the copy of the *Times*, folded to page two. She pointed to the headline: *Dying Confession of Vidalia CEO*

Kathleen held the paper for him to read his letter of disclosure, printed in full for everybody in the county to read. She patiently followed his eyes and turned the pages accordingly.

When Floyd finished reading, a tiny smile creased his lips. And then he began weeping. He took hold of Kathleen's hand and gripped with the strength he had left. "Please forgive me," he wheezed. "If I could go back in time, I would…"

His words were cut short when he suddenly curled up in acute pain.

Kathleen beckoned the nurse again.

That evening, a local TV station out of Macon, in an air of sensationalism, reported all the talking points of Floyd's public confession. Kathleen's real name, Angela Marie Carter, was included in the breaking news.

Over the next two days, Floyd's two primary attorneys spent time at the house reworking his will.

Floyd dictated that upon his death the deed to all the church property be passed to the congregation and held in perpetuity by the church trustees, according to the original agreement.

His house, guest house, land, and multiple vehicles, along with three million dollars placed in a trust fund, would be given to the Middle Georgia Home for Children based out of Statesboro. The Vidalia location, to be christened *Floyd's Estate,* would be strictly used for "transitional living" for foster girls turning eighteen and wanting to attend college. A hundred percent of their tuition for all four years would be paid if they agreed to attend Ailey Bible College, the private Christian College fifteen miles away. The house, guest house, and property could house ten girls and a "foster couple" during any given semester. Floyd had floated the idea to the Ailey Bible College board of trustees a year or so ago. They had unanimously agreed to his proposed terms.

In addendum, an attorney would be available at *Floyd's Estate* at any time to help the older teen girls find, and make contact with, their birth parents or their closest biological relatives if the girls so desired and if the birth parents or relatives were sympathetic to the notion.

Floyd's privately owned company Prime Vidalia Onions, his bank accounts, and all his investment instruments—valued collectively at twenty million dollars—would go to Angela Marie Carter.

Regarding the inheritance of Prime Vidalia Onions, Angela—at her absolute insistence and with Floyd's heartened endorsement—made it clear that she would keep all the present-day employees in place. The current Vice President would simply step up to the position of CEO.

Regarding the vast amounts of cash coming her way, she would use a portion of it to fund her planned organization in Mali that would bear the name S.W.A.N.S - Strong Women Against Non-essential Slicing. She wanted an acronym that sounded feminine and beautiful. Yet, she wanted the actual words to sound brutal, as the very act itself.

Floyd was enthusiastic with all her plans, as much as a dying man possibly could be. Kathleen even managed to capture a few of his smiles on camera.

* * *

A week later, as Floyd was declining faster than anyone had expected, he beckoned Ian, who was visiting in his home one evening, to sit down beside him. He whispered into Ian's ear, "If Angela is truly the love of your life, then don't stop pursuing her. Don't make the mistake I made when I was in your shoes. Pursue her at all costs. Don't let anybody or any circumstance stop you."

Following Floyd's advice, Ian reiterated to Kathleen in private that he would wait for her to return from Africa, even if he had to wait three, four, or five years. Then he intended to marry her. He was elated that Kathleen approved the idea with an unfeigned smile and emotional hug.

*   *   *

Three weeks later, on the clear, brisk morning of January 27, 2017, Floyd, who hadn't eaten in three days, feebly motioned for the on-duty nurse to leave his room so he could be alone with Kathleen one more time.

"Billfold. Pants pocket," he mumbled to his granddaughter.

Kathleen retrieved his billfold from a pair of beige pants hanging over a chair back.

"Behind driver's license," Floyd said in a soft cough.

Kathleen found his driver's license. She inserted a fingernail beneath the legal certificate and pinched the edge of another item. She pulled the object from the sheath. It was a worn and faded black-and-white photograph.

"Bernadette," Floyd wheezed. "Your grandmother. Five weeks pregnant. Nineteen-years-old. My only picture."

Kathleen stared at Floyd for four or five seconds then, with her mind whirling, gave her undivided attention to the photo. The image that stared back at her was one of the most striking female figures Kathleen had ever seen. The attractiveness wasn't the runway-model-type beauty with thin, symmetrical proportions. Rather, it was a raw, exquisite beauty punctuated by flawless skin, gorgeous long hair, and the most stirring smile imaginable.

Floyd motioned with his fingers that the photo was now hers to keep. Kathleen swallowed hard. Every love story was unique. But passionate love, no matter where it crystallized in the world—she knew from experience—always stole an epic portion of a lover's heart and would never give it back. Never. Not even in one's dying hours. Kathleen instantly thought about Scott Nicholas Carter.

She took Floyd's hand and squeezed it. She then prayed aloud for Floyd's peace of heart.

Floyd, with bone-tired eyes, looked at her when she finished praying and blinked as if to say *It's nearly time now - the final moments of regret on this side, the soon-to-be moments of unimaginable discovery on the other.*

Only a few hours later, Floyd's breathing became erratic and forced while his heart rate soared. He started fading in and out of consciousness.

The nurse on duty summoned Kathleen who was in the kitchen preparing herself a small bite to eat. She also called the three people from the Prime Vidalia Onions office who Floyd had requested be present at his death - the Vice President, soon to be CEO; the senior accountant who had been Floyd's close friend and confidant for thirty-five years; and Floyd's secretary, Mable, who had worked for him since the beginning of the company.

When everyone arrived, they gathered around Floyd's bed and with tears in their eyes watched as the body of their friend and co-worker gave way in its struggle for life.

At around 3:45, Floyd, beneath the covers of his own bed and surrounded by his granddaughter and friends, gasped seven or eight times with closed eyes and breathed his last breath.

Kathleen was holding one of his hands at the time. The nurse was holding the other and had a cool, damp rag pressed to the old man's forehead.

Continuing to grip his hand, Kathleen closed her eyes and sobbed.

66

The closed-casket funeral was held four days later on Tuesday afternoon at two o'clock.

The simple pine-box coffin stood at the base of the church platform where Floyd had stood many times to lead congregational business meetings, make announcements, and occasionally teach.

The auditorium was filled to capacity, with people both from the church community and the business community. Many of the people present had known Floyd well and had loved him dearly. Others had known him only as an important figure in the community. Others were former church members who were drawn to the service simply for the sake of nostalgia.

Outside, six professional security guards, hired at Kathleen's insistence, were working undercover to patrol the parameter of the property.

Sitting on the front row of the church, Kathleen felt herself submerged in broken-heartedness. It would be her only time to step foot back on the premises. And Floyd was the only reason she was now present. Blocking out the assembly of faces, she stared at the coffin and lost herself in the emotion of all that had transpired over the last two months. She wept without restraint.

Lowering her head, she sniffed and squeezed her eyes tightly. It was her fate, wasn't it - irrepressible grief was going to find her wherever she went.

The memorial service, right on time, began with a couple of a-cappella songs that Floyd had preselected. Both hymns were presented by a choral group of seven women and four men. The first song was *Be Still My Soul.* The second was *O Love That Will Not Let Me Go.* Both renditions created a feeling of God's somber majesty that brought several people to tears.

The new CEO of Prime Vidalia Onions, Bob Sutton, then went to the microphone and gave an impassioned fifteen-minute eulogy. He talked mainly about Floyd's influence and integrity in the business world over the decades, along with the unquestionable fairness Floyd had exhibited from day to day to all his employees, even the field workers. In conclusion, he shared a humorous work-place episode that involved Floyd, simply to insert a moment of emotional reprieve.

The story indeed evoked a few tempered laughs.

Kathleen was the next speaker on the program. She was glad she had made notes that would help maintain her focus. Floyd—with unimaginable guilt over his longtime secret—had told her more than once in his final days that she did not have to speak at his funeral; he would understand and he would be okay with that decision. But now that she was at this stage of the unfolding chain of events, she wanted with all her heart to speak to the crowd.

When the CEO took his seat, Kathleen moved quietly up the carpeted steps to the podium.

"As most of you know by now," she commenced, "My name is Angela Marie Carter. And I am Floyd's biological grand-daughter. The fact that I'm his granddaughter is something I learned only six weeks ago. But that's a whole different story." She pursed her lips. "Anyway, I've been living in Lyons for almost two years, serving as the pastor of the church here. Floyd is the one who hired me for this position. And the experience has benefited my life in ways I would have never thought possible. Over the past few weeks, I've made sure to thank him over and over again for his decision. And I will now miss him terribly."

Keep it together, she told herself.

"When we consider the number of people scattered all over the planet, it seems that those who are characterized by true generosity represent only a small fraction of the population. Floyd was not only a member of that minority. He, I believe, was a leader in that small number of individuals. He supported me, for example, when I was in a foster home. He paid my college tuition in full. Every automobile I've ever driven, even the ones I drove in Africa, were his gifts. He supported me and my husband when we were missionaries. He gave us more than seventy-five percent of our monthly support. Here in Lyons, he provided me with a salary, a home, and a car. If you know my story, you might say, yeah…but he helped you because you were his granddaughter."

Kathleen paused and flipped a page of her notes.

461

"Not all wealthy grandfathers, need I say, help their grandkids so abundantly, if at all. But he not only supported me, a granddaughter. I have learned in recent weeks that he has been supporting more than fifteen different missionaries around the world for decades. Of course, as most everyone here knows, he built this beautiful church facility with his own money, on his own property. And in a few weeks time when his will is probated, the deed to the property will go debt free into the hands of the church trustees. He not only built this church building as a gift; he also—I learned just a few days ago —built a debt-free facility for a black congregation in Claxton. When he didn't have to, he constantly gave salary increases to his employees at Prime Vidalia Onions. And he has bequeathed his beloved house and property to the Middle Georgia Home for Children, based out of Statesboro."

Kathleen offered another five minutes of tributes that highlighted Floyd's specialness. And then concluded her part in the program with the words, "Floyd was a good-hearted man who helped many. Perhaps more people than we will ever know. He was one of those prized individuals who truly helped make the world a better place."

She nodded down at the coffin and held back her tears.

"He was my grandfather. And he will be sorely missed." And then straying from her notes, she added, "I love you, granddad. I wish we had had more time."

* * *

The following four weeks for Kathleen were a blur of activity, chalking off items on an extensive to-do list.

She first had to be present for sundry meetings as Floyd's will went through probate.

She was granted permission in the meantime from the Middle Georgia Home For Children to stay at Floyd's estate until her planned departure from the U.S. on Saturday, February 25. She continued to hire security guards to watch over the property during her stay.

The small house that had been her residence on West Oglethorpe Avenue went to the church, to be used as a guest house. All the furnishings stayed in place.

She met several times with the Prime Vidalia Onions board of directors, board of trustees, and executives. As the new owner of the company, she quickly needed to become acquainted with all the key people and all the different aspects of the day-to-day business. Plus, she had to sign a lot of papers.

To help bring her ministry at the church to a gracious and not-so-blunt close, she met privately at off-church locations with multiple families and with a host of college students—for meals or simple conversations—to say a personal and precious goodbye.

She also convened a couple of times with Walter and the deacon board, at their request, to give suggestions about the next steps for the church, and to pray for the ministry's continued wellbeing.

In her spare hours, she mapped out a route back to Mali that she believed would be nearly impossible for Ansar Dine to track. She would initially fly from Atlanta to New York City where she would layover for two days. She would then take a taxi over to New Jersey to the Newark airport. From there she would fly to Reykjavik, Iceland. She would spend a full week in Iceland's capital city, doing nothing but sleeping and decompressing. She would then fly to Frankfurt, Germany. From Frankfurt, she would fly to Dakar, Senegal. On each leg of the journey, she would fly with a different airline carrier. From Dakar she would travel by train, 450 miles, to Kayes, Mali. And from Kayes, she would hire three or four different taxis and, without giving her identity, traverse the remaining 400 miles to Bamako— Mali's capital city. Overall, it would be a brutal and taxing journey. But certainly, Ansar Dine would not be able to trace it. And she would have at least a couple of trouble-free months inside Bamako, with the protection of hired body guards, to set up her new organization S.W.A.N.S. and get it legally established with government recognition. By that time, she would hopefully have the backing and protection of the Malian government which had been supportive previously of her independent efforts.

And then…

Before she could hardly blink, her final days and hours in Lyons had been spent.

On Friday, February 24, 2017, Kathleen's last full day in America, she and Ian spent eight hours together—meandering around the Vidalia estate, sitting at a cafe, and walking along the foot trails at Partin Park—relishing each other's presence and dreaming aloud about reconnecting in a few years and maybe starting a family of their own.

Ian was almost beside himself, trying to maintain a normal composure and trying to squelch his emotions that wanted to run wild.

Their time together finally ended late in the evening with a tearjerking prayer, repeated prolonged embraces, and repeated passionate kisses.

Kathleen could barely sleep that night. How could she, with Ian and a thousand Georgia memories running through her head?

Saturday, February 25, would prove to be the coldest day of the year in Lyons. Yet, the Walmart parking lot was crowded en masse with over a hundred teary-eyed adults, college students, and teenagers who gathered to give Kathleen an emotional send-off. Even Ray Huxley was present. Like everyone else, he was unable to keep a dry face.

Personal hugs and personal "goodbyes" were shared one at a time in a deluge of unrestrained tears and cracked voices.

When Kathleen, after about thirty minutes, finally stepped into the car that would be chauffeured by Walter and Troy, a clamor of spontaneous voices erupted from all directions.

"We love you, Kathleen!"

"We will never forget you!"

"We will be praying for you!"

"Please don't ever forget us!"

Kathleen settled in the backseat and for a moment rolled down her window. The expressions of love and heartfelt emotion were nearly overwhelming.

As the car slowly pulled away, a few of the teens and college students ran alongside her blowing kisses and waving as if they were losing their best friend in the world.

Kathleen wept all the way to the Atlanta airport.

67

On the following Tuesday, people all over Toombs County —in their homes, doctors' offices, beauty salons, barber shops, grocery stores, convenience stores, nursing homes, library, and other public venues—were greeted by another "Eric Sawyer" article on the front page of the *Vidalia Times*.

At noon, Eric Sawyer was eating a greasy burger at Roxy's diner where he had conducted his first interview with Ray Huxley almost two years ago. He wiped his hands with a handful of napkins and unfolded a copy of the newspaper. He slowly read his article, now in its published layout.

A Forlorn County

Pastor Kathleen Rose of the International Baptist Church, formerly Central Baptist of Lyons, has only been gone for four days, but the whole town seems eerily empty without her, as if we have lost a big portion of our heart, character, and prudence.

It's not a common occurrence for someone to come along in one's county or one's life who can so quickly redraw

the lines of the social landscape, who can
change the colors on the palette, who
can reshape the way people think. But
Toombs County was privileged beyond
measure to be visited by just such an
inimitable individual. As brief as her
stay was, a scant twenty-three months,
Kathleen Rose helped turn our small
world upside down. With her no-holds-
barred approach to ministry, she
challenged the status quo and convinced
us that we had been blind. She helped
close racial gaps, generational gaps,
and social gaps. She showed us that
the local church can be more than just
a boring, passive audience; that it was
from the beginning meant to be, and
can be, a vibrant, interactive, family. Her
insatiable hunger for God's heart and
God's truth, constantly reflected in her
sermons, inspired us to hunger after
God's heart and God's truth. One can
only imagine what the ramifications
will be long-term for our county and
town. Her fingerprints will still be all
over our community even when most
of us are no longer around. Thank you
Floyd Baxter, now deceased, for intro-

ducing us to this one-in-a-million specimen of life changing prowess. To the next American town that welcomes Kathleen Rose, be prepared to have your world shaken. Because when she arrives, your world will definitely be thrown off kilter. And that will be a good thing.

Eric grinned. He was proud of himself, especially for the last three sentences. He had added those six extra lines to intentionally create a red herring for any so-called "killer" who came into town looking for the lady who had single-handedly revamped Toombs County and won the undying love of all those who gave her a chance.

He then thought of Walter. He had in no way wanted the man who had been voted in last Sunday as the new pastor of the church to feel overshadowed or belittled in comparison when he read the words of the article. So, he had called Walter in advance and read the article to him before it went to print.

"I just want to make sure you're okay with it," Eric told him.

"Are you kidding?" Walter had laughed and cried at the same time. "I'm the lady's biggest cheerleader. I will sing her praises till the day I die."

Eric then stared at the big, bold picture of Kathleen accompanying the article. It was the first time her photo had been printed in the Vidalia newspaper. As Eric stared at the image and got lost in the eyes that were staring back at him, he thought, *She really must be the most beautiful woman anyone in Toombs County has ever seen.*

He then raised his Coke as a silent cheer to the good fortune of the church as they all dealt with their sadness and looked ahead.

Following the weeks-long, cumbersome communications between Ansar Dine and his handler, the executioner—a highly-skilled sniper from Saudi Arabia—arrived in Lyons after sunset on Friday evening. He knew the small-town people would be occupied with weekend activities - parties, meetings, dinners, movies, or simply locked away inside their homes with the TV blaring.

Once inside the city limits, he quickly and easily found the church building.

His next task was to scout out the town and find a commercial rooftop that would give him an unobstructed two-to-three-hundred-yard view of the outside office-entry to the church building.

He knew a person could stay on a commercial rooftop for days without anyone knowing he was there.

68

Eight Months Later

In early November, 2017, Bob Sutton, the CEO at Prime Vidalia Onions sat down at his company desk to place his regular call to Kathleen in Africa. The time in Vidalia was 1:00 PM Eastern Standard Time. It was mid-evening in Mali.

As planned prior to Kathleen's departure from the States, he and Kathleen spoke once a month by phone, usually around the tenth of the month. He would give Kathleen a running update on the status of the Prime Vidalia Onions enterprise. Kathleen, in return, would brief him on her well-being and on the development of S.W.A.N.S.

Sutton had regularly passed along Kathleen's news to Walter at the church.

As the Chief Executive Officer of the multi-million dollar company, Sutton had grown more fond of Kathleen with each call. His appreciation for Kathleen's understanding of business had only been enhanced further when in their call the previous month he learned that S.W.A.N.S. had at that point become a legal entity nationwide and would begin receiving government funding the following week, and that the Legislative Branch of the Malian government had even expedited approval for her group to produce a weekly program on ORTM, the state-run radio that would be heard by millions.

He himself had never been off the American mainland. So he couldn't begin to comprehend how this solitary woman in a foreign country, and in a foreign language, could have pulled off such a feat in only seven short months.

"Yes, sir, she's something else," Sutton whispered to himself as he punched out the number to her home line. He was definitely proud of his new boss.

When Kathleen didn't answer, Sutton made a written note to call her the next day. When she didn't answer over the course of the next four days, he grew seriously concerned. When she didn't answer on the seventh day, he called an emergency number that Kathleen had given him. The number was a private number that belonged to Sisko, the director of the Bible college Kathleen's late husband, Scott Nicholas Carter, had founded. Sisko was a Malian native who Kathleen had known for several years. Kathleen had told Sutton that Sisko was one of the few Malian men she felt she could trust.

When Sisko answered the phone, he reported that he had not heard from Kathleen in more than a week, but that such a time lapse in their communication was not uncommon. He promised he would personally go to her house and try to make contact with her.

Two days later, Sisko called back saying that neither Kathleen nor her body guards could be found, that Kathleen had even failed to show up at the ORTM radio station for her latest recording session.

* * *

Ian, when he learned Kathleen was missing, booked an immediate flight to Mali.

Once on Malian soil, Ian worked with the police to find the love of his life. He talked to people at the Bible college and the radio station. He talked to the staff at S.W.A.N.S. He even talked to the families living around Kathleen's place of residence.

The last person who had seen Kathleen was one of the staff members at S.W.A.N.S., a young mother named Chloe.

"It was late in the afternoon and Angela had just led us in a company prayer," Chloe clarified. "A government official had agreed by phone earlier in the day to be a supportive guest on one of the up-coming radio recordings. And Angela wanted us to pray that the official's voice of authority would help legitimize everything that S.W.A.N.S. was saying."

Chloe explained that when Kathleen left the office with her body guards, she was headed home for an evening of rest. "But she never showed up at her house. And the body guards have gone missing as well."

Ian spent days walking the route Kathleen most likely would have taken to her home address. He showed a photo of Kathleen to bus drivers, merchants, street beggars, and residents. No one could offer a single bit of helpful information.

When Kathleen partially awakened, her head felt foggy. The drowsiness was absurdly heavy. Yet, she deciphered—half in and out of her awareness—that she was gagged and blindfolded. Everything was so dark. She discerned, or thought she did, that she was sitting upright and that her wrists were strapped to the arms of a chair. As she tried to lift her hands and move around, it became obvious that her ankles were tied to the chair legs. Her feet were bare and were touching what felt like a dirt floor. She wanted to panic, but the grogginess overtook her. She felt her head droop and everything went black again.

The next thing she knew, cold water was being splashed in her face. She gasped and jerked. Her head felt so wobbly. As she attempted to stiffen her shoulders and steady her neck, she registered that her blindfold had been removed. She squinted. There were people in the dimly-lit room. Her hands and feet were still bound. And then, almost instantly, spotlights were turned on her. She closed her eyes and moaned. Her gag had been discarded.

"Please help me," she pleaded through a dry and groggy voice.

Another bucket of water was thrown in her face. She flinched and inhaled strongly as the water drenched her.

"All right," a man's voice said in the Bambara language, "We'll start again." The man stepped in between her and the spotlights. The man was an African male with a turban wrapped around his neck like a scarf. "You are now a prisoner of Ansar Dine," he said bluntly. "So, you are going to look into the camera." He pointed somewhere between the spotlights. "And you are going to say that you are an enemy of Islam, an

American spy, and that you have intentionally tried to deceive the women of Mali with your western lies. You are going to say that every one of your radio broadcasts, television specials, and live seminars have been a calculated attempt to mislead the women of our country. You will say that the Malian practice of cutting is honorable and good and is the will of Allah. You will say that it is right for the women of our country to obey their husbands and Imams."

Kathleen tried to snap out of the dream. She sensed her heart racing. Her head ached terribly. Had she been knocked out? Had she been drugged?

And then she remembered.

She gasped again and burst into tears.

Her fear returned in full force.

"Dear Jesus," she begged, "Give me strength to keep saying 'no'."

She clung to the memory of her son, and his unspeakable death, to give her courage.

* * *

Weeks later, on December 6, Kathleen was finally found.

In the dead of night, her body was dumped in the center of the city, in the middle of a major street. Her corpse was headless. Her body showed signs of torture.

Ansar Dine claimed responsibility.

Further police investigation concluded that Kathleen's body guards had in all probability been paid an irresistible sum to sedate her and deliver her alive as a trophy to the Ansar Dine leaders.

The body guards, it was believed, had since fled the city.

Over six hundred Malian women, along with the staff and student body of the Bible college and several government officials, attended Kathleen's funeral conducted outdoors at the college. Kathleen's body, in a somber ceremony, was buried in-country, next to her husband, Scott Nicholas Carter, and her son, Jake Elliot Carter.

Ian's grief was inconsolable. For two weeks after returning to Savannah, he took unpaid leave from work.

He drove I-16 several times to Lyons to relive memories, alone in his car.

Mostly, he lay around his condo or sat and stared out his windows and wept.

Food was not palatable. Sleep was not restorative. For the first time in his adult life, God seemed faraway. Life felt totally dark and empty. He felt harrowingly pressed inside an emotional straight-jacket with no way to escape.

At some point he began to think seriously about suicide and it frightened him. He somehow found the doggedness one afternoon to pick up the phone and call Dr. Blitz. He made his first appointment for grief counseling. He wasn't convinced the appointment would help one iota, but it gave him a smidgen of bland hope, just enough to keep him breathing.

The thing that would keep him moving in between therapy sessions, and there would no doubt be many of those sessions, were the flashbacks of the way Kathleen had fought her own grief. She had been the model of spiritual fortitude, immoveable faith, and miraculous resurgence.

He placed photos of her throughout his living quarters. It would be her example, her legacy, her quiet roar that would inspire him each morning to put one foot in front of the other and keep living.

The hole in his heart, though, would never be completely healed. He was certain of it.

At the International Church of Lyons, sorrow and dismay over the news of Kathleen's death permeated the congregation like rain water inside moss. The shock and tears throughout the congregation were immeasurable - in the lives of everyone: Walter, Troy, all the deacons, the college students, the worship team, Eric Sawyer, Willow, Ida Mae, Alexa, Evelyn Huxley, Billy Huxley, and everybody else. Even Ray Huxley. Everyone who had known Kathleen, even in the slightest, wanted desperately to deny the report. They simply couldn't conceive of what had happened, and that their hope of one day seeing Kathleen in their pulpit again had been totally obliterated by some despicable low-down force of evil. The vocalized heartache and anger was incessant all throughout the county.

The people knew collectively, however, that there was one thing they could control; the woman who had changed their lives would never be forgotten.

Not in their town. Not in their lifetime.

They would make sure of it.

Especially Pastor Walter.

On the first Saturday evening after receiving the news of Kathleen's demise, Walter went early to the church to mentally prepare himself to lead the weekly Bible study for college students. Inside the building, he sat alone in the semi-darkness on the front pew and wept unashamedly. Through a cascade of tears, he found himself staring at the podium. He couldn't shake the hoard of memories of Kathleen standing behind that sacred lectern. Overcome by a new wave of pummeling grief, he pulled out a pocket knife, stood up, and pushed the communion table aside. He sat in a nostalgic daze on the edge of the platform and—without thought of expense, appearance, or consequence—slowly dug his knife into the face of the podium. Fully committed to his impulse, he sat there and worked diligently through his tears until two ragged letters, each about six inches tall, marred the old piece of furniture standing at the focal point of the auditorium—the letters K.R.

"We will never forget you," he whispered.

EPILOGUE

In early March 2018, three months following Kathleen's death, it was made known by Bob Sutton, the CEO of Prime Vidalia Onions—and revealed publicly in the *Vidalia Times*, with Sutton's permission—that before Kathleen had returned to Africa, she had worked with the Prime Vidalia Onions attorneys and drafted a new will.

In case of her demise, whether by natural or unnatural causes the document declared, the following distributions were to be made. The ownership of Prime Vidalia Onions would be transferred in full to the top four executives, named in the will, along with Floyd's secretary, Mable, who had served faithfully under Floyd Baxter for over thirty years. Each of the five would receive an equal twenty percent ownership of the company.

One third of all her inherited liquid assets—checking accounts, savings accounts, certificates of deposit, stocks and bonds—would be placed in a trust fund for Floyd's Estate, the new branch of the Middle Georgia Home for Children. The money would be used to maintain the property and to give a $25,000 head-start grant to each of the girls in the home who, while a resident, graduated from college.

Another third would go to the Bible college Kathleen and her husband had founded in Mali. The money, among other specified usages, would provide grants to poor Malian young men who wanted to study to become Christian pastors and evangelists.

The final third would be given to S.W.A.N.S.—if established and adequately staffed by the time of her death—to insure the perpetuation of her vision to help millions of precious Malian women stand with knowledge against the age-old devastating practice of female genital mutilation.

In April, the following month, the legislative branch of the Malian government—motivated by Kathleen's widely-known sacrificial death and martyrdom—ratified a new nationwide law that was effectuated on June 1. The new piece of legislation was called the Angela Carter Law. The law forbade forced genital mutilation on any female younger than eighteen. A violation of the law would be punishable by five years in prison and a fine of 2,900,000 West African Francs, the equivalent of 5,000 US Dollars.

By the end of the year, the ancient Muslim practice of female genital mutilation in Mali—to the absolute outrage of tribal leaders and Imams across the country, and amidst widespread confusion—was being abandoned by more families than anyone would have ever imagined.

The millions upon millions of Malian women, for generations to come, would be forever indebted to an American Christian woman of mixed race who stood and fought, at all costs, for what was good and right.

Final Notes

(1) Some protestant denominations, such as the Methodists and Presbyterians, commonly allow ladies to serve as senior pastors in their congregations. In order to create a sense of realistic tension and controversy in this story, I needed to select a denomination that <u>typically</u> does not permit ladies to serve as pastors. I could have chosen the Evangelical Free Church, the Missouri Synod Lutheran Church, or others. Instead, I opted to use the Baptist denomination simply because it has a larger footprint in society and has a larger audience. With that said, the Baptist denomination is not a target in this narrative. I have no personal agenda to undermine Baptist Churches. As a matter of fact, I believe that the tens of thousands of Baptist Churches across our nation have through the years—with their belief in the authority of Scripture—been a pillar of moral strength in our culture.

(2) It's officially reported in multiple sources that female genital mutilation—FGM—is practiced in at least 30 countries across Africa, the Middle East and Asia. FGM is mainly performed on girls between the ages of 10 and 15. It's estimated that 3 million girls are cut every year across the world. The World Health Organization defines the practice as *"all procedures that involve partial or total removal of the external female genitalia, or other injury to the female genital organs for non-medical reasons."* According to a

2007 World Health Organization report, 92% of the girls in Mali at that time had been subjected to the knife. Many of the practitioners believe the cutting is a religious requirement to ensure proper sexual behavior.

Female genital mutilation is classified into 4 types. You can research these types online.

There are several organizations around the world which are currently working to educate women about the long-term hazards of FGM and to help stop the practice all together.

(3) If you found A Quiet Roar to be meaningful, please promote the book on your social media accounts. This will be appreciated more than you know.

Acknowledgments

I want to say a giant thanks to the twenty-one test readers who proofed the original manuscript and offered feedback that was invaluable. Their insights and suggestions improved the story beyond measure. Those twenty-one individuals are Sherri Dodd, Dawn Daily, Jacque Lederman, Anna Strawn, Pastor Tommy Hargrove, Julie Beacham, Pastor Butch Entrekin, Leslie Shivers, Billy Lord, Dr. Linda Foltz, David Daniell, Gina Hardy, Brenda Bair, Dr. Sandra Hutcheson, Dr. Denice Colson, Angie Vittur, Rheta Duren, Rosemary Ahonen, Jimmy Cochran, Dave Lambert, and Shanda Dodd. Thank you, thank you, thank you.

Reviews for Randall's Other Books

Wisdom Hunter

"I read about 250 books each year, and Wisdom Hunter is the best I've read in ages. It blows the doors off 'packaged' Christianity. If you only read two books this year, make one the Bible, and the other Wisdom Hunter." - Paul Griffin, Senior Vice President, Multnomah Bible College

"I can honestly say that next to the Bible Wisdom Hunter has been the most influential book I have ever read. I have told hundreds of people about the book." - Dr. Ben Gates, executive director, Greater Fort Wayne Campus Ministry at Indiana University, Purdue University

"Wisdom Hunter and The Shack are for me two books that forever changed my life." - Bobby Dowde, founder and CEO, ChristianCinema.com

"This fictional book will teach what thousands of sermons fail to achieve! A must read!" - D.L.

"Several pastors in the area took up the cause of banning this book, demanding their congregations to 'not under any circumstance read it, or else.' It has been 17 years since I first read Wisdom Hunter. It radically changed my life." - J.S.

Jordan's Crossing

"Jordan's Crossing is an absolute must read. Randall Arthur writes obviously from experience. This is a captivating, no put-down book." - A.C.

"Wisdom Hunter is one of my all time favorite books. I have read it three times. Jordan's Crossing is in many ways a more powerful book. If you are looking for a hard hitting, in-your-face story full of hard truths, then you are in the right place." - T.T.

"I have read this book 4 or 5 times. I love it! It touches on the nature of GOD and His love for us, and how He will not let us go!" - A.C.

"I have read few authors that gripped me the way Randall Arthur has in his three stories. Thank you for being honest about the good and the bad in the church and our lives, and about God's grace and His presence through both." - M.M.

Brotherhood of Betrayal

"The books I have read through the fastest in my adult life have come from the pen of Randall Arthur. I just finished reading Brotherhood of Betrayal and was simply floored." - J.W.

"Rough and raw all the way down. This is without a doubt one of the most-real Christian fiction books out there." - C.F.

'Randall has once again written a book that I could not put down. Words cannot explain how wonderful and life changing this book is.' - Anonymous

"It was so therapeutic to read Brotherhood of Betrayal. I was counseled to get a divorce, but since I read this book I could not do it. As a result, my husband finally came to brokenness and is now leading us spiritually." - P.W.

"Brotherhood of Betrayal is such a life impacting book. I sat in my closet with the lights on till 3:00 A.M. the first time I read it. I'm a bookstore owner, and Brotherhood of Betrayal is my all time favorite work of fiction." - E.K.

Forgotten Road

"This is the first novel I've read by Randall Arthur. Forgotten Road has risen to my top 10 all-time favorites. The story is mesmerizing. I encourage everyone to read this novel." - Tom Marchinowski

"I am generally not a fiction reader, but once I started it, it was difficult to put down. Breathtaking. Chilling. Pulled all my emotional strings" - Nancy Kelly, Educator

"This book touches my heart and spirit like nothing I have read in a long time. I am not usually so personally affected by a fiction narrative." - Jo, ChristianFictionShop.com

"I just finished reading Forgotten Road by Randall Arthur, a book I can't stop thinking about. I keep reminding myself it was only fiction. That is how real and organic his writing is." - Cheri Swalwell

"I finished reading Forgotten Road at 1 AM this morning! It has been a long time since I read a book that was able to invoke so many different emotions. Thank you for such a fabulous read." - Sharron Lanham

46 Stones

"46 Stones is full of the right questions and will lead the reader to consider his personal view of God, especially the reader with an open mind." - Apologist Dan Arsenault, Church-For-Skeptics International

"46 Stones is a home run! Prepare to be convicted, challenged, and inspired to look closer at the true nature of the Christian Gospel." - Jeremy Morton, Senior Pastor, First Baptist Cartersville, GA.

ABCs On the Move

"ABCs On The Move is a book that generates wonder and imagination. The beautiful use of alliteration throughout the book makes it the perfect tool for introducing this literary concept to young students." -Felecia Spicer, Award winning teacher, and principal

Purchase from Amazon or from www.RandallArthur.com